CW01064555

Earthshine

Alliance, Volume 5

Kadee Carder

Published by Addison Multimedia, 2024.

Earthshine
by Kadee Carder
Published by Addison Multimedia
This is a work of fiction. Names, places, characters, and events are fictitious in every regard. Any similarities to actual events and persons, living or dead, are purely coincidental. Any trademarks, service marks, product names, or named features are assumed to be the property of their respective owners, and are used only for reference. There is no implied endorsement if any of these terms are used. Except for review purposes, the reproduction of this book in whole or part, electronically or mechanically, constitutes a copyright violation.
EARTHSHINE
Copyright © 2018 KADEE CARDER / ADDISON MULTIMEDIA
Cover Art Designed by Addison Multimedia. Special thank you to Pexels.

For Cheyenne. I'll always remind you of the conqueror I see before me.

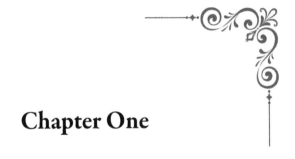

Chapter One

MONSTERS
Saylor

Sitting on my stool at the dry cleaner's, my foot tapped along the ground in a steady rhythm. The humid, thick air wrapped around my face and up into my hair like a bath towel. I grinned a little. My heart thrummed. It was *safe*. Not deadly. I haven't heard of many cleaning-related deaths. One guy in the back burned his hand real bad because he shut the press lid too quick, but I don't do the presses. Just the buttons. Unbuttoning the shirt buttons, buttoning the pant buttons, zipping the zippers, pinning on the tags. Tag it, bag it, and repeat. It's simple. Again, not deadly. It's practical. Comfortable.

The wooden, swinging door to the back thrust open toward me. A screeching stack of hangers filled with clothes, covered in plastic, swayed along the rail mounted to the ceiling.

"Rack these and you can go," Crystal called out from behind the bags as the door shut between us. "Slow night. I'm closing." Her voice faded behind the rattling of the steam-powered presses.

Nobody had come in for the last half hour; surprising, for a Wednesday night. Crystal was right. The hand of the clock on the wall ticked to seven. Finishing up the last tag on the shirt, I tossed it in the silky red bag. Drawing the string tight and yanking it into a knot, I pulled the lumpy sack up from its stand. Red meant rush. Following where Crystal exited, I ducked around the plastic bagged laundry and tossed the red bag into the big red bin by the metal wash tubs. The last of the presses hissed, winding down, and the back room seemed to sigh in relief. Usually the area rang with conversations of the ladies cleaning and pressing. They'd gone already, booking it to dinner with their families.

Crystal was probably in the office counting the registers.

Shoving back through the door, I wound over to the front entry and glanced out the windows. Clouds made the sunset hazy. Three small trees lined the edge of the parking lot, their flimsy branches and leaves flopping about in the soft breeze. Golden flecks of light pranced upon the blacktop in the empty parking lot. I snapped the lock on the door. *Closed.* A burly black truck rumbled into the drive, gleaming black rims on the tires tagging the shadows.

Tucker.

I couldn't help but grin then, and tossed a wave to the dim interior. Holding up a finger, I spun on my heels and ran to the clothes rack.

"Crystal!" I called, grabbing the heavy hangers. "My ride is here."

Ten bags for customers whose last names began with *M* later, Crystal slumped through the swinging door. "What'd you say?"

"My ride's here!"

"Oh. Alright. See you tomorrow."

"Okay. See you!" Yanking my thick time card out of its slot on the wall, I penciled in the time for the day.

"What shift you working?" she asked.

"Early!" I whined. "I'm the six crowd. Have to open."

"Fun for you!"

"You know it."

"I bet Earl brings coffee."

"Eh. I guess it helps." I shrugged. The lights from Tucker's truck shone through the front doors.

"Nice truck."

"Yeah. Nicer looking driver inside." I jiggled my eyebrows at her. She giggled. "You go get it, girl."

"You bet I will."

"Here, I'll lock the door behind you."

After last waves and condolences for opening so early the next morning, I ducked out of the glass entryway and flung open the truck's passenger door. Tucker hunched over a pile of papers stacked up in his lap and propped against the steering wheel.

"Whoa." I breathed out. "That's a lot of paper, yo."

"Hm." Tucker tapped a pencil against his forehead. He squinted at his other hand's grip on the wheel.

"Are—hey? Hello? Everything okay?" Hefting myself up into the body of the truck, I hauled the door shut behind me. Cool air drifted around us. I sighed, liquifying against the soft seat. "Air conditioning." I breathed in the sweet, crisp wind. A last beam of sunlight meandered across the dashboard, renewing the cab with the fragrance of freshly ground coffee beans. Wiggling my throbbing toes against the soles inside my hot shoes, a shudder ran through my spine.

"Sorry." Tucker glanced up. "I have to finish a project before we can grab dinner."

Dinnah. Dinnah with Tuckah. I'll take it. His lovely Aussie accent. Say anything, Tuckah. "What kind of project?" I asked.

"Hold up." He held out the eraser end of the pencil for a moment, then sighed, and scrawled several sentences on the paper.

While he finished, I buckled my seat belt, untucked my white polo shirt from my khaki pants, and re-did my ponytail into a fabulously unkempt messy bun.

Tucker gathered all the papers, shuffling them into a huge stack, and dumped them into a box in the back seat. "Have you talked to your dad today?"

"No. But he'd be happy to know you have a huge box in your back seat."

Tucker huffed out a laugh as he twisted back to face the steering wheel. "Too right."

"You don't need a back seat in a truck, Thompson," I mimicked Dad's stern concern. "A vehicle serves as transport and nothing else."

Tucker furrowed one eyebrow, lowering his voice. "When you take Saylor out in that truck, imagine I'm right there in the back seat."

Giggling, I rolled with it. "Is he in the back seat? In the box?"

Tucker's humor loosened then, and the one eyebrow rose.

"What? *Is* he in the box?" I glanced back at the box. "Did you kill somebody?"

He rolled his shoulders back, and sniffed. "Let's eat." He forced a smile onto his chiseled jawline. "Starved. Absolutely ravenous."

"Did—did you kill a guy?"

Tucker's emerald glance rolled over to me and then behind him as he reversed the truck away from the front of the building. "I'm in the mood for pasta. Something saucy. And bread."

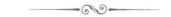

His hunched shoulders swelled into tense arms, gripping his menu. In the three months he'd been working with the new recruits, he had spent a lot of hours in the fitness center. Those muscles on the sides of the neck, the perfect place to rest a head or nuzzle a kiss, had become more defined along with his shoulders. His camouflage uniform jacket didn't hide it.

A single candle in a red glass holder flickered between us upon a red and white checkered plastic tablecloth. Only a block down from the dry cleaner's, we hadn't had a chance to say much. But the waiter would be bringing our water glasses any time and Tucker just stared at the menu like he wanted everything on it. Maybe he did. That was entirely possible.

"What's in the box, Thompson?" I breathed out the question.

"The tears of my ancestors."

"Wow."

The waiter stalked up then, carrying two ruby jars filled with icy liquid. Setting them down before us, he offered a quick smile. "Have you decided what you'll be having this evening?" He readied a notepad from the black apron at his waist.

Tucker tossed the menu onto the table, the cardboard slapping onto the plastic. "I can't. I'm sorry." Tucker ran a palm across his forehead and jerked his head my way. His eyes stared through me. "Here's—let's—I need to—"

Tucker slid his chair out while the waiter stared. Tucker grabbed my wrist and heaved me toward the door. I mouthed a silent "apologies" to the stunned man, as the muggy evening air filtered around us. Tucker charged onward, until he stopped short at the bench on the front porch. Robotically, he sat, stiff, on the edge of the metal furniture.

"Are you alright?" I asked. "Seriously, what is in the box?"

"I have to leave."

"You should eat dinner. I think you're having a hangry moment. Hungry and angry. All at once. Hangry."

"It's not like that."

"We all get cranky. The waiter—"

"I've been called up for duty overseas. On the seas. Away. Not sure exactly where we're going."

My tongue melted into the roof of my mouth. "The—why? What?" All the questions I wanted to ask clung to my ribs, sticky with dread.

"We need to find—" He stopped, licking his lips and then clamped them shut. "I'm not supposed to say. It's a high-level clearance assignment."

"Do you know who's going with you?"

"Your dad will be assigning duty recs tomorrow." He heaved out a heavy breath through his nose.

"But. You. You just—for how long? How long will you be gone?" As the sun sank behind the trees, so, too, my heart tugged into the horizon.

"Until we finish the assignment."

"You can't tell me?"

His palms wrapped around my cheeks, guiding my eyes to his. "If you were to join us, I could tell you everything. And we wouldn't be apart again. We'd be side by side on the field. Together. Working as a team for a greater good. And I wouldn't have to garner secrets or confidences or keep information from you. You'd be right there."

"I can't. I won't." Shuddering away, I had to break free from his warm, pervasive grip. He'd have me sunk in an instant. The chill helped. "You know I can barely walk by myself. I've spent months, *months*, getting to where I can stand up for an hour at a time without leg braces." Anger welled up, underlining all the words as they tumbled out.

"You'd see it all for yourself." He continued his line of thought, ignoring my argument. "You wouldn't miss out on anything, because you would be on the front."

"Can you not hear what I'm saying?" I cried out. "You hear me, Tucker. If there's one thing I love about Tucker Thompson, it's that he hears me in all the noise. No matter what I said, you heard it."

"That's the thing." He pleaded back, just as sunk in his own case. "You will be heard. By getting back out there, standing on your own, you'd be free."

"Stop. You haven't seen me broken. I'm broken. Remember those months you traveled the world doing missions for Alliance? While you were out exploring, I recovered from nearly dying. Wheelchairs, leg braces, endless dark nights where my voice refused to meld with my mind. The words refused to come out, but they've started to come back. But look at me now. I'm done with *adventure*!"

"You aren't, Saylor! Remember the nanocomputers! I brought them back for you. Those weeks when we injected the serum of nanocomputers back into your blood, they changed you for good. You are a whole new person."

"No! I am not. I've lost."

"Why do you continue arguing a moot point? Quit being dramatic about the pain and use it. Move into it. Make it a stepping stone and not a crutch."

"Easy to say." I spat out the words. *He doesn't hear me.* The idea drove burning and blurry tears into my eyes.

Tucker stepped back. He studied his shoes and lowered his voice. "You need to come with us, Saylor." He planted his balled-up fists in his pockets.

A man and woman walked up to the front door, eyeing us discreetly. I offered a tight smile as they entered the restaurant. Tucker sank onto the bench.

"You might want the old Saylor to come with you. The one who was reckless and bent on destruction. She stole a boat and convinced everyone she could save the day. That Saylor didn't know her limits. She didn't realize how tall the heights truly are."

"You have—"

"But I'm not Yesterday Saylor anymore." I held up a palm to stop his beautiful voice from bickering. "I've built big walls and I ripped them down. I did my hard thing: saved the world from a global wave of solar radiation. And it struck me down. I cannot do it again."

"Why do you believe that lie?" His voice breathed out question after question, unhearing, misunderstanding.

I can't face any more giants. "Some people face death and it makes them stronger. It makes them want to live each day fully and do big things. But I did those big things. I gave away my time for people who hate me now, and who say I'm this despicable creature."

"You're not despicable. Why do you care about what strangers think of you anyway?"

"Stop. You are not listening to the words coming out of my mouth."

"I'm hearing you."

"No." Quaking in my white tennis shoes, I bit back loathe for his thick-headedness. "You used to hear me. I'm not sure—"

"Saylor, I refuse to leave on a bad note again. I've left twice, wait, three times from a bad spot. I won't do it."

"Maybe it's our fate."

"And since when do you believe in fate?"

"When have I not?"

"Who am I even speaking to right now? Where's my Saylor? The Saylor who forges her own path, come what may?"

I let out a quick yell, a quite unladylike grunt, and tossed my fists in the air. "Do you not see I'm losing this battle inside of myself? Do you not see I've got nowhere to go? I've got nothing to give. I don't care about the things I used to dream for. Now I dream of blood stains. Now I dream of falling into darkness. My losses outweigh any wins I've ever had. My clothes don't fit. My knees always hurt. And I can't train. And I can't run. And I can't be who I used to want to be, because I tried, and it ripped me apart. I cannot face the darkness again." The tear spilled out of my eye, running down the side of my nose, dragging a river of black mascara with it. I didn't care.

Tucker sprang up from the bench, wrapping his arms around me. His coffee scent devoured the hunger and wrenched hope. Whatever spices of cinnamon or leather or mountain forests he'd used earlier, bound the splinters of fear. He held me, resting his cheek against my ragamuffin hair.

"All I want," I whispered, "is to sit on a porch with you, watching a sunset together."

He swallowed, breath ragged. One of his hands buried into the back of my hair. "We can find a sunset. *That* I can do."

He laced his fingers through mine and we wound over to the truck. He parked us by the small pond over the hill from Fort Story, and we sat in the back of the bed, legs dangling over the gravel, while stars dropped into their places above the trees.

We didn't say much.

The stars didn't either.

But Tucker held my hand the whole time, even as he walked me to the door of the house, and kissed my cheek. I ached for more. I wished he'd said less. His eyes, oh those eyes, they shone with questions and unstated opinions.

That night behind my closed eyelids, black pools of wide oceans quivered with unblinking eyes and hollowed cheeks. Somewhere someone laughed, but it silenced with a quick crack. Somewhere in the deep forests, monsters lurked, snapping and flapping their vicious wings, heaving fire at those who'd charge against them.

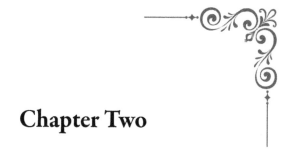

Chapter Two

MUTINY TO THE WRATH
Tucker

"What's she been doing all this time?" Canaan sipped from his white ceramic mug, the liquid inside the same color roast as his skin. Steady, almond eyes gauged the Commander's reaction. He sat across the dining facility table from me, munching on bacon and eggs.

Commander McConnell licked his thumb and flipped the top paper over on the legal pad resting on the table before him. "I gave her the option to renew her contract as a specialist with the Alliance Military Guard, to suspend the contract, or to terminate it. She chose to work at a local dry cleaner and laundromat."

"Are you—why would she want to do that? Between the nanocomputers swimming in her blood, years of training and experimentation, and tech developed for her, she's worth millions in Alliance investment. Not to mention man-hours."

McConnell's shoulders held steady but I saw the flinch cross his sun-seared face. The topic had been a source of contention among the family, unspoken, obstinate, and infinite. The Commander didn't want to push Saylor, but she vacillated on an hourly basis. Restless. I called her restless. Her brother Logan called her annoying. He said she was milking it. But he never said a word to her, as far as I knew.

How can you, after all, lecture the person who single-handedly saved your life?

I shoved the eggs on my plate around with my fork. Not hungry.

Burkman coughed to my left. "How long's your layover, Canaan?" His booming voice caused some men from the next table over to crane their necks our direction.

"Layover. Nice way to put it."

"Now that your whole squad's been reassigned, I suppose I wanted to be easy on you. Just the one time." Hulking hands rustled over his charcoal scalp.

"'Preciate it." Canaan tried to huff out a laugh, wrapping his fingers around his fork. "Can't say I know. Meeting with Fulbright and Blagojevic in ten."

"Blagojevic?" The Commander jerked his chin toward Canaan. "He's here?"

"Notified me late last night. Guess he ranked up. Four stars now."

"Thought he'd stayed in Washington."

"Red eye. They want to tap out the leak. Find out who's pacing our shipments and why they want 'em."

"Gray markets, Canaan," the Commander sighed, his sapphire eyes holding a hollow ache. "More computers, more parts, they can trade it all."

"It's more than that," Canaan insisted. "I feel it in my kneecaps. Three shipments of these particular parts, the replacement pieces for them, these pirates continue to confiscate this particular equipment and none of the others? It's improbable."

"What do they want you to do about it?" I edged in.

"I helped design many of the parts. The prototypes are registered as my patents."

"Nice work," I cheered. Took a big swig of the black coffee in my brown mug. Darker than the highway's morning commute and just about as tasty.

Canaan bobbed his head side to side. "Except I'm under pressure now."

"What if—" Burkman cleared his throat. "Nah." The hearty volume tapered out.

"Can't begin a sentence with 'what if' and end it there." Tapped my eggs with my fork.

"I was just thinkin' Canaan needs some security help. Maybe a team should recon the security leak, take care of some unhospitable outflow, and get our property back."

"Burkman," I negated.

"It could be a good training platform." He shrugged.

Across the table, beside Canaan, Commander McConnell's blue judgement flicked up to me. I returned it. He refocused on the papers before him, tapping his pen against his jaw.

Canaan tossed a confused glance my way.

"Burkman," I sighed. "The recruits haven't finished their training yet. They've only just come out of the first phase of reintroduction. I haven't been a drill instructor long enough to think I'm *that* good with them. Sure, they're not green, but without their GRIPS, they're lost."

Burkman snorted. "None of them are lost. Guarantee it."

Canaan continued gauging my reaction.

I answered his silent question. "My squad consists mainly of reassigned Alliance students. Each one of them has been a part of Alliance since they were age five, trained up to incorporate psychological and physical warfare as their main priority. They were Project Reboot, and Burkman here helped me *realign* the program."

"That's where Steele—"

"Yeah."

Canaan nodded, dropping his gaze in memoriam.

"They had two unique tools, a set of mechanized gloves called GRIPS, and an ocular mapping display for their eyes, called VISTAS. They worked together to create a killer punch."

"Pretty unique."

"Rapton thought so. Before he died at the wrath of the tech he helped create."

"Heard stories. Rough. You say your squad's in training?"

"Yeah."

"For what?"

"The ones who were old enough needed to be assessed and evaluated before reintegrating to normal life once we got them back stateside."

"Heard they call themselves Dragons." An amused grin crossed his face.

I tilted my head to the side. "For now. I'm working on another title for them."

"So, you're, what, taking the soldier out of them?"

The idea crawled across my forehead with spindly feet. "No. Not exactly."

"What are you doing with them, then?"

"Correcting their worldview. Retraining them to protect and serve, rather than simply assassinate. Taking the monster out of them."

Canaan scratched the back of his neck. "Seems like they might want to get out of the classroom. Obtain some hands-on experience to ensure they've learned properly." He shoved a piece of bacon in his mouth and crunched it up.

"The reintegration program only began a couple of months ago. I couldn't say if—"

McConnell contributed his opinion. "Thompson, we'll discuss the idea. I'm not sure Blagojevic would go for it anyway. He's a standard ops sort of guy. Doesn't like to test the waters. Especially when so much coin is at stake. Have the troops do a longer run this morning. Get them ready for the Surveys."

"Yes, sir."

Boots shuffled. Bodies stirred from seats. Plates around the dining facility began clattering louder, as men prepared to head out for the morning's Physical Training. Good mornings begin with PT. Most mornings begin with PT.

I squinted at the Commander. "Do you think Blagojevic would want them to do a trial run? Send them out before they've completed Phase Two?"

"No." The Commander shook his head. "He's a tried-and-true planner. Doesn't go rogue on any ops he's ever done. He'd have no interest in dealing with the repercussions of putting our crew on a trial run."

"**B**lagojevic wants to send the Dragons." Outside the fitness center, Commander McConnell caught up with me, holding up a palm to prevent me from arguing. "He said they need to get some field training and this serves as good a time as any."

"They're not Dragons anymore," I argued. Narrowing my eyebrows at the idea of the ubiquitous Blagojevic, I yanked the front of my sweaty PT shirt away from my skin. PT had been brutal, with a five-mile run and a thousand sit-ups. Maybe it was seventy-five, as well as seventy-six push-ups, and ending with even more squats and a dash of pull-ups. Burkman had a way of amassing excruciating workouts. But we were still alive, so they must have helped.

Meanwhile, the Commander sighed, flipping through a manila file folder thick with white and yellow papers. "He said we ship out tomorrow. Gather your best ten."

"What else do we have? Who will be operating this excursion? Ten rookies and a prayer?"

"You, me, Burkman, Canaan, Logan McConnell, and Micah Fortuyn. I've got five from Delta Red unit who have been working with Canaan, and Fulbright's asked me to handpick from the coastal unit. Plus, your ten."

"Micah's been back but she's on desk duty. Logan's waiting on his assignment."

"This is it."

"But why—"

"Think of it as an opportunity." The Commander tucked the folder under his camouflage sleeve. "Pick your top ten students. This will initiate them into the realm of Alliance. Blagojevic made a good point. They've been training for years. While they've had different tactics and mindset, they received top marks in their classes and trainings with some of our best men. If they're not ready now, then they should reconsider their future with Alliance. All your students signed contracts, remember. They're of age to decide for themselves what they can do."

I wanted to shake my head or argue. Cleared my throat.

"I've been in your shoes, Thompson." He stated it clearly enough. Those azure eyes lit with his honest opinion. "My children fight battles I wouldn't have picked for them. While I encouraged all of you to consider Alliance, I didn't force you here. Saylor jumped in with both feet."

"Would she say the same?"

"How so?"

"You gave her limited options for joining Alliance. Either she join or she join."

A grin wiped across his face then. "And I've heard quite a bit of flack from Bette. She thinks I'm abhorrent for doing it." He shrugged. "I had no idea she'd be so good at leading a troop and fighting her worst fears." He dropped my gaze then. "I didn't know she'd be so courageous. I figured she would want to leave after a couple of weeks and go back to the States. Instead, she rose to the occasion, which is what she does."

Swallowing the hard lump of dissolution in my throat, the silhouette of her limp frame in my arms welled up around the memory. "What about her now?"

"She has to keep fighting those hard battles."

"And we leave."

"Son, one thing I've learned about life as Alliance: plan as you go, and plan for traveling. It's a progressive work we do. I almost lost Esmerelda to it; she tired of all my relocating." He shrugged again. "But this is important."

"Is it?"

"What are you saying, Thompson?"

"Alliance seems to take and take. What are they giving back?"

"They secure. They round up the threats and put them away."

"Sir, with all due respect, seems to me I've spent too many years mopping up our own messes. How can we be doing any good if we're simply dealing with our own rogue operatives?"

"Alliance has many kindles in the fire. Bigger projects are coming. Like your Dragons."

"Speaking of, they need a new name. I think it would help morale."

"Up to you, Thompson." He checked his watch, and then surveyed the empty field. "You've got twenty-four hours before we roll. Prepare your troops to be gone for at least three weeks, if not a month. I'll gather everyone else. Assemble in Fieldhouse Four by 1500 tomorrow."

"Yes, sir."

"And Thompson, Saylor—"

"Yeah?"

He flinched, then grit his teeth, the words rolling around his mouth before they came out. "We're headed out to investigate piracy, missing tech, and missing crews. It will be dangerous. A lot of unknowns involved. We're on high alert here. Somebody knows something they're not supposed to, and someone else is a traitor. Keep this close to the vest. Be prepared for the worst."

"Always do, sir."

He nodded, and tossed his shoulders straighter. "Yes, you do." Gave a quick, knowing nod. "Hoo-rah."

Something had happened between my Dragons and me in the time since I'd brought them back from their dungeon. The Solaris program training facility at Camp Kissinger, beneath the sands of the hard Outback in Australia, had been decimated. But they'd come out alive. Most of the younger ones had gone back to their families, and those who had no guardians were placed in homes of other students or Alliance families. Those ages sixteen and over were given the option to sign up with Alliance in a training program to refocus their abilities. And I'd worked with them since their feet touched the ground. Scraggly and hardened, they'd become something like a family to me. Twenty-two Dragons took on every challenge I passed their way. Burkman, General Fulbright, Commander McConnell, and I worked with them to reign in the ideas upon which they'd been educated—such as the fact they believed they were alive in order to destroy the weakest of humanity. Many of them, especially the oldest, had killed other Dragons during their Assessment tests back in Australia to advance ranks. Bridging the gap between protecting and assassinating proved to be no easy task. But yet it served as quite fulfilling when they made progress and didn't opt to rip the heads off the mannequins during target practice.

I lay their name cards on the ground in the center of my room. Headshots and their testing scores added to the Dragon nickname scrawled above each actual name. Picking the first few was easy—I needed the oldest ones. Eagre, Wring, and Flight. All nineteen, same as me, and all remembered me from when I'd been at their side in the program. All watched when my "parents," actually undercover Alliance operatives, removed me from the Solaris program. And they knew another set of Alliance agents had taken me to be with Commander McConnell on Isla Barina to begin my training outside of the program. Saylor had mentioned she thought Eagre never took her eyes off me. Saylor'd be happy to see this mission happening for a myriad of reasons.

Rubu and Weyr would have to come. They loved a good adventure. Both eighteen, fans of sailing, lean, and salty. Those guys came in a package. And they believed Logan to be godlike, so they'd follow his orders well enough. Clutch's brown and gold-streaked curly hair pled for action, so I added her card to the stack.

Pacing around the cards, I studied the rest of the eighteen-year-olds. Thunder and Case managed to ace their marksmanship assessments, their hand-to-hand combat, and their psychological evaluations. Like hot coffee and chardonnay, those two. They often bickered, and tied for last place on the obstacle course because they couldn't get each other over the climbing wall.

Hazard was a muscled ox of a warrior. Headfirst, he'd grind whatever chore Burkman sent his way. He definitely had to go. He stormed with a fire in his eyes. Fire for loss and for what never would be. His parents died in a tsunami which devastated his hometown on the eastern coast of Japan. That fire would help our team. Hazard often stuck right by my side and got the others in line when they stepped out.

Nine.

After tucking the nine cards in a neat stack, I hooked my thumbs through my belt loops. I paced. Arguments about what these students could handle crisscrossed over each other, a knotted tangle of conflict. Their scores reflected similar results. Who could handle more pressure without breaking at this point?

My eyes landed on Shadow's card. Ebony hair flung over her left shoulder, those pale blue eyes burning into the camera. Seventeen. Five-foot-five. Shadow only spoke after I commanded her to. Hazard once told me she'd had a lisp and been tortured by their previous commander, so she refused to speak. But Shadow held her ground in all areas, following orders and whipping out a rifle faster than the others. She'd succeed.

I flicked her card onto the stack. Here were my ten, and there we would go, crossing the world into the murky unknown. Many of them were leftovers, children without homes or families, the unwanted; many of them preferred the ranks of the elite, just like most of us in Alliance. Unwanting of ordinary. The zeros of the normal world. Discredited, rejected, above average. The rulers of the underworld. Dragons they were, and exactly what we needed, a collection of mutiny to the wrath about to be poured out upon the earth.

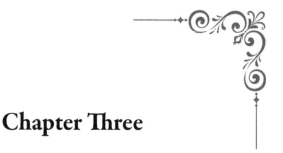

Chapter Three

WITHDREW
Saylor

"What's got your peas in a pinch?" Micah asked, a huge bowl of cereal bobbing on the table before her. She scooped up a heaping spoonful and slurped it into her mouth.

The tea kettle whistled from the stove before me. Starting, I blinked from my hazy fog. Outside the window, morning continued resting under its black blanket. Five o'clock came too soon. Every time.

"Besides, seems like you were asleep early last night," Micah continued, her mouth full of slushy flakes. "Didn't even talk to Tucker when he came over."

"He came over last night? Why didn't anyone wake me up? What are you eating? It sounds like death."

"Ha."

"I need my tea."

"Yes, you do, Hot Cross Buns."

"If you're saying I've got a nice—"

"Good morning, ladies," Dad interrupted, striding in to the kitchen. "Is coffee full steam this morning?"

Micah winked at me. "Of course. Long day and all."

"Quite."

I poured the bubbling water from the blue kettle into the rosy ceramic mug containing the tea bag. Dad shuffled around, grabbing a mug from the cabinet and then sliding beside me to access the coffee pot I blocked.

"Sorry," I mumbled and slid aside.

"Thanks." He poured the black liquid into his blue cup. "Whatever you said to Tucker the other day had him up in arms."

"I did?" I questioned, still blinking my heavy eyelids.

"He stopped by to give you this." Dad dug into his uniform pocket and fished around, then tugged a small white envelope out. "He insisted I give it to you first thing."

"Thank you," I mumbled.

Dad sauntered out of the kitchen with his mug. His boots thumped up the squeaky stairs.

"Ooohhh," Micah sang, "A love note!" She somehow lilted the phrase into a ten-syllable journey.

"Har. Go make fun. Eat your cereal." Tucker had sealed it. Slipping my finger under the glued flap, I ripped through the seam. The scrap of paper inside unfolded in my clammy, fumbling hands. He must have used some of his box paper. The penciled cursive spelled out a simple sentiment:

Fear is a liar.

– Thompson

My resolve took the weight of his sentence and tumbled to the floor.

"What's the smell, bluebell?" Micah had twisted in her seat, watching me stand still like a bewildered weed.

I shook my head.

"You should come up to the camp before we ship out," Micah was saying. The words were hazy, clouded. "We've got debriefing a little after noon, but you could come have lunch with me."

"Ship out?"

"You missed everything by going to bed before dinner. We're leaving this afternoon for several weeks."

"Who?" I studied my white socks.

"Me, Logan, Tucker, Canaan, Burkman, the Commander—"

Tightening my jaw, I held in any quivering lips which may have betrayed my lackluster morning demeanor. "I might do that," I found myself saying. The words muddled. A tremor rumbled through my hand as I carried the tea upstairs. My wrist locked up, aching in a pinch. They didn't understand. Fear may be a liar, but hope can be a monster.

They'd gathered at their long table, another dining facility on another continent, all the same and yet so different. Micah, Logan, Burkman, Canaan, Tucker, and various other semi-familiar faces Tucker had shown me pictures of before. They'd grabbed their servings and started in on the meal. My stomach gnawed at me, confuddled and indignant I wouldn't be joining them. In more ways than one.

Tucker eyed me and jumped to his feet. His face lit up, bright and airy.

Heat rushed to my cheeks, my heart shoveling itself into a deep pit in my chest. "I'm not here to—I, um, took a long lunch. To see all of you off."

Tucker's gaze dropped to the pink purse in my hand.

"I wanted you to leave on a good note," I uttered, emboldened. "I agree. We've left badly before, and I wanted you to want to come back this time."

The corners of his mouth shimmied up. "I'll always want to come back to you. Doesn't matter where you are."

"Even if I'm a laundry cleaner?"

He focused on my hand, and sent his to claim it. "If you're on a fox or in a box."

A small smile wrapped over my cheeks. "Mind if I join you? I won't be in the way?"

"Nevah."

The seat across from him sat empty, so I settled into the space. Conversations bobbed in and out, witty, and rife with life. The uniformed guys down the table from Tucker held up a hand in a brief salute as Tucker introduced them with weird nicknames. Something about a purse or a thunderstorm?

Canaan sat beside Tucker, often pausing his fork over his plate, as if he wanted to say something, but he'd just watch me.

After catching his glance for about the fifth time, I giggled. "Canaan, if you want to say something, please do."

"I've been instructed not to cross lines."

The lanky, caramel-colored, tech-savvy man hunkered in his spot, shadows lining his deep-set eyes. He'd been restless as well.

"Canaan, you've gone to the ends of the earth with me. I don't know many more lines you can cross."

"Glad to hear you're more of your eloquent self."

"Bah. I don't know who you're talking to."

"Commander McConnell informed me you utilized another dose of the nanocomputer serum Breame constructed."

Clearing my insta-dry throat, I offered a quick bob of the head. "Um. Yes. They—one more vial had been recovered. And I—used it."

His curious gaze flicked to Tucker and then back to me. "How's it been?"

Tucker studied his half-empty plate of meat and lettuce.

"Over about the course of six weeks, I injected myself with the nanocomputer serum to see if it would help me recover from my injuries after the solar flare in Dubai. The flare wiped out all the nanos that had been in my blood, so I lost my sight, talking and walking capabilities—It's a pretty long story, Canaan. And pretty uninteresting."

"Not to the right person, ma'am." He leaned closer. "Seems like the injection worked. I'd like to hear more from you on the matter. The sooner, the better."

"Any time, Canaan. When you all get back, I'm happy—"

"It might be too late then. If you came with us, if you re-upped with Alliance, I could share a project with you."

"Hey, Canaan!" Logan yelled from the corner of the table. "Tell Micah about Tweehouse. Tell her what you told me yesterday. About the bags."

"Ah, yes, Tweehouse. An entire pallet of tea fell on top of him in the warehouse—"

The conversations multiplied then, laughter roaring and Logan snorting into his drink. Micah didn't believe a word Canaan said, but then she did, and then the guys beside Tucker needed to know why Tweehouse was such a hoser.

Their words faded in and out, old stories mixing with new life. Tucker chuckled often, taking bites consciously, and only after we hadn't said another word to each other, he glanced up at me.

The room whirled with jittery excitement.

Friendly voices claimed history and collided like confetti.

But there sat my world. Across from me, around me, the family, the glitter, the people who made my days ripple onward, they flickered amid the faulty air.

And in those moments, Tucker saw me.

His eyes said it.

He saw more parts of me than I understood. He saw me fearful and he saw me fearless. Those marbled green eyes lit with the sheen of life.

My heart applauded, and then shuddered.

Tucker slid his hand across the table and I reached out, accepting his fingers against mine. We waited, a silent bridge of loss and redemption.

As I blinked away the deep breaths which engulfed me, my heart lurching within its crate, the seconds ticked onward.

He saw, too. He released his soft grip with a quick squeeze and a brief nod.

Dad strode up to the table, welcoming and being welcomed. Canaan gave a hearty hello.

Surprised, Dad jogged to me and offered a deep hug.

My heart lost its hold.

"I've got to get in a last meeting with Blagojevic before debriefing, sir," Canaan said rising from his spot. "Did they call you too?"

"I am on my way. Thought I'd catch Thompson. Blagojevic would like to confirm some parameters with you."

Tucker nodded, wiping his napkin across his lips.

"Sir." The uniform beside Tucker boosted his hand to garner attention. "What if some of the squadron doesn't return? What then?"

Tucker exhaled, clicking his tongue and using the second to confirm with a glance at his commanding officer. "We have few guarantees. As with every assignment, we adhere to the warrior ethos. And we continue forward."

The twitching inside my gut began again. *Nobody said anything about not coming back.*

My eyes began to burn. Taking in the faces around me, the red began to set in. They had to come back. Every one of them.

Dad's eyes met mine. Concern again crept into the deep blues, rattling around the black cores. He knew something. He knew something particular that he wanted me to know. And I couldn't know it if I wasn't—

"We need to go." Dad clapped his hands. "Saylor, I'm so glad you came to see us off. Makes my heart proud." He offered his arms, and I buried myself in his hug. Tightening his strong arms around me, the warmth spread through the thin layers of my cotton cleaning uniform. He whispered by my ear, "Be safe, kiddo. Take care of Bette and Cadence and Patricia. They're used to being home while the troops are out. You can offer them a unique perspective."

Of what? I wanted to ask. *Of all the existence they're missing out on? Of all the nightmares they're not garnering? Of all the late-night calls-to-arms? Of all the action-packed, heart-wrenching, bone-breaking, adrenaline-scurrying flutter of accomplishment?*

Blinking quicker, I nodded. Scorching bubbles welled up in my throat and my eyes.

One by one, they stood, my unit, my family, my people, and one by one they offered a sad nod, a hearty handshake, or like Micah, a mind-crushing bear of a lifeline to the earth.

"I'll miss you, Saylor. Seems wrong without you. But I understand."

My mouth began to clamp up, filled with a skittish reflex to run far away as fast as possible. I followed my people to the door of the dining facility, and with last waves, they continued down the sidewalk into the afternoon sun. I shoved the long strap of my purse over my head, onto my shoulder and down across my chest.

"Be there in one moment," Tucker called out to Dad, who gave a brief smile, and paced away.

Tucker twisted back to me. "Thank you for deciding to venture out."

"Of course. I had to say goodbye. Also, I didn't want to fill my lunch break with sweeping."

"I understand not wanting to sweep."

"It's every day! Every. Day."

"Right so. Too much." His arms wrapped around my back, circling my waist.

"I guess you better go grab some coffee. I figure you and the guys need to discuss Alliance things."

Tucker set his jaw. Clamped teeth. Arid desert. A glimmer of a smile rustled across his lips. "Coffee o'clock." He drew his arms tighter around me. "The darkness within will whisper lies. The darkness will always be loud. But I'll be louder, Saylor. Don't lie to yourself and say you want to sweep your days away. You hate sweeping. Be honest, deep down."

"I know it. Not so deep down. Right here." I patted my shoulder.

He matched my grin. When I gave my bottom lip a gentle nip, he brought his forehead down to mine. "I'll be there when the darkness tries to drown you. You've faced it before and won. You have this remarkable life. I'll never stop reminding you of the truth."

The air around us could have scorched and sparked, and it probably did, as he shelved the conversation with a kiss. His lips met mine, reserve ditched, ache dissolved, as warmth flooded through my spine. The scent of warm coffee and tangy spices lingered around us. My fingers settled upon his neck and the stiff fabric of the uniform dividing us.

Before long he tore his tantalizing lips away from mine. "Own your choices. Own those decisions. They make you who you are, and you're phenomenal. Your super power, Saylor, was never nanocomputers. Or oxinals. Or that chip Breame planted up in there." He slid one hand over my forehead, brushing a couple loose strands of golden hair out of the way. "Your power exists as heart, and faith. You conquered the sun. You throttled death and rescued your family. You dug your way out of a mountain with your fierce resolve. Now you've got time on your hands, and instead of evaluating, learning, you're second-guessing. Warriors don't get to evaluate in the crux. You acted. You reacted. And now you need to compile your arsenal. Forgive yourself for the broken parts. I'll always remind you of the conqueror I see before me. Especially when you can't see her."

"Tucker—"

"You're going to argue with me right now, but I haven't had enough coffee for it."

He cupped my smooth cheeks in his hands. Those teal eyes sparkled. "Your story carries powerful weight. Somebody needs to learn from your story. Maybe it's you. You've only got so much time on this planet. Don't waste it looking back. Create a new ethos."

I withdrew one statement from my arsenal. "Never quit?"

"Keep that one. I've found it useful."

"I think I'll keep it."

"Do it." His dimples deepened on the edge of his sly grin.

Tucker slid closer, his warmth mixing with mine. His hands explored the back of my neck, my cheek, his thumb massaging my jawline. "Perfect." He muttered in that alluring accent and brought his lips to mine. Fire couldn't contain him, and neither could gravity. His kiss carried me closer to the stars and drew me into the earth. My greedy lips melted against his, ebbing life, and thirsty for more.

He had to come back.

He might not come back.

Air tore away from my throat. I gasped for its loss. Loss.

"I'll do my best to contact you while I'm gone." Tucker cupped my face in his hands. I threw my arms around his neck, surging against his chest in the most awkward way ever. Somewhat stumbling back, he steadied himself. Then he returned the gesture. His heart thumped, pounding. So did mine.

Fear wouldn't bind me anymore. Neither would the shadows.

Tucker released his grip, and withdrew for both of our safety.

"Wait," I stated. No—I commanded. "Wait."

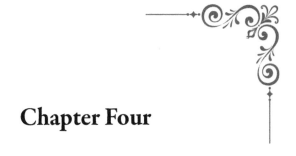

Chapter Four

LANDFALL
Tucker

S he said she would stay at the back of the line. She said she wouldn't be in the way. Words tumbled out of her mouth, one hand landing firmly on my wrist. Her tranquil eyes lit up, the shutters opening.

"No," I interrupted her. Stopping the smile winding its way on to my face, I strapped down the balloon inflating within my chest. "That's not the way this works."

Her face fell.

"You come with us at full capacity. You come with us ready to ride the line."

"But, Tucker—"

"That's the deal, Saylor. You commit yourself here and now for a new contract. You'll commit to probably two years with Alliance. Your coming with us serves as a new start. It's not a chance to be the kid at the back of the class, the weak link. This is your reboot. This is Day One, all over again."

She worked her jaw, considering the words. Her gaze flicked back and forth between mine before finally dropping and studying my boots. "You're saying you don't want me to come?"

"Not at all. I want you. Right on the line beside me."

"But I have to be a rookie again?"

I shrugged. "You keep your rank. Just re-upping your contract. You'd need to be able to match the Dragons. Also, don't mention the word 'Reboot' to them. They don't react well to it."

Those hungry eyes roamed up to my name badge. "But they react well to the term dragon? And they don't mind their nicknames?"

"They have their days. But most importantly, they're willing to risk being here."

"As opposed to what?"

Before I let any words roll out like they wanted, I licked my lips. "You aren't like them. You've seen different challenges. But I know, *I know,* you belong on this undertaking. As an equal part of the force."

Swallowing hard and squaring up her shoulders, those eyes narrowed. "Alright. What about uniforms? And do I have to change what I call you? And let's talk about the accepted hairstyles. I think we need to renegotiate the low bun."

Relief began building up that balloon again. "I won't be your commanding officer. You'll have to take it up with him."

Saylor stuck her hands in her pockets and nodded her chin toward where the Commander had exited the mall. "I guess we need to follow him, yeah?"

"Yeah. I think he'd like to know about this development."

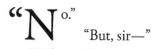

"N o."

"But, sir—"

"Why did you press her? She doesn't need this." The Commander stalked away, pacing the room outside Fulbright's office. He ruffled his sandy high-and-tight under one palm.

"She does. She's withering away."

"She's doing just fine at the laundromat."

"Do you hear yourself?" Perched on the edge of the chair beside the door, I jiggled the heel of one boot. Saylor had gone with Micah to find sundries and other paraphernalia.

"You'd best remember who you're talking to, Thompson."

"Sir, I hold you in the highest regard. As does Saylor. She needs you to believe in her."

"Oh, I believe in her," the Commander stated. "But I also believe in recovery time. I believe in letting her have time to figure out what *she* wants from life, rather than what I've lent her to desire."

"You do realize she writes her own story, right? She'd have ended up in a battlefield somewhere. How *fortunate* she ended up under your instruction."

"You know just as well as I do Breame constructed that meet-cute, don't you?"

"I know Breame meant most of his projects for harm or his own personal greed. I believe good can come out of bad. He brought Saylor back to you and reunited your family." Clamping my pearly whites closed, I fought back further arguments. Forcing the issue did no good. Here stood the great Commander William McConnell, master of his fate and that of his company. Present company included.

He exhaled. Grunted. The Commander strode to the chair beside me and sat. "Will she be received well?"

The Dragons. They'd, well, they'd react. "Of course, sir."

He eyed me. Linked his fingers together and settled his hands in his lap. "Once her Hancock hits that piece of paper, you must relinquish your fraternizations. Understand?" He almost seemed relieved.

I grinned. "Yes, sir." *Our lives aren't awkward at all.*

"Have you told her?"

"About being her superior?"

"About—about the—"

"Oh." The reports and their findings flashed in the back of my mind. They hadn't been far away since studying them. "No, sir. It's classified. I've kept my word."

His chin bobbed up and down. "Best keep it that way for now."

"Agreed."

The door to Fulbright's office yanked open. The general's secretary wandered out, black heels scuffling on the carpet. "Sorry to keep you," she whispered as the door fell shut behind her. "He's on a call. Shouldn't be more than a few minutes."

"While we wait," the Commander rose from his seat, "would you mind gathering some paperwork for me?"

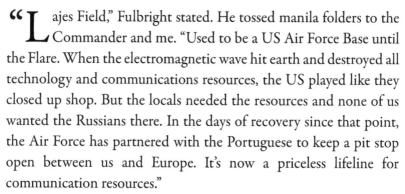

"Lajes Field," Fulbright stated. He tossed manila folders to the Commander and me. "Used to be a US Air Force Base until the Flare. When the electromagnetic wave hit earth and destroyed all technology and communications resources, the US played like they closed up shop. But the locals needed the resources and none of us wanted the Russians there. In the days of recovery since that point, the Air Force has partnered with the Portuguese to keep a pit stop open between us and Europe. It's now a priceless lifeline for communication resources."

"Where's Lajes Field?" the Commander asked, flipping open the file cover.

"The Azores islands. Smack dab in the middle of the Atlantic."

"Seems like we lost our ships due north."

"Not as far north as you'd think." Fulbright perched on the edge of his desk, intertwining his fingers and settling them on his leg. "But it's the closest location where we have been able to track activity. Your team will have to seek out intel and use their resources to recon. Our satellites have done what they can, and we will continue to hunt from here, but these islands are prime ground."

"The pirates must be located near Lajes?" I asked to confirm. "Without a doubt?"

Fulbright nodded. "The Azores islands are a grouping of nine islands off the coast of Portugal. Since all three ships went down to the north, we assume it's the best place to begin."

"Has the official word been concluded? They sank?"

"You're right to confirm," Fulbright sighed. "We have no conclusive evidence of anything other than they didn't meet their port and sent no distress signals. We've got ghosts."

"And tech worth its weight in gold to the right person." Commander McConnell closed his folder.

"Especially worth it to the wrong person. Your contact at Lajes, General Titus, as noted in your documentation, will have additional information as to known whereabouts of those wrong people. And their—associates."

"Yes, sir," McConnell offered Fulbright a hand. The two shared one firm shake. "We'll report in at landfall." Fulbright nodded, and I returned it.

Fulbright pointed to the Commander. "And you've gained an extra set of hands?"

McConnell cleared his throat. "Seems so, Fulbright. She'll be able to supplement with some unique insight on our other guest. I'll make sure to keep you in-the-know."

"I'm looking forward to reading that transcript."

Chapter Five

IT'S BEEN A WHILE
Saylor

"Y ou're coming along?" The leggy blonde whipped her ponytail over her shoulder. Marbled brown eyes stared me down.

"I am." I sat on the bench in the room lined with lockers, waiting for Micah.

"Like as a cook or something? Journalist?"

"I'm not a cook."

"So, what then? You're out for the count, right?" She slammed her locker door shut, then shouldered the strap of the faded green duffel bag.

"Well, I wouldn't say that, quite."

"What's your role?" She did seem genuinely confused, I'll give her, but the innocent twist to her coy questioning drove spikes into my spine.

"Journalist. Ha." My line of thought didn't keep up with her.

"You're writing it all down? Maybe you're the secretary, then?" The smile flipped on her lips then, and I saw it. The curl of contempt.

"No." I didn't stamp my foot, but I let the edge roll out a fine line in my tone. "I'm a specialist. I ranked up right before I saved the world from a global catastrophe and it nearly killed me." My turn to flip my hair over my shoulder. Tilted my chin down at her. *Punk.*

She slid the edge of her jaw into a sly grin. Sunlight streaming in through the high windows glinted on her white teeth. "My apologies. Tucker doesn't speak about you much. Figured you were done."

"I'm not done."

"Seems like it would be hard to come back from something like that."

Clearing my throat, the liquid stuck around, like fire in a matchbox. "What's your name again?"

"Eagre."

"Eager?"

"As in, a flood."

"That's your real name?"

"That *is* my name." Her slim chin settled with discontent at my conversational ability. "And you? Seriously, what will you be doing on our mission? Tucker's our trainer. We've got medics, tech, and all of us Dragons are the muscle and brainpower. You're—what—the—?" Her eyebrows peaked over her forehead. Her shoulders settled into an annoyed slump.

"I'll be read in on the mission at debriefing, just like everyone else."

"But there's no way you can catch up with where we are physically, can you?"

"I—"

"Mentally?"

"I'm perfectly fine, mentally."

"You don't want to endanger the mission. Do you? Or are you just coming for more face time with your boyfriend?"

"Hey, you are out of line."

"I've read all about you and your story and your hopeful, star-crossed ideology. We're nowhere near the same line, Miss McConnell." She dropped her arms and straightened up. "I'm a fine-tuned warrior. I'm a machine of power and poise. I've spent the last five years tagging slackers such as yourself in the ring and taking them out."

"You should know better than to speak to your superiors in such a manner."

"You're not my superior, sheila." She stirred the words around her mouth like venom in a cauldron. Her mock-Australian accent made the words cute, and loathsome. "You're yesterday. You're burned up, burned out, and you know it."

A renewed, fiery drip dried up in the back of my throat. "Are you threatening me?"

She chuckled. "You wish me insecure enough to threaten. I'm stating facts."

"Tucker sure would hate to hear about his trainees acting like you are right now."

"Oh, and I'm *sure* he'll believe every word you say."

"He would!"

"Because you telling my chain of command serves as the best way to show him you're so much better than me. As you obviously are not."

The door cracked open, Micah's energetic, large shadow filling the void. At least she was tall. And on my side. "Got your uniforms, Saylor! They had to discharge new ones."

"Good luck breaking them in," Eagre added, the friendly tone in her voice infiltrating the conversation. But I heard the sentiment underneath. "I hear they take a while to adjust to. Just like the company."

❧

"Is someone throwing shade in here or is it just me?" Micah held out the green duffel bag when the door latched shut. Her cocoa eyes studied me longer than they needed to.

"Summer's empty room. I understand Dickinson now. Summer's empty room. Because summer couldn't stay anymore. Winter moved in like a storm and stole it from her."

Still holding out the duffel in her fist, Micah asked in a lilting voice, "Is your medicine wearing off? I'll make sure to let Logan know you're going batty."

"That's why they call it rough sledding," I continued. Crossing my arms over my stomach, my fingers clung for solid matter. "Because winter. No more summer. And the sledding in the winter, it's because the hills are covered in boulders and dead animals. Covered in snow. Rough sled rides. No fun."

Micah let the bag drop to her side. "I'm going to find Logan now."

"No." I dropped my arms. "I'm sorry. I'm—maybe I am going loony. I probably am. I'm standing here about to suit up again for a job I told myself I'd never do again." I found the nearest bench and collapsed on it. The locker room didn't have a lot of options other than the gray lockers and the two benches. And the shower on the far wall. But a shower only would have made me look even more unprepared than I was.

"What do you mean?" Micah held her position, those boots holding sturdy beneath her.

I sighed. "I've spent a lot of hours sitting on the couch wondering if I could ever try to join up with Alliance. I'd decided no, I couldn't. Didn't want to. Didn't want to help a Guard which eagerly put its people into such harm and happily experimented on them."

"But you know they're changing, right?"

"Yeah. Right. I do. Tucker showed me how he's working with these new recruits, and he says how they're a whole new hope for Alliance."

"Okay. So?"

I jacked my pointer finger toward the door. "Her? Blondie just proved she's exactly like the people I'm determined not to bend to."

"She seemed nice enough."

"You didn't hear her entire sales pitch."

Micah strode over to the bench and thumped the bag into my lap. She plopped down beside me. "Well, I suppose you haven't signed the papers just yet. You can always back out."

"Hmph."

"What's in your bag?"

"My bag?"

"The one you've been clinging to, strapped across your shoulder."

I glanced down at the pink strap crossing my chest and noted how I was indeed gripping the strap at my hip. Swallowing hard, I swung my head to face Micah. "It's my carry-all. It has the things it always has."

"Which is what?"

"My ID cards, my point card, my lip gloss. A tube of mascara. Gotta have that."

"Of course."

"There's a cross-stitch Trish wanted me to finish."

"How's that coming?"

"Well."

"Let me see."

"Micah, we don't have time for this."

"Let me see the cross-stitch."

"Fine." Huffing out a deep breath, intertwined with a groan, I tugged the black and white polka dot bag out from under the duffel. Sticking one hand inside, I fished around for the stiff, itchy fabric and the— "Ow." The needle stuck my hand. Grabbing the small square, I withdrew the project. It ducked its head in shame in the fading light of the room.

"That square supposedly will be what?" Micah asked, holding out her hand. She pursed her lips.

I tossed the cloth into her palm. "Hey now, Hallie Homemaker, I don't see you attempting any needlework projects."

Micah let a cackle creak out of her gut. "No, no you don't. Is—is this a cat? A monkey?"

"It's supposed to be the Alliance logo."

"No, it's not!"

I grabbed for the fabric. She held it up over her shoulder, still studying it.

"This doesn't look like the letter A at all, Say."

"Gah! I know. I'm no good at cross stitch."

"Then why are you doing it?" Micah brought the fabric back down and pushed it toward me, as if it smelled like a dog's wet dinner.

"Because Patricia said I should try it."

"And Patricia always has the right answer?"

"I needed something to do while I sat on the couch. I couldn't sit and turn into a lump of potatoes. I had started to sprout leaves. She told me to try sewing or quilting or photography or painting or crocheting or knitting."

"Did you?"

"You know I tried knitting."

"And?"

"Micah, you saw my scarf."

"That was a scarf?" She giggled and bumped her shoulder against mine. "What about the sewing?"

"Again, you saw the button hole debacle."

"Logan was so mad."

"So was Dad."

"Photography? Did you try pictures?"

"What point are you making exactly?" The duffel bag began to lean away from me, prepping for a nose dive against the concrete. I grabbed it with one hand, the other still fingering the traces of cotton strings against linen.

"I'm not making a point. I just wondered what you were holding so tight. Looked like you have been guarding it with your life."

"Not really."

"What are you guarding with your life? People-weaving has always been your thing, Saylor. You're the guardian. You're the glue holding us together."

"I keep you all in line, right?"

"Exactly."

We giggled.

The sink dripped.

Micah cleared her throat. "Trying new things. Distraction works. And you should. You should definitely keep Logan away from any kitchen."

More giggles crashed out of our lips, but I tore my eyes away from the cross stitch to follow her argument.

Micah's big brown eyes widened. "You are good at hanging in. That girl, Eagre, she may be a blonder, taller, skinnier, fiercer version of you."

"Your argument's not making me feel so fabulous."

"You are good at protecting your own. You're good at being available when everyone else runs away."

"But I'm not good at cross stitch."

"We can't all be good knitters."

"Like you're a good knitter."

She shrugged. "If I ever start knitting, please take the needle thing and stab it in my heart. Just kill me then. My life has ended."

"Don't diss knitters, man. They *will* stab you."

"Don't I believe it, too."

Shoving the fabric back into the black bag, my free hand withdrew from the darkness, free and clear. "We're not knitters."

"We are not knitters." Micah swung her head side to side.

Swallowing a lungful of air, the cool room seemed to thin out. I studied the green duffel bag. "I'm not sure I am ready to be a fighter again. What if I fail? What if I fall? What if I get hurt again?" Sticky, the lump of doubt welled up in my chest, curdling my throat. The room seemed to satiate with steam.

Micah placed her hand on my shoulder. "Saylor. You *will* fall. You *will* fail. The first time you try to take on Logan in hand combat, he will probably drop you like a taco on Tuesday."

Licking my lips, I sighed. A girl knows truth when she hears it. Truth hurts the most.

"But," Micah added, squeezing my shoulder, "I'll be with you. Logan will help you get back up. Tucker will probably have chocolate waiting."

"He better."

"I saw his stash."

"Good."

Micah stood up then and held out her hand to me. "We win. We defeat. We finish the mission."

"Hoo-rah." I offered a brave smile, and nodded, grabbing her hand. "Wait. When did you see his stash?"

———— ❦ ————

Micah led me to the briefing room, a stale meeting space with gray walls and a low ceiling, filled with rows and columns of desk-chairs. Camo-clad bodies filled most of the seats, facing the front. Large green duffel bags lined the back of the room, and Micah and I added ours to the pile. She coasted into the last row and patted the back of the chair beside hers. I slipped into the blue plastic seat. Familiar pounding of anticipation wadded up behind the many layers of flesh and fortitude. This one little heart didn't know if it could take another round in the ring.

Micah dipped her chin. "Hey."

Shaking away the fog I'd let myself begin to slip into, I blinked over at her.

Those serious brown eyes studied me. "It's basically just like Fort Prospect."

"Oh. Good!"

"Except it's totally not."

"Oh."

"So." Micah blinked.

"Thanks for that."

"Sure thing."

Logan strode across the front of the room, over to Dad, who buried his attentions in a thick file in his hands. Tucker stood beside him, engrossed in some conversation with a brawny Asian kid. A good head and shoulders shorter than Tucker, he made up for it with his muscled shoulders and steady stance. His wiry black hair fell across his forehead, those black eyes locked on Tucker. The guy folded his arms across his chest, dropping his gaze to his black boots.

"His name's Hazard." Micah nodded over to the guys. "He's one of Tucker's trainees."

"Looks pretty intense."

"All of them are."

"Goody."

"They didn't get to have our carefree home life, Say."

"Oh, right." I somewhat snorted. "It was so merry."

She chuckled. "As merry as a berry."

"Under the boot of a—under the—huh."

"You're off your rhyming game."

"What can I say." I shrugged. "It's been a while."

Dad strolled up to me, placing his warm palm on my shoulder. His serious eyes held a dark secret. That jaw set in a firm line.

"Yes?" I asked.

"Come with me for a moment."

Bobbing my head in confirmation, I tossed a sideways bug-eye to Micah, who threw back a thumbs-up sign. Dad patted another muscular set of shoulders as he passed the guy, on his way out the door. My Commander then stopped right outside the door. I followed. The shiny white tiles glared up at us, curious.

Dad clasped his hands on the edges of the green folder, white pages sticking out of the edges. I'd forgotten how impending his uniform looked on him—bright-colored badges tagging his chest for the hero he was. McConnell. Under the name tag, his uniform rose and fell as he let out a deep breath.

"Yes, sir?" I peered up at him.

"I need to show you something. I'm not sure I can explain."

"Okay?"

"I don't want—I don't want you to worry. What you're about to see might bring up some issues with others who don't comprehend your history, or may bring your loyalty into question, but not with those who understand the situation."

"My loyalty?"

"Without question, I've ruled you out."

"For what? What do you need to show me?"

He held up the file. When I didn't budge or scream, he sighed, and opened the front, flipping through several sheets, before withdrawing one crisp, thick paper. From the back of it I could tell it wasn't a report, but a photograph, in grayscale.

As he flipped the paper up and around, the image of three people walking pointedly across the deck of a boat became clear. One of the people had a long, blonde ponytail tied loosely at the back of her head.

Dad held out the photo to me. "This was taken by satellite three weeks ago."

"Okay?" I accepted it.

"These are some of the people who've been capturing our shipments and disappearing."

"Ghosts, then. At least we have some sort of a target."

"Look closer." Dad cleared his throat, with a grunt, and then held up a second page.

"Three people? Two males and a female. The female appears younger than the males." Glancing up from the image in my hands, I had to blink at the paper he held. The girl stared up toward the sky, suspicious, one left hand pointing to the edge of the paper. Even in the gray lines of the image, I knew her eyes would be green and she'd be using that left hand to throttle someone. It was me.

Chapter Six

WICKED
Tucker

"**W**hat did she say when you showed her the file?" I ran a hand over my hair. The long, copper parts on top curled up, a bit unruly, the way I like it.

"I simply showed her the picture." McConnell pressed the button on the elevator door.

"You didn't show her the whole file?"

"I'll get to it soon, once she's ready. One big bite at a time." The doors closed before us, with a slow grinding sound. The lift lowered us closer to the ground floor.

"She won't like finding out the story one piece at a time."

"It's what she can handle."

"Possibly."

"Trust me. She's got a lot on her mind. Today was her big step back into Alliance life. You know as well as I the step was much bigger for her than any of us realize." He leaned against the back wall. "I'm not sure she's aware of what she's done." Amusement lit his cheeks.

"Are you glad she accepted?"

He paused a moment, considering before answering. "It's what she needs. I've let her take the time to recover. I'm for pushing a person forward if necessary, but I wanted her to take these steps on her own. She needed to believe in herself, to have her own reasons to accept the challenge, to believe in Alliance, in order to sign that contract and suit up again. It couldn't have come from me or from anyone telling her to do it."

"Although, technically, we did ask her."

"Asking isn't the same as ordering. We requested. We motivated."

"And she chose."

"Indeed." The elevator thudded to a stop and the doors whooshed open. Glaring light beamed through the glass doors down the hall to the front lobby, facing the port where our ship lay docked.

Another boat. Another journey. A new enemy.

"All set?" McConnell asked as he stepped out into the hall. Several crewmen stood waiting.

"Locked and loaded, maestro," one of them confirmed with a salute.

"See you at the helm."

"Aye, sir."

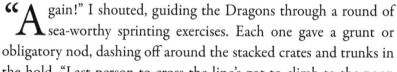

"**A**gain!" I shouted, guiding the Dragons through a round of sea-worthy sprinting exercises. Each one gave a grunt or obligatory nod, dashing off around the stacked crates and trunks in the hold. "Last person to cross the line's got to climb to the poop deck carrying Burkman on your back!"

I chuckled to myself as they groaned amid their gasping for air. I've got to admit, I enjoyed the mental image. Especially if it would be Rubu or Weyr.

Burkman must have relished the idea too, because his hearty laugh rocked up behind me. As I clamped the timer into the prongs of the clipboard in my hand, I wrote down the time signatures for each Dragon. "Would you like a ride up to the best view in the house?" I called to him.

He stopped at my side, rubbing his chest with one meaty hand. "Any other time. This ship's smaller than I prefer. I can feel the waves this time around."

"Ah. Don't blow your groceries in here. It'll be a chain reaction."

"What do you say—no worries? I'll be better once I get to boss these guys around the benches. McConnell needs you in his quarters."

"Again?"

"The younger one."

Just then a yell resounded from across the hold, and a crunching of trunks collapsing. I darted around the stacks, navigating through the maze we'd created. Burkman followed on my heels. A mess of fists and boots rolled around on the floor, along with the smacking and crunching of flesh scraping flesh. Shrieks and shouts assisted the two bodies grappling against each other, as two or three others watched.

"Break it up!" I hollered, dropping the clipboard to the ground. "Break it up!" Grabbing a pair of shoulders, I readied for a flinging fist or two. I dodged just in time, and instead tugged harder against the rally. Burkman bounded up to the other, dragging him away from us.

"He tripped me!" Flight spat out the words, red-faced, and slippery as an oyster.

"Did not!" Case clawed at Flight, but Burkman restrained his arms with his hands, which covered almost the whole length of Case's upper arms.

"You were in my way, you canker!"

"Shove off!"

"Hold it!" I hollered again, and wrestled Flight's arms behind his back until I pinned his wrists. "You two are done for this exercise.

Points withdrawn from your folio if either of you says one more word." Staring them down, I heaved in a weighty breath. "Burkman. Will you guide the others through about ten more minutes and a cool down? Somewhere in the cooling down they need to re-establish the restraints on the trunks so they don't shift during our voyage."

He cleared his throat and released Case, who ducked away from him. Case grabbed his elbows. Burkman then clapped his hands. "Gather round, Dragons! I've got a treat for you."

"Now," I declared, also releasing my prisoner's potential weaponry, "Case, Flight, let's chat. Thatta way." I pointed to the far portal. The two silently stormed beside me. Winding around stacks and crates, the air steamed with not only the humid, Atlantic air, but the seething hormones reeling through the two minors at my sides.

When we reached the doorway, they parted to the opposite sides of the exit.

"Now." I hooked my thumbs through my belt loops. "Case. Say your piece."

He muttered a string of hushed words, which possibly could have been Latin, and I held up a palm. "Case. I'm giving you one chance to bring light to the situation before I judge it completely without any input from you."

"That punk tripped me. He grabbed my shirt and crowded ahead of me."

Flight's usually amicable face narrowed at the accusation, his wide mouth sneering in disgust. His pale nostrils flared even wider than normal. Unkempt blond curls matted to his forehead. But he kept his mouth shut.

"What's your version?" I asked him.

"My boot caught the corner of the trunk. My hand caught his jacket. It happened real quick. Then he just outright shoved me away and started punching."

Case's thin, dark nose wrinkled, his square jaw shadowed in the dim lighting of the hold. Two lines of sweat rolled down his smooth, chocolate temples.

"Is this a competition then?" I questioned, staring them both down. "Your first instinct reacts to take out the man beside you?"

"You said it was a race."

"The race you run requires you to challenge today's self against yesterday's self. You rage against the old you, the slow you, the weaker you. Today you are stronger. Act like it. You don't race against your squad."

"Then what's the point of threatening us with losing?" Case almost spat out the idea. He backed away from us.

"To inspire you to fight your good fight. To inspire you to be the strong links in the chain."

Case snorted.

"Torr, you can't be serious." Flight's eyes ticked side to side as he studied my face. "We train to be the best. Somebody's gotta be at the front. Somebody's at the back. That's the way it goes."

"And you would be at the back, Flight."

"I know."

"In fact, you would have taken out your fellow Guardsman in the process."

The side of his lips twinged in disappointment.

"So, what's more important?" I swung my head toward Case. "To get there first, to get there having beat down your falling squadron, or to get there, period?"

Case exhaled, his shoulders slumping. He dipped his head to the side, releasing a *crack* from his knobby spine.

I flung my glare back to Flight. "We train hard to toughen you up. You've got to be ready to carry your weight. But don't forget your team may be the weight you've got to carry. You carry them, they carry you, and together we finish the mission." Swallowing down further words and a renegade rant, I slammed my jaw shut. Did they understand? These Dragons were so far away from where they needed to be. They were still quite untamed.

"Understand?" I punctuated the speech.

Two nods, slow and scruffy.

"Go cool off. Hit the showers. Rest up. Be ready for TAWT at 0700 tomorrow. We've got some new tech to work with, and I need my squad to be at their tops. Can I count on you two?"

"Yes, sir," they murmured.

"Say it only if you mean it." The words snapped out. "We've been at sea for the better part of two hours. If you can't handle close quarters now, it's best you went back before someone dies."

Case cleared his throat. "Yes. Sir."

"Attention!" I heaved my voice out, and my hackles. The two popped into a line before me, boots together, left arm to the side, right hand in a salute at the brow line. "Can I count on you?"

"Yes, sir," they shouted. The rumblings from the other side of the room hushed.

"Dismissed."

As they dropped their arms and shuffled through the open doorway, I wiped a palm over my own moist cheeks.

"Flight," I called over my shoulder.

He paused.

"Call me Thompson. Or Sergeant. I don't go by Torrent anymore. That was my Dragon name, and I'm not that any longer."

"Yes sir." His voice faded away, as did his hushed footfalls.

Sticky wicket. The air, the endless damp, I hadn't missed it. A sigh escaped. Micah's head ducked around the corner. "Sounds like you're having a good time."

"Too right," I agreed.

"So's Saylor."

"Oh?" I aimed a glance at Burkman, whose loud yells, some string of lessons at the other Dragons, resounded around the gray walls. Heads bobbed among the crates.

"Logan's already got her working on, well, everything."

"I hear you saying I should intervene."

Micah snorted a laugh. "Only if you want to lose an eyeball. Commander McConnell asked me to come get you."

"I need a radio. He already sent Burkman."

"Said it's important and I should bring you myself, even if I have to drag along your ten extra spinal cords."

"Gross. All right. Where's he at?"

"Well, interesting you ask. Come with me."

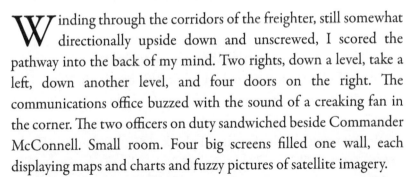

Winding through the corridors of the freighter, still somewhat directionally upside down and unscrewed, I scored the pathway into the back of my mind. Two rights, down a level, take a left, down another level, and four doors on the right. The communications office buzzed with the sound of a creaking fan in the corner. The two officers on duty sandwiched beside Commander McConnell. Small room. Four big screens filled one wall, each displaying maps and charts and fuzzy pictures of satellite imagery.

"They've gone to the mess," one of the men was saying. "When the round's up, we'll make sure everyone knows to keep a look out. I'll post notice."

"Affirmative." Commander McConnell punctuated with his normal no-nonsense nod. He stopped short when he saw me. "Thompson—good. Thank you, Fortuyn."

"Sure thing, boss."

"Our rickies settled in?"

"Pretty much," I nodded.

"I wanted to get you and Canaan squared away on coms. I want to have a trial round with our new tech."

"Yes, sir."

"Did I hear someone say coms?" Canaan's rich voice blew in from the hall.

"How much time do you need with Thompson?" McConnell swung a curious glimpse toward Canaan, who held a water bottle in one hand.

"Depends on his reflexes." Canaan grinned over at me, chewing. He swallowed the remainder of a snack.

"Then no time at all." I regarded the challenge.

McConnell set a stack of papers beside one of the communications officers. "Fortuyn, stay with them and pay attention. I'll need you to catch Saylor and Logan up when they join us."

"Yes, sir."

"I'll be in my office. Sorting through our itinerary."

"Enjoy," Canaan interjected. He wiped his hands off. "Now. I've been waiting months to see those fancy blue lights I keep hearing about."

With a smug twitch of my lips, I plunked one hand nonchalantly into my pocket. "It'll cost you one quick stop by the nearest coffee pot."

"What've you got in here? A dead body?" I grunted. The black case thumped against my leg.

"Don't you wish you'd have put on your GRIPS before volunteering?" Canaan carried his own weighty trunk in both arms, stepping in an unsteady rhythm along the corridor.

"Yes. Without question."

"Here." Canaan paused beside a closed metal door and leaned the trunk against the wall.

"The fitness center?" I asked.

"For now." He grabbed the handle on the door and twisted, the door releasing to the sound of imminent shouting and groans and thumps and bumps. Ah, the fitness center. My favorite room in a structure. The clinking of iron against iron. The wash of heat and sweat and resounding initiative versus gut. The making of immortals through the means of tension and tenacity. A place of power.

"What're you daydreaming about, Thompson? Get in here." Canaan lugged his crate further into the room and off to the corner, away from the bodies building themselves into shredded force.

"Move it, soldier!" Logan's familiar shout echoed from the opposite corner, where a messy blonde bun jumped up, raising her hands to the heavens, and then ducked down to the ground in a pushup. Ah, the burpee. Saylor didn't look too happy about it.

"If you'll move your crate next to mine, I will give you the rundown." Canaan had opened the lid on his rectangular box, squatting down beside it and digging through assorted boxes and cords wrapped around themselves. "We sent a man to the moon, and still have tangled wires," he muttered to himself.

Plodding over to him and settling the trunk beside the other, I scanned the room for what we had available. The Dragons would need the machines. So would I. A large square platform presented itself in the corner beside us, with mesh siding for those boxing within. Beside it, lining the wall, were racks of hand weights and weighted discs for the lifting equipment in the corner near where Logan and Saylor established their...interaction. She yelled something at him and then he clapped at her twice. She grunted and punched his shoulder. Ah, siblings.

Chuckling, I squatted beside Canaan. He handed me a black rectangular box, the size of a quarter, rounded on the thinner top and bottom edges.

"What's this?"

"One moment." He continued sorting through cords and placing them on the ground beside his boots.

Turning the box over in my palm, one shiny side caught the glare of the lights overhead. The other consisted of a matte black surface. When I touched the shiny side, it lit up with a bright white light. *"Welcome"* the display read in blue letters.

"You got your VISTAS in?" Canaan asked.

"I want to know what you know about it all."

"When I heard about the mission, I had Fulbright send over every bit of information you discovered and brought back. Nearly memorized your debriefing report. Fascinating stuff. Wish we'd had this tech at Prospect."

"Agreed. You make a good point. Too bad McConnell and Rapton didn't communicate better."

"That's what's so out of the ordinary. Rapton took regular reports from him."

"But they disagreed about Breame. Rapton obviously kept information from McConnell. Guess they returned each other's favors."

"Shows you where good team work gets you." Canaan stood up, stretching his arm over his head. The camouflage ironed itself out as he did.

"Huh."

"About those VISTAS?"

"No, mate, I don't meander about wearing any of it. Too dangerous. 'Specially for doorknobs."

"Clock's ticking. I'll get your WiCoDe ready."

"My what?"

Impatient, he waved me off with one hand. "Suit up!"

Impenetrable. Barbaric. Maleficent. Invincible. The mix of the VISTAS, GRIPS, and the NEXIS shaped me into a humming, deadly force. The VISTAS worked as a glass shield within my eyes, as a display mapping and reading all before me in vivid hues of purple, blue, and neon greens and yellows. The GRIPS, a pair of black gloves with a latch on the back of the wrist, lit up with a vibrant blue outline. They linked up to the VISTAS, as well as the Networked EXoskeletal Infiltration System suit. The GRIPS gave me brute force strength, snapping wooden beams like toothpicks, and crushing bone like candy. Of course I didn't aim for crushing bones, but my enemies could if they ever got their hands on the tech. The NEXIS linked up wirelessly to the GRIPS and the VISTAS, working as a cooling, armored suit. We'd used them in our battles against the oxinals at Fort Prospect on Isla Barina, but as far we knew, Saylor had taken out most of the spherical androids in her takeover against the globally devastating solar flare. The electromagnetic wave shot the nanocomputers in her system, and crushed her from the inside out. The tech fried within her veins. She had been so different since then.

Snapping the latches on the gloves, the blue outline illuminating in the white light of my quarters, I took a moment to accept all we were about to do, and to honor those fallen before in the name of the tech I commanded. Few could wear the assembled gear. My Dragons. Myself. We'd been injected with what Rapton called "FIRE" serum filled with nanocomputers, which linked our blood to the equipment, powering us up like warmongers.

Clamping my jaw to harness the visceral yet ethereal feeling of absolute dominion, I shoved my boot on my right foot and tossed the buckles onto their hooks. Go time.

Canaan rose both hands over his head when I strolled into the fitness center, and for a moment the room quieted. Curiosity beat my way, some obvious, some not, until the action restarted.

"Now, what equipment do you have to add, Canaan?"

"You'll appreciate it."

"Good on ya."

"Let's attach it to your neckline here." He cornered me, removed one L-shaped corner piece, and clipped the box into a silicone section near the Alliance logo. "I'd begun work on these coms but found myself lacking in motivation." He snapped the box into what looked like a spot designated for it.

"You were in Washington, right?"

"That's the black room where they sent me, yes, before Fort Will."

"You liked it, then?"

"D.C.'s a pit right now. Didn't think I was going to get out. Thought I'd be stuck manufacturing walkies for our guys forever until Blagojevich reassigned me."

"Sorry to hear that. Did Fort Will offer some fresh air?"

"Eh." He shrugged. "Gave me time to rethink what I wanted from Alliance."

"Another five years of innovation!"

His eyes fell for a second, before he cleared his throat. "Let's see how your WiCoDe works with the system."

"Canaan?" I saw his hesitation. Wanted to let him know. He wasn't the kind to hesitate.

He scrunched up his nose, peering down to a slick black box in his palm. "Okay. You're channel eight. The WiCoDe works like our old coms but with an added feature—you may now tune in to one individual's encrypted channel and have a private conversation. We have our group channel and then the individual. Saves time and patience."

"Wicked."

"It is, yes."

"No, what are you calling this thing? A wicked?"

"Wireless Communications Depot. WiCoDe."

"I kind of like *wicked* better."

"Call it whatever you want, Thompson. But you're channel eight. The earpiece for the audio." He held the black, L-shaped silicone tab between his thumb and first finger.

"They're getting smaller."

"That is the way of it. Pretty soon we'll just implant them. Or maybe we're almost there. Who knows?"

I huffed a laugh. "Well. Some of us." I palmed the squishy item and then situated it into my right ear. A slight, high-pitched *beep* resounded.

"Headset connected," a female voice confirmed.

"It's on," I stated. "Ridgy didge, mate."

"Has it linked up to your system?" Canaan squinted his eyes to stare into mine.

"You're being creepy, Canaan. I need a three-foot perimeter."

"I'm trying to see if you can read its signal."

Scanning my display, an extra icon appeared, like a circle with an upside-down capital A over it blipped up on the top right corner. "I see a new signal, yes."

Canaan studied his handheld computer. "We're gold!" He tapped on the shiny display in his palm several times. A written message popped onto the top right side of my peripheral. "Let's see those GRIPS in action."

With a quick scan of the room, delighted, I dashed over to the weight racks. I lifted one of the green hundred-pound circular weights and tossed it into the air above my head. The disc soared up to the ceiling, where it just missed denting the metal bulkhead. I caught the disc behind my back and then flung it heavenward again, this time jogging to where it flipped head over heels. The thing landed in my hands with a meaty thud. I whipped it up to my chest, wrapping my arm around it and twisted. My right side faced Canaan from across the room.

"Catch!" I called to him, and prepared to toss the weight like a disc.

Canaan's expression was worth all the points I'd have lost if I did throw it at him. Cackling at his stumbling out of the way, I reset the green disc with the others, and jogged back over to the techie.

"I need a picture of your face," I laughed, clapping.

"Remember, Sarge, I have the capability to control your vision," he muttered. "And dipping your fingers in hot water while you sleep."

"Big threats." True. He was my bunkmate, along with Logan, Burkman, and the rest of the male Dragons.

"What about the audio?" I asked, somewhat winded from the excitement. "And what else do you want to see?"

Canaan had stooped over to the other crate and raised the lid. One half of the crate sat filled with a gray, spongy material. Metallic silver pieces rested embedded in it, nestled in carved-out hollows for each unique shape.

"What's that?" I pointed.

Canaan whipped his chin over his shoulder. He lowered the lid. "Nothing."

"So it's something exciting."

"It's something still in development."

"You'll have to tell me all about it."

"If I get it working right. Still a lot of issues with the software." Canaan tapped his tablet.

"Ah."

"Meanwhile, let's test out our new coms and the integration. I'll give you some orders from the next room over to see how our connectivity works out in this metal box. I don't want your rickies to get disconnected on their first flight."

"You and me both." I agreed.

"How are they doing, by the way?"

"The newbs? Ah. Well. You know."

"Not really." Canaan stood again, holding two more WiCoDe boxes in his hands, along with his tablet.

"They're having trouble adapting, some of them. The ones who were in my class, they don't always understand or appreciate that they have to follow orders from me."

"Makes sense."

"It does. But they don't care about sense. Their first instinct tells them to kill, regardless. Insulted? React. Criticized? React. Loud noise? React. Soft footsteps? React. Switching their gears has been a harder task than I imagined."

"Sounds like it. But this is war, Thompson. One battle doesn't determine the outcome."

I shrugged. "True. One battle does not quantify total success or failure. But here they possess the opportunity to prove themselves. Me too. If they fail, I've failed them."

Chapter Seven

TRIFECTA
Saylor

———————

"I think I'm dead."

"Nope," Micah shifted her head on her pillow from the bunk across the aisle. "You've already done that."

"But I feel like I'm dying."

"I guess you'd know."

"Ugh." Every muscle in my poor body cinched upon my bones, groaning and pulling and pinching. "I can't move. I don't want to move. Ever."

"Too bad. Dinner will be served in like, five minutes ago." Micah sat up, hands flying over the loose strands on her low, brunette bun.

I lay on my bunk, still in my slimy gray shirt and navy shorts, tennis shoes still strapped tightly on my fiery feet. "Go without me."

"I've been instructed—"

"You're not my keeper."

"But."

"Hey. I'll talk with Dad about it later. Let me rest in peace right now." I gulped in a deep breath of humid air.

"You know that phrase is reserved for—"

"As I said."

"What did Logan do to you today?" she asked.

"If you want a recap, I'll write a book about it one day. And make it drag on and on talking about what it takes to stand on the line beside Logan."

"Um."

"Bring me back something?"

Micah straightened up, tugging on her jacket and buttoning the top button. "On it. I'll scope out the duds, tell the O-I-C you're S-I-Q and I want a C-A-K-E to G-O."

"Ugh. Don't tell Logan I'm sick in my quarters. He'll just make me run more sprints or something."

"You ran sprints today?"

"No. But I know they're coming. I was proud of myself for keeping up with all the pushups. He let me do the pansy pushups, fortunately."

"How has PT been, honestly?" Micah perched on the edge of my bed. "You haven't done much physical work in a while."

"I know." I sighed. She twisted her mouth. That face. Concern. Intense. "My upper half feels better than the lower. Shaky all over. I'll be okay. These first few days will be killer. But I've done it before."

"And you'll roll again. It'll come back."

"It will."

Micah laid her hand on my shoulder. "And hey. I will bring back cake. Come what may."

"Ugh!" I stuck out my tongue. "I just want a big tub of cold water."

"If you're sure." She shrugged.

"And maybe some ice cream."

She winked. "Deal."

You know the sound of dusk, when the winds have wrapped up, the birds duck into their nests, and the sun yawns one last time for the evening? The sound, the song of it, the feel of it, rubs into the skin like a goodbye kiss. The night, the blackness of the space, permeated the swaying pitch of the vessel and our bunks. Some slight squeaks from bolts and their nuts stirred in the rise and fall. Someone rustled in crisp sheets, and someone else's nasal passages groused about the sea air. My brain decided it needed to get back to shore.

With heavy, thick breaths, I sat upright, jolted forward in spite of the creaking timbers of my bones. Some piece of my uniform plopped down into my lap, glowing with a bright white brilliance against the black. The small square-ish item hadn't been there before. Picking it up between my fingers, the white screen illuminated again, with the text: *Call me when you wake up. Channel eight. -Tuck*

Lowering my sneakers flat onto the floor, I considered the stink emanating from around me. Figuring it wasn't Micah, but could be, I began the tedious process of removing the shoes with my numb, swollen fingers. Lifting weights had been a good idea at the time. I needed my gloves, though.

Proud of myself for not whimpering, I straightened my backbone. Time to go locate the showers. The black square on my rumpled sheets illuminated again, a white reminder of the message.

But how do I call you, Tucker?

Tapping my finger against the screen, the message flashed again. I pressed it and the message disappeared. Another screen displayed, with channel numbers and green circles beside some of them. Seeing Channel Eight, I pressed the green button, then glanced around the room at the slumbering faces. I skittered over to the hatch portal and pressed down the latch. I slipped into the dim, metal passageway. The cool flooring helped my aching feet, flat and hard as it was. That's one thing about the ground I'm grateful for, even on the sea. The hard surfaces remind us we are alive to feel them.

"Hey." Tucker's voice rang out behind me. Twirling to face him, the empty corridor greeted me.

"Tucker?"

"It's working then?"

"Um? I think so? Where are you?" I asked.

"Technically, in your head."

"Ha ha. Where are you?" I glided over to the next hatch, which sat closed.

"Canaan set up a new com system. He said yours should hook up to the—to your—the nanos." His Aussie accent had gotten stronger since his mission to Camp Kissinger. The warm sounds stirred up around my chest.

"So you're in my blood, rather than my head."

He chuckled. "Guess you're right."

"Either way."

"How are you feeling?"

"Mediocre."

"Aw. You're not." His rich voice sounded so confident.

"Don't let Logan hear you."

"Nix feeling down about yourself. You're starting over. You get extra points for that." His tone had an edge to it, like when he instructed the Dragons.

"If you say so."

"I do. And right now, I outrank him."

"Alright, sir."

"It's good to hear your voice." He had to have smiled then.

"You too. I feel like I haven't seen you in several days. Even though it's been hours." I attempted a laugh. It came out as a sigh.

"I mean, you sound hopeful."

"You think so?"

"I do. I see big things happening for you, Saylor."

"I gotta admit, I've missed hearing your voice over the coms." I strolled further down the hall.

"And we can talk whenever with these coms. Canaan set it up so the conversations are private instead of through the group."

"'Bout time."

"I said the same thing," he agreed.

"You could come meet me. We could have a late-night training session. Hand-to-hand combat." A frisky smile fluttered onto my lips. Let's call it combat.

"I *am* at the fitness center."

"Right now?"

"Yeah."

"Tucker! What time is it even?"

"I've gotten in the habit of lifting in the evenings. Take a nice walk on the 'mills."

"But it's like the middle of the night." I studied the metallic gray hallways around me, to the left and right. Still new. "I'm not sure how to get to the fitness center."

Tucker let out a quick breath. "Saylor, I don't think it's a good idea. I'm on a short leash right now. Your dad clearly expressed we're to keep our space."

"I know."

"And I have to be a good example for the Dragons."

"I know."

"And it's already in my record three times I've tossed aside protocol to do my own thing with you."

"It is?"

"And these Dragons—they need to see that following orders can be done. They need an example."

"Tucker. Don't worry. I should get to the showers anyway."

He paused. "Screw it. Take two lefts and go down two levels."

I giggled. "Should it worry me when you say you enjoy the idea of me being sweaty and stinky?"

"Ah, the smell of Saylor in the morning!"

"Ew!" A warm laugh escaped, and I covered my mouth with a hand as I turned the first corner. Dad stood in the middle of the hall, facing me.

My laugh cut short. "Hi, Dad."

"Saylor?" they said simultaneously.

"Where are your shoes?" Dad asked.

Glancing down, I shrugged.

"See you in the morning, Saylor." Tucker's voice lowered through the channel. "Sleep well, love." A slight click followed.

"What are you doing?" Dad shifted weight on his feet. "Are you alright?" He'd taken off his jacket, the green tee-shirt tucked into his camo pants.

"I'm all right. What are *you* doing?"

"I—I'm the one who gets to ask that question right now."

"Woke up a little confused. A little hungry. Totally missed dinner." I ran my hand through my tangled, loose hair.

"I noticed."

Scuffled my toe against the floor. "Sorry."

"Wanting something now?"

"I'm not sure. Think I want a shower more than anything."

Dad rubbed his forehead as he nodded. "I understand. Don't let yourself get too distracted. You need rest."

I wasn't the one who seemed distracted. "Are you alright? Do you need anything? Or are you patrolling the hallways?" Offering him as big a grin as I could manage, I glided my hands over my elbows, crossing my arms over my empty, aching stomach.

"I've been hashing out some paperwork for the Board. They're wanting a rewrite of the mission statement, the organizational goals, all sorts of records, as we move forward. Eliminating the last branches of Breame and Rapton's FIRE Initiative to catapult the globe into the next technological awakening has been somewhat earth-shattering."

"Simple things, then."

A slight laugh bounced out of his mouth. "Exactly."

"Anything you need a sounding board for?"

"You want to be a sounding board?"

"I've become a decent one. With all the ironing I've had to do lately, I've learned a thing or two about the importance of pressure and all of its friends. Sometimes a body just needs a surface to rest against."

"Was that an ironing analogy?"

"I don't know. Logan really knows how to make a girl exhausted. My brain's bushed."

Another chuckle. "If you're interested. You sound tired."

"Nah. I'd love to give some input. Or just to hear what you're working on."

"Alright. Come with me."

He nudged his head indicating the hall, and I followed by his side past three more doors, until he pressed down the latch on his hatch.

Dad's room offered much more space than the girls' bunk, and his starched sheets on the made bed indicated he hadn't even sat down on the thing yet. A desk built into the wall and footboard of the bed sat clear of elements, but he seated himself at the chair bolted to the floor in front of it. Pulling open a drawer, he withdrew a stack of black and green folders, overflowing with papers, many edges wrinkled or rumpled.

"Wellington Breame and Ram Rapton created many of the original mission statements, organizational elements, and modus operandi for Alliance. I gave opinion, as did the other board members, but the two transcribed their insight for an over-arching intent. They viewed Alliance as a world-builder. A control. An empire."

"You didn't?" I seated myself on the edge of the bed, trying not to muss the crisp surface.

He shuffled through the drawer, searching for something else. "I saw it as an opportunity for those who needed a second chance. Here we were with the world in disarray, with people lost and forgotten, who needed order."

"Breame did like to give the lost a home."

"He certainly adopted a herd mentality. He needed a herd to accomplish his feats."

"Ram too?"

"Indeed." Dad stopped rifling through his drawer and closed it with a sigh. "I've lost my pen."

"What were you working on last?"

"The mission statement."

"Remaking it?"

"Rewording it. Alliance needs to be unified once more. Our mission statement requires more meat to create a steady, beating heart within the organization and its members. With these new recruits, and the outlook of Alliance being at stake, I've determined to rally the Board for a higher goal."

"More than as a military guard?"

"We are so much more than a policing organization. We are progress, research, creation, expedition, protection, service."

"And well-read."

Dad let out an amused snort.

"What are you having problems with? Sounds like you know what you want to do."

"For the most part. I want to simplify it."

"Makes sense."

"See—" Dad scrunched his forehead up into three deep lines. Those turquoise eyes, thoughtful and pensive, questioned the words hiding behind them. "May I tell you some ideas you may not be ready for? Are you willing to listen to what I'm not prepared to tell you?"

"Um. I guess?"

"I have wanted to share this with you—I wanted to tell you later. You've got a lot to deal with, training and refreshing your abilities for our mission. But I can see it in your eyes you need to hear this."

"Well, I hear they say the truth will set you free."

"Indeed. But first it will sucker-punch you in the gut."

I withdrew, my shoulders tilting away from him. "What are you going to tell me?"

"Three elements combine to create the balanced objective for every human. Each human maintains a cup, a cross, and a yoke. A cross to bear, a cup of wrath to drink, and a yoke to share."

"That's—that's a lot. Of. Words and things."

"Let me show you." He picked up one of the green folders from the pile and tugged a white sheet of paper from the middle. Opening the second drawer down, he exclaimed and then held up a black pen. Settling the stack on the desk, he drew a triangle. At the top point, he wrote, *Cup of Wrath*. "Every warrior must fulfill three protocols in order to fulfill his mission. He won't become who he must be, he won't be able to discover his ultimate objective, until he understands or experiences the combined unity of these three things. The cup of wrath, first, equals suffering. All humans face suffering. It's our lot. Like it or not, the suffering exists. We can complain about it or accept it, but we must drink of it. When suffering, when wrath erupts, the warrior sees it as the crucible shaping the mettle. Perhaps you can consider it fate, what has yet to be written, or what will be. The battles you face, whether mental or physical, make you into the warrior you're supposed to be. They're learning opportunities. A catalyst for growth. Without those battles, without the gift of your suffering, you wouldn't be able to stand and face the fires yet to come."

"You mean, like me. Here I am, relearning how to walk, how to stand on the line with my family. I needed to experience my crucible in order to, to what?"

"That, my dear, I will explain. Let me continue." Beside the second point of the triangle, he wrote, *Cross to bear*. "Desire. Desire can control you, contain you, or confirm you. Each man has a unique skill set or desire embedded within his essence. Control desire, make the necessary sacrifices, and the warrior stands tall upon assessment. In ancient days, murderers, thieves, and even innocent men died atop crosses. They died for their misdeeds or they died in the name of something greater than themselves. Desire fuels that cross you bear. What cross will you lash onto your shoulders? Carry it with humility. Carry it for the good of those around you."

"So...You're saying my crucible helps fuel my desire. The trials guide me to the things I'm most passionate about."

"Your trials serve to shape your weaknesses into strengths." His eyes dropped to the sheet, studying the triangle. He wrote the last words, *Yoke to share*. "A yoke fulfills the role of an instrument of control and connection. Originally constructed for beasts of burden to plow a field as a team, a yoke unifies. A yoke connects workers to better carry their burden and accomplish their labor. Without a partner, the weight of the work will be overwhelming under the strain of the load and the unused yoke. But with the unified team toiling toward a single objective, incorporating guidance and wisdom, they accomplish their task."

Swallowing hard, my heart pulsed in a charging rhythm. For all he was saying, as hard as it sounded, it made sense.

"I like to look at it as the elements creating the ultimate objective." Dad continued, and drew a line from the bottom left point to the top third of the triangle, and then added a line from the bottom right point connecting to the top third. It looked like a capital A with a wonky middle bar.

"Kind of looks like the Alliance logo," I stated.

Thoughtful, his gaze skimmed through the air to study me. The wrinkles released from his forehead. "Exactly."

"Those three things are what Alliance is all about? Suffering, crosses, and yokes?"

"Desire. Intention. Teamwork. Alliance will be more focused." His brow furrowed again. "Or will be. If I get my way now."

"Pretty intense."

"As the warrior recognizes the gift of suffering, in fact drawing strength from it, and fulfills duty within gifting, as part of a unified Alliance he completes his ultimate objective. He's a trifecta of power. He cannot be stopped. He defeats, because he has no other option." He glanced at me. "Or she. She defeats, for she dominates her objective."

Shivers pounded upon my arms then, swishing down into my stiff gut. His words were for me, and the fear trembling within my marrow.

"What do you think?" he asked.

All I could do was nod.

"I've written up a statement." He seemed to hesitate then. "I'm not sure if the board will agree."

"No? Why not?"

"Some of them haven't been on the battlefield, Saylor. They prefer to close their eyes to the pain and hurt. Some of them haven't experienced their crucible yet."

"That crucible will certainly take you places you never imagined." My words were humbled. I hadn't considered being grateful for my story, my weakness, my lacking. But in them, I'd become, well, I guess stronger. I mean, I had built up the gumption to climb on that boat.

Dad opened a black folder and tapped a sheet of yellow paper. "I typed it out."

"The mission statement?"

"Yes."

"May I read it?"

He lifted it up and gingerly placed it before me. I accepted it, two sweaty palms reaching, tentative, unprepared. I scanned the words, reading them aloud. "I've got this deep wrestling within my dark soul: a hunger for the oppressed; an almighty beckoning for the broken and bent; a writhing which cannot be tamed by silence. No; the silence, the hush, the hustle, cannot squelch the fire to share light for those trembling in the depths. I cannot stop giving of myself for my mission, for to stop is to suffocate. To quit, impossible. To surrender, unattainable. No. My wrestling therefore occurs not in the loss, but the gain. Loss no longer exists. All movement, all attempts, fulfill the mission. My mission.

"For I have been redeemed, and I defeat the darkness within me by each lent hand and rescued soul whom I reach. I am Alliance. I defend freedom, defy injustice, and deepen creative productivity to enhance mankind's survival. In living victory, I bear my burden, a warrior for my objective: Be powerful. Be consistent. Never quit. Finish the mission."

I glanced up from the words to my father, then back down, reading, re-reading. Recoiling. Rerouting. "I guess with this kind of mission statement, there's no room for fear."

"There's no need for fear. It's not part of the mission."

"I am Alliance. I like it."

"I am Alliance."

"Hoo-rah."

"You're sitting awfully still." Tucker sat down a tray on the table beside me the next morning in the mess hall.

"It's because I can't move."

"Explains it."

"How do you do it? I forget the pain goes away."

"It does. One of these days you'll be freewheeling like the rest of us. Until Burkman gets hold of you and makes you drag this freighter around a beach."

I nearly coughed up the sausage I was chewing on. "Sounds intense."

"Don't mention it to him. Might give him ideas."

Micah tossed her tray down on the table to my left and huffed into her seat. "I think someone owes me an explanation."

"What?" I asked.

"You said you wanted ice cream last night. I got it for you. Brought it back, all undercover and hijinx-y. Then I get back to the room and you're so out cold I shook you like an earthquake's uncle, yelling at you, but did you wake up? No." She chewed on her lip for a moment. "And here you sit, nice and chipper way before I've even had a chance to tell you about the device you're supposed to hook to your uni."

"What happened to the ice cream?"

"Don't change the subject, MacTavish."

"Um, pretty sure you owe me some ice cream and not a lecture."

Micah grinned, toothy and forgiving. "I see you've had your coffee already."

"Just the one cup."

"Good girl!" Tucker patted me on the shoulder, then let his hand drop to his lap.

"It was a mandatory commodity today. I abruptly awoke when the ship dropped my stomach into the ocean. Couldn't get back to sleep because I knew what torture awaited me."

"Is it that bad?" Tucker rested an elbow on the edge of the table, right inside the raised lip which kept our trays contained on the surface should the ship waltz about.

"Logan's training? Um, yes."

"How so?"

Unable to contain a laugh, I spurned the hot air blowing out of my guts. "Let me count the ways."

"Maybe I can have a talk with him. See if he could ease—"

"No!" My shout made Micah jump, and some guys at the next table glanced over their shoulders for a moment. "No." I quieted, shaking my head. "I can do it. I've done it before. I just need to buck up and get through it."

"You can do it."

"People keep saying that. I'll keep believing them for the time being."

Micah bumped her shoulder into mine. "Maybe I should hang on to the ice cream while you try to regain your muscle tone. No need to add those extra pounds on the old knees."

"I'll tell you exactly where to put the ice cream, Micah."

"Ooh, burn!"

Stabbing three pieces of sausage on to the tines of my fork, with each one I forced the words to at least feel true. *Yes, I can.*

But then Logan knocked them back into the sea. He wrung me out like a wet mop on a sinking ship. Three days later, I leaned against the back wall of the fitness center, taking a break. I'd wedged between the weight racks, trying to be as out-of-sight as possible. Logan had marched out of the room to find us some water, but I had plenty in the corners of my eyes.

All those moves which had been so familiar and close were fumbly, awkward losses. Once again, Logan moved quicker, lifted heavier, and pounded louder. He towered over me, a shadow I couldn't phase.

Rubbing my eye with my sweaty palm, the salt stinging, my vision blurring, I rested my elbows on my knees. Heat welled up in my forehead, pounding, resounding, as the tears began to burn in a slow drip down my cheeks.

"Saylor?" Tucker's voice dispensed beside me. He took a knee at my side.

"I'm fine."

"Are you overheating?"

"No. Yes. Maybe. Yeah."

"Have you had water?"

"Logan went to get some."

The weight machines slammed in their spots, clankings and thunkings of the weights and their enforcers echoing around the large arena.

Tucker cleared his throat. "You know what I miss? Your X-11, Slingstreet. You made it look effortless, swinging that bat around. Remember when we'd drill our strats? I kind of miss someone screeching out a name and then we got to knock those mocks till kingdom come."

"Banana split. That was one of my favorites."

"Probably because it was named after dessert."

"Probably."

He settled down into a seated position, one knee still up, his elbow resting on it in a casual way. "Want to hear what I think?"

"What?"

"I think you're stuck trying to recreate something you once knew, but need a different way to do it now."

Licking my lips, I tilted my face just so I could peer at him, curious. "I miss being strong."

"Saylor. You are strong."

"No, I'm not." My head hung, my defiant chin weighty and ashamed.

"Are you sure? Is that the utter truth?"

Dropping my hands from my face, a trailing drop of sweat rolled down from my temple along my jaw. I batted it away with the back of my hand. Sniffed.

"Permission to speak?" Tucker dipped his chin, those emerald eyes searching mine. "Honest? Because I like you?"

My heart rallied then, wibbling within my ribs. "Go for it."

"You've got to stop letting your doubts win. You've got to knuckle down and quit listening to the lies fear whispers. Are you strong? Yes, you are."

"Tucker, I—"

"Do you have muscles in your arms? Yes. Do you have a story packed with perseverance, moxie, and results? Yes. Have you grown up into a more capable, enduring human over the last few years? Yes. You are strong. The lie whispers you're not. Don't lie to yourself. Who would you be if you stopped listening to the lies?"

My throat dried up, more parched than before. Placing my palm on the back of his hand, I wrapped my thumb around his.

"You are She Who Hears The Enemy, if I recall," he added. Those eyes twinkled. "Therefore, since you know the lies, and know the attack, then you own the advantage. That's your power. You *are* strong. Be the person who counterattacks with truth. If you tell yourself you cannot accomplish the task, then you won't accomplish it. But you win by pushing past the doubt. If your thoughts make you feel less than you are, they are wrong. Flesh them out as the enemy. Deny them. Defy them."

"Man, I almost wish I could knock some oxinals around now."

Tucker's shoulders relaxed. The side of his lips quivered into one charming, dimpled smile. Even the sun itself couldn't warm my soul like he did.

"How 'bout a round in the ring? I'm about to lead the Dragons through some drills. Demonstrate with me?"

Hesitating, I studied the lining of his boots.

"They understand the moves, essentially. It's a refresher for them. I just need a body who can navigate around mine."

"I guess I might remember them."

"The Flare took your pride. Don't let it take your spirit."

My nose scrunching, I blinked back a shiver. He was right. "Okay, Thompson. I'll trust you. Use me as you will."

"I would, but I think we aren't permitted."

A giggle flitted out of my lips. His uniform, with its coffee and spice scent, brushed my elbow as he rose to a knee. Ragged breath caught in my throat, aching for the room to be empty.

Eagre herself, snappy and cute with her shiny boots and rolled sleeves, settled one firm hand on her waist in the center of the room. Her eyes zeroed in on Tucker. And me.

I didn't mind showing her I knew up from down. "Let's go, Thompson! What were you demonstrating?"

"Kali."

"Oh." My hope stuttered. I'd left the Kali sticks behind long ago on Isla Barina. "Well. It's been a while."

"Basics, Saylor. I've introduced them to our moves, but yes, it's been a few weeks."

"Weaving in and out of the arena with swords has been off my doc's physical activity prescription."

The side of his mouth slid up into a grin. "Don't tell me you've lost your touch."

"Never." Some hair slid down my sweaty temple. "I'd hate to disappoint your students when they see me smack you around like we used to."

"Actually, I think they'd love to see me get smacked around." Tucker caught Eagre's stare and waved at her. Her eyes had already lightened by the time he'd circled. That cold chill must have been saved just especially for me. So great.

Tucker meandered over to a gray trunk beside the door and picked up the lid. I followed.

Eagre strolled over to the trunk, cutting in front of me and sidling up beside him. "Need any help?"

"Not just yet, Eagre. After we demonstrate the activity, I'll need some assistance, if you don't mind."

"Demonstrate what activity?" She studied the nails on one hand.

"The art of Filipino war."

"Mm. Okay. I'm happy to demonstrate with you, as well."

"No worries. Saylor's going to help this afternoon."

Eagre's eyes almost appeared to glare with a golden sparkle. If she'd have had fire to launch, I think she would. "Let me know what you need." She spun a shoulder away from us and wandered over to the dark-haired Dragon leaning against the wall. The two girls owned their ferocity. Obviously, they hadn't dealt with the weight of true pain yet.

"Gather round," Tucker called out then, and my spine tingled. The rumbling trembled from the roots of my hair and down into my boots. Time to dance.

"What's the plan, boss?" asked the tan one, whose eyes slanted with a hushed torment.

"My good friend, Saylor, will be helping me demonstrate the art of Kali for you today. We're expanding our arsenal. At Fort Prospect, they incorporated a unique skillset and you'll do well to learn a new tactic. Specialist McConnell and I have had many rounds of this before, but it's been a week or two since. We're going to start with the basics I've shown you, to remind you of where we begin. Once you have those down we will advance." Tucker held out a wooden rod. The light brown sticks, each one-inch in diameter and just a little over two feet long, shone with etchings of the takedowns and combat they'd seen in their colorful lives. They must have come from Prospect. Taking one, I waited to follow Tucker. The stick warmed in my palm, whetting the familiar but dusty barrels of coordination and control.

"Ready, Saylor?"

Nodding, I swung my weapon before me.

Tucker held up his. He guided us with his words and I slowly wielded my stick through the air. "First you cross them at the top once." Our sticks smacked in the air between us. "Flick the forehand in a downward diagonal, then bring it around for a backhand downward diagonal." With a click, they whacked again around our knees. The exercise began to feel comfortable. "Do that three times. Hit high, in front of the chest, and retract, bring it around, hit before the knees, and retract." Tucker took a step back and held out a palm to his students. "Then combine the two exercises once you've gotten them in a rhythm. One chases the other. Switch. One advances, and then the other. Circle it around. Keep your rhythm! Keep count! Master this first, and then we move on."

Muted nods and blinks of agreement answered him.

Tucker grinned at me. "Shall we?"

"Just the one stick? Going soft on them?"

"Basics, Saylor. One stick at a time."

Raising my stick into the air, Tucker brought his forward and we began the tapping around, a step forward, a step backward, with swinging sticks rattling through the arena. The Dragons appeared bored. Raising an eyebrow, Tucker counted faster, *one, two, three, one, two, three,* into a frenetic, pouncing beat. I swiped hard and lost my footing. The counts frazzled in my mind. My knee twisted under the hurried, foreign tango and Tucker swung a stinging blow to my side. I stumbled. One knee hit the ground hard, and the Kali stick clattered from my hand onto the black, crusty flooring of the fitness center.

Groans or gasps or some kind of recognition might have been easier to face than the looming silence radiated by the ten Dragons. They saw me as weak. It flared toward me, hot and loathsome, and prickling like a porcupine in my stomach.

"Are you alright?" Tucker flew to my side, offering a hand to help me to my feet. "I'm sorry. I guess I lost count."

"No." Blood pulsed around my achy kneecap. "I'm fine."

"Do you need—"

"Again."

"Saylor, can you—"

"Again!" Swiping down a gritty hand to grab the fallen stick from the floor, I then straightened to a room full of observing faces. Slapping the side of my thigh, brushing away the dust, I cleared my dry throat. "This exercise I can do. We do it again until I'm proficient."

Tucker dipped his chin. "Yes, ma'am. Again."

And through the steps we swayed, opposites, yet in sync. The dance became the game, and the game became the weapon. One swipe, one click, one rapping tap at a time.

The Dragons joined in at some point, teaming up in pairs of two and advancing, retreating, chasing, clanking Kali sticks and defeating their own invisible enemies. After several rounds, and even into some more advanced moves Tucker talked us through, the old devices began to rebuild themselves.

By the time sweat dripped down my temples and down into my socks, the sound of laughter, including my own, rippled around the room. Tucker and I finished a round with a flourish, and then checked on the Dragons as they reciprocated the strategy. As I sought out Tucker and the next round, Dad's and Logan's crossed arms at the door made me freeze in my steps.

"Hey!" I raised a stick to them.

They nodded.

"Just what are you doing?" Logan called.

"Helping."

"She was just about to help me demonstrate the double stick drills. Let them see what they can look forward to." Tucker stated from beside Eagre and the other girl Dragon.

"Oh yeah?" Logan tilted his forehead down, narrowing his eyes. "Let's see this. Sounds enlightening."

Tucker sauntered up beside me. "How're your wrists?" He smelled like greasy socks, crisp garlic, and coffee. He smelled like yesterday.

"My wrists are perfect."

Without even glancing at me, he tossed a second stick through the air. I caught it.

"Double weave?" Tucker slid a boot backward, holding the sticks in both hands. "Plan it out? Or free form?"

"I'd love to be coy and flirty right now, but I've already fallen down once in front of these people today. Let's stick to the drill."

"Yes ma'am."

"Today only. Tomorrow, you better watch out."

"Understood."

He smacked me several times with the sticks, and I flinched ungracefully, but then I followed back through and swung wide and far with mine. As our sticks passed in the flow of meetings and partings, feet stepping in just the right places, balancing a united front of control, technique, and coordination, Tucker called out, "One last time!" My staggered lungs thanked him with a wheeze. Both arms and shoulders ached. My legs must have been like lava tubes. But it was life. It was moving. It wasn't collapsed within myself like I'd been.

"Never stop moving!" Tucker hollered, as we finished the last few jabs and hits. "That's what I'm talking about!"

Grinning, he tossed aside his sticks. He grabbed my right wrist and held it in the air. "There she is!"

With a laugh, I ducked my head.

A white bottle of water appeared in my periphery. And a pair of big black boots. "If I recall, I instructed Logan to train you. And here we are, in a sparring session with Thompson."

"Dad. He asked for my help while I was taking a break."

His blue eyes glinted, a flash of a smile on his lips. He held the bottle higher, closer to me.

Taking it, I slugged down as much as I could handle.

He cleared his throat. "Saylor. I think it's time to shake things up. What do you think about changing your training partner?"

Chapter Eight

ALLEY-OOP
Tucker

"Who's the girl in the picture?" Saylor placed her fingertips on the top of the file folder in my arm. Her skin tapped against the paper in a wave. "You know that's not me."

We strolled down the hall toward the communications office. A light flickered overhead. I cleared my throat. "Part of me hoped you could tell me."

"I've been sifting through each memory I've created over the past two years. I cannot figure out how this could be possible. I have another twin?"

"Surely not. Surely we can't have three of you McConnell's running about, wreaking havoc on the planet." I gave her a small smirk.

"Surely not." She stuck her chin out in joking defiance.

Our boots clunked along the metal thoroughfare, taking the final right turn before meeting Commander McConnell outside the open door.

"Yes, ring him up," McConnell stated, tossing a wave in our direction, and sliding into the office. "We're here."

"Having trouble connecting." The officer clicked his receiver and tapped on the number pad beside his radio.

"No storms on the horizon, right? We shouldn't have any interference." Canaan rose from his seat and leaned over the officer's computer monitor, examining the screen.

"Something to do with the receiving end. Not sure. I'll restart the system and see what's going on."

The Commander's eyes wandered to Saylor's face. "Anything new?"

"No," she said. "Tucker showed me the intel we've got. All those pictures from the satellite, the ships in the port, the almost-instant disappearance of our perps once they get off their ship, the infrared scans of those islands, it's so little information. These guys are ghosts. How do they know our shipment plans? Do they have access to our transmissions? How do we find them?"

"Titus should have more for us," the Commander answered. "We were hoping to find out."

"It's back up." Canaan seated himself.

"Hello? Sorry about the disruption." A man in a green camouflage uniform filled the screen in front of the communications officer. He wiped his cheek with the back of his hand. "We've been having some irritating brown-outs lately. Our com system has been haywire."

The communications officer, Jett, propelled his chair away from the desk. "It's no problem, General Titus. I'm leaving you in the capable hands of our Commander McConnell." Standing, Jett offered McConnell a nod, and the two exchanged places.

"Hey," I whispered as Jett passed me, backing out of the room. "Are you going to the canteen?"

He gave a sly grin with a subtle nod.

"Would you mind nabbing me any drink dispensed in a big container?"

"Just about to get one myself, Thompson. I'm assuming when you say, 'any drink,' you mean coffee?"

"Is there any other?"

Good guy, that Jett. He understood the bare necessities, especially in running the com office. I didn't envy the man. Jett offered a quick head bob as he headed off down the hall.

"— nice to meet you, sir," Canaan was saying to the man on the monitor. "I'm happy to help however I can."

"I appreciate it. We can't seem to figure out why the power's been thin." He rubbed his thumb across his square, midnight chin. Two thoughtful, charcoal eyes studied the camera before him. "I've requested a meeting with the town council, but you know how those meetings shuffle around."

"Don't I know it!"

The Commander seated himself beside Canaan. "Any updates on the case?"

Titus shook his head. "You'll be here in about one week, correct?"

"According to our plan, yes. If the weather works with us, of course."

"Of course. We've had a fair spring so far. All the best as you progress."

McConnell nodded. "Thank you. I've got my other staff leaders with me, Sergeant Tucker Thompson, and Specialist Saylor McConnell."

"Nice to meet you." We gave a quick salute and settled in behind McConnell. "I've got a few leads on your spooks and their location. Hopefully my scouts can dig deeper before you get here so we can team up for a quick raid and return your equipment. A charter boat went missing with some French tourists on it, and France wants answers. We think they're connected. Similar execution—the charter had some tech on it headed to the mainland, along with the tourists, and the cargo, vessel, everything, just disappeared in a blink.

Our sats couldn't track it. One minute they were visible, another vessel approaches, and then they're gone."

"Unusual," McConnell murmured.

"Indeed. We're wondering if an EMP is somehow involved."

"Electro-magnetic pulses?"

"Right," Titus' eyes shifted to the edge of the screen, and then gave a swift but slight shake of his head. "The boats seem to stall in the water, the pirates overtake them, capture what they want, sink the boat. It all happens within thirty minutes or less."

"Understood. We will have to move fast."

"And have several protocols organized. Your men are prepared to deal with unusual weapons, correct?"

"Yes. It's their specialty."

"Just to be clear," Titus leaned closer to the screen. His intense bronze eyes narrowed. "I don't lose men. I'm prepared to work with you, and am happy to do so, if it's for the protection and safety of the people of our great nations. My men are prepared to do whatever it takes to recover your tech, as long as you're not leading us into the wolf's den."

"I understand your concerns, Titus." Commander McConnell straightened his shoulders, uprighting. "We're cleaning up the wreckage. My men have also prepared to do their part to recover our valuables and get everyone back to safety. These vandals are not affiliated with Alliance's current commission and directive. We believe them to be rogue, and unfriendly. If at any time you determine your men to be putting themselves at unnecessary risk—"

"Oh, we don't walk away from the danger, McConnell," Titus interrupted. He reclined in his seat. "But we will judge our risks accordingly."

"Agreed. As it should be."

Titus rolled his tongue around his mouth, considering further words, then waved a finger to someone behind the screen. "We'll see you in about a week, then."

"Yes, sir. We'll continue sending status reports as we go."

"Thank you. Until then. Godspeed."

The monitor went black before any other words could be spoken. The four of us watched the screen click over to the gray and black program screen.

"So," Saylor spoke up, "he's excited to work with us."

"I think so," I agreed.

McConnell glanced up at the two of us. "We'll have to prove it to the world, one person at a time. Alliance has a new statement. The whole world watched us try to burn it down."

"But—" Saylor began to argue, her mouth wide open.

The Commander held up a palm. "You sacrificed for us all. They watched you and respect you. Now Alliance has to catch up."

Saylor's eyes widened, her nose scrunching. "Do you know who's in those pictures?"

McConnell didn't even cast a look my way. "We don't. We have some suspicions about possibilities, but no confirmations."

"Please clarify."

McConnell's weighty gaze seared my direction.

I cleared my throat. "I've spent several hours deciphering conversations with the Dragons. I had some curious conversations on my escapade to Camp Kissinger."

Saylor licked her top lip, waiting. "Okay?"

"We've had a founding board member go, somewhat, missing."

"Somewhat missing?"

"His last known whereabouts link back to Washington, but his file states otherwise. After I returned from Kissinger, I looked him up. He's been missing-in-action for about three years."

Saylor pursed her lips. "Didn't anyone in Alliance notice?"

The Commander shrugged. "He worked closely with Breame and Rapton. They all kept tabs on each other. The other board members, Buchanan, Chevalier, and Ibrahim, all slowly stepped away. Those three were on my side with the disagreements with Breame, but Rapton and Adenauer formed a strong partnership and overrode them or convinced them one at a time to give in. Traded favors."

"I'm glad they've stepped down."

"Yes." The Commander cleared his throat. "Continue, Thompson."

Running a hand over my head, to clear away the cobwebs inside, I jostled around the faded memories. "In a conversation with Rapton, he'd mentioned Adenauer, and how Adenauer lived on an island like a king, or lion, or something. He mentioned Atlantis."

"You—are you saying Adenauer lives on Atlantis? Are you saying he's dead?"

"No." I shook my head adamantly, but then considered it. "Or, at least—I don't think so. I think he's up to something nefarious. Or he's dead."

"Just the two options?"

"Probably. But a decent guess suggests perhaps Adenauer wanted this Alliance tech for some reason. Note we're headed to an island."

"Mm hm." Saylor waited, expectant. She balled up her fists and placed them on her hips.

"And it so happens, one location where experts researched Atlantis' origins exist on or near the Azores."

The Commander angled his head toward Canaan at this news. I hadn't exactly followed through on the report I'd meant to send him before now. Oh well.

Canaan's pointer finger poked the heavens. "I believe I can look at some old documents from early project proposals. Look for anything substantial."

"Thank you." Glancing at the clock on the wall, the time glowered its disapproval. The Dragons needed herding. "I've got to check in on my own council. They've got their own deadlines."

"Please do." The Commander strummed his fingers along the edge of the desk. "I've got to check in with Burkman. Dismissed. Thank you for your help."

"Saylor," Canaan swiveled in his seat. "Speaking of proposals."

The Commander and I both jerked our shoulders toward Canaan.

He chuckled. "It's so easy to mess with you people."

"What's up?" Saylor asked. She slid her hands in her pockets.

"I need a moment of your time. Shouldn't take too long. May I borrow her?" Canaan eyed me.

"Of course. I'll be in the fitness center with the Dragons."

"So, Kissinger was an escapade, was it?" Canaan raised an eyebrow.

"Like a parade on steroids."

"Sounds fun."

"I don't know if we can use the word 'fun' to define it." My forehead wrinkled at the remembrance of those sweltering days in the Aussie outback.

"Like doomsday's baby cousin."

"With that thought, I'll let you be." I clapped him on the shoulder. "I see you've captured its essence."

Dealings with Dragons are never simple. Titans carry prideful tendencies, smirking with power, and wallowing in diva-ishness, particularly when secured together in close quarters. Hazard's black hair flung over his forehead as he leaned against the hallway wall, shoulders slumped forward. He clutched his elbows in front of his chest.

"What's the deal, mate?" I asked.

Hazard continued staring at the floor.

Silence emanated from behind the door to the room we used as a classroom. "Did you all finish the assignment?"

"Things kinda got out of hand," Hazard mumbled.

A rich scream sliced through the steel wall. Shoving the door inward, I readied my fists to separate or pummel some wayward punches. The Dragons circled up in the middle of the room around the desks anchored to the floor. Weyr stood atop the large desk at the front of the room, pointing to the crowd, his eyes wide in disbelief. He shut his mouth mid-yell. The others I parted through, some of them standing on chairs to see the ruckus in the midst of the group. Shouts, hollers, and a second round of shrieks filled the small space.

Wring and Rubu kneeled on opposite sides of a desk, slouched forward, stuffing white sticks into their mouths. Rubu's wild hair bounced around as he grabbed another handful and jostled it into the wide mouthful already protruding from his head. Wring's dark eyes widened when he saw me and he paused with one arm in the air, holding three more of the paper items, which turned out to be straws.

"What are you doing?" I shouted as loud as I could over the noise.

One by one they hushed, a shocked and awkward silence ensuing.

Clear liquid drizzled out of the straws crammed between Rubu's lips. His blue eyes blinked once. He snickered, and some straws fell out.

"Gross!" My voice echoed through the room.

Eagre giggled. I shot a look to her. To everyone.

"What is this, a contest? Who has the biggest mouth? Who can waste the most straws?" How did I sound just like the Commander all of a sudden? I cleared my throat. Ah, to be young again.

"Wring." I pointed at him. "Who's the mastermind here?"

Wring wrapped his palm around the straws and withdrew them from their recess. He wiped his mouth with the other hand. "We'd been talking about the integrity of structures like—"

"Your mom!" Weyr shouted, cupping his hands around his gaping noise hole.

Rubu shot Weyr a two-handed finger guns and winked.

"You people are children," I muttered.

Shadow sat down in a chair opposite me, her lips curled up in a shy way. Her shiny, raven hair fell loose over one shoulder, eyes tracking the movements of her fellow squad. The shy motion resonated deep within my chest. Clutch leaned up against Flight's shoulder, and she whispered something in his ear. He chuckled, then paused, considering Rubu, who now had a wad of white paper balancing precariously on top of his head. Rubu had no idea about his new hat.

"You *are* children." Shaking my head, I let reality kick in for a moment. "We've been on this boat for quite a few days, eh?"

Groans, moans, and a resounding *yes*, along with Weyr's hand-microphoned *boo*, echoed.

Shadow's eyes met mine. Sky blue and hopeless. Waiting. Eagre jumped onto the nearest desk, seating herself for the lecture. Her jaw clenched, with one eyebrow quirked. By the door, Hazard slipped his hands into his pockets.

"I've been running you ragged, yes?"

"Yes." Most of them nodded or agreed too heartily.

Hazard shook his head.

Withholding a grin, I scanned these warriors in their various states of disassociation. "We've got at least seven more days afloat. If the weather cooperates. I need someone to tell me your favorite memory from your time at Camp Kissinger—at Solaris."

Heads uplifted, eyes narrowed in confusion, faces twisted to check others for confirmation. Reticence.

"Someone share a favorite activity. A happy moment from the years in the lair."

Flight spoke up, raising a hand. "One time, I beat Exit arm wrestling."

Eagre held up a palm and slapped him a high-five. They nodded at each other, smiling. She ran her fingers through the golden waves lounging upon her shoulders.

"No." I shook my head. "Not what I mean."

"What?" Flight slammed his fist on the table. "He was impossible to beat. When I did, he stopped having dibs on the first in line. I had a whole week of getting the big slice of steak before he did."

"I'm not talking about incorporating violence or training, or your classes."

"Wasn't much else," Eagre interjected.

"I realize this. But you had some free time. What did you do? Favorite memory. Go."

"Addison and I exploded half the lab with those fire paintballs." Case nudged Thunder, who snickered at the memory. "Trigger got so mad. Destroyed all his work on that batch."

Shoving my palm against my forehead, I tried to wipe the sense from my skull into theirs. "No. That's not how this works!" I began to laugh. "The beach. Sandy waves. Watching the stars at night with a friend. Taking a walk on a mysterious, woody path. Tracking thunderclouds. Dancing with a beautiful girl to a song repeating over and over and over. Anyone?"

They blinked back at me.

"Fine." Crossing my arms over my chest, I straightened my shoulders in a stubborn way. "Your assignment this afternoon, then: go make a memory. A *good* memory. Go watch the waves of the ocean. Study the clouds and the wind patterns. Don't stare at the sun. Find a book to read, one that consists of the word 'fiction' on the back cover. Write a poem about the rocking of the boat upon the waves. Write down ideas you want to one day make into memories."

Some jaws dropped as I spoke. Eagre's lips swayed up into a smile. Clutch frowned.

"If you don't have a story, a life you want to lead, then what do you have to fight for? Alliance protects life. What are you protecting? What are you fighting for? Why be here? What do you know? You've got to know your why. You've got to choose your why. You're all old enough to understand and to begin planning. Your reason may change over time. Mine has. I hope you're here because Alliance offers you a life greater. And greater means full—full of laughter, of thrill, of knowing the essence of what makes us human. When it gets tough—and it will—why do you keep fighting? Stop being Dragons for about two hours, and go be humans. Report back to me at 1700 in the mess. They're serving enchiladas."

One by one they stood or slid away from the chairs. Some whispering slipped between them, and Eagre grabbed Clutch's wrist to drag her into the hallway. A chill settled around the room. Hazard began wiping down the chalkboard.

"Thanks!" I called. "I'll get it though. You can go be with people."

"I don't much care for people." He grunted and parked the eraser. Slapping his palms to rid them of grime, he grimaced.

"I understand the sentiment."

"Can I help with something else?" Hazard asked.

"I've given you your assignment. Seems like you should find a way to do it."

"I go along with what you say most of the time, sir. But I'd rather not. I want a job to do."

"You don't find reading a book to be a worthy task?"

"Don't have any books."

"You can write something, then."

"Not creative." Hazard's eyes shuttered then, and his head jerked. The shiver rattled down the seams of his uniform.

"What's going on?" I sat on the edge of a desk.

"I know why I'm in Alliance and why I was a Dragon. Strength and power are my wheelhouse. I wage war. Fluffy things and thinking about them do not make me win wars."

"I feel like you're making fun of my examples full of expounded imagery."

Hazard clamped his mouth shut.

"Come on, Hazard," I bargained. "You don't enjoy doing anything but sparring and studying?"

"I like structure."

"Understood. But surely you enjoy other things."

"No."

"Is that true?" I eyed him.

His eyes relaxed to my face. "I—I like following instructions. They don't disappoint me."

"The rules?"

He nodded.

"Rules are for rookies, mate."

Hazard swallowed hard.

"Look, I'll give you a tip. Most people around here won't tell you. All these rules and guidelines, they're to help you get where you need to be as a warrior. People let you down, you say? Do they? Can they? Why would you expect them to be what they're not? Dragons are unreliable. Humans are unreliable. Unpredictable. Don't worry about what they're doing. Focus on what you're doing. Then do your best. Once you get the rules down you can swing around them like a ropes course. Know which rules work best for you and know which ones challenge your weaknesses."

"I don't know how to do that." Hazard's arms dropped to his side.

"I know what you need. I've got just the book for you." I passed him on my way to the door, cuffing him on the shoulder.

"Which book—"

"Nope!" I interrupted. "Won't ruin the surprise. It's in my bunk. It's the worst book. When I say 'worst,' I mean it's the best book I've ever read, and I hate how much I love it. It's a book of modern poetry."

"Poetry is pointless."

"Ah, Hazard." I rested a hand over my heart. "How I felt similarly before I read this book to the girl I loved as she lay unconscious."

Hazard followed me through the door. "What do you mean?"

Striding through the hall, our boots clunked along with us. He kept pace beside me.

I shrugged. "Saylor nearly died. Twice. Her friend Denise stuck this book in my face and told me to read it to her the first time. Saylor stayed in a coma for a couple weeks and we didn't know if she would pull through. The words in the book—they told a story I wouldn't have understood if not for Saylor. The second time in the coma, destroyed, for some reason, those words brought me great comfort. I was sent on a mission across the earth from where she waited in the hospital room. I'd taken the book with me. I read it on the darkest nights. It helped me pause. It showed me, somehow, all of us had this great thing in common: our humanity. Our written lives. Our vivid memories. I found, because of one poem in one book, written years before I was even born, I could manage the hand I'd been dealt. Even if in a small way. It's magic, mate. Poetry does that."

"I don't like poetry."

"If you don't mind me saying, Hazard," I sighed, "give this one a try. Imagine who you could be if you didn't believe those words. You may one day need a reminder to take a breath, and enjoy life's continuing, even when you feel like you can't."

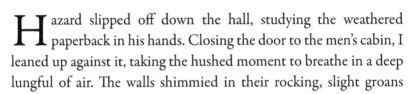

Hazard slipped off down the hall, studying the weathered paperback in his hands. Closing the door to the men's cabin, I leaned up against it, taking the hushed moment to breathe in a deep lungful of air. The walls shimmied in their rocking, slight groans slipping through the steel joints.

A quiet knock on the door behind me jolted me back to the ship, my cabin, and the stack of reports I needed to roll through.

Eagre whipped her head to face my door as I opened it. She held up two paper cups of coffee, raising one closer to me. "Figured you needed one of these."

"Thank you." I accepted the cup, noticing she'd taken her own version of the assignment in a direction I'd not intended.

"Clutch wanted to read. Weyr's climbing in the rigging somewhere. Shadow never says a word, and I couldn't find the others." Eagre fluttered her eyelids. "As if they'd be exciting to make a memory with."

"So you brought me coffee?" I arched an eyebrow.

Eagre raised one muscular shoulder and angled her coy chin over it. "What if I did?"

Blackest black enveloped us. The lights evaporated. The walls and floor shuddered around us, a thick, grinding ripple inundating each surface. As quick as I'd breathed in, a brain-shattering *boom* thundered. It echoed and rolled. It swallowed all my senses. I tripped on the door frame. Not sure what happened with the coffee. Red lights blinked on and off, accompanied by a blasting siren in a staccato rhythm matching my heartbeat. I grabbed Eagre's arm.

A voice filtered through the loudspeakers over the alarm. "All hands on deck. This is not a drill. All hands! On deck!"

"What's going on?" Eagre shouted. She yanked her arm free, but then gripped my hand. A hollow void filled her eyes, darkened in the glaring red lights. Dragon mode engaged.

We ran.

We charged, I should say.

We coursed through the hallway, as the noise continued purring, grinding, and flopping about beneath our boots. Turning corners. Our pounding feet sought the surface of the ship before we were under it.

Having drilled all the shortcuts into my skull the first few days on the craft, I guided us up to the deck within what may have been seconds but dragged like eighty-seven spellbound years. My heart jumped all directions within my ribs, and my wits tried to catch up.

On deck, the bright sunlight slapped our faces like a bottle in a bar fight. Burkman bounded up to us. He pointed at the starboard side of the ship. His mouth appeared to be spewing words but all I heard were muffled yawning moans. He grabbed my face in both his hands and shoved my face toward a glassy patch mid-deck, and a sack of cloth beside it.

His warm lips shoved against my ear. "We've been hit. Ship's going down. Get your Dragons on that life raft!" His first finger then pointed straight before my face across the deck. Two forms wrestled with rigging and ropes beside a white raft.

"The weapons!" I shouted at him.

Burkman's face twisted in confusion.

"We need the GRIPS. VISTAS. NEXIS suits! They're the last of their kind!"

"People first, Thompson!"

"I know. But—"

"I'm checking for survivors below decks. I'll grab what I can." Burkman clapped my back and blasted into the darkness.

"The black trunk in the armory," I called out after him.

Our vessel pitched and swayed, rocking in a precarious angle. Eagre and I fought the uphill climb, seeking the raft.

"Get in the raft. Stay there," I ordered her. The two people handling the ropes turned out to be Weyr and Rubu. Weyr bellowed commands to Rubu, who followed with a swift alacrity. Clutch hopped over to the raft just as we bolted up beside it on the deck.

"Anybody seen the others?" I asked, trying to reign in the volume on my panic. The rustling ring in my ears made it difficult.

Heads shook side to side.

"Battle ready, Dragons." I demanded. "Watch your six. I'm going to look for the others. If they get anywhere close on deck, make sure they get in here. We've got to be free from the ship before it goes under. Can't be too close because it could take us with it. You work as one. Understand? Weyr, you're in charge."

Heads bobbed.

Uniforms scurried across the deck, an organized chaos to their running and hauling of injured persons and equipment boxes.

Who had we passed, laying on the deck?

Jogging over to the figure, the glassy pool beside it clearly a crimson glow. One of the men from the engine room.

Logan, breathless, flung his arm up to my shoulder. "You made it. I've got Saylor, Micah, the rest of our squad on Raft Four."

"Dragons are on Raft Six."

"Need help?"

"Yeah."

Thunder and Flight scrambled toward us. I gave them the thumbs up with one hand, and pointed to the raft with my other. "Hurry. Raft Six."

Nodding, they focused their wild eyes on the inflatable and sprinted.

I ran a hand over my hair. "We're missing Case, Wring, Shadow, and Hazard."

"Attention, Alliance!" One tempestuous, echoing voice rang out above the chaos. A screech. "Your ship will be under water in less than ten minutes unless you carefully follow my instructions."

Activity on the deck ceased. Everybody froze, ears analyzing the loudspeakers. The siren silenced, followed by a gaping hush.

One body strolled along the deck. Gray, slick pants, and a zipped-up gray jacket didn't hide her flowing blond hair. She held a small black box radio in front of her mouth. As she lowered it, the silence grew even colder.

Saylor.

More confident than I'd ever seen her, her smile radiated while her glare sizzled around at her captives. "Bring all the cargo from Hold Fourteen," she called out. "You brought it to garner my attention. Nicely done. Let me have it."

"We don't have a section fourteen," one of the deckhands shouted.

The left side of her lips curled in a smirk. "Yes, you do."

Hot winds whipped around the deck. Water splashed up beside us, small drops wetting the edge of the raft.

"What do we do?" Logan whispered from beside me. "That's the Dragon tech."

"I know," I murmured.

"Where is it?"

"I just sent Burkman after it."

"Great."

Two men in gray suits similar to Saylor's marched up to her side from the back of the boat. They stood close enough I could see the glimmer in their eyes, and far enough away I couldn't consort with Logan about a plan. Saylor scanned the deck occupants, and her glare landed on us.

Raising her chin, straightening both shoulders, her boots marked a straight, uncrossable line.

She wore so much more makeup than Saylor normally did. Heavier mascara, thick black upon her wide eyes. Glowing cheeks. Deep red lined her full lips. Her hips swayed as she walked, an easy and firm swagger. Not even a hint of wobble or hesitation.

"Tucker," she stated. Her eyes flicked to my partner. "Logan."

"Who are you?" he asked, begrudging.

Her laugh flittered about, as if on bird's wings. Delighted.

I squinted in the bright sun toward her. "Let's have a sit-down and talk about whatever you've come here to take."

"Oh, I've missed your voice." Gliding up before me, she tipped her head back. She rested a hand on my wrist. "Tell me something I don't know. Tell me anything."

"Who are you?" I asked.

She giggled, her voice jingling, and ducked her face for a second, only to wrap her arm around my neck. Her other hand gripped the back of my shirt. She smelled like vanilla and strawberries, mixed with cinnamon. Like a full meal and dessert. Like beaches and blankets. Like yesterdays.

My heart couldn't help but hammer within my chest.

Her lips, so close to mine, nuzzled against my cheek. "I'm your fantasy. I'm what you always wanted."

Even with her warm, soft words, the threat glistened in the hot sun before me. With both hands, I grasped her upper arms, considerably thicker and stronger than I'd known them to be. Her nails scratched my neck as I pushed her away.

"Pardon me," I breathed out. "I believe you've confused me with someone else."

For the slightest breadth of a second, a question flickered in her dazzling sapphire eyes. Then she grinned. "And I believe you're losing time. I want the tech from Hold Fourteen. And I know you're just the man in charge of it."

"You can't have it."

The vessel beneath us shuddered, swaying. Saylor whipped out a gun from a holster on her backside. She held the barrel less than five inches from my chest, point blank for some impulsive negotiation tactic.

I calmly stated, "You realize you're on a ship full of soldiers. I could disarm you in less than three seconds."

"Not if you're dead."

"Saylor wouldn't point a gun at my chest."

"And you know this for a fact?"

I clamped my jaw shut.

She winked. "A girl never forgets being jaded. You leave a girl to fly around the world without a proper goodbye? The next time, you don't get off that easy."

Logan spoke up. "What do you want from us? Some empty boxes?"

The two men behind the girl aimed their rifles.

The girl backed up, still aiming the gun at the center of my chest. "You've got three minutes before your socks get wet. Get me the cargo."

"It was a ruse," I admitted, twisting my face in pain. "To see who was listening in on the coms. We knew someone had hijacked our network."

Pounding air buzzed from behind us. Several rounds of gunfire shattered the quiet.

"Too bad." She shrugged. But she continued studying me, her eyes locked on mine. So blue and clear, just like they'd always been. Especially when she needed help.

The noise thickened overhead, and a shadow passed by. Logan and I hoisted our chins, the impenetrable, hot air swirling around us. Overhead, a dark gray object soared, a bulbous body with four arms extending like compass points. Each arm ended with cross-blades chopping the air.

"Inbound traffic?" Logan exhaled.

"Have a nice swim home," the Not-Saylor sang. Three ropes containing two thick straps looped onto them plummeted onto the deck with a *thud*. Our three gunslingers each placed a foot in the lower loop, and laced their free hands through the other loop, clutching the rope. In a rapid, smooth motion, the aircraft lifted them up. On their way, they slapped several rounds of ammunition into the deck, to keep us from retaliating. The machine arose and pitched itself away from us, the blades buzzing and whirling as they surged overhead.

And they were gone.

Ghosts.

The ground beneath us quaked, rising and diving faster than my stomach could tumble.

"Abandon ship! To the life rafts!" someone yelled.

Before the sirens could be reinstated, the ship groaned the warning—our phantoms had rigged explosives beneath us.

I dove for my Dragons and their life raft. Hazard plunged at the same time. We jumped in to the boat, and the group of us lowered the craft. Logan disappeared. So had the quiet. So had my sense of up and down. Just as rubber met water, another explosion rocked the body of the craft. The *boom* bubbled out, along with a heat wave, soaking us, throwing us, flipping calm into cacophony.

The cold ocean engulfed us.

My ears didn't handle the volume or the sudden deluge of water. Muted screams and splashes encompassed me.

As I surfaced, wiping the stinging liquid out of my blurred eyes, I welcomed a few quick, hearty breaths of air. The white raft bobbed in the water not more than twenty feet away, upside down. I heaved my anchor-like boots, kicking through the water.

Logan's sandy head of hair emerged from the water and grabbed a rope hanging off the edge of the craft. He then shook water droplets off his face. "They really hated that boat."

"We need to get this thing right-side-up," I called.

Several other dark-haired heads dipped and rose, heading for the raft. Hazard surfaced on my left, spitting water out of his mouth, gasping for breath.

"You alive?" I shouted to him.

He tossed his chin up and down, but he seemed to be lacking in response time. His movements slowed and his eyes closed.

"Come on, buddy," I veered for him. "Let's move. I need your help to get our raft useful."

"O-k-k-kay." His teeth chattered.

Although cold, the water wasn't getting the best of him. He needed to be on some solid ground before the shock dragged him under.

"Talk to me, Hazard."

"Ab-bout what?"

"Swim to me." I spit out a splash of water attempting to climb into my gut. "How far did you get into the poetry book?"

"Three poems in."

"The one about the dog?"

"The one about the coat."

"It's a shame you didn't get to read more." I reached his side and placed his hand on my shoulder. "Hold on. Swim with me and don't let go."

He nodded, blinking heavily. "I'll find you another copy some time."

"It's a plan."

"Heads up," Logan bellowed. With a splash, the raft raised up, gigantic in the air above us, and then toppled down into the water not five feet away. "Alley-oop!"

After a few more shoves through the miry blanket enveloping us, I gripped the rope on the edge of the raft to park Hazard and myself in place.

"One more big push, alright, Haz?" I asked him.

He nodded, gasping from the efforts.

"Take this rope in your fist. Hold tight." I guided his hand up to the rope and closed his clammy fingers around it. He did not hold tight. "Logan!" I gave an extra loud shout behind Hazard's form. Logan paddled over. We jostled Hazard over the edge of the raft.

Wring slung a leg over the edge just as we rounded the other side of the raft. Eagre swam our direction from the wide-open waters of the Atlantic. Her eyes narrowed in concentration. Flight lay on his back in the water, loosely gripping the rope.

"You alright, Flight?" I questioned.

"I'm trying to figure out if I want to get in the raft yet. I think I lost my lunch somewhere mid-flight just then."

"Understood." I wiped my face clear of more water drops. "Unless you're about to lose it again, I vote on getting into the raft."

"Yeah."

"Need help?"

"Nah, boss."

Other bodies approached the vessel. Jett, from the communications office. Rubu. Weyr. A lady from the mess hall. With a helpful hand from the Dragons, we boosted any nearby bodies up and over the sides of the raft.

Oxygen shuddered within my flustered lungs. My mates rested beside me, dripping, digging through the emergency kits to find thermal blankets and rags to dry us off.

Sunshine swung down, clouds drifting away from the whirling star's vision of us. We were a pitiable lot, but had seen worse.

Logan wrapped a silver blanket around his shoulders and kicked off his boots. "Well." He clicked his tongue. "Found the bad guys."

Chapter Nine

STARFALL
Saylor

One droplet of frigid water trailed along my scalp, through the roots of my wet hair, down my temple, along my chin, and finally hurtled itself down onto the black box in my lap. Sitting with my legs tucked under me in the bobbing white life raft, my eyes couldn't seem to close or focus. They just wanted to watch the far, flat horizon. Where blue meets blue. The lines nibbled at each other's cheeks until they became one hazy infinite.

Like when *She* had rubbed her cheek against Tucker's. She'd opened her eyes then. And focused on me. And smirked.

Heat wove through my ribs, intermingling with the fire in my blood.

"Looks like nine rafts total." Burkman's gritty assessment filled the air.

Canaan plunked a box closer to me. "Can't determine a body count yet."

"We need to collect the rafts," Dad added. He laid a heavy hand on my shoulder. Lowering his voice, he asked, "Are you alright?"

Still unblinking, locked on the horizon, I offered one quick bob of the head. It'd have to do.

"Micah's in the next raft over." Dad pointed with his other hand.

"Good," I stated. Blue on blue on blue.

"Never seen a craft like that before." Canaan wrestled with a silver package in his hands. He wrenched it apart from itself, the thing doubling and then quadrupling in size.

Dad handed one to Burkman and the other crew in the boat. Eight of us total. One guy had a red gash on his forehead and slumped forward. Burkman dug through the raft's first aid kit, a white box with a big red cross on it, to find supplies to fix him up. The guy didn't look so good.

"Anybody else need a thermal?" Dad asked. Some nods, some grunts. A hush tossed aside hairs in the ocean's cool breeze. Sunshine warmed our shoulders, the blue surrounding our souls. Throttling the rafts. I tugged at the wet collar of my uniform.

"We should have some collapsible paddles in one of the compartments," Dad said, searching through one of them. He closed a latch and opened another lid, searching. "We need to gather closer so we don't lose anybody else."

"Here we are," one of the crewmen said. He pulled out a bundle of orange poles, snapping them together. One had a wide, oar-like piece. He slapped it into the end pole and handed it to Dad.

"It's possible," Burkman began, "we need to discuss the great white shark in the raft." He tossed a quick glance from Dad to me before shifting back to his wound victim. The soldier grimaced as Burkman wiped a strip of tape over his forehead.

Dad paused.

Our small craft puttered in its spot. Water slapped underneath us and at the edges of the boat.

I grinned at Burkman. "Are you saying I'm great? Or that I'm white? Or that I'm a shark? At least it wasn't another blond joke, I guess."

Canaan laughed.

Weighty grimaces followed.

"We now know she's real. And she's pretty—" Other words clung in my dry throat. She seemed *more*. She was all the adjectives I'd want to be. Pretty beautiful, strong, threatening. Amazing. Pretty much all over Tucker. *Hmph.*

The crewman held up the second paddle. Dad gave him a thumbs-up. The two of them settled to the sides of the raft, placing the thick paddle ends in the water and shoving off.

"Do you recall what we talked about the other night?" Dad asked.

"Um. Alliance's new mission statement."

"Guess I'll have to work up a new copy of my notes, eh?" He glanced over his shoulder at me and then refocused on the water.

"Stinks."

"Maybe my notepad and paperwork will miraculously float to the surface?"

"I bet. Suppose you can wish for it."

"To spend time hoping for what logically does not exist distracts me from my mission. My notes are gone. Our boat, gone. Now we move forward with what we do possess. Now we create new options."

"We sent out several maydays," Canaan added. "Got Lajes on the line before we went down."

"Good." Dad held his paddle still for a moment, resting the stick on the edge of the raft. "We should have a radio and flares on board."

"I've been working with this one I had in my case." Canaan held up a book-sized device, a flat, black, shiny rectangle. "Got wet. I've got to get it aired out. We'll need it." Canaan risked a furtive look my way, and I blinked as my answer. We required his tablet. I gripped the black box in my lap with my jittery, wrinkled fingertips. Good thing he'd made it water-tight.

"Every man faces a battle," Dad sighed. He placed his paddle back in the water. He and the crewman resumed their strokes. "Sometimes he faces one important battle, but often he's got a whole life of struggle. That's his cup of wrath. Let him drink it with pleasure."

"Sounds tasty," I ventured.

"Here we find ourselves at a crossroads. We can give up, or pursue our attackers."

"We have the option to give up?" I asked.

"No."

"That's why we're here."

"Exactly." Dad let out a thoughtful breath. "Our mission has taken an advantageous turn. We've received proof. Indeed, we have a recognizable enemy who thinks they have the upper hand. And our enemy had been intercepting all our transmissions."

"Sounds like it's not such an advantageous position."

"On the contrary." Dad's words came in a slight gasp, as he inhaled to continue his task of rowing. "We'd been planting each transmission, using various channels to communicate with Lajes. Canaan and I broadcast different messages on those channels at a variety of times and with multiple misleading communications."

"They wanted the cargo from Hold Fourteen," Canaan added. He offered a brief nod toward the large black trunk at the end of the raft. "We broadcast using the encrypted Alliance network."

"Two days ago." Dad returned the head bob. "They're using our system."

"Is it truly Adenauer, then?"

"Got to be. Either him or a protégé."

"We never rescinded his security clearance," Dad clarified. "I wanted proof he was in contact."

"So he is." Canaan dropped his hands in his lap, the tablet reflecting the sun's glare in Burkman's face.

"And we've got proof of life."

"I can track the message, if I can get this puppy back from the dead." Canaan held up the device.

"Then by all means," Dad grunted, winded. "Please do."

We drew up to another white raft. They cheered, and we looped some ropes from one craft to the other. Another crewman accepted the paddle from Dad, and they took turns, along with the other raft, journeying closer to a third, and a fourth.

Dad leaned back in his seat beside me. Burkman passed him a bottle of water.

"Thanks." Dad accepted it with a grim smile.

Water trailed down into the small of my back. Far off in the distance, across the space where our ship used to be, Tucker, Logan, and many of the Dragons settled into their raft. A shiny, blonde head leaned against Tucker's shoulder. Why did so many people out here have blonde hair? Why didn't Tucker shake her away?

I chewed on the inside of my lip.

Dad lowered his voice. "The measure in which you trust others often illuminates the measurement of how much you trust yourself."

Swallowing, I eyed him. We both scrunched our eyes in the bright light of the afternoon. Light mirrored off the choppy water surrounding us. The glare offered a strobe-light disco inferno.

He continued. "Tucker's in the other boat. I see you trying not to stare."

"Yeah."

"Do you trust him?"

"I don't trust her."

"Who?"

Not being a first-grade playground gossip, I puckered my lips. "No one in particular. It's just something I've been dealing with. Any *her*."

Dad thought about it, and jogged his chin. "If you trust him, then you have to trust your reaction to his interactions. He'll be surrounded by other people, by *hers*, all his life. Jealousy imbues a cruel color. It doesn't look good on anyone."

"I know."

"Bring it back to yourself. Would you trust yourself surrounded by a boat full of *hims*?"

"You've got a point." I licked my lips. My inside self grinned at the premise. I *was* in a boat full of *hims*.

"You choose." Dad shrugged. "You can't control how the other people act. But you can choose what you do. You decide to be someone trustable. Someone honorable."

"What if he's not trustable?"

"At some point, he may not be. But you can't decide for him, or determine it ahead of time, or avoid it if it happens. You, however, decide your integrity. That's your win. Every time."

"Sir," Burkman spoke up. "Over there?" He pointed to a green and brown camouflage jacket in the water by a pile of boxes and ropes. Some cargo had been connected to a raft in the middle of its inflation, and the upside-down body had been thrown with it.

With a revered effort, our grouping of rafts drifted near the wreckage. The other boat reached the soldier first, and one of the men rotated the body in the water, checking for a pulse. They slipped the dog tags over his neck.

"Specialist Daehly, Commander," the man read.

Dad's face held firm, a line of solemn acceptance. He held out a palm, and the soldier placed the tags and chain in Dad's hand. His fingers wrapped around the wet metal. He'd collect six more. Four sank to the ocean floor.

Stars, brighter, fuller, bolder than I'd ever seen them, lit the heavens above us. They whispered secrets only they understood.

I lay on my back in the raft, covered with a thermal blanket. The wind hustled overhead, adding to the song. Water knocked against our tiny island, attempting to threaten us. But you can't threaten the dead.

Canaan continued tinkering with a tiny screwdriver and his tablet, murmuring to himself every so often. He'd put it down only to eat a ration for a quick meal and to transmit a message to anyone nearby. The Army should have been on their way. We hoped.

Snores darted in and out of the slouched soldiers and sailors filling our nine little rafts. Thin ropes bound us in a clump. I'd been able to wave to Micah, and she to me, and we made some hand signals about our thoughts on the whole thing. She ended up in a boat with the main cook, a boy and girl Dragon, and three men from engineering. She seemed happy with her lot, particularly the muscled one who'd removed his shirt and needed help with a cut on his chest. She'd spent the better part of the evening helping him tend to his wound.

But in those hours, I stared at the passing, mutinous clouds, and the many faraway places we could have been. We could have been on any island, or ship, or backyard, or beach.

The stars and their song spun above us, first as a whipping wind, and then as an orchestra of voices, of those who'd left and those who'd gone before. It shimmered as simply as the evening starfall. The speech of the stars and all they know vibrated around us. They have seen the world blossom and continue their song, showering down in the most brilliant and barren of nights. And they spin onward, again, again, again, until their master rests his staff once more upon the ground. What were they saying? I strained my ears to hear. Dad's words added to the symphony. *Where is your unity? What is your battle? How will you fulfill your desire? This is your mission,* they hummed. *This is you. This is you, returning light into the ether. Here you discover who you are meant to be, in the intrinsic net of humanity.*

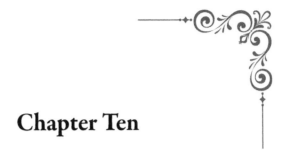

Chapter Ten

A BIT MORBID
Tucker

N oisy pinpricks of light bounced around my eyelids. They only stabbed the headache swelling behind my forehead.

Shadow.

Case.

We'd done a head-count. We'd screamed until our voices went hoarse. We'd sent up a flare, we'd used binoculars to dredge the horizon, seeking any signs of life away from the ship.

Shadow's blue eyes followed me from beyond the stars as my frame slumped against the hard lining of the rescue craft. Gone. Her ebony hair had slid between her and the rest of the world for the last time. My stomach didn't stop churning, boiling, wringing, with the thought I'd brought her to that end. I'd lost track of her. She was one of the youngest of my Dragons, and I led her to her doom.

While the stars hammered down, I'd scanned the horizon. Clouds faded into the inky dawn. My throat couldn't take it. My chest couldn't bear it. My insides burned with a heavy chorus strumming. I'd have to tell her mother, with those same intense eyes.

At one point in my frantic search, Eagre leaned over to me. She gripped my shoulder with her hand. "I have a cramp in my neck from trying to rest on the edge of this life raft. For just a few minutes, I need a shoulder."

I nodded.

Her weight eased against the white vinyl, and she rested her head against the crinkly silver poncho wrapped around my torso. "You're scaring the others," she whispered. Those turquoise eyes echoed the hollow reflection of the ocean around us. Terror shone through. She'd never have admitted it with words. "You need to take a break." Her voice broke. "We can't look for them anymore."

I nodded. A sigh, burdened and broken.

To my left, Logan crossed his ankles. He tilted forward. "Eagre, how did you all deal with—I mean—what was the protocol after—after Assessments? Or if you lost a fellow Dragon to illness or an accident or something?"

"We didn't lose anyone on accident. Not that I know of, anyway. After achieving Level Two, and we dropped our names and moved into the numerical category, the instructors methodically ingrained certain, well, I guess you'd call them affirmations, if they weren't so morbid. They taught us the six statements of the dragon code, an acronym of DRAGON, to draw back focus. If we found ourselves in any uncertain scenario, we return to those for our—our instructions, if you will."

"What were they?"

A slight smile wavered in her tone. "Tucker's spent the last six months yanking those out of our brains. He replaced them with their opposites."

"And what are they?" I asked her, nudging with my shoulder.

She relaxed her head, straightening her shoulders. "Duty, respect, action, grit, overcome, never quit."

"Nice." Logan's amused lips rose in a crooked grin. "Did you put that together on a whim?"

"I couldn't very well let them continue reciting six reasons to kill people, could I?" I shrugged.

"There's more to the cadences, I mean the statements," Eagre added. "But you get the gist."

I filled in the blanks for Logan. "Duty to Alliance; Respect for all; Action as service; Grit throughout overwhelming odds; Overcome doubt; Never quit. I'd considered changing the O to a U and including some quality about unity or unifying. I couldn't bring myself to have them spelling 'dragun.' Sounds like something a pickup truck would do on a dusty road—dragun around."

Logan blinked at me. Maybe it was just the sun.

"What?" I asked.

"What were the original?"

"Don't worry about it."

"No, I'm very curious now."

"I've been telling my students to let them loose all these months. It's about time you did the same."

"But you haven't told them to me." He cleared his throat. An audacious smirk leered on his face. "D stands for ... deadly. Daring. Daunting. Direct. D...angerous."

"You don't need them, Logan."

"I might, when we find these boot-licking scumfilchers."

Overly horrified, I jokingly placed my palms over Eagre's ears. "Young ears listening nearby, Logan."

She giggled.

He clicked his tongue in reply. "I bet R stands for Roar. Relentless. Really strong."

"You're ridiculous." I let my hands drop and settled them on my knees. "No looking back."

"Dangerous renegades addictively going on—nadventures." Logan punched the air with a fist.

"No doubt. What other better acronym could it have been?"

He dropped his fist and the act. Added a quick nod. "Sometimes what could have been intended for evil can be turned around for good."

"Most certainly. I've got a lot of hope in these Dragons. We've all invested in each other. I'm honored they've been entrusted to me. They're soaked in knowledge and skill. They just need a chance to prove themselves. Active duty's where we find out if any of this has worked."

"Currently, they're also soaked with salt water."

"Thank you, Logan."

"Glad to bring you back to the raft."

"You're truly a gift. Quite a bit heartless."

"Don't I know it?"

Restlessness stirred up almost as quickly as the next breeze. Shadow's silhouette often popped up beside the survivors. Case's sharp wit and punchy persona haunted the slapping waters beyond the canvas borders. I'd jump whenever the raft shifted.

We'd cabled our rescue crafts in a formation like a grid, and assigned individuals to shifts so some could sleep while others rested. During my shift to sleep, the stars stared down at me, at all of us on those cloudlike vessels, buzzing with energy. They blinked messages, stories of the lives surrounding me who needed a guardian. And they mourned for the loss beneath us.

Sitting up, I shook away the dusk and the twilight, hoping for some fresh air unhindered by apparitions. Saylor's face popped up in the adjoining raft.

Jumping back, I grappled at the air around me before toppling over.

"Sorry," Saylor whispered, reaching over the side of her boat and extending her hand. Panic welled up in her wide eyes. "Apologies. Didn't mean to startle you."

"Trade places to be with Micah, eh?"

"I did." She glanced over at the brunette snoring softly at her side. "I fell asleep earlier but now I think my heart has caught up to the shock. I traded shifts with Thunder."

I settled back in my spot and leaned out, grabbing Saylor's hand. Her fingers were soft and chilled.

"Glad to see you're learning their names."

"He made a face when I called him Lightning earlier."

I held back a laugh. "You'd be surprised at how often he gets called that. It's a running joke."

"Oh, man!"

"No, it's too right. He probably thought I put you up to it."

"Oh, well, okay. Maybe he'll think I'm more part of the inside joke."

"Maybe."

She rested her other hand on the edge of the raft and placed her chin on top of it. "How are you?"

"Made it off the boat."

"In one piece."

"Just the one. I think."

"But how are you doing?" Her eyes flickered around my face, analyzing my reaction.

After a pause, I admitted, "We lost Shadow."

Her eyebrows pinched over her nose. Concern. Her voice softened. "I know."

"I don't—"

She squeezed my hand.

"She was my responsibility."

Saylor nodded, her eyes never leaving mine.

Air chilled within my throat.

"You know," she tilted her head, eyes reflecting the starlight, "you fiercely adore your people. Even in this puddle. That's one thing I like about you. Part of your power plays out in how you're so good at your position."

"I'm not so sure."

"I am. These kids needed someone to argue their case and you took it on. You gave Shadow an opportunity."

"For what?"

"We all know the risks involved."

"Do we?" Suddenly I wasn't so confident. Even after the wreckage I'd seen in my years, floating on that lonely ocean, the depths surrounding us...

"Now's not the time to rethink it." Her tone sounded stronger than I'd heard in quite some time. "Why do you think I'm here?"

"Why did you decide to come, Saylor? What was the final push?"

She chewed on the inside of her cheek for a moment. Her focus drifted around us, taking in the scene, then zeroing in directly on me. "Because you're my adventure. It's possible I could sit back at the house with Mrs. Schuring and Patricia and Cadence. It's possible I could sweep day after day after day and exist. It's possible I could walk out the back door and the ground could open up beneath me. It's possible I could get on the bus to go get groceries and we wreck."

"A bit morbid thinking, McConnell."

"All that to say—you traveled the world over to discover you wanted to be on the line with me. I say, let's travel the line and see what we see along the way. It's bound to be more exciting than sweeping."

"Guaranteed." I held in a deep breath, letting her speak, truly speak, for what felt like the first time in years.

"Anything is possible. But when I had the chance to pick my own destiny, then, I couldn't *not* pick going with you."

"Using those double negatives, mate."

"See?" She grinned. "You get me all muddled. My life would be grammatically correct without you."

"Now we're a grammar joke." I shook my head, feigning disappointment.

"You and me. I figure we deserve a chance. Wherever we go. Whatever we do. Riding the line, getting the bad guys. Defeating the fires, one at a time." Her eyes shone.

"You're beautiful, you know it?"

"Eh. I'll be cute and you just talk. Talk about anything."

I crawled as close to her as I could without disturbing the raft's contents and inhabitants. The Commander lay asleep across from Saylor. Lowering my voice, I dipped my chin, "I'd kiss you now, if I could."

Saylor nipped down on her bottom lip. Casting a quick glance around, she hoisted up on the edges of our rafts. Her face lowered to mine, and she breathed out, "This one's for still being part of what is. You're my perfect present." She pressed her soft lips against mine. A warm embrace for a cool night. Hot and flickering. Her eyelashes brushed against my cheek as she eased away.

I continued holding her hand. "I'm glad you're here, Saylor."

She settled back down in her raft. "I don't know if I should say 'me, too,' but, I'm glad I'm not sitting back at home getting news your boat sank. I'd rather be in the puddle with you."

I cringed at the idea of Cadence and the other females at the plantation.

"May I ask something?" Saylor swallowed hard.

"Of course."

Her gaze darted around the raft behind me, landing on the sleeping bodies and one bored Hazard. I followed her line of sight. Hazard had pulled out a knife and appeared to be whittling a block of some white foam into a shape.

Saylor's eyes locked on mine again when I collected my senses. "What was she like? What did she say to you?" Her voice was nearly inaudible.

"Who?"

"The girl."

"The Not-Saylor?"

"Ye—right. Is that what we're calling her now?"

I shrugged. "Why not?"

"And?"

"She was powerful. Confident. Demanding. Arrogant."

"So then...a lot of great things I am not."

"It's not like that, Saylor. She was similar to you, but thinner."

"Phenomenal."

"Not—you're misunderstanding me. Like before—before the tower. Remember how much you'd been training and working? You'd hardened up. Once you've been in the field you'll find your stride in no time. Already on your way." *Good work keeping your boots out of your teeth, mate.*

Saylor released her grip and shimmied her fingers. Our palms had gotten clammy over the water. She wiped her hands against the raft.

"Why'd you call this a puddle?" I asked, not letting the conversation get away from me. My voice rose over the waters. Micah stirred.

"Shh!" Saylor held up a finger in front of her lips, her eyes wide.

We paused.

I mouthed, "You think of the ocean as a puddle? It's a little bit more."

"I'd rather not think about being one of a few people hovering over a yawning breadth of endless, watery death."

"Makes sense."

"I have this fear of falling into holes."

"Good thing you can float in this one."

"Ha. Why don't you talk about paint drying? Or the process of building a nanomite?"

"Did you know the shutters on a ship are called the deadlights?" I tossed out some of my latest reading material at her.

"Um, oh yeah?"

"Yes. They're screwed onto the outside of a ship's windows to protect it in a storm."

"Ah. Cool. Collecting some nautical knowledge, I see."

Letting a grin ride across my cheeks, I offered a nod. "Pirate history, actually. Deadlights can also be a term for 'eyes.'"

"Because the eyes are the windows to the soul?"

"I suppose? Regardless, you've got lovely deadlights."

Saylor scrunched up her nose. "I'm not sure if that's a compliment?"

I narrowed my eyes, seeing past her, and squinted.

She paused, and then leaned back slightly. "Wha—what? What are you doing?"

"Is—" I blinked at the murky waves beyond the raft, "—is that a shark?"

Chapter Eleven

OF WRATH UNFURLED
Saylor

Tucker's finger pointed straight across the glassy plane. Trembles welled up in my chest and shivered down my spine. The water around us sparkled in the starlight.

"Where?" I squeaked.

The grin flowing across Tucker's cheeks lingered long enough to vault my shudders into fury.

"You did not just—"

His eyes widened, and those wicked dimples lit his cheeks. "Thought you could use a chuckle."

"Oh, sharks are funny now?"

He shrugged. "I'm short on comedy routines lately."

I balled up my fist and slammed it against his shoulder. In an effeminate, appreciative, joking way, of course.

"Guess we should get some shut-eye?" Tucker reluctantly sighed.

I squeezed his hand. "Think you'll sleep?"

"One can hope."

"Pretend you're back at the beach."

"Under the stars." A slight smile perched on his lips.

"Under the stars."

———— ⚬ ————

The helicopters came, one by one. Pounding across the horizon, the beasts brought rippling waves and ferocious winds. And water canteens. Lowering rope ladders and small, sling-like platforms, the Army rescue op loaded the first batch of Guardsmen into the six green choppers. They'd come back for the second load—and I found myself perched in a harness, swinging through the whirling winds above the Atlantic Ocean. As the rope whipped upward, my feet hanging beneath me, I studied the upturned faces of my squad.

Dad's eyes crinkled at the corners. He stood in the center of his raft and offered a brief salute.

Logan shielded his eyes with his hand.

Tucker assisted a woman, the one who served in the mess hall, helping her lock the harness around her shoulders.

The females went first. Our Guardsmen did indeed maintain their insistence on it, and to be honest, I don't think anyone argued.

When my sling approached the aircraft, a soldier reached down and helped me slide up on the horizontal skids. His thick fingers wrapped around mine, and was I ever so grateful his arm was as wide as my thigh. With a quick shove, he boosted me into the body of the fuselage, where two benches faced each other. Another soldier inside helped me out of the harness, and then wrapped a bright orange towel around me. He pointed to the bench, and I sat beside Eagre.

The weight of gravity sank into my boots. We suspended mid-air, fighting a war against nature and the murky depths of the seas. Closing my eyes, I inhaled a deep, heavy breath. *Try not to think about how small this helicopter is.*

Clearing my throat, I yanked my arms deeper into the warm towel, pulling tighter around my shivering core. I'd seen wetter, colder, less hopeful days. Micah slid onto the bench beside me. The other Dragon—Clutch?—shifted in her towel, coughing.

The soldier who'd helped me into the helo signaled to the pilot, his lips moving in conversation, and then slid the door shut. We soared through the air, turning tail, heading back from whence they came. Bright sunlight drifted through the small square window. The thunderous rotors overhead blocked out any conversation we might have had.

After what seemed like hours later, the chopper's skids hit the ground with a gentle bump. Eagre jumped to her feet right away, dropping her towel in her place. When the soldier opened the door, she was the first to hit the tarmac. Fists on her hips, she glared at us, while we slowly hopped to the blackened pavement.

"Let's move," she declared. "We've got to get a lead on these guys, they think they've taken our men out. The faster we move, the more surprise we have on our side. If they see choppers and a rescue party they'll have more time to prepare another attack."

"Calm down, Eagre," I said, still holding my towel. I stood beside her, watching the soldier help the others down. Taking her elbow in my palm, I intended to pull her away from the swift kicking of the rotors against the air.

She yanked her arm away from me. "You're not to touch me."

"Didn't mean to—" Jumping back, I held up my hands in surrender. I dropped the towel.

"You spend your time wishing and wandering. We don't need you here," she spat. "Toss off."

"Eagre, they will be okay. The guys will be back in no time."

She snorted and tossed her fiery gaze around the tarmac. "Look around, blondie. We're here because of you. You and your lookalike. I sincerely can't understand why anyone would want to be around you, let alone make a copy of you."

"What are you talking about? Make a copy of me?" My insides ground to a halt, and the air rested thickly inside my lungs. Heat welled up in my cheeks.

"Oh, come on. Obviously something shonky's been trickling through the line. You have to know more about this."

"I truly don't."

Her spurning laugh burned. "Right. Keep telling yourself that. Meanwhile, I've lost all I had. We lost Shadow. We've lost a good deal of intel. And now what? What will you do to fix this? What can *you* do?"

"I—I don't know." My shoulders slumped. She voiced all the questions I'd been letting stomp all over my mind.

"And you continue to be of no help." Eagre pointed a finger at me, her knuckles white, stretched tight. "You're not needed here."

"Hey!" Before I could stop the words, they tumbled out, hurt, angry, red, and hot. I yelled it over the bellowing insult and jealous loss. "You don't know me. Eagre, you haven't seen my dark days or my lost nights. You don't know what I'm ready for and what I can do. I can do more with my little pinky than you can do with your eight claws. Why do you think you can judge me? How would you feel if someone just outright decided you weren't worth a shot? What makes you judge and jury?"

Her eyes glinted. "I validate myself. I say I'm good enough, and therefore, I am. Nothing you, or anyone else, can say will change that. I prove I'm ready for my battles because I train, I show up, and I give doubt a hearty handshake and a back-handed slap. I'm a Dragon. With every breath, I live it, and I know it. I've got nothing else I need to prove."

Her heel ground against the pavement. She sauntered toward a red-brick building with a large white sign labeled, "Hangar Six."

A large part of me envied her then. Some of me pitied her because of what I'd seen as loneliness or arrogance. But the bulk of me absorbed her words and her strength.

I am so much more than these two arms. I am more than my deadlights, open to the abyss. I am more than a battle cry. I am Alliance.

"Wow." Micah cleared her throat and stepped beside me. Her tall shadow hovered over me.

"I think she possibly could be a dragon."

"I think I saw smoke coming out of her face-holes."

"I've never felt so small or jealous before."

Micah slapped my back. "Welcome to the party. We've all been here for a while."

"About Eagre?"

Micah let out a surprised laugh. "Saylor. Don't be ridiculous."

"Ladies," a man called from the door through which Eagre had disappeared. He held his camouflage cover in his hand and waved it in the air. "This way!"

Behind me, the whirling crescendoed, chopping through the air louder and more intense. I twirled to watch a second helicopter land, and the one we'd emptied began to take off. The soldier from our craft waved, and I held up a hand to offer a salute. He nodded with a smile, and slammed the door shut.

"Hey, Micah," I called over the ruckus. "You go with them and make sure a medic sees to our friend from the mess hall. I'm going to wait for this next crew to unload. I think Canaan was on this helo."

"Sure thing. Why are you waiting for Canaan?"

"I need to check with him about our trunks."

"Alright." Micah flung her orange towel over her shoulder. "I feel like I'm missing something without my pack. I've never gotten off a chopper without my bag before."

"You've been on a helicopter before?"

"Well, no."

"Ah." I nodded, my mouth puckering.

Micah shrugged. "But I feel like I would have had a bag with me. Usually I have a bag."

"I know what you mean."

"I guess I get to finally pick out one without holes." Micah grinned at me, and then jogged off toward the office. "Dibs on the one without holes!"

"Just the one?" I called out after her, but the roaring wind whipped away my words. "Why have you had holes in your bags?"

The side door of the green helicopter slid open, and men began unloading, jumping to the ground. They jostled away from the aircraft, carrying their orange towels. Some wore boots, some swiped their covers on their heads, and some lacked all but their camo pants and green shirts. All carried their shoulders high.

Canaan climbed down from the fuselage, twisting back to face the chopper and the men inside. They shoved black trunks from out of the depths of the beast. Two others helped Canaan unload the trunks and carry them several yards away. A crew lugged a thick black hose attached to a large drum on wheels beside the chopper and began the refueling process.

Under the hot, rushing air of the slowing rotor blades, Canaan raised the small black box in his hands, signaling for me to join him.

"Glad you made it safe," I shouted, jogging to him.

"You too, kid." He offered the box to me.

I accepted the box, gripping it in both hands like the treasure it was. "Anything else I can help carry?"

"This satchel. If you don't mind." He tugged a gray bag with a long gray strap off the top of the stack of trunks. Two Dragons, one with scrappy blond hair, the other a scowling mass of tan muscles—*I seriously need to learn their names*—hopped from the hold and each seized a handle of a trunk. Canaan called to them, "Hangar six. Where everyone's headed!"

They nodded. More of our Alliance guys grabbed cargo, unloading.

"I'll see you in there," I called to Canaan, tossing the satchel strap over my head and across my chest.

He winked at me. "You better. We got some training to do."

I returned the look. "Yes, sir." As I strode away, I studied that black box. Using my thumbs, I unlatched the black, shiny, clasp locks folded back on themselves. With a metallic *clink*, the clamps popped free. I cracked the lid open.

The ten mirrored shapes lay in their padded spots, each one surrounded by a thick layer of foam. Their blue tinting reflected the bright sun. They hummed, awakened by the solar energy; I could feel it tingling in my fingertips and swirling into my marrow.

Closing the lid and snapping the latches back into place, I tucked the box under my arm. *You're home now.*

Tucker and Logan slid into the doorway of the mess hall, rumpled and haggard. Their eyes lit up at the large portions on their plates and the short amount of time it took for them to receive it. A herd of Dragons followed Tucker around, and he directed them to eat as well, and he only dove in after everyone else had begun.

I strode over to them with two fresh cups of steaming, hot coffee. "Gentlemen. Your liquid happiness."

Logan brought his hands to his shoulders. "She knows us all too well." He closed his eyes, a wide smile plastered across his face. Then he quickly accepted the cup in his palms.

"She understands." Tucker twisted in his seat to face me. He placed one hand on the coffee mug handle, and the other on my hand. His smile dropped, the exhaustion clear in the shadows under his eyes. The green wasn't so bright. "Thank you, Saylor."

"A little less cheery than I thought you'd be after leaving those sharks behind."

He studied me, a small glint of cheer at the joke radiating on his cheeks. "I'm truly grateful for the coffee. Thoughtful of you."

I wanted to throw my arms around his neck and squeeze tight. Anything to help wipe away the sorrow he carried. It lingered. Everyone's eyes lingered as well. "Can I get anyone else coffee? This serves as a one-time offer. I don't do drink service."

Five guys glanced at each other with their mouths full of food, bleary-eyed, and starving.

"Well, since you're offering." Micah bounced over to me, tossing a soft fist onto my shoulder. "I'd love a large—I don't know, what's one of those special coffee drinks? A cappe macarena? Mocha thumbelina?"

"I'm going to need you to calm yo'self." I held up a palm. "You're more excited than a mirror on a disco ball."

"They have chocolate chip cookies." Micah almost squeaked.

"Ooh!" I perked up myself.

"I want cookies," Logan said, his mouth stuffed with meat.

Two of the Dragons across from Logan and Tucker raised their hands.

"I'll get cookies." I nodded. "But I'm going to need you guys to wear name tags."

"We do normally have them on our unis," one of them said. His short, sandy hair had been scuffled with salt and sea breezes. A streak of black grime tapered along his cheek. "But I'm Weyr." He whipped his hand up to his forehead in a miniature salute, then arced his eyebrows. His teal eyes shone. "Not like you 'wear a coat' or 'wear a uniform,' but as in w-e-y-r, a collection of dragons."

"Ah." I clicked my tongue. "Nice to meet you, Weyr."

"And you, McConnell." He gestured to my name tag.

"But what would your uniform name tag say?" I asked.

He swallowed. The side of his lips rose in a smirk. "I've answered as many names. But now I answer to Weyr."

"Duly noted."

"Thank you."

"Two cookies?"

Weyr's grin widened. "Too right."

Micah raised her hand. "I'll count. Raise your hands for how many cookies you want?"

While she took a count, I bent my knees. My face lowered closer to Tucker's. Quietly, I studied his jawline as he chewed.

The skin near his ears had freckles on it. I'd not noticed before. His ears burned red as he chewed. He carefully set his fork on his plate and tilted his face my way. He swallowed. Those emerald, marble-like eyes. So normally full of life and ease, they strained to focus on mine.

"Do you know Dad's whereabouts?"

"He's meeting with the base commander and such. Should be in here once he gets some details squared away."

I nodded. "Good. Also. I know you're not a huge fan of chocolate." I stated it, deadpan. "So I can get you lemon pie if you prefer."

"If you get me lemon pie," he zeroed in on my face, then blinked once. "I'll have to call off this whole mission. Deal breaker."

"You're saying, then, yes to cookies?"

"As many as you can stuff in your pockets."

"You realize they'll end up salty."

"That's how I like my cookies. And my women." He grinned then, those dimples simmering on his cheeks.

I winked at him. "Don't I know it."

D ad gathered us all about an hour later, in one of the conference rooms off the backside of the mess hall. Beside him stood Tucker, Burkman, and two Army officers in green camouflage battle dress uniforms. Their name tags read *TITUS* and *WOJCIKOWSKI*.

"Since we've arrived sooner than planned, our hospitable friends," Dad motioned to the Army men beside him, "have helped me set up a place for us to stay for the next couple of nights until our barracks are available."

The towering, brawny Titus stepped forward, holding up a hand to greet us. His skin, even more ebony than Burkman's, hid the curve of the muscles in his frame, but his uniform sleeves almost screamed to be increased a size so as not to bust apart. He cracked his knuckles. "I empathize with your loss." His voice rumbled across the silent room. Even my bootstraps understood his authority. "We will do our best to aid your search. We've sent a freighter out to recover what we can from the wreck. I understand several of your men went back out."

Dad nodded.

"You've experienced a swift hardship. Expect our full cooperation. We're happy to work in tandem to rid our area of these pirates." Titus settled both balled up fists upon his belt.

"Thank you."

Dad motioned to the other man. "Our strategic systems coordinator, Woj—wochi—I'm sorry, how did you pronounce it?"

"Most around here call me Dub," the man answered. A southern drawl spun around the words. A wide smile marked his thin, strong cheeks and steel jaw. "Been all over the world. Settled in the midwest. Found myself out here, seems to be near heaven." His dazzling smile and meticulous eyes studied the men in the room. Chocolate brown hair settled back in a wavy peak. Friendly. But sharp. Like his nose. "While I too am sorry to hear about the circumstances, I'm excited to work with you. Heard a lot from the papers about Alliance." He let the word Alliance roll off his tongue as four or five syllables. "What you'll find on this island are humble people, horrific humidity, and sunsets more brilliant than your momma's pearly whites."

Some of the men chuckled.

Micah leaned over to me and whispered. "He can get on my pearly whites."

"Micah!" I mouthed, my eyes popping wide.

We caught his attention, as his gaze settled on us for a moment longer than on the others. Then he studied Dad. "We've found some accommodations which will be to your liking. When our barracks have been cleared, I'll provide a tour of our campus, registration, and anything else you need. Say the word, I'm your man." Dub focused on us again. "We've got a supply of uniforms and personal hygiene items you may be needing. And we're prepared to assist in whatever manner you may require."

"Thank you," Dad stated. "The Army has been more than accommodating. We cannot express the depth of our gratitude."

A murmur of agreement from all of us followed.

Dub held up a hand, wiping away the adulation. "It's what we do. In a few moments I'll be escorting you to your accommodations, but, Commander McConnell, I believe you wanted to say a few words?"

"Yes, Dub." Dad cleared his throat. "Guardsmen, take a knee."

After a quick snap of movement and shuffling of bodies, we hushed. Dad scanned the room. He held his chin high, absorbing the attention and condensing it. A restrained intensity emanated from the deep pools of his eyes. His forehead wrinkled in concern.

All breath in the room awaited, enrapt in attention.

"Along the path for truth, we have found an enemy who seeks to intimidate and destroy. We have lost some of our own. We are missing material possessions. Yet we continue to seek and battle our foe. I tell you now: we do not battle the hands who dare strangle our efforts, but the fear and confusion which led them to this action.

"We do not embrace fear or linger near its cousin timidity. In the heat of danger, we forge onward; dauntless; united. In the taunting of weakness, we push back stronger. In the whispered regret, we shout our forward progress. For we are not seekers who lose our mark, but protectors of life. We maintain our mission, should all else fall away. Amidst the turmoil, we pursue the vein of our ethos. Our protocol holds strong regardless of location, spirit, or company: Be powerful. Be consistent. Never quit. Finish the mission.

"We find our target, tear down their armory, and reclaim our property. We take as few lives as possible. But we must clean up our house. You and I embody the symbol of Alliance. We are the message to this world, proving Alliance operates powerfully, presently, and better than ever. Carry that symbol proudly, serving those who have gone before, and honoring them with our actions. They've given the ultimate sacrifice. Now we finish this task to which we've been commissioned. We will not rest, come bully or bounty, until we have served our objective in full. This is our statement, our rally. We satisfy our duty, through day and dark night. We are the Guard. We are Alliance."

All paused heartbeats clamored together, men surging to their feet, some clapping, and some confirming with a hearty, "Hoo-rah!" Many bumped each other on the shoulder, while others bobbed their heads.

My chest filled with heat, with a shimmering fire of battles past. Here rose my father, my family, my forged privilege. The deepest corners of my soul resonated a thrumming pulse, a war cry.

My boot bumped the black box at my feet as Micah threw her arm around my neck.

In the scalding torrent of wrath unfurled, even my blood screamed what I could no longer quell or deny. I'd have no more looking back. I didn't want to.

I am Alliance. I am the Guard.

Chapter Twelve

YOU'RE NOT ALONE
Tucker

Relegated to the front of the room, I saw the truth behind their eyes. Our loss weighed upon each body, and yet...resolve padded the bruises. Saylor's eyes locked with mine. She gave a slight nod. I returned it. I wasn't sure I even convinced myself.

Eight Dragons. At the back of the crowd, Shadow ducked behind Hazard, whose black eyes stared at the ground before him. Case's dulled eyes studied his folded arms, leaning against the back wall. I blinked. Shadow's profile disappeared.

Commander McConnell divided us into groups, and we followed Dub to a line of rough and tumble vehicles, mostly jeeps with open tops, which had seen their fair share of wet, hot, island days. Each Dragon took a seat before I climbed aboard the last vehicle. Slamming the door behind me, I squished into the back seat of a jeep beside Wring and Clutch.

Sultry winds whipped through Clutch's loose, curly hair. She yanked it back, wrestling it with one hand. "I'll be glad to get the ocean out of my skin. Doesn't smell so great."

"I'm looking forward to sleeping in a bed," Wring admitted. "Although I'm still rocking. I may fall out of it."

"Sea legs will get ya," I agreed.

The soldier gunned the engine. We drifted out of our spot along the drive, following the other vehicles through the winding streets around the island. The hills rose on one side, the other sloping down to a city. Farmland surrounding us divided the acreage into colorful green and brown patchwork squares. Wind curled around us, hurtling through the open air. Rich, golden light tangled among the towering clouds. Pinks mingled with the oranges of the sunset, cascading over the island. The road wound over a corner and a small town of stucco buildings came into view. We passed a bakery, a weathered church, a butcher shop, a multitude of open doorways, shutters and window casings painted in bright blues, pastel yellows, beiges, and shades of purples. Second story balconies lined both sides of the roads, laced with ivy, colorful flowerboxes, and red and green flags. Villagers milled along beside the road. They watched our convoy, stiffly eyeing us.

"Welcome to Angro do Heroísmo."

"Are the locals friendly?" I leaned forward in my seat, gripping the roll bar by my head.

Our driver called over his shoulder, "They're used to us being here." The wind nearly ripped the words out of his mouth. "Angro do Heroísmo serves as a key shipping port. However, they get sticky when seeing an influx of military personnel. It's not exciting for them to have more tourists around using their resources, but they also appreciate how we pay them in exchange."

"Seems like it'd be a good deal for them."

He shrugged. "With the increased rate of piracy nearby, the resources are scarcer. Makes them a little tense."

"Ah. Piracy does pressurize a situation."

The road led straight for the crystal, waving ocean. He shouted over the noise, "Eliminate the pirates, eliminate the tension. Hopefully."

"Aye." I gave a quick bob of my chin. "And eliminate we will."

Our driver wound around a turn, following the caravan down a tar-paved road, and a large cement edifice rose before us. The building, not a square, contrasted as a stark force against the green, lush grass surrounding it, and the sparkling blue ocean beyond.

"What's that?" Clutch gasped.

"Used to be an old fort, built in the 1600's, then renovated to be a luxury hotel."

"It's a hotel?"

Our driver nodded. "You don't happen to know Portuguese, do you?"

"Just so happens," I answered, "We do not."

"The culture's rife with history and legend around here. On a clear day you can see three of the other Azores islands from the lookout. The fort served the island well, and you'll be glad for the rooms. Don't expect anything so nice back at Lajes."

"Do they have a pool?" Wring asked, his eyes lighting up.

"Yes, indeed."

"Yesss." Wring made a fist and pumped it by his chest.

"Don't get too excited just yet," I cautioned. "We may not have time to use it. And what about your swim trunks? Pretty sure they're at the bottom of the Atlantic."

Wring offered a devious smile in return.

Clutch shook her head and rolled her eyes. "Gross."

Our driver rolled to a stop in a rounded drive, behind the other vehicles, and shifted the gear to park. "Welcome to Pousada Forte."

Gray cobblestones on the road led to a gray brick and cement wall rising from the electric green grass beyond. The wall, covered in moss and years of patching jobs, sloped away from us to a flat top. Two wings on each end jutted toward us at a ninety-degree angle. In the middle of the wall, the cobblestones led over a stone bridge through a single arch containing a black tunnel to the mysterious beyond.

"Where are the windows?" Wring asked.

"Well, it's a fort," Clutch stated matter-of-factly.

"Not too welcoming, for a hotel."

"Wait until you see the other side," our driver laughed. "Enjoy your stay."

I hopped out of the jeep and landed on the ground, my boots thumping against the gray stones. I stuck out my palm. "Thanks for the ride."

He nodded, gripping my hand. "You bet. I'm sure I'll be seeing you tomorrow."

"Right so. See you then!"

Wring and Clutch each tossed their legs over the edges of the jeep and grabbed their brown paper sacks from the back end.

"Do you have everything you need for the night?" The driver twisted in his seat to face us.

"I believe so." I glanced at Wring and Clutch to confirm with them. They nodded.

I held up my own paper bag. "For the night, anyway. As long as they have coffee in there."

"Sir." His eyes widened. "First, what's your cup of choice?"

"Hot. Blonde. Strong."

Saylor strolled up beside me, her blue eyes bright, cheeks flushed. "Hey."

I grinned at her, then refocused on the man in the jeep.

He chuckled. "Sounds about right. Here you'll find coffee unlike any other in the world. What you're used to, ask for, '*Um café Americano.*' It's luxurious, smooth, and full-bodied. If you want the flavor of an espresso with a mite less viscosity, order, '*Um abatanado.*' For a lively double shot of the nectar of the gods, order, '*Um café duplo,*' or '*Um café cheio.*' The kitchen here will know what to do. If you find the time, *Café do Rei* three streets over has the island's best cup."

Just the idea of the forthcoming lurid swig drew satisfaction to my gut. I offered a hearty thanks.

"Welcome," he beamed. "If you go, tell Aleixo that Nuñez sent ya."

"Yes, sir."

He gunned the engine, then shifted back into gear.

"Thanks again!"

"My pleasure." Nuñez waved and followed the two other empty jeeps out of the circular drive. Their rumbling engines died away in the hot breeze.

"Did I hear the word café, as in coffee?" Saylor asked, her bag slung over her shoulder.

"Aye, mate."

"You're too easy to predict."

"Nevah!" I declared, reaching for her hand, the many eyes around us watching.

Her blues studied mine, as she drew her hand away, and forced it into her pocket.

I did the same, wadding up my fist within the folds of fabric. "Right. Coffee later. Now, room assignments."

The Commander finished his lively engagement with Dub, who pointed over to the fort.

"How was your ride here?" Saylor asked. Her head tilted away, studying our surroundings, and then she inched closer to my side. "Our driver didn't stop talking about the history of the island. Fascinating place."

"Seems like it."

"Beautiful."

"Agreed."

Her voice had a melodic hum to it. She analyzed the sunset beyond the gray wall. A breeze tossed some stray hairs around her temples. She wrinkled her forehead for the slightest of moments, and then the thought blipped away.

"What?" I asked.

Saylor blinked, then focused on me. "Sorry?"

"What's going on in there?"

"I just love the sunset, is all. It's such a magical time. All the colors. A star's out already." She tipped her head back.

I followed where she indicated, the bright spot stuttering upon the impending navy horizon.

"You haven't said the word *magic* since Barina."

She cleared her throat. "I guess I'm drawn to islands."

"A fair assessment."

"Haven't experienced much magic since Barina." Her lips parted, a slight breath drifting out and up into the atmosphere. Then they tumbled into a rigorous smile. "I know we just lost almost everything. But it affirms I needed to come. You were right."

"I was right?"

"Circle up, everyone!" The Commander clapped. "I've got room assignments, keys, and basic instructions." Our group crowded closer. Eight Dragons. Check.

"Ordinarily," the Commander began, straightening a stack of papers in his hands, "I'd keep us on mission, on task, and with a rigid schedule." He glanced up, exhaling deeply. "And tomorrow, we'll do that. For now, we need a brief period of rest."

An audible sigh of excitement murmured among the troops.

The Commander held up his hand. "Tomorrow morning at 0700 you report for duty, bright-eyed, bushy-tailed, and more prepared for action than you've ever been. Our accommodations have two restaurants which will accept your room key for payment. Lights out by 2200. I will personally be doing room checks. You must stay with a buddy. Should you leave the campus, you must check in with me, Burkman, or Thompson. Don't make a scene, leave this place better than you found it, and remember at all times you represent Alliance Military Guard. Otherwise, you've got free time."

More excited grunts made their rounds.

Commander McConnell held up the stack of white papers. "Form a line."

"Your rooms are right past here." I waved to my Dragons. Their boots padded along the tile hallway. I pivoted in my spot to face them. Wring and Flight stopped short behind me. Following them, other camouflage jackets strolled along, searching for their rooms along the bright corridor. The beige walls echoed with stirrings and rumbling conversations.

"While we're here, your roommates are your traveling buddies. Stay in groups of two at minimum. Do not go anywhere alone."

"Who's your travel buddy?" Rubu leaned against the wall, crossing his arms. A smirk lit his cheeks.

"Your mom!" Weyr cackled, and punched Rubu in the arm.

Rubu tossed his arm around Weyr's neck to wrestle him to the ground, and I held up a palm. "Quit muckin' around. These other guys need to think you've got some semblance of order."

"Oh, we keep order alright." Weyr straightened and released Rubu.

Rubu nodded, wiping the wrinkles out of his uni, and held up his pointer finger. "I'd like to order a ribeye and a side of whiskey, neat."

"You can't order whiskey, Rubu," Eagre chided from beside me.

"He wouldn't know how to drink it, anyway," Clutch murmured from the edge of the group. She rested one ankle over the other and adjusted her bag in her palm.

"No alcohol. I can't even believe you're bringing up the idea." I held out a white card to Eagre. "Eagre, Clutch, you're rooming with Saylor and Micah."

Eagre snorted.

"Careful around Micah. She bites."

Eagre rolled her eyes.

I tossed a white card to Wring. "You, Flight, and Rubu. You're here." I tapped the door to my right. "They're bringing up a cot."

They accepted their assignments with a nod.

"Thunder, Weyr, you're across the hall. Hazard, you're with me."

The team began dismantling. Before they'd taken too many steps, I bellowed "Dragons." One by one they paused, acknowledging my voice.

"While the Commander gave you leave, I want to reinforce some rules. You're not to leave this property without letting me know where you want to go, and you must take a buddy. Your travel buddy will ideally be over the age of twenty-one."

"We can't even go with you?" Eagre questioned, and then chuckled.

"Look, if I thought I could get away with it, I'd toss into my bed right now and stay until morning. As it is, I've got to meet with the Commander to get tomorrow squared away. I'm unavailable for escorting tonight."

Saylor, Micah, Logan, and the Commander strolled up, the Commander pointing them toward the girls' room.

"We good?" Wring asked. "I'm starved."

"Go!" I held up my empty hands. "Eat, drink *water*, be merry."

"I heard your subtle hint," Weyr admitted. "And I beg you to reconsider."

"Oh, the steak's ridgy didge. In fact, order one for me and I'll see which of us can eat it faster."

"You're on, boss."

"Dismissed."

They settled into their rooms and I slid the key card into the slot on my door, when Canaan marched through the hall, muttering to himself. He grabbed my shoulder. "Thompson! Just who I was looking for."

"Fantastic."

"I hear your sarcasm. I'll be quick. Come with me."

Hazard had stayed still, observing the whole scene since we'd arrived at our section of rooms. His charcoal judgment flicked around. I blinked pointedly at him. "Can you buddy up with Thunder?"

Hazard nodded. "I'd like to sleep. If I must eat, I can, but I'd rather not."

"Feeling alright?"

He bobbed his chin, his eyes dimming. "I want to rest, like the Commander said."

"No worries, Haz. Sleep some for me."

His lips skewed a wee bit. "Yes, sir. I'll take your bag, sir."

Canaan called from down the hall. "Thompson!"

"Canaan!" I twisted back to Hazard. He stuck out his palm. I set the strap handle in it. "Thanks," I mouthed.

He gave a quick nod and disappeared into the room. As he exited, I jogged down the hall.

Logan sprawled across the white comforter topping the double bed. His eyes squeezed shut. "I admit in the last twenty-four hours I thought I'd never sleep in a bed again."

"You are not alone," the older McConnell answered, navigating his bag into the closet. "Remind me to get our crew new bags." He stopped moving then. His shoulders slumped.

The closet door swung shut, clicking in the silence. The Commander lifted his hand to his forehead, covering his eyes with a limp hand.

Curtains flapped in the open window, the twilight's breeze allowing in a briny, soft swath of air.

Canaan had perched in a chair by a small round table in the corner, and he watched the scene, waiting.

The Commander stumbled to the bed and sank onto the edge of it, his hand still shielding his eyes from the light.

"Canaan," the Commander began without moving, "what were you able to salvage? Do you have a specified list?"

"Yes, sir. I've made notes on everything."

"Do we have our coms?"

"Enough for a small team."

"Did you get your computer working?"

"The tablet's still airing out. But she's durable, sir. I'll get it up and loaded in no time."

The Commander nodded. His hand fell onto his thigh. "We need bags."

"Our men are durable too, sir. You've inspired them to continue. We're all committed."

"They're Alliance's best, no question."

"Yes, sir."

The Commander studied the ceiling. "My wedding ring. It's gone." His left thumb traced the empty space on his ring finger.

Logan opened his eyes and raised his head from the comforter.

"I keep thinking of items I need to get from my bag, and they're buried in the ocean. Gone." Command ran a hand over the sandy stubble on his chin. The shadow hung over his countenance, deepening the lines of fatigue.

A knock on the door.

Logan jumped, sitting straight up.

Since I was closest, I plodded over to the door and opened it, revealing one Saylor and a Micah right behind her. "Ah. The welcoming party!"

Saylor lifted one eyebrow. "If by that you mean the dinner party, yes. Gimme food."

"I'm starved," Micah called over her shoulder. "I heard someone mention steak earlier."

"Have them come in," the Commander stated.

Waving the girls in, I closed the door behind them.

The Commander gripped his knees, still seated on the edge of the bed. "One quick word before we go."

"Is everything okay?" Saylor whispered to me, brushing against my arm. Behind her back, she caught my hand in hers and intertwined our fingers. She leaned against the wall, casual. I placed my free hand on my hip, trying to appear nonchalant. Her warm skin against mine. Hot and blonde. My ribs ached suddenly.

"Team," McConnell sighed, "tomorrow we split up. We'll need a re-supply unit, a recon unit, and an intel unit. Recon needs to check out several areas of interest our friends at Lajes have investigated in their offices. Logan, Tucker, you'll head out for recon with a local translator who's meeting us at 0700. Intel will head to Lajes in order to follow the paper trail. Canaan, I'll need you at Lajes with me. Saylor, Micah, if you can head up re-supply, I'd appreciate it."

Micah folded her arms across her chest. "You want us to go shopping?"

The Commander just flicked a look in her direction.

"Isn't that a little...cliché?"

"You'd rather trek three kilometers into the forest reserve to photograph rocks? Interview locals? Analyze tactical spreadsheets and feasibility reports?"

"I'll do whatever you ask me to do, Commander McConnell." She eased back, her voice softening.

He tilted his head. "I'm entrusting this task to you. You'll find a certain enjoyment in it, I'm sure."

"Yes, sir."

"Now." He straightened his back and sought us all, those piercing, steel eyes slicing the façade. "In a way, we've made headway on our intel, even though we lost most of our data in the process. I got a call in to Fulbright and he's collecting copies for us, hopefully to be sent within the next few hours. So, we wait for tonight, and charge ahead full steam tomorrow. Our enemy thinks they've got a lead on us. Let's use it to our advantage while we can."

"And the motivation for giving everyone the night off?" Logan asked, almost burning in his tone.

The Commander shook his head. "Everyone needs a few hours to recuperate. Even the most experienced of us must let the shock wear off to perform at maximum aptitude. We demand every ounce of capability at our command to apprehend Adenauer and his team." The exhaustion wore through his words. Thinly veiled, the deep shadows under his eyes relayed the facts. He was worn out.

Saylor squeezed my hand, let go, and edged closer to the Commander. She dropped to a knee beside her father. Ducking her head for one brief moment, she then glanced up to catch his line of sight. "Dad. Once upon a time you told me you'd never leave me. You said you had my best interest in mind, even if I didn't understand it. When I needed it the most, you reminded me I wasn't alone. I had Alliance, you, and these squibs." She grinned up at us, then stared at the Commander. "I still trust you. I trust you more now, because we've been through fire together and you literally hung in with us. Our enemy tried to take our courage, but they've only stirred it up. I'm not the smartest in the room, but I say we celebrate. Tonight we take one more night to pluck the strings."

Saylor rose up on her knees and wrapped her arms around his neck. He gripped her back, enfolding her within his grasp.

She'd seen death. She'd seen the end.

She had nothing to lose.

She had everything to lose.

"I think I hear steak sizzling in the kitchen." I jutted my thumb over my shoulder.

"Second the sizzling," Canaan agreed. He rocked in the chair.

The Commander released Saylor, and she stood, knees cracking on her way to her feet.

"You're dismissed," McConnell murmured, with a gentle wave. "Thompson. Stick with me for a moment, please."

The others drifted out. Logan hopped off the bed. Micah pressed down a patch of hair on Logan's head that shot out wildly. Logan smacked her arm away. Canaan chuckled as he strolled through the doorway. Saylor shot silent questions our way before scuttling after them.

"Yes, sir?" I asked, standing at attention.

The Commander stood, adjusting his belt. "I'll tell Burkman to help enforce the Dragons tonight. I understand how difficult losing two of yours must be."

My voice cracked as I confirmed. "Yes, sir."

He exhaled a gusty breath. "I'm mighty sorry to lose them. We'll give them a proper memorial when we get home."

"Their families deserve closure as well."

"Of course." He ran a hand through his hair.

"If it helps, I've been there."

"Hm?"

I had his attention. "I've stood in the scrub, penniless, homeless, without a trace of anything familiar."

He arched an eyebrow.

"Turns out, with the right company, even the most daunting paths can be dominated. Borrowed uniforms or none."

"Those monsters still haunting you at night, Thompson?"

"Not so much. Only when Burkman's my bunkmate." I offered a slight grin.

"Now you've harnessed them. Go." McConnell tossed an amused glance at the front door. "I'm pretty sure a hopeful soul in the hallway awaits you. Go be young for a few hours."

"Sir—"

He grunted. "I won't repeat myself, Thompson."

Chapter Thirteen

A THOUSAND DARK NIGHTS
Saylor

The worn, earthy tiles on the walls reflected the candlelight from each table. As if we dined within the hollows of the earth itself, the marbled pillars suspending the high ceiling echoed with murmurs and trills of laughter. Floor-to-ceiling windows to our left filled the wall, starlight in a midnight sky humming through the glass. Black calm crept around us. Red hot electricity vibrated throughout the fabric of my uniform. While nanocomputers throttled throughout my veins, Tucker's hand brushed against my own. Craving scraped against the outer crust of my resolve to finish the plate of greens resting before me. His warm, smooth skin settled against mine, on my right thigh under the table. Burkman wrestled with his knife across from me. Logan's eyes darted around the room as he drank from the stemmed glass he held in his right hand. At the head of the table to my left, Micah chuckled.

"What?" I asked absently, skimming the back of Tucker's hand with my pinkie.

"Remember when..." Words tumbled out of her mouth but I couldn't tell one from the other.

"Anyway," Micah sighed, "Clutch asked me if I wanted to try out the pool. You in?"

"Hum?" I glanced up at her. "I'm not sure. I wanted to explore around the hotel a little. See what the fort looks like." *Lies.*

Clutch stopped by the table then, and Micah left with her. *You're being a bad friend.* My fingertips lit with heat, each tiny crevice of Tucker's skin a ripple of thrill.

Tucker tilted his hand so our palms aligned, and he interlaced his fingers, squeezing. Releasing, withdrawing, he picked up his napkin and wiped his mouth. "Logan, you said you wanted to go run some sprints, correct?"

"You're nuts!" Logan shoveled a big bite of beans and rice into his gaping mouth.

Burkman jabbed Logan's shoulder with a fist. "Oh, come on, McConnell. I hear the island air is good for cardio!"

"No way, Burkman. I don't care. I'm crashing upstairs after I finish this plate of goodness."

"Saylor," Tucker turned to me. "You wanted to explore? I'd like to see the grounds too. I need to track a run for the Dragons in the morning. Join me?"

"Sure thing." Dropping my fork, I tried to swallow the grin away from my cheeks.

"A run. Right," Logan muttered.

Somehow we made it into the spacious lobby, the bright lights glaring around us.

"I have to brush my teeth." Tucker grimaced.

Laughing, I knocked my palm against my flushed cheek. "Please. Go brush your teeth."

Running my tongue against my gritty teeth, I giggled. "You've got a point."

We dashed up the stairs, slinking into our rooms. My room, voiceless and shrouded, breathed shallowly around me.

After a refreshing session of toothbrush versus tooth and a quick running of the brush through my shiny golden tangles, I ran my fingers through my thick blonde roots. Fluffing the tendrils, I tossed my head upside down and then back again. The room spun. My cheeks still held a rosy glow.

Grabbing the soft gray shirt with a large black ARMY scrolled across the chest, I tossed one arm and then another into the clean material.

A calm knock on the door.

My heart tumbled around behind my ribs. Breath scuttled through my throat, catching in the ache and query of stolen moments.

Tossing the door open, I grabbed Tucker's wrist and tugged him inside toward me. With a soft laugh, he slid in the slim entry, shutting the painted white panel behind him. He lifted the chain and slid it in the lock. *Click*.

Then his hands wrapped around my waist, drawing my body against his. The soft cotton between us sighed. He radiated heat. I was a sponge hoping to melt. My arms enfolded his neck. Closer. His lips brushed my cheek. Breath unfolded against my skin and broiled around us. Tucker slid his kisses down my jaw, nearing the base of my ear. My skin trembled, tickled, the soft hairs pulsing.

A girly squeal escaped and I beat it back, matching my lips with his. Shoving onto my toes, I slid closer, relaxing my weight onto him. We sank against the wall. A shiver shook along my spine, from the base of my hair and straight into the floor.

His fingers traced my neck, down my shoulder, along the shuddering line of fire, to where my lower back disappeared beneath my belt. Parting my lips open further, I dipped my tongue against his, pressing harder, pushing past forbidden lines. He thrust back.

Tucker's chest rose and fell, deep, windy breaths mangled between us. His hand trailed to my neck, his thumb drifting along my cheek. "They could come in any time."

The red heat flickered to white. "The door's locked." A fervor welled up in my chest, livid, lurid. The idea bounced around us. Little bumps bounded all over my arms.

"Can't." He withdrew the slightest, his lips parting, before melting against mine.

"Can." I gasped between breaths.

His grip tightened, hands triggered, exploring. "Saylor." Murmuring. Unwound. His sigh caught against my lips and I nipped at it.

"Let's be irresponsible for just five minutes."

He chuckled, the rumble pulsing against my lips. My hips dipped closer into his space, and he drew me in tighter in his arms.

Without warning, he tilted his chin to the side, inhaling deeply. He threw his arms in the air, palms facing the heavens. "Mayday."

I moaned. "Mayday, yourself."

"Our squad needs us to have our...heads on straight." The words slithered through inhaled exhaustion. Tucker straightened, tossing his shoulders back. He couldn't back up any further from me for the wall behind him, but I'd seen his resolve before.

My lips dried. I bit down on my bottom one before answering. "You don't want to get caught with me?"

"You *have* to understand by now." His hands settled on his hips. His eyes dropped, his gaze studying the carpet by the door.

"Why won't you look at me?"

"I'm trying to. Just give me a minute."

A smile peeked onto my lips.

"You're much too difficult, Saylor McConnell."

"Nah." I considered the idea. "Well, you're probably right."

"I will not ruin the years I've spent working for a few minutes of recklessness."

"You can't be irresponsible at all?" I stepped back, crossing my arms over my belly.

"I'm young, but youth carries no excuse for doing things I know I shouldn't do. I've got temptation, and I've got a mission. My mission gets the better of me right now."

My mouth dried, the cool air wrestling to dive down into the fiery pit strangling my still-racing heart. "I'm just a temptation?"

Tucker's verdant eyes pierced the dim space, flashing. "You know you're so much more to me than dark corners, and hands. Lips." His lips curled up. "Skin."

"If I was Eagre, or the other version of me who kissed you on the boat, would you do the same thing?"

"Saylor."

"No, I'm serious."

He rolled his eyes up to the ceiling and sighed. "Will we keep coming back to this self-doubt? To this dismissal of who you are?"

Clamping my jaw shut, I steadied for impact. I narrowed my eyes.

"There's a difference between confidence and chemistry." Suddenly, he was everywhere. His arms enveloped me, hoisting me up into the air. One arm around my back and entwining in the hair at the nape of my neck, his other arm grasped my leg, shoving it against his hip. Surging his lips against mine, his smoldering kisses melted the sweat and salt from our last few days.

He surged me onto my back on the soft bed, and we bounced there for an endless moment, his weight resting on me, forcing deep breaths from the oxygen to escape my wild heart. My lungs screamed. My skin bristled at every ounce of contact between us. He wound one leg around mine.

Our eyes locked. He dipped his forehead down until only emerald blurred in the closeness. Raging oxygen lurked, roiled, electrified, as his lips strained against mine.

He pulled back. "If you could hear the screaming inside this brain of mine, you'd understand. I would say I'd take you right here if you wanted, but I cannot. It's not that I don't want to. More than that, I want to fulfill my role better. I've got this moment to prove I can stick to my word. Long ago, I told your dad I'd be your safe place. I'd make you stronger. Get you back on-mission."

"You did?" I scrunched my eyebrows.

"I did." His pulse rattled, pounding through his chest.

"So what about after this mission ends? What then? As long as we're contracted with Alliance, we can't—?"

He shook his head, cramming his eyes shut.

"I love your battle, Tucker Thompson."

His eyes popped open, forehead crinkling. Those slight freckles shimmied.

"All your shady corners and your inner criticisms, and those ghosts haunting every doorway. I love your focus. I love how you care so much. You are my safe place." I blinked up at him. "You do make me better." Running my hand along his cheek, I allowed the quiet of the room to swallow us. "But can I also run my hands along your abs? Because I'm pretty sure it makes me a more cultured person."

He chuckled.

"No, I'm kidding. Somewhat."

"Are you up for exploring the fort?" Hot breath simmered in the closeness of our lips.

"I am. Are you?"

"I might need a moment." He unwrapped himself from around me and sat up. He cleared his throat.

"Take all the moments you need."

"You might want to brush your hair."

"Just think about Logan and Burkman in the hot tub. That'll cool you off real quick."

I ran the brush through my hair, counting to fifty, and came out of the bathroom. Tucker took my hand in his. We made our way down to the rear terrace. Illuminated by yellow lights, the twilight glowed, twinkling with laughter of voices beside the pool and at the patio tables. We seated ourselves beside Burkman and the shaggy-haired blond Dragon, at one of the small, square metal tables under a big, red, round umbrella.

"Thought you were headed up for the great sleep of a thousand dark nights, Thunder," Tucker stated.

"I tried," the Dragon replied. "Heard all the noise out here and had to see what I was missing."

"What's on your plate?"

Thunder's hand had settled around the base of a small, clear glass with yellow liquid in it, beside a square white plate upon which rested a flaky pastry. "Cornucopia. The sign just said 'Cornucopia. With pineapple jam.'"

"What kind of cornucopia?"

"It's some sort of bread thing filled with sweet cream. Eat it."

"I—"

"I've already eaten four of them. Just try it."

"Alright." Tucker shrugged, analyzing it.

I studied the cement wall lining the edge of the terrace. "What's over there?" Faint white dots of lights bobbed far beyond where the lights glistened upon the ocean waves.

"The Atlantic." Burkman's rumbling voice offered the obvious answer.

"Thank you, Sir Geography. What are those lights?"

Burkman reclined in his seat, crossing his ankles. "The dawn, then. My youth. Pick one."

Thunder guffawed. "Your dirty socks' nightmares."

"My silver tooth's headache." Burkman's gaping snicker reflected the yellow lights.

Tucker grinned. "The second star to the right and straight on till your mom! Oh!"

I rolled my eyes, letting a slightly amused chuckle pop out. "I'm going to examine the evidence." Escaping the terrible puns, I padded over to the low wall. Soft breezes dove in from the cliffs and the gusty shore below, well out of sight. Wet rocks piled up beneath the horizon took the brutal bashing of water crashing, brackish and distempered, as if the ocean could wear them out. They remained, unyielding. Wind whipped through my hair. The waves hummed the lonely song of the souls resting within them.

A warm hand slid down my shoulder and gently wrapped around my wrist. "I hear the south lawn would be a good place for drills in the morning." Tucker's silky voice sliced through the calm.

"Oh?"

"Care to investigate with me?"

"Sure, Sergeant."

His lips rose, one cheek dimpling in amusement. I followed him along the bricked path, past a crumbled statue which once must have been majestic and towering. The skewered edges thrust upward into the hazy night.

Tucker's pace didn't lag, and I had to quicken my steps to stay at his side. "Where are we going?" I huffed.

"You've gotten over that fear of heights, I believe?"

"Standing on top of the world changes a person."

Along the perimeter of the wall we strolled, past the pool, a pentagon shape filled with glistening blue water. Micah and Clutch sat on the edge of one side, dangling their feet in the water. Deeply involved in their conversation, they didn't even notice us pass by. The bricks led us along a ramp sloping upward along the outer wall of the fort, surging us to the second-story level. The marina and its white and golden lights popped into view to our left, boats rocking in their slips.

"Where are you taking us?" I asked.

In the quiet solitude, occasional orange lights illuminating the red path, Tucker slid his fingers between mine. "Truth? I wanted to get you away from the crowd."

"Ah. I'm fine with that."

"Also, I did need to find a place to run drills."

"Glad I'm along for the ride."

He slowed then, and the walkway opened up onto a wide platform, which offered a lookout over the road and down the steep hill to the marina. Around the corner, another long walkway stretched straight.

"This fort is like a triangle shape," Tucker stated. "I thought we might be able to see the best space for some cardio. I want the Dragons to stretch out. Burkman said he agreed we all needed to start our day off with a little chain dragging."

"I hope that's a metaphor."

"You never know with Burkman."

A shiver crashed up my spine into my shoulders. "Great."

"Actually, expect chains."

"Good to know."

"Eagre!" Tucker stopped short, as a shadowed body darted away into the depths of the walkway before us. Tucker's hand flew up to his forehead, seeking the forms lurking in the distance.

A second body stepped toward us, lithe and fearless. Eagre's face slid into the dim yellow glow from the overlook behind us. "You rang?" With a swift and subtle brush of her hand, she wiped the corner of her lopsided smirk.

"What are you doing?" Tucker almost exploded.

"Our instructions were to relax." She bore her weight on one foot, the other stuck out begrudgingly by the wall. One fist balanced on her hip. "I find physical contact soothing."

"You cannot—" Tucker made a fist and buried it against his closed mouth. "Ah!"

"I'll head back to my room now. Sir." She ran her tongue along her bottom lip. "I'd certainly hate to miss bed checks."

"Who were you with?"

She sauntered past us.

"That's two, Eagre." Tucker didn't move or turn to face her.

She continued her stroll. "I know." Before she disappeared out of sight, she paused, silent, cataloguing her own assumptions about our evening stroll.

Tucker exhaled, frustrated. A grunt escaped between his challenged breaths.

I said the words low. "I suppose you can't lecture her for making out with anyone on the squad."

He spun to me. His eyes wild, the exasperation glowed even in the dim light. A grin pitched across his lips. "Come here." He held out his hand.

I placed my palm in his, and he yanked me in one smooth motion against his chest. Close to his pounding heart, mine pummeled its outer limits. He released my hand. I wrapped my arms around his neck.

His lips met mine, a hardened resolve, an itching desire, for control within a mortal realm. "Five minutes," he murmured among breaths.

My fingertips caught up against his steamy neck, burrowing in his hair. "You don't feel terrible about being totally hypocritical?"

"I'll burn it out tomorrow during drills." One of his tantalizing hands slid along my back until his palm settled in the hollow behind my belt.

As if we danced a waltz only we could distinguish, he guided us against the wall, melding into obscurity. Surrounded by moss and ire, for our own infinite section of eternity, we drank of the molten invitation.

"Tucker?" I asked, coming up for air. "If that was two, what was one?"

Chapter Fourteen

RESERVE
Tucker

G ritty. I wiped my palms against my starched pants. Sand throttled itself toward the earth, joining the sediment beneath my boots.

"You want to show these Guardsmen you're the stuff? Show them you are the Dragons you've been bragging about? Now's your chance." I stared them down, as they each took a knee. Full eyes, widened and hard, glowered back. Eight heartbeats thundered beneath the second-hand black shirts we'd wrangled from Dub. They'd started the drills early morning, as usual, some bickering, some silent, some weighted by the impending sunrise. As the morning progressed and we'd traveled to recon the forest reserve, they'd become incorrigible, hungry, sniping mugs.

"You're tired." I spat the words at their feet. "You're in a foreign country, nothing's familiar, and for the second time you can remember, you've lost everything you've known."

I studied their faces, each set of eyes glaring at me. Hazard's almond eyes filled with rage. Eagre's, pride. Rubu, arrogance. Wring, pure lackluster. "Sticky wicket, mates. Here's where you show up, grow up, and get up. This is where it's hardest, and where you dig in. Not for yourself, not to pass some test, not for somebody approving of you, but because you have been chosen. You're the best. Time to shove it in your pack and use it as fodder. That must fuel you now, and nothing else. I'm looking for the leaders among you. Understand?"

"Yes, sir." Mutters, confirmation, semi-complacency.

"Now." I cleared my throat. "Who's going to get us out of this hole? Rubu, Hazard, since you two lost our map and wrestled our walkie into the well over there, who wants to take the lead and navigate back to camp?"

Thunder raised his hand.

I nodded.

"Does the forest reserve have a patrol? Could they send out—"

"We don't rely on anyone else's help." I crossed my arms over my chest. "Alliance has to own the field. Our missions, our lives."

Rubu's glance dropped down to his boots. "I'll lead."

"You can find the path to the cave?"

"Yes."

"Then take us." I took one step back, waving an arm to the surrounding overgrowth. Moss covered trees, towering overhead, to a canopy of branches blocking out the gray skies. Hot, sticky air cowered beside every Dragon, but they propelled up to their feet, shoulders tossed back.

"Okay." Rubu faced them. "Apologies, mates. Haz."

Hazard nodded. His lips stayed slammed shut, jaw braced. His knuckles dripped with a single line of blood by the scraped skin.

Rubu waved over his shoulder and started off out of the shallow, grassy hollow where his rumble with Hazard had taken us. Without saying a word, I visualized the mental picture I'd memorized of the island reserve, hoping to stumble upon the pirates' headquarters. No such luck. Instead, the Dragons scuffled and we had ourselves a happy little lesson in hormonal teenage protocol. I scanned the area for the lost radio. Vanished.

The Dragons followed Rubu in a southbound line, and I allowed him silent credit for his sense of direction.

Hazard took up the back of the line. I fell in step beside him.

"We didn't train to work together," Hazard grumbled. "Our lessons focused on initiating orders and ultimatums in combat."

"That's the most I've ever heard you speak about Kissinger, Haz."

"I don't want you thinking I'm trying to make trouble. Rubu's been overbearing and just plain annoying."

"Understood. However, he's your mate."

Haz made a hollow, grunting sound.

"You blokes are a team. He loses, you lose."

"He loses his temper, so I lose, too?"

"In a way."

"Can you fix this problem you've got with him?" Twigs tore at my gray pants.

"I don't have a problem with him!" Hazard burst out, his arms flinging to the sides. "He's supposed to be the example. He's supposed to be this amazing marksman and the likeable one."

"He's *supposed* to be that way?"

"Yeah."

"In the weight room, is it the barbell's job to lift itself?"

"What?"

"Does a hand weight raise itself up off the ground?"

He scoffed. "Of course not."

"So then, whose job is it to lift the weight?"

"The guy working out."

"Right. Are you the guy working out?" I stuck my thumb through my belt loop.

"Um. I guess?"

"Yes, Hazard. The answer's yes. Some complication comes along? That's *your* weight to press. Lift it high. That's your job. Find yourself in a rough place? Realize it's where you're supposed to be."

"Rubu was being a wad."

"Right. But no matter. How was Hazard being?"

He made his grunting sound again.

"I picked you to come on this mission. You're ready. Do not let some morning grumpiness ruin the long strides we've made."

"Yes, sir."

"What's our ethos?"

"Duty, respect, action, grit," he sighed, "overcome, never quit."

"Now, are any of those things found in wrestling on some island forest?"

Hazard stopped. He rammed his hand into his pocket.

I paused after a step. "What?"

He shimmied a black rectangle out of the side pocket of his black backpack and held up the radio in his hand. A giant grin smeared across his cheeks.

"You had the radio the whole time?"

"I told Rubu I'd carry it, but he didn't hear me, and then before I had a chance to tell him where I put it, he shoved me."

Blinking. My jaw fell open. I pointed to the walkie. "He shoved you. He teased you. He stood within arm's length and you didn't take him into a headlock and snap his neck."

"Yes, sir." Confusion wrapped around his forehead as the grin softened, lopsided.

"You didn't kill him."

"Found the beach!" Eagre's voice echoed from the green beyond.

"I didn't." Hazard's smile vanished.

"You accepted his shouting until he pursued the action."

"Yes."

I considered the soldier before me. "So, in summary, Hazard acted honorable until he had to physically defend himself."

Hazard swallowed hard.

"Good work, Hazard." I held out a palm to shake his hand.

He returned the shake, one eyebrow raising. "You won't write me up for this?"

"Bonus cookies. I'll even let you have extra desert today if you like." I let go, and then patted his shoulder. We slogged to the clearing of trees ahead.

"I'd rather have an extra side of protein. I've been starving."

"You're one strange taco, Hazard. You want extra protein, I'll get it for you."

"Thank you, sir."

"No extra cookies?"

"Sugar makes me emotional. Clutch says."

"**A**lright." I shook out the new, crisp map the Commander begrudgingly handed me after lunch. "We've checked out three leads from the peninsula reserve."

My Dragons stood watching over my shoulder, surrounding me. They smelled seriously of sweat and mud.

"You're breathing right in my ear, Weyr." I swatted by the side of my head.

"Sorry, boss. How many more do we have?"

"For today? Depends on how long it takes us to travel. And how long it takes Dub to get a convoy."

"Total."

"They had seven leads for this island: several caves, an abandoned building, an underground bunker, and various spots known for illegal activity. At the port on the other side of the island we will have to interview the locals and see if they've noticed increased activity."

Thunder raised his hand as he spoke. "How are we supposed to interview people? We don't speak Portuguese." He rolled the last word on his tongue like the locals who'd shaken their heads at us earlier in town and held up their hands in sympathy.

Of course, if I'd been a local trying to tell some smelly group of haphazard misfits how to find the nearest shower, I'd have probably done the same thing. No room here, mate. No speak the English.

"We'll get a translator." I nodded. "Dub said he has someone who can assist us this afternoon."

"Until then?" Eagre worked her finger through her loose ponytail.

"We've got some tunnels and dingy warehouses to explore."

"Fun!"

Weyr bobbed his chin. "When will we get to test out our suits? Make sure they work after being dunked in the ocean."

Agreement resounded around me. I held up one hand. "We'll get there. Patience."

"But if one of these leads follows through into a warehouse full of warmongers? What then? Shouldn't we be doing all this in our gear?"

"I thought a Dragon *was* a weapon?" I clicked my tongue in amusement.

Weyr smirked. "Oh, I am. Especially when I have my GRIPS."

"And without those GRIPS?"

He tossed his glance to the sky and then back to me. "Still stronger than the average bear."

"Show me. One of these days you'll have to face your monsters without your gear. While Canaan works on fixing up our tech, we have to use what the Army gave us. Body armor will have to be your best friend for now."

"But the tech—"

"I navigated a round in the ring with Exit without tech." I stated. The shadows of battles past riddled the backs of my eyes. Exit had been the biggest of them, the best, and I'd faced him. He almost won.

I held in the shudder for the missing bodies we never recovered when we infiltrated Camp Kissinger. "You've got to be capable without the tech. Your mind, your ability to strategize, your perseverance, those keep you alive in the crux."

Weyr licked his lips. A slight nod confirmed what I'd thought. He didn't believe me. He'd find out I was right soon enough.

"Keep with your buddy," I commanded them.

Nods.

The warehouse rose before us, dark, dusty, decrepit.

"Built after the Flare," Truly reported from beside me. The islander pointed to a faded sign. His broken English worked well enough I could understand him. He'd given me another name when Dub introduced us, but Truly was all I understood. He was okay with it.

"Has it been closed long?"

He bobbed his head, wild and loose. "Locked ten year. Owner gone."

"Gone, gone? Like, dead?"

"No one know. No more on island." Truly shrugged. "City put boards on windows, doors."

I pointed at the non-boarded back door which we'd approached. "Except this one?"

"This where they go in."

"Who?"

He shrugged, his lips pursing. His dark chocolate eyes rolled back and forth, studying the clouds, as if to find the words. "The men who go in."

"Alright then." I cleared my throat. "Dragons, watch your six. Just like the other locations, we're looking for signs of life, activity determining whether our friends have been operating out of here recently or currently."

"If we see anyone?" Flight slid his palm over his hair, ruffling the russet curls.

"Do not engage."

"Yes, sir."

"Understood?"

More nods.

I surged ahead, twisting the hard handle and shoving the latch down. It gave, with a gigantic, rusty squeal.

"Someone remind me to get a tetanus shot tonight."

"You got it, boss," Weyr murmured, at my right. "Of course, if you had your GRIPS on, you wouldn't need to worry."

I shot him a knowing look, and then stepped into the shadows. The wooden slats of the grimy floor shook, shirking their duty. Crumbles from the door frame dusted our heads as we ducked inside.

"You ever been in here, Truly?" My voice echoed around the space. I lowered my voice. "Seems like a place people would explore for recreational activities."

His forehead pinched over the bridge of his nose. "I no come in?" He motioned to the door.

"No. It's fine. You stay with us." I waved for Hazard. "Hazard will be your guard." The Dragon tossed a quick wave, frowning.

Beyond us in the depths of the void, dashes of light slung like ropes from the few windows along the four walls, and through small cavities in the ceiling towering at least three stories above us. Dust sprinkles shimmied along the light beams and crashed into the ground in a silent waltz. Far in the gloomy corners, behind stacks of metal scaffolding, shuffles clawed away upon the cement floor. Tap, tap, tapping.

The door slammed behind us with a bang.

"Sorry," Clutch whispered.

Echoes rummaged around, clattering against doorways and dusky hallways. Gray covered everything—empty shelf units, up-ended furniture, and the skeletal remains of jagged, dismembered machine parts.

One careful step at a time, we made it into the back of the first section of offices. Along the way, we found one locked door which Wring picked. His thin fingers nimbly worked some metal clip he just so happened to have in his pocket.

I lifted an eyebrow at him.

He shrugged. The door squeakily yawned open and a giant grin wrapped across his pleased cheeks.

My Dragons and I explored the dank space, moldy air crunching underfoot. I had to pinch my nose shut between my first two fingers to hold back a sneeze.

In the far back corner of the office, a rusty, green metal desk sat covered in boxes. Cobwebs ran amok.

"Nothing like a good breaking-and-entering to end a day of busy grunt work." Rubu leaned against the wall, tapping his fingers in rhythm. He kicked up one heel and settled it against the paint, but must have used more force than he expected. Crumbles burst out from behind him, and his top half disappeared into the hollow of shadows. Snapping, smashing sheetrock disintegrated, filling the room with a sudden dust cloud. The yelling, the grumbling, the coughing of our immersed crowd covered up Rubu's screams before we heard him from his spot in the hole, cinched between two scraggly wooden support beams.

Chapter Fifteen

OF YESTERDAYS
Saylor

"This is hard."

"It's shopping, Micah."

Micah's shoulder slumped. "Why would he put us in charge of this? We are not fashion people." She tossed a blue shirt onto the small stack on the display.

"I thought you typically wore clothes."

"Um, girl, you're telling me. I wear them. If you haven't noticed, I don't spend my time styling guys. And most of my closet consists of green shirts."

"Okay, well, we're about the same level of interest in this. Let's just consider it our adventure for the day. Shop or die. That's got to be somebody's catch line somewhere."

She snorted and rolled her eyes. "Five blue shirts. Done. Bam."

"This store doesn't have very much." I eyed the small shop's varied racks and their contents. "According to Dub, another shop's available down the street."

"What do we have so far?" Micah clutched the blue shirts in her two hands.

I studied the list in my hand. It flopped backward. "We got socks for everyone."

"I thought we had some pants."

"They're on the counter." I jabbed my thumb behind me.

"Well, get them!" Micah slung a fist onto her hip, annoyed. She pressed her lips together and huffed a breath out one side of her mouth.

"But do we get everyone the same clothes or do we get a different outfit for everyone?"

"What do you think?"

"We have to pick out clothing for about forty people."

"We've discovered my great nightmare. I do *not* care."

I giggled, and then sighed. "Everybody gets to matchy matchy! Yay!" I waved my fingers in the air by my head.

"Let's get these shirts." Micah scooped up a pile of primary-colored button up shirts from their rack. The wooden hangers clattered.

"Well, you can't just take them all. What sizes are they?"

"What's on your list?"

"Dad didn't sort them. It's just a collection of who wears what."

"Super." Micah tossed the shirts over her shoulder and grabbed more from another nearby rack. "Floral. Somebody'll love this."

"I wonder what size Eagre wears," I mumbled scanning the list.

"I'm picking out this special shirt for her." Micah held up one black shirt with lace ruffles across the front.

Chuckling, I shrugged. "I didn't say a word."

Micah slung the pile onto the basket at my feet. "Well, I guess this isn't so hard after all."

"I'll get the pants. You get the shirts."

"Think Logan would like a yellow banana shirt?" Micah held up a flowy men's shirt, the color of the sun, with printed pastel bananas all over it. The wooden buttons down the front matched the brown spots serving as the banana ends, which took on a polka dot pattern from a distance.

"I think our goal should be to not make everybody hate us."

"So, yes to the banana shirt."

"Oh, yeah. Most definitely."

Our pile continued to grow, the shopkeeper eyeing us from behind the counter as we cleared out items from shelves and racks. At one point he sent over a younger girl to help us, but she spoke no English. She picked up the pile, her forehead wrinkling, and I whipped the card Dad had given me to pay for everything out of my pocket. The mid-morning glare streamed through the window, glinting on the strip on the back of the card. She smiled shyly, nodding, and backed away to the front counter. One item at a time, she began folding everything.

"They're out of men's larges." Micah searched through the hangers, the wood scraping against the metal racks as she checked shirt tags. "We've cleaned them out."

"Check."

"They have a few more men's mediums and a lot of smalls. I guess the islanders are smaller than our guys."

"What about shoes?" I stood over a large tub of shoes, boots, sneakers, heels, and flats of all shapes and colors piled up within. "We're supposed to get everyone a civilian outfit and a uniform outfit. Get two pairs of shoes too?"

"Probably. Get a pair of runners for PT and the standard issue boots at Lajes."

Stooping down, I sifted through the options. "The shoe sizes are weird."

"Well, look for ones anyone could wear."

"Like these sensible running shoes?" I held up a pair of sparkly pink high heels, the thin, four-inch long stem under the heel ending in a silver, metallic tip. The toe end pinched down to a stiff point.

"Exactly like those sensible running shoes."

The girl shuffled over again and stood awkwardly beside me as I rifled through the shoes in the tub. I set aside two pairs of shoes which could be used as running shoes. She let loose a string of words I couldn't understand. Pausing my search, I looked up at her from my spot, frozen. She waved her hands, pointing at the basket.

"Are these not for sale?" I asked.

Her brown eyes lectured, and she tossed her head back and forth, still letting loose a barrage of Portuguese. Or Russian. Didn't matter; I had no idea what she meant.

"One." She finally said and held up her pointer finger.

"For sale?"

The girl dug through the bin and wrenched loose a white piece of cardboard with black etchings scrawled on it. The number 10 stood out, surrounded by a mix of letters which had no meaning to me.

"Are these ten credits?" At that point, the idea dawned on me. Dad's card may not have utilized the same monetary system the islanders did. Surely he wouldn't have sent me to buy clothes without a way to purchase them. I dug for the card again.

The girl shook her head. "For sale." She pointed to the shoes. "One."

"I'm not sure what you mean." I apologetically shook my head, curling my lips in a dejected frown.

"Ten for one." She stated. She pointed to the sign again.

"Ten points? For one pair of shoes?"

She shook her head. "Ten for one." She held up her pointer finger.

Micah meandered up to me, a large pile of multicolored shirts bundled in her arms.

The girl held up one shoe. "Ten."

"Ten points for one shoe?" Micah asked.

The girl nodded.

I eyed Micah, who eyed me back. Twisting back to the girl, I confirmed. "Ten points for one shoe?"

The girl again bobbed her head, still concerned, and took the shoes I'd set aside, adding them to our pile at the counter.

I blinked at Micah. "Ten. For one."

"I guess they buy shoes one at a time here?"

Giggles rolled up my throat. "Island life, mate!"

Micah tossed her chin back, and we both laughed at what we didn't understand. Maybe we were getting ripped off, maybe they were overcharging, or maybe they bought shoes one at a time. I mentally shrugged.

We stalked out of the shop, the man and girl quite confused and befuddled, shaking their heads as they lectured in their foreign dialect. The man quickly began to straighten up the emptied racks from behind the shop windows, staring at us.

Tears welled up as I continued to chuckle, the ridiculous unknown constantly tapping me on the shoulder. Dad wasn't as amused when I told him about it later on.

With our paper bags crammed full, we made our way down the road to the next shop and found a few more civilian outfits. That shop owner spoke English and pointed us to a nearby shoe store.

"Do you have to pay for them one at a time?" Micah asked the man as he pressed the number buttons on his card reader machine.

His forehead crinkled in concern, unsure of the question.

"Never mind," I called out, nudging Micah's elbow.

She beamed at me. "Ten. For one."

I burst out laughing, then smacked my palm against my mouth when the shopkeeper again looked quite concerned.

"How you take all this?" he asked, piling up a stack of striped shirts on the counter.

"To go?" Micah offered a friendly smile.

"You have bag?" He nudged his chin toward the many bags by our feet.

"Um, I guess we can add these." I started mumbling words, squishing down the other clothes and stacking the newest ones on top.

The man handed Micah more, and she tried the same.

When the brown paper started to rip, Micah picked up three of them. "Stack some on top.

I did, and she stuck her chin against the pile to keep it in place. She grinned at me.

"Okay." I sighed and took the last large pile of folded clothing from the store owner. "Thank you."

He offered a hesitant nod and shuffled back through a darkened doorway.

"My stomach's trying to claw its way outside of my body," Micah said, keeping her jaw tightly clenched against the pile of clothing in her hands.

I juggled the three other bags, one which fortunately had a paper handle, and wobbled through the maze of racks. While reaching for the door handle, the paper bag dangling from my arm scraped along a shelf with kitschy knickknacks and baubles on it. A palm tree sculpture wobbled. A pair of sunglasses toppled from a foam display shaped like a human head and smacked against the glass shelf surface.

In trying to spin through the door without knocking into any other breakables, my arm grazed the edge of the wooden door frame, and the handle tore from the bag. I missed the slightly raised edge of the door frame and stumbled out of the shop, the bags pitching forward, the one bag wildly scampering into the cobblestone street.

Micah's amused guffaw rang out from behind me. "I'm sorry, I shouldn't laugh. Are you all right?" She kneeled, resting her bags against the pink stucco wall.

"Fine." I grumbled other un-proper words, gathering my fallen comrades from their misshapen resting places.

"We need more bags." Micah bent over and grabbed a semi-folded stack of pants.

The door creaked open behind us, the bell inside jingling. Mr. Shopkeeper popped his head out of the opening and cleared his throat. "You leave without car."

"Yes. No car."

"You need car."

"We probably do." I agreed, uprighting, with the last of the shirts in my grip. "But alas."

"Here, car." The man edged out of the door, and dragged a squeaking, mangled, mesh cart out behind him. "For you. Keep."

"Oh." I scrunched my nose, about to shake my head. "How much does it cost?"

"You keep."

"But how many points will it cost?"

He waved a palm at me. "Take. Keep."

"Well, thank you."

A bright, wide grin settled across his cheeks. "Thank you." He bobbed his head and vanished back inside the door. The bell jangled behind the slam.

"Okay, then!" Micah tossed her head in the breeze to clear some stray hairs away from her eyes. "Now we're cooking with butter."

The cart, which had long before been painted with a cream-colored paint, sloughed paint chips and red chunks of rust off its body as we piled the bags up inside the wire mesh. Taller than it was wide or long, the bottom contained four small wheels, which had rusted in on themselves, and the thing wobbled and bobbled as we took turns dragging it from the "handle," a frayed rope tied along the bottom rung between the front two wheels.

"Hold on to the wires so it doesn't fall over," Micah instructed me. She tugged on the rope, the cart rattling along behind her.

"Do I have to touch it?" I gingerly pinched one wire with my thumb and pointer finger.

Micah shuffled forward, the wheels squealing, one of which seemed to not turn at all, but instead served as a brake for the clothes car. No wonder he didn't want it back. Down the street beyond Micah, I noticed a faded green jeep turning into the square several blocks away. The sun shined off the driver's glossy silver sunglasses.

"Hey, there's Dub." I tossed my free hand in the air.

"Where?" Micah stopped, heaving a breath, and searching around us. She stared at me.

I pointed past her. "I bet we can catch him and snag a ride." I darted after the open-air jeep, judging if I could make five blocks before he continued on his merry way. Sure, I could make it.

"Saylor!" Micah called from behind me, the wind whipping her voice away.

Pressing forward before Dub disappeared and we had to drag the cart all the way back to the hotel, I pumped my fists, faster, faster. Four blocks. Three. The sprint unfolded in my spine, heart thudding, feet shoving away from the bumpy cobblestones below. A soft, warm breeze trembled through my hair. Freedom. I hadn't experienced it in so long.

The hazy golden afternoons on Isla Barina appeared around me, palm trees dancing against the distant horizon. As if they were ghosts, my Alliance crew rounded the bend in their black NEXIS suits, throttling forward at my side. We charged onward, ripe with calamity, triggered by precision. I could almost taste the fire of the charred oxinals I used to banish. An outburst of sweat dripped into my eye and I smeared at it with my fist. Oxygen tumbled in my throat like it used to. My knee cracked. The jarring bump of the spasm drew me back into the stone street, alone, gasping for air. Reaching the open space of the corner square, a few harried walkers crossed by a fountain surrounded by purple flowers dancing in the breeze.

Twisting in a circle, reaching down to steady my pulsing knee, I searched for Dub and his jeep. Gone.

The unfamiliar buildings towered, surrounding me, whiter and starker than before.

Dry heat caked my throat. Licking my lips, I spun, seeking Micah.

Four blocks away, the cart stumbled behind her. She caught it as it pitched to the side and flung the loose clothing back in its pile. After another few steps, it faltered and pitched the other way, and with a crashing squeak, the whole thing dumped over. She spun in her spot and kicked the cart, yelling.

The cart didn't budge.

She slung a fist at it in the air, lecturing it for its impudence.

By the time I reached her, sweat had built up along her red forehead. "I'm leaving it," she shouted. She pointed at the cart. "It's fired!"

More laughter welled up in my gut and I couldn't help but laugh at the frustration. "Ten. For one!"

She picked up the cart in both hands, launching it over her head in victory. "Death! Death to the cart!"

"No! Let's carry it." I snagged one of the black pairs of pants which snuck back onto the cobblestones. "I'll get the back, you get the front."

"I hate that idea."

"Well, either that or we leave behind half the stuff we just bought."

"This cart makes me want to become a cage fighter." Micah slammed the cart on the ground, wheels first. One of the wheels popped off and slid across the street.

"It could be worse."

Micah grunted.

"I think it's more of a gravity situation than this particular island." I slapped the edge of the cart as it started to fall over.

"Gravity is stupid." She grumbled, shoving pieces of clothing and one shoe into the cart.

"I think we need food."

"I'm *starving*."

Nodding, I searched the street for the fastest way back to the hotel. Straight it was. "Onward, ho!" I pointed ahead.

"No calling names." Micah glowered, disgruntled. Her forehead rumpled into three solid lines of anger. Then she grinned at me, the left side of her face scrunching into a wink.

"Thar be my Micah." Pirate references got her every time.

"Also, I'm not the one who disappeared until late in the night yesterday." She wound her fingers around the edge of the cart.

"I was helping with research."

"Yeah, I'm sure. Researching Tucker's face."

My brazen lips relayed my blushing answer.

"Sir, we accomplished our objective. For the most part." I dropped my salute in time for Dad to glance up from his chair. Beside him, the closed doors of the hotel restaurant hid rattlings and clankings.

He twisted from the clipboard in his hands. "All of it?"

"Well, the civilian half of the assignment. If we can get a ride to Lajes, we'll gather the remaining items."

"You were to collect everything today. It's supper time. Why didn't you organize a ride earlier? Dub has made several rounds today already."

"I—I didn't know. I thought we had a while to work on this." My grin vanished behind the ice storming at me.

"Do we require everyone to wait on you to get it organized this evening? What do they wear tonight? Tomorrow? After they've spent the day dealing with roadblocks, dead ends, and muddy fields?"

"I'm—"

"Half of our crew has spent the day searching through tunnels, shuffling through paperwork, and cleaning off water-logged evidence. We had a medical emergency with the Dragons. The other half has been in offices, sweating out intel and networking with civilians. And you mean to tell me, you and Micah have spent the entire day shopping, only to have a few items to supply our men? What about the sundries? The toiletries? You didn't get to the BX at Lajes at all?"

"Um. I radioed in an order. Thought I could go this evening to pick it up."

"The BX closed already for the day."

"I didn't know they closed early. I thought—"

"Saylor." Dad slung his clipboard down to his side. The pencil rattled from its holder at the clip and flung onto the ground, bouncing away.

"I'll get to it first thing in the morning."

He clenched his jaw. "I'm disappointed. I asked one thing of you and Micah. You joked about it. Didn't take it seriously."

"We did! It was harder than you'd think."

A sigh let me know exactly what he thought about my performance. Burkman bumped through the restaurant's double doors and strolled up to us. "They're ready for us. I told them to be ready at 1700 sharp and they are."

Dad whipped his face in Burkman's direction. "Thank you. Good to know some of us can follow directions in a timely manner."

"Dad—" I held up a hand as if to volunteer for a second chance.

"You're dismissed, Saylor. I'll get Burkman on it."

"I'm—"

"Canaan needed to see, you, I believe. Mark my words, Saylor." He waited, and I forced my resolve to meet his stare. "Focus. I warned you this was the rallying point. You carry your weight right now. You're part of Alliance. Act it."

Quivering lips muzzled any argument. A quick nod. He and Burkman stalked off with a sideways glance from Burkman.

My shoulders slumped.

As soon as they rounded the corner, Micah slid out of the hallway leading to the staircase. "I guess I'm glad we didn't get *him* the banana shirt?"

Gripping the black box in my trembling hands, I exhaled through my nose. Steady. I knew what Canaan wanted to see me about. Testing the box. Testing my underlings. I liked calling them that.

Glancing to the chain cuddled snugly in its sheath, I mentally confirmed with myself the door was locked. Nobody could know about these yet. I wanted to be able to control them better before anyone saw.

Don't drop them on the carpet.

Flipping open the lid, I set the box carefully on the bed. I released both hands at once. Rubbing those two chilly palms together, the heat zipped through my fingers.

Ignite.

Nothing happened.

It worked on the ship. What's going on?

Replaying the memories from when Canaan had first shown me the pieces, I mentally checked the list he'd rattled off. Focus on the transmitted network. Engage with the network, lock signal, ignite.

Wrinkling my forehead, I wiggled my lips. *Hm*. Biting my bottom lip, I closed my eyes, releasing the stress, the laughter, the noise, the chaos. A hush whiffed through the room.

Hear the network.

The buzz had long since quieted between my ears, a faded ringing which rarely nuzzled against my brain.

Dad's angry eyes burned in the background. He yelled. I watched our conversation occur again. Why hadn't I said more? Why hadn't I defended myself?

Focus.

Squeezing my eyes shut tighter, I shoved away his disappointment.

Swallow.

Taking a hefty breath in, gulping the brackish oxygen, I heard the echo. It resounded, far off.

Come to me, friends.

Opening my eyes, I studied the ceiling. The quiet blue grid of yesterdays surrounded me. Horizontal and vertical blue lines hummed. They vibrated the essence of life and logic.

A shiver welled up in the base of my neck and rumbled down my skin, into the base of my heels. Gnarled fear clawed at my ribs. My heart knocked, knocked, pinching the fear until it cried out. Awed.

I grabbed one of the smaller pieces in the top left corner. One side had a smooth, rounded edge, with a row of spikes lining the concave edge. The other side had a rectangle protruding from the center. Holding the cool, blue-ish silver metal piece in the palm of my hand, the faint ricochet of the network vibrated in a chord around me. A red light on the outside of the rounded surface began blinking.

A small smirk dribbled over my lips. The smirk tethered to my spine.

With a ginger shove, I tossed the piece into the air. It popped to life, buzzing, a slight blast of air surging out of the spikes. It floated, hovering in space amid the blue grid.

"Hello," I whispered.

The piece clicked, gears whirling, the microengines cycling, awaiting my command.

"It's been a while," I stated. "Haven't commanded my own little army in over a year. I'd lost faith I could do it."

The red light blinked.

"My brain keeps saying I'm not good enough. Can't seem to ever live up to what I need to be."

Lifting a finger, I directed the little floating piece, bigger than a thimble, smaller than my palm, in a line to the open window. It followed the line exactly.

"Maybe with you little buggers I can finally do something right around here."

The red light blinked.

"Why, yes, you are right. Thank you. I'm your superior, after all. I'm already qualified."

A breeze wound inside the window, shoving my little friend, and I surged the piece against it. The piece held steady.

I offered a slight, congratulatory nod. "Hoo-rah."

The piece floated where I guided my finger, and I tossed it every which way, focusing on the grid. If I concentrated on the flashing metal, the coordinates seemed to resonate around the piece. The gridlines dissolved into commands, measuring the piece's location.

Canaan had said he'd manipulated the network so it would connect to the nanomites within my blood only, and more clearly than it had before. He had spent months studying data Breame collected on me and figured out how to include a signal booster in each of the ten pieces so they'd connect with each other and also to my internal network. The closer they were, the stronger the signal, the easier for me to operate them. And when I formed them together to create a fist-sized ball, they'd function similarly to the oxinals, minus the external fire of the oxinal cloud.

I let the piece hover in the sun, the solar-friendly material absorbing the energy needed to operate. One by one, the other pieces buzzed, awaiting my commands. The more sunlight available to them, the faster they charged.

Having only spent about twenty minutes with them and internalizing all the information Canaan had thrown at me before we were overrun by my other evil twin...my eyes glazed over, the ringing between my ears growing louder.

The piece stuttered in its spot.

"Hold it." I shot my pointer finger to the piece.

Focus. No distractions.

The last of the six spikes on its smooth, rounded surface stuttered. The piece wobbled for a half-second, then recovered.

"Do not be glitchy on me," I ordered.

The red light on the piece blinked.

"You need a name."

The last piece in the box beeped. All ten ready for action. Canaan had said each SIMPL possessed a unique trait. Solar Intelligent Matrix Powered Logistics. I fingered the second piece and its cross-like shape. I tossed it into the air. It shook the grid. I had to squint, the spark shining on every crossing blue line. We'd started testing the ten before the alarm sounded.

"Okay, okay. I'm getting ahead of myself." Lowering the pieces to shoulder height, I listened. "What do I do now?"

As if the pieces would answer.

When testing them with Canaan, the ending had been so abrupt. He'd just grabbed them and chunked them into the case, and then told me to hang on to that box like it was my own soul. I'd whimpered some kind of answer. And then we were on deck.

"How do I control you?"

The red lights blinked.

I smacked my lips. "Okay. I can do this. You are like the oxinals. You operate from menu commands. Somewhere. Menu."

My eyes flicked left to right, searching the blue grid surrounding me, the bed, the small round table in the corner, and the dresser.

I clicked my tongue. "Show menu. Display menu."

As I heard myself saying the words, I appreciated the door lock.

"Show menu." I called louder.

Scanned the room again. Nothing.

"*Menu.* Options. File. Operator. Help!" I sighed, as loud as possible. "Quit. Save. Open." I held up my other hand and snapped twice into the air. "Close! Chocolate!"

Out of the right corner of my eye, a word blipped for a moment and then disappeared. Swatting my eyes to the right, I whipped my head to catch it, but it was gone.

"Chocolate!" I kept my eyes snapped to my right peripheral. *That'd be funny, Canaan.*

Nothing.

"Well, it's a good thing you guys aren't on fire."

The first piece suddenly burst upward, five of the six spikes riddled with blue flames.

"Stop!" I jumped back. "Quit! Ah!"

The piece zoomed around the room, in zig zag patterns, a small wisp of black smoke following its course.

"Command," I shouted the word. The piece halted, still enveloped in electric blue flame. "Quit."

The floating flames shuddered, and one by one the flickering stopped, except for the middle spike's spurting.

"*Quit!*" I pointed at it. The other piece zoomed over to it and knocked against the other with a clank. The two pieces dropped to the bed, silent.

I darted over to them and scooped them up, expecting to face some hot, hot consequences, and as fast as I could, dumped them into the black box. They tumbled into their spots.

My heart a wreck of disheveled chaos, I exhaled to slow everything down. The grid faded from around me. I clicked the lid shut.

Chapter Sixteen

TO FINISH YOUR MISSION
Tucker

------ ✖ ------

"**I** don't know what to do with them." I buried my forehead against the top of my hand, flat-palmed on the cool marble bar countertop. "They don't listen. They aren't listening. They haven't listened."

Burkman sipped from his glass, the tumbler smaller than his ebony hand. "Team work makes the—"

"Don't." I held up my free hand, releasing my own slick tumbler. "Don't. Even. Say. The. Phrase. There's no dream. The dream's dead."

"Someone's sounding jaded."

Raising my head, I straightened my shoulders. "I've spent months trying to un-brainwash this group, teaching them they can be so much more—"

"Thompson, can I be honest with ya?"

"Burkman, I would never try to stop you. Probably couldn't if I tried."

"You gotta stop trying so hard."

"I can't stop."

He twisted his stool in a semi-circle so his shoulders faced me. "You can't force change in others. You want them to be Alliance? They *are* Alliance. Maybe it looks different than planned, but they're

184

what Adenauer and Breame and all those board members wanted it to be. *They* wanted killers. They wanted a manhunt."

Wrapping my swollen fingers around the chilly glass, I let the words do their own tumbling among the orange, bubbly liquid. Some kind of tonic water mixed with juice. Not great.

I scrunched my nose, sensing the prickling on the back of my neck along with the sticky assault of sweaty, wrinkled bandages, and crusty socks. "Dragons, assemble," I stated. I didn't turn around.

Weyr's voice rang out behind me. "We wanted to talk to you about today."

Burkman rested his forearm on the bar. "You look a mess of swamp people." He sipped his drink, draining the glass.

"We know." Weyr sounded apologetic.

"Sir, we helped Rubu back to his bed after the clinic released him." Clutch's fingers nimbly strummed some curls behind her ear. "We realize we've done the opposite of what you trusted us to do. We're going to do better from now on."

"Yeah." Thunder tussled his head, his blond locks unkempt. A streak of mud caked on his cheek. "The Commander ripped us a new one."

Flight corroborated. "Guy's scary." His nostrils flared at the memory.

"I can't see that I'm the guy for the job." I disagreed, swallowing my pride and a dash of orange zest. "I'm your peer. You don't think of me as your leader. That's apparent now."

"Rubu fell through the wall on his own." Clutch shifted her hips, her chin tilting in defiance. "We worked as a team to get him to the clinic. Isn't teamwork what you wanted to see?"

"It's more than one round in the ring." I began to shake my head.

Burkman cleared his throat. "From where I'm sitting, I see three things." Leaning back against the countertop, he rested his thick elbow on the surface and upended his palm like a flag, shooting one finger up at the sky as he prattled off his list. "One. You found a new method of destroying public property today. Congratulations. You owe the city of Sao Sebstiao hundreds of thousands of points." He scanned the group. "Two, you have spent the better part of a year waiting to prove yourselves to this guy right here. Three, this guy right here's about to lose his position because you knuckleheads can't get your stuff together."

"Sir, we—" Thunder rushed forward while Burkman held out his palm.

Burkman's upper lip curled. "You're Alliance. A team. Your team's the best when you're the best."

I could almost feel the tremors wrestling inside their ligaments.

Hazard's dark eyes darted from Burkman, to me, and back to Burkman.

"You'd rather have this guy here as your CO?" I jerked my thumb to Burkman.

They quickly shook their heads, lowered eyes, and murmured a vigorous round of 'no' and 'nuh-uh's.

I chuckled. "So, what, then, the Commander?"

Burkman interrupted. "Point is, Dragons, how can you prove you're worth all Alliance has invested in you now? You keep resisting protocol."

My hand flew out to Burkman's shoulder. I studied their disengagement. Their cool dismissal of authority. I tightened my grip upon his muscled uniform. "You're right, Burkman."

"I know I am."

"They're not what I've tried to get them to be. They're more Dragon than anything."

Hazard brought his steady gaze up to mine. "I gave back the radio."

"What would Rapton have you do?" At the name of the man who'd raised them, the man who'd died to create them, their shutters dropped. Eagre's shoulders straightened. Weyr's chest lifted, his nostrils flaring.

"What did Rapton teach you about the end game?"

Wring licked his lips before answering. "Littleton was the base commander. He taught most of the protocol and directed our training program."

"Did he have specific methods? An ultimatum?" I pressed. Heat welled up around my jaw line. It buzzed into my ears.

"Dragons win. They defeat." Wring rubbed his chin against his shoulder and retreated. "The ultimate definition of DRAGON was—"

"No." I sliced my hand through the air like a knife. "I don't want to know the acronym. Did Rapton or Littleton give you a directive? What's the point of the program? What's your failsafe?"

"Do you have a napkin?" Hazard whispered.

Burkman slid a small white square over to him and reached over behind the bar counter. He nabbed a short pencil, offering it to the smaller soldier.

Hazard accepted the items and placed the napkin on the counter. After scratching several lines upon the surface, he held it up. "Control. Containment. Consciousness." He'd outlined a neat triangle shape, with the words lined along each side.

"What do you mean?"

"This is our providence, our union as Dragons." His words, lathered with his accent and heritage, dripped of years ripe with the repetition.

"Tell me what those three C's mean, Hazard." I requested it softly. "What does this triangle mean?"

His eyes glazed over, one shoulder slumping. He leaned closer to the napkin and added faint lines from the three pointy corners, to the center, drawing a thick dot at the intersection. "Littleton spoke of Atlas, the burden-bearer of the ancient world. He signifies strength, power. So, too, as Dragons, we carry—he told us the strongest of us carried—the freedom of the new world."

"The strongest of you? He wanted to end up with only one of you?" Burkman wagged his head, shuddering. He squeezed his eyelids shut. "Such a short-sighted man."

"No." Hazard solidified his resolve, tossing his head upward. The dim lights from overhead caught on the calcified sweat from earlier in the day on his cheeks. "They retained the heart of the warrior. For backup. For the rest of the mission."

"Why am I just now hearing about this?" Burkman's voice leveled out, echoing around the chamber. Conversations quelled around the room as wandering eyes sought out the disruption.

I held up my palm to him. "We'd just had the program stopped. I didn't dig in before, because the psychologists instructed me to retrain their thinking. Instead of diving into what they'd learned, I'd been told to teach them a new way, maneuver them in a new direction." I whirled to Hazard. "What do you do to finish your mission? Where do you go?"

"To suspend the pillars of the universe."

Chapter Seventeen

SOAR
Saylor

—⊸⊷⊶—

"What in the Johnny Appleseed's jumping jacks did you do with the command system on this?" I held the black box up by my ear, waving the thing around.

Canaan jerked his chin to the side. "Get in here." He stepped back to let me into his room. "I tried finding you earlier."

"I was busy being a complete failure to the human race." I strode by him and halted just past the door leading to the bathroom.

"Bummer." Canaan wrestled with the buttons on his uniform jacket, yanking the camo taught against his chest.

"But I bought a banana shirt. Should count for something."

"Do I want to know more?" He finished slipping the last button through its hidden slit. His fingers strummed against the folded fabric, smoothing away any straggling wrinkles.

"It was a banana shirt."

"Tell me what you've been doing with my precious here."

"I wanted to practice with them."

"Good. Where?" He gripped the back of the stuffing of the chair beside the dresser with both palms. One boot slid behind the other as he crossed his ankles, digging one boot toe into the carpet.

"Moot point. I was being careful. The more important thing? I can't remember how to get these things going. Or, well, how to turn them off."

"We can't practice here. Too many wandering eyes."

"And flammable items."

"Saylor, what did you do?"

"Where can we go? I can go by myself if you're busy."

Canaan straightened his shoulders, rolling his arms in a stretch. Beaming, a smile lit his cheeks. "You don't quit, do you kid?"

"I quit when I thought I was broken. Now? I'm just getting started, Canaan."

"These ceilings should be high enough." Canaan's voice echoed in the quiet fitness center. Dub had been so nice to send a driver to take us to Lajes. We had one hour to practice.

Weight machines and racks of barbells filled most of the main room. About six guys in black sleeveless shirts operated the machines, pushing, pulling, tugging, lifting the bars and gray cylinders and machine levers. The occasional weight clinked upon the other. A black utility fan as tall and wide as me sat angled in the corner, buzzing air across the space, rustling the pages of an open book on a nearby chair.

The door to a large classroom at the end of a wide hallway gaped open. A sign on the wall notified us in black, bold lettering, the room would not be available unless requested ahead of time. Canaan waved us into the area.

He snapped the light switch on the wall, and the long white tube bulbs flickered on overhead one at a time. Every other bar hummed to life, leaving us surrounded in a dull, blueish glow.

"Ah, the essence of nighttime," I joked quietly to myself. "Sweat, weights, and fire."

"Shouldn't be too much fire, if you operate these correctly." Canaan set down his instrument case and rubbed his palms together.

"Yes, sir."

He indicated the black box tucked under my arm. "Show me how far you got."

"Alright." I squatted, resting the box on the ground. My new dark gray pants rustled. "I got this one to fire up, but it—I think it has a problem." Unlatching the locks, I flipped the lid away from the body of the box. The pieces shined up at me, reflecting the light from their blue surfaces.

"Which one?"

My fingers brushed along the smooth exterior, extracting the piece from its spot. I pinched the metal between my thumb and first finger and lifted it toward him.

"Show me what you did." Instead of taking the piece, he stepped away from me and thrust his hands in his pockets.

"Okay." Resting the piece against my palm, I held it before me. I closed my eyes. Focus on the grid. Unwitting or not, I held my breath. My chest tightened.

"Having trouble seeing the grid?" Canaan's friendly voice ghosted through the black.

I opened my eyes. "Having trouble seeing the grid."

"It's not always visible?"

"Nope. When something engages the grid, I see it activate around me."

"Hm. Good to know." Canaan sounded thoughtful.

"Thought I'd relayed that at some point."

"It's all new territory." He sidled up to my left. "Two ways to engage." He touched the round tip of his pointer finger to the darkened red light on the end of the gadget. "Manual activation. Press here."

"Ah. It's more than just a light."

Canaan gave a quick bob of his head. "Vocal activation. I've attuned it to your voice and mine, so by chance someone tries to commandeer them, they'll have a difficult time of it."

"Awesome. Smart." I continued holding out my palm, the piece warming against my skin.

"Do you remember the vocal commands?"

"I do not."

"Need to memorize them."

"Yes, sir. I lost the manual in the boat explosion party." I pursed my lips.

"I hear your sarcasm, and I'll raise you a fun fact. I *do* have a manual, and it's in my bag." He stuck out his chin in defiance.

"Oh yeah?"

"Yeah, smarty. Memorize it tonight."

"Will do."

Canaan sniffed. "For now, seeing as I have already memorized the manual, because I wrote it, let's start with basic commands."

"Yes, please."

"Activate SIMPL One." The metal shivered in my palm. The red light blinked. Hushed blue lights of the grid swallowed us, and the tremor shuddered from my palm and across my skin.

Flickering around the room, each surface's measurements contained exact dimensions, the blue lines counting distance, dismissing threats. The tremble continued wavering into my gray running shoes. Ten for one.

I couldn't stop the thrill rubbing across my lips. My cheeks flushed.

"You see the grid?"

"Yes, sir."

"Lock on your target piece. Center it in your vision."

I tilted my head, the little awkward chunk warming in my palm.

Canaan shuffled away a step and whispered, "Engage."

"Engage!" The piece blasted up, with a quiet rush of air brushing against my palm.

"Your next audible command is 'Initiate menu.'"

"Initiate menu." A blue and white square appeared to my right. "Ah!"

"Now you have a menu full of commands you can use to visually manipulate SIMPL One."

"Focus my eyes on the command and hold to select, correct?"

"Yes, ma'am."

"Abs fabs." A purple dot lined up on the menu box, indicating where my focus rested. I scanned up and down the different options of commands.

"See what you can make it do."

"No need to tell me twice!" I opted for *Fly*. A corresponding menu popped up to the left of the menu, closer to the center of my vision. What looked like an opaque blue plus sign, with arrows on the top, left, right, and bottom, and a circle in the center, hovered where I could touch it. Holding up my right hand, I almost tried to press the imaginary buttons.

Canaan saw the hesitant motion. "You can use your hands."

"Can I move the tools around?"

"The controller?"

"Yeah." I swiped at the shape. It fluttered into the center of my vision, a blue spectre. "Ah, I can!"

"Yes—"

"Good." With my left hand, I grabbed the center of the plus sign so the thing sat before my left shoulder. Pressing the top arrow, SIMPL One fluttered away from us, without even a hum. Testing the different arrows, One hovered on an invisible plateau. It retracted to me with the bottom arrow, and left and right with those corresponding arrows. "How do I make it go up or down?"

"The middle button switches the controls to height."

"Kind of clunky." I tapped the buttons, my finger meeting no resistance, the SIMPL darting every which way.

Canaan cleared his throat. "You can use the visual controller to pinpoint where you want it to go."

Raising my eyes from the faint blue shape, the purple dot again appeared in the far back corner of the room, where a rope hung suspended from an exposed beam. SIMPL One surged toward the nut anchoring the rope to the beam. "Well. Much easier."

"Simple, right?"

"Aw, Canaan. A pun."

"Now, how do you turn it off?" Canaan stepped back into my peripheral and slung his palm along his forehead. "Man, I could go for a brisket right now."

"That's random." I withdrew the SIMPL from the ceiling, whirling it in a spiral across the room.

"Tuesdays, I like to have brisket. It's not so random."

"Guess not. Also, didn't know it was Tuesday. Haven't you been stationed in Italy?"

"Spain."

"Do they eat a lot of brisket in Spain?"

"Not so much."

"I guess Tuesdays are hard for you."

"I am not in Spain any longer." Canaan gave a slight chuckle, then cleared his throat. "Let's see how you handle more than one SIMPL."

"I'm going to name them."

"Alright?" Street lights flickered upon Canaan's face. A warm breeze thundered around us, the jeep engine gunning, shoving us back to the fort.

"Can I change their names in the Settings?" The black box bumped in my lap as the tires thumped over some rough stones on the street.

"Yes. Don't make it too hard for yourself to place a command."

Dub glanced over his shoulder to Canaan, who sat beside him in the front. Wind whipped around us, plugging my ears.

"Dub?" I leaned forward so he could more easily hear me. He swayed backward in his seat. "I need to get to the BX first thing tomorrow. They should have a load of items for me."

"Not a problem. I'll send my second to assist you."

"Thank you." I relaxed for a moment, waiting for the stars to collapse on us from their blanket overhead. They winked back the reminder my company would have to wear three-day old uniforms the next day and it was my fault. Funny how the mind can soar and stumble in the same second.

"Get your task accomplished for the night?" Dub asked, his eyes flicking in the rearview mirror to seek my face.

"Yes, sir." Canaan bobbed his chin up and down. "Thanks again for the ride."

"I was going to head over to speak with your Commander anyway. We received some new images and I think you'll be glad to see them."

"Oh yeah?"

"Yes, sir." Dub gave one solid nod. "Looks like we found some activity off the western coast of Sao Miguel."

"Unusual activity?"

"You can say that again. Looks like a large submarine or other sub-aquatic transportation device. Satellites caught it surfacing and releasing a four-armed drone which headed toward the mainland."

Chapter Eighteen

BRISTLED
Tucker

I held up the white, crumbled napkin upon which Hazard had scribbled the faint penciled triangle. "Have you seen this before?"

The Commander studied the napkin. The blacks of his eyes expanded, eyebrows raising. With a precise motion, the Commander placed the pen on the table. He held out a palm for the napkin. "Thompson, may I look closer, please?"

I cleared my throat. "Have you seen this?"

"I've seen triangles in my days, yes."

"In regard to Rapton. Or Adenauer. Or any of the board members."

McConnell waved his fingers as if to draw the napkin closer.

"Hazard drew this. It's the mantra, or a map, if you will, which Rapton taught the Dragons."

"A triangle has often been used as a symbol for some kind of—"

I lowered myself into the chair opposite him at the dinner table, long since cleared of dishes and flatware. One single white ceramic mug, drained, with a brown ring around the inside edge, signaled the cold after-dinner remnants of an endless work day. "What interests me is I've been clearly instructed to stay far away from the teachings Rapton used. The very symbol of our uniforms contains an element similar to this one. I've got my trainees muttering nonsensical protocol which they do not understand but seem to have some bearing on our productivity. Note how if you look at the global positioning of Breame's financial holdings—Fort Prospect, Heart Mountain, and where we are right now—you get this same shape. What I'd like to know, sir? Will you give me any relevant information pertaining to this particular premise?"

"Tucker."

"With all due respect."

"Let me see the drawing."

I smacked it on the table and slid it over to him with my first two fingers.

He hunched, his head dipping over the square. "Tell me your thoughts."

"I'm not sure what to think." I perched in the chair, my spine fused into a rigid pole of taut concern. "I'd like to trust Alliance. I'd like to trust my gut."

"What's your gut saying?"

"Says this is key."

"Alright. Could it possibly be you partially remember this from your days in the program?"

"No. I don't know. I don't think so. I've got no particular bent for triangles."

The sides of his mouth wobbled for a moment. "Nice wordplay."

"Sir."

He cleared his throat and swallowed the humor. "I see we're past the point of discussing this in a lighthearted manner."

"I need answers. Do you know about this?"

"You're asking if you can trust me."

I splayed out my fingers. "The last time I trusted blindly was when you threw Saylor in the reformatory on Isla Barina, naming her as Breame's mole. I trusted she wasn't."

"So, your gut's got good instinct."

My shoulders tightened, a crick in my neck needing to be released. "Meanwhile, the real mole pocketed my points and bought herself a pair of shoes with them."

"Thompson, you've got to let her betrayal go. She stole your points, too?"

I slid one hand up to the back of my neck to rub away the muscle twinges. "Noticed it after the gala when Twila disappeared. Thought it was payback for not going with her."

"Here's the straight. Are you ready for it?"

"Anchors aweigh," I said.

"Alliance's initial logo and branding included a primitive triangle shape, then quickly morphed into a simple letter A. We've utilized the idea of a triad in our goals and mission statement."

A waiter picked that moment to arrive at our table with a small white ceramic cup. He replaced McConnell's empty cup with one filled to the brim with thick, steaming liquid. When I raised my hand to ask if he'd bring one more, the man set a white saucer with a matching cup before me.

I gave him a solid thumbs-up. "Thank you, sir. You've made my night."

With a quick nod and a small smile, he grabbed the empty cup and skidded out of view through the swinging door leading out of the dim, hushed café.

"Are we in paradise?" I asked.

The Commander huffed a small laugh. "Following Rapton's not-so-gentle exit, the board and I had a long discussion about our goals."

Remembering Rapton as he collapsed to the floor, in the heart of Camp Kissinger, electrocuted by the artificial intelligence he'd helped create with Breame and Adenauer's help, I could almost smell the burned scent of iron and blood and flesh. Swallowing hard, I shut my eyes to void the vivid image.

The Commander sipped at the espresso. The liquid sloshed through his lips as he breathed upon it to cool it rolling along his tongue. "The board approved me to create a more purposeful, positive mission statement. We brainstormed ideas of what we wanted, and they'd charged me with improving the final draft. I'd been crafting it and just so happens lost my copies during our friends' volatile visit."

"Control, containment, consciousness," I stated, blindly eyeing the papers skewed upon the table. "Hazard said the words as if they'd been etched into his basic understanding of language."

"It's possible Rapton reinforced the ideas in a different way than I did with my men."

"Seeing I've never heard you state those three things in one sentence, I'd agree," I said.

"He's not far from your basic understanding. Mission, perseverance, unity."

"We defeat. Never quit."

The Commander nodded. "Yes. I suppose Rapton—"

"And Littleton."

He coughed. "Yes, and Littleton. I suppose they simply made it easier to remember."

"Consciousness is not the same as perseverance. Control is not the same as mission-oriented."

"No. You're right."

"Perseverance is lasting even when you don't think you can. Perseverance endures, regardless. Despite. Because of. Perseverance builds upon itself. Consciousness...I'm not even sure how it relates."

McConnell shrugged. "Well. Consciousness, mindfulness, keep the soldier aware of his mission. Helps him see the bigger picture."

"Consciousness made Cello a killer."

McConnell licked his thumb. "Rapton helped build that device. Maybe it served him right that Cello turned on him." He patted through a stack of papers until selecting one. "After you returned from Kissinger, I printed out a report summary of Rapton's activity logs."

"That was almost a year ago."

"I know. It piled onto the end of my list, and then got pushed back. I'd recently sent it to analytics and they replied with—you know what, I won't bother you with the minutiae—he'd gone MIA after he sent you out on that mission, do you remember?"

"Indubitably." I eyed the curls of white smoke still ruminating from the bronze liquid before me.

"Well, one particular payment on his Alliance charge account never made sense. I thought it was an error."

"What?"

"Rapton purchased a boat pass to New Zealand. Ten hours after his time of death."

"To New Zealand?"

"To Jackson Bay, New Zealand." McConnell eyed the paper, reading the findings filling the page.

"Seems odd. Why would a ghost need a boat trip to New Zealand?"

"I suppose he had unfulfilled business to attend to."

"I hear they have beautiful mountains."

"Thompson, who used Rapton's card?"

With one bold move, I hoisted the espresso cup into the air and brought it to my lips. The bitter scent of roasted plans and bristled remains thrummed against my skin. "Indeed, the question of the hour. I have a feeling whoever it was planned to use a helicopter and something went terribly wrong."

C anaan, Saylor, and Dub stalked into the café, to the waiter's grimacing hand-waving. Dub pointed at us with a smile, and the waiter sighed, motioning to us, continuing his sweep of the tile floor. Someone in the back switched the window lights off, and the sounds of splashing water in the kitchen, along with a lonely singer wailed behind the swinging door.

"Late night delivery." Dub held up an orange envelope he had tucked under his arm. "I figured you would be up anyway."

"It's never too late for good news," McConnell confirmed, and began to draw the chair beside him out from under the table.

Dub waved away the movement. "I can't stay. Believe it or not I have a meeting. I knew you'd want to see these right away. The satellite request you submitted? Turned up some good intel. Notes are in here, with a findings report and photo analysis." He slapped the envelope on the table. "Merry new year."

"Thank you, Dub."

"I expect we will hear from you in the morning first thing. I'll keep an ear out on my radio."

"You bet."

Dub tossed a polite, quick salute, and pivoted on his heel. With the swagger of a man who knew his place in life and didn't envy a soul, he made his way out the door.

"What's that?" I asked Saylor, nodding to the black rectangle she'd been clinging to since the accident.

"Oh?"

All eyes dodged from me to her.

She elevated one shoulder, studying the box. Her eyes never budged from it. All ten fingers whitened on her tight grip around its edges. "It's, well—not, um—you know."

Squishing my eyebrows together, I accepted she didn't want to say anything, but hadn't a clue why not. Nobody present held a lower clearance level. Unless she didn't want me to know, specifically.

Canaan intercepted the awkward silence. "Dub said we'd want to see those photos immediately."

"Yes." The Commander unwound the red string tied around an orange clasp on the backside of the tall envelope.

Saylor pulled out the chair beside me and slunk down into it. She successfully avoided any eye contact with me.

Canaan dropped into the chair beside the Commander, groaning as he did. "Gettin' too old for this."

"If you're too old," the Commander stated, "then don't even think about what I am." He slid a thick pile of papers out of the envelope. The slick, colorful photos, and hand-written reports dropped and rested before him.

"Dub said it was a submarine off one of the nearby islands," Saylor blurted out. She craned her neck to see the photos.

"What?" McConnell spread them out. Sure enough, five photos revealed a compelling narrative. The satellite had captured a dark gray cylinder appearing off the western coast of a bean-shaped island. The next photo closed in on the scene, revealing a green landscape of the island with a fresh beach, and a curiously shaped cylinder just beyond the shallows. Following that photo, a closer shot revealed the cylinder to appear to have an item resting on top of it, a square-ish triangle with arms. The shape resonated with a not-so-distant memory and the large drone which had allowed our mysterious compatriots to nearly kill us all before disappearing without a trace.

"Gotcha." McConnell jabbed his finger against the glossy photo.

"How's it proof of anything?" I asked.

"It's proof enough to provide a last-known-whereabouts. These photos were taken this morning." He tapped on the time stamp on the bottom right corner.

"Good. So which island are we looking at?"

"Sao Miguel," Canaan answered. "Check the next photo."

McConnell flipped the next to the top of the stack. The picture revealed a shadow where the cylinder had been, and the blurry cropping of a squarish blob hovering over the bottom of the photograph, over the water.

"Dub said the drone headed mainland, which falls due east."

"The satellite didn't track it because we set certain coordinates, which did not include Portugal itself." McConnell closed his eyes, thinking.

"We head to Sao Miguel tomorrow?" Canaan asked. "Or waiting for more evidence?"

"I'm going to read through the reports this evening. See what I can glean from them. We still need to finish gathering our items as well, so our group can travel for a few days." McConnell's forehead wrinkled while he considered Saylor. "I'm headed to my room. I believe these men would prefer to have us out of here for the night."

The waiters sang in the kitchen, cleaning, scrubbing, and a laugh followed before the song continued.

"Sounds good," Canaan agreed.

Saylor stood, her chair screeching on the tile underneath her. "See you in the morning." She grabbed at the black box, gathering it tightly in the crook of her arms.

"I'll go with." I stood as well, but she waved me away.

"I need to make a pit stop at the front counter," she said, still avoiding eye contact. "Have to arrange a special wake-up call so I can contact Lajes and collect the last of our uniforms." Clamping her jaw shut, she strode off.

"Sleep well," I called after her.

She waved one hand over her shoulder.

Canaan observed the exchange and held up a palm to me when I exhaled. "She's working on an intense project. Takes a lot of mental fortitude."

"What's the project?"

"Sarge," Canaan grinned, "she'll tell you when she's ready. Never underestimate a powerful woman."

"Oh, I never underestimate her."

"Rest assured." He placed both hands on the table and hoisted his body up out of the chair. Some muscle around his knee popped. He winced. "Whatever you're thinking right now, it's nothing compared to reality. If you don't underestimate her, then why would you let her walk away without a proper goodnight?"

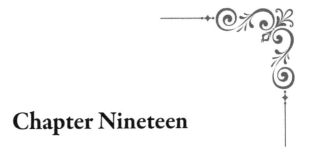

Chapter Nineteen

CAUGHT
Saylor

———❧———

"This order cannot be correct." My elbow dug into the worn wooden countertop of the hotel front desk. The telephone receiver curled against my skin. "Sir, my radio request consisted of forty-two black canvas duffel bags, and you supplied twenty-six; I requested all the black socks available, to which you helpfully provided ten pairs. I also requested as many boots as possible, unisex, in sizes four through fourteen."

The man's voice crackled through the line. "You asked for the left." His thick accent did not help.

The pile of black leather boots lay stacked at my feet. "I asked for what you had left!"

"Yes. Here is left."

"These are left boots."

"You Americans have strange orders all time. I do what you ask for."

"I need both of the boots. The left and the right. A pair. A pair of boots consists of the left boot and the right boot."

He replied with a string of unrecognizable words, and the line squealed with cackling static. I angled my head away from the noise. The lady behind the counter focused in such a neat matter on filing her papers I nearly believed her, and chose to ignore the smirk tipping her lips.

"Sir, I cannot pay for left boots. Left boots do us no good." My finger curled around the white, twisty cord.

"You must speak to manager. You ask for left boots, I send."

The line went dead.

I stared at the phone receiver in my hand, red as sin and snickering just as hard. Pursing my lips, I stuck the handle within its indention on the white plastic phone body.

As I stepped away from the desk, mumbling a thanks to the woman for lending me the phone, I stumbled over one stray boot.

"Stupid boots!" I yelled at them. Sighing, I picked up the renegade I'd tripped over and studied it. *Do they buy shoes singularly here? What a strange place.*

"What's with the shoe pile?" Eagre, in a white tank top and a pair of fitted black capris, sauntered beside the desk. Her loose blonde hair curled around her shoulders and down her back, waves absorbing the golden sun streaming in the windows behind her. She held a gray ceramic cup in one hand, and a matching saucer underneath it in the other. The coffee inside the cup licked the edges of the mug, taunting the morning sun.

"I'm working on collecting the remaining necessities for the rest of our trip." The words oozed out, hateful and snappy. "Where did you get coffee?"

The left side of her cheek rose for a moment, lithe and unamused. "I'm taking it outside to the leadership meeting."

"Leadership meeting?" Leaning around her, I craned my neck to see who might be waiting on the patio.

"If you have them, I need a size six."

"What?" I rubbed my eyes, fazed.

"I wear a size six. Do you have those?"

"No. Not yet."

"Fine." She huffed an impatient breath through her nose and stepped away.

"Eagre?"

She paused, tossing me a backward glance.

"Where did you get that outfit?"

"What are you, my keeper?"

"No, I didn't mean—"

Eagre flipped her hair over her shoulder and strutted off to the brave horizon of the patio and whatever pair of lips awaited her gauzy flirtations.

"Leadership meeting," I muttered under my breath.

Gathering the boots, a long check-list tumbled through my brain of what I needed to do to get enough right boots to outfit my squad, when Logan appeared at my side.

"You've been talking to yourself for about five minutes, and I think I can help," he said. "Want to go and lift some heavy things with me and Tuck?"

"I surely do. Will you help me pick up these ridiculous boots?"

"Why are they ridiculous?" He reached down and picked up two in one hand, eyeing them.

"Why have you been lurking around watching me for five minutes instead of helping? Come on."

He gathered boots and helped me place them back in their appropriate boxes. "Where are the matches to these boots?"

Adopting an innocent Southern drawl, I slammed two boots into one box. "Why, whatever do you mean?"

"Here are two size eights, but they're both lefts."

"Just put the boots in the boxes and let's go hit things."

"Alright."

After assembling all the shoes into boxes and stacking them up, Logan tapped his empty wrist. "Dub should be here any minute. Want to go grab an extra set of clothes? We're going to stay at Lajes to work some logistics before coming back. Dad said he'd meet us there."

"Yeah." I sighed, eyeing the stack.

Tucker strolled into the lobby, a brown paper bag slung over his shoulder. His black shirt snuggled against his chest, and those eyes studied the tile floors.

"I'll be right back," I noted. "Who's here with the Dragons?"

Tucker raised his head then, drawn out of his thoughts. A small smile crossed his lips. He lifted his chin in a nod. "Burkman's going to work with them. They're discussing all things Dragon."

"How 'bout that." I pivoted to dash upstairs, when I paused. "Why aren't you working with them?"

"Dub's pulling up," Logan interrupted from the front door. "Get your bag and meet us outside."

"Sure thing." I called out over my shoulder, feet already sprinting ahead of me.

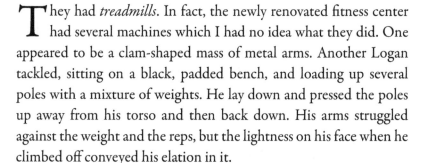

They had *treadmills*. In fact, the newly renovated fitness center had several machines which I had no idea what they did. One appeared to be a clam-shaped mass of metal arms. Another Logan tackled, sitting on a black, padded bench, and loading up several poles with a mixture of weights. He lay down and pressed the poles up away from his torso and then back down. His arms struggled against the weight and the reps, but the lightness on his face when he climbed off conveyed his elation in it.

Meanwhile, I grabbed my own set of thirty-pound barbells and ducked over to an empty corner of the room, away from the bulky men and their slick, muscled shoulders. Sweat dripped down my forehead, along the small of my back, and down onto the black flooring. Push-ups, overhead presses, and pull-backs, I chucked the barbells around, gravity verses my arms. Gravity usually wins, but on some occasions, my grit pulls one over on it.

After my therapy session with the barbells ended, I climbed on the treadmill. The machine followed my button presses, and I strolled along the looping belt under foot. Music played from overhead speakers. The pulsing drums and electric guitar wailed, fueling the room's heat.

Tucker grabbed a large gray disc from a pole sticking off the side of a large black rack. He stacked the disc against two others on a thick black pole he'd set on the ground, and then slid a shiny, silver clamp beside the disk. He navigated several steps to a chair. With a smooth motion he yanked the bottom edge of his shirt, rolling it up his back and over his head. A gray undershirt attempted to fling itself up his smooth skin, but he tossed the black shirt on the chair and tugged the wrinkles out of the gray sleeveless shirt. I bit my lip, somewhat disappointed.

Attempting not to ogle, I studied the face of the treadmill instructions.

Tucker settled his hands on the bar and weight plates resting on the ground, and he steadied his palms against the metal rod. Adjusting his fingers, he set his jaw, with his eyes fixed on the ground about twenty feet in front of him. He saw the challenge and owned it. In a smooth motion, he straightened his legs, lifting the bar off the ground, then hurled it up to his chest, elbows forging as steel underneath. Every muscle in his body carried the weight, shoving it heavenward. He surged the pole overhead, victory shimmying through his wrists, rounding down his slick, bulging shoulders, and into his heels.

He brought the bar down to his chest, then touched the tips of the weight plates to the ground, and repeated four more times.

Forcing the weight to submit to his will, dogged jaw and gritted resolve, he tossed the bar to the ground after the last rep, and the bar bounced in relief.

The taut muscles in his arms and shoulders glistened under the lights. Air caught in my chest. Tucker rested his hands on his hips. Blowing a deep breath out of his lungs, he lifted his eyes, catching my reflected glance in the mirror. Maybe it was a gawking stare, so what? He arched one eyebrow. Caught. I winked at him, then pressed my teeth against the edge of my bottom lip.

Tucker's chest heaved from the exercise, and a grin lit his cheeks. Shaking his head, he dropped his gaze, focusing on the work yet to be done.

"I'd like to thank you for the banana shirt," Logan's voice tumbled from behind me. He climbed up on the treadmill beside mine and pressed several buttons.

"You're quite welcome. I saw it and thought, 'Logan needs that.'"

"How could you think anything differently?"

"I just know you well."

"You talk to Dad this morning?" Logan asked. The belt under his shoes sped up. His feet churned faster, in a not-so-relaxed walk.

"I have not." The words caught in my throat. Dry air welled up against the heat soaking through my skin. "What's up?"

Logan swayed his head. "I haven't seen him either. He'd disappeared before I got up. He left a note saying he wanted to meet with us at 1000 hours."

I checked the clock on the wall above the front door. "That's half an hour from now." A new trickle of sweat rambled down my temple and meandered into the corner of my eye. I swiped at it, the burn tickling the whites of my eyes.

"I figure we can hit the BX on our way?"

A hefty sigh wove itself out of my lungs. The shoes. "Copy that. We need to stop by."

"Maybe we—"

"I'm not a screw up."

"What?" Logan shot me a confused look.

"The guy at the BX didn't understand me."

"Okay?"

"Everybody misunderstands things from time to time. We're dealing with a huge language barrier."

"I think—"

"I mean, communicating with any human being carries the option for a miscommunication. Even you and Cadence probably bicker, even though others don't see it. You're always gushy."

"Wow." He scrunched his nose.

"It can't *just* be me. Surely."

"Saylor. We are in a new place. And yes, there's a language barrier. Is that why the shoes aren't matched?"

I shrugged. "I don't know what—yes. Yes."

"No big deal. We'll fix it. Team work."

"Okay."

"We need boots." Logan pressed a button on the face of his machine, and the treadmill slowed.

"I know! And now you can rescue your sister the screw up."

"It's not a rescue. And you're not a screw up."

"Hmph." Another torrent of sweat built up across my forehead. With my left hand, I flicked the water down to the floor and away from me.

"Besides." Logan cleared his throat. "Cadence and I did bicker. Quite a lot, especially—" He paused.

"What? You *did* bicker? What does that mean? Just the one time?"

He sighed and pressed the buttons in front of him two more times. The belt of the treadmill slowed. Logan placed a hand on the arm of the machine. "I didn't mention anything to anybody before we left. I've tried—we've tried—to not make a huge deal about it."

"Did you break up?"

He tilted his head to the side, lifting his free hand, and then dropped it. His palm slapped his pants leg.

"But you love her!" I could feel my voice raising to be heard over the whirring of fans and machines, so I lowered it, leaning closer. "What happened?"

He forced another guttural sigh out. "You know, it's been this evolving thing. We're both different than we used to be, on Isla Barina. She's walking now, almost fully without any help. She cannot get enough of her independence and we disagree on many topics that ignite her passion. Between taking courses at the university and wanting to go live in Asia, she has little room for me. Cadence wants to start a non-profit for children who have lost parents, working directly with the children, training them how to sew so they will have an income."

"Pretty amazing goals."

He nodded. "Oh, I agree. But she wants to accomplish them on her own. To prove herself, or something. She doesn't approve of my working with Alliance. She hates Alliance."

"I understand. Alliance killed her father."

"No. He served in the Army, Say, long before. He lived a life of service and sacrifice, purposefully. Colonel Schuring deserves only honor for his career, not sympathy. The man thrived because of Alliance."

I nibbled on my bottom lip.

"My world revolves around the Guard. She constantly talks down about it, and wrote an essay for one of her classes about how it's the ultimate evil and all the people in it are pawns and warmongers."

"Dude." I wiped a stray hair away from my cheek.

"Yeah."

"I don't think you're a warmonger."

"Thanks." His shoulders slumped. "I'm moving forward, though. Cadence and I were good together. She helped me see who I wanted to be. We were best friends. And I hope she finds success."

"No wonder I haven't seen or heard from you much lately."

"What's up, Tuck?" Logan bobbed his chin regarding one dripping, mussed-haired Tucker approaching us.

Tucker held out his arms like he wanted to give a huge hug. "Why the serious mugs, mates?" That lopsided grin.

"Saylor was just telling me about her obsession with bananas."

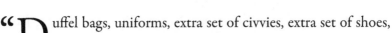

"Duffel bags, uniforms, extra set of civvies, extra set of shoes, socks, undies, toiletries, and both the left *and* right boots for every member of our company. Sir."

"Not sure why you had to distinguish the left and right boots," Dad mumbled as he checked his list, "but good work. Are you ready for distribution?"

"Yes, sir."

"Good."

Dad set his clipboard down on the table which we all sat around. The circular table filled one corner of the assembly room at Lajes, the rest of the space occupied by chairs in rows facing away from us. The white bulbs overhead stammered, and then buzzed bright.

"I've set a time table for our trip." He slid a file folder to each of us around the table—Logan, Tucker, me, and Canaan. "We fly out at 1210 hours, land at Ponta Delgada at 1310 hours, where a convoy will take us to Sete Cidades. They've been experiencing similar brown-outs at this island, and I've got a meeting with the local authorities to discuss their theories."

Canaan propped his chin on his fist. "They wouldn't discuss over a satellite conversation?"

Dad shook his head. "They were hesitant. They nearly refused to speak to me once I'd mentioned I was with Alliance."

"Odd."

"Indeed," Dad agreed.

"It's possible their superstition supersedes their desire to utilize technology."

Dad cleared this throat. "Whatever the cause, we have to go in person to make any headway. After we meet with them, I hope to get some time to speak with locals and follow up on some leads Dub has tried to investigate. But again, the connection between these islands is limited and Sao Miguel has been quiet."

"What does that mean?" Logan asked.

Dad shrugged one shoulder. "Not much news coming from them. Not much leaving the island. Limited activity on the west side of the island, from what we can tell in the satellite images and thermal scans. Although Sete Cidades has been lighting up like a lava lamp in a couple of the images. I want to see if those correlate to the brown-outs."

"What's a lava lamp?" I scrunched my nose. "Sounds dangerous."

Dad huffed out a quiet laugh. "An antiquated type of lighting device."

"Ah."

"What are we wearing on this little shindig?" Tucker rubbed a hand over the top of his hair, drawing the freshly-showered front hairs to a slight peak.

"Time to suit up," Dad said. "Canaan has your NEXIS suits, which you'll want to layer under the fresh civvies Saylor procured."

"Wear our civilian clothes over the NEXIS?" Logan rubbed his forehead with the back of his hand.

"We saved the NEXIS suits?" I pumped a fist in the air. "What's the plural form? NEXI? Nexises?"

"Barely." Canaan rubbed his chin. "They're what our blonde friend was demanding before she destroyed our ship."

Tucker cleared his throat. "And the GRIPS. And the VISTAS."

Canaan pointed at Tucker. "And the SIMPLs."

"The what?"

Canaan twisted in his chair. "You ready, kid?"

I rolled my fingers until they splayed up to the sky. "Your creation. You pick the reveal."

He nudged his eyebrows up and down on his forehead. "I almost feel like we should taunt them with it a little. Needs some buildup."

"I'm sayin'. A bit of teasing always helps, right?" I leaned on my elbow. "Like, this project took you several years and a whole lotta points, right? Might as well make them sweat a little bit."

"I like it." Canaan rested his arm on the table before him and twisted, taking in the others. "Anybody interested?"

Logan sighed.

Dad held up a hand.

Tucker's eyes shifted back and forth from Canaan to me, and his jaw worked as if he chewed on the idea. "You're killing me, Crackerjack."

Canaan shot him a grin.

I grabbed my bag and opened it up, lifting the black box. In a smooth motion, I squeezed my eyes shut and focused on the grid. Without a word, having memorized those oh-so-crucial commands, I thumbed open the lock and released my SIMPLs. My new friends. One by one they shot up into the space above my head. I blinked up at them, dazzling in their brilliant manners.

To give my fellow Guardsmen credit, they didn't even shift in their seats when my SIMPLs flew over their heads. Dad's eyes widened, the blacks in the centers welling as he tracked their movement with his eyes.

I spun the SIMPLs in a dance, whirling around, waltzing among each other. Forming them in a line, I introduced them to the gang.

"I've named them," I announced. "Canaan created these, in the same vein as the oxinal, but more chill."

"Unless she wants them to be otherwise."

"Exactly." I raised a palm to present them. "Unless I want them to be otherwise." I waved my fingers. SIMPL One came forward. "Meet Glitch. This one catches on fire. Sometimes."

As if on cue, the flames sputtered out of the middle spike with three short bursts of blue flame.

Drawing out each one, I shared their names. "Sparks elicits electricity, Zee, shaped like a big letter Z, contains magnetic capabilities. Chunk serves as the main processor but hovers nicely and records all the action on his tiny camera. Turner contains a lock-picking mechanism. Striker can straight up hammer his pointy end right into your skull, and Razz illuminates nearly any dim space. Moon is a shield, Lief is a filter, and Brian, well, I'm still figuring out how I can use him effectively."

"Brian?" Canaan's nose flared out in annoyance.

"Once upon a time, this cute guy in my class moved to Canada. I always wondered what happened to him."

"What's—"

"It's better than Von PoofleBurg."

"You're a strange character, Saylor."

I let a wild smirk sear across my cheeks, chattering my front teeth. "Now I kind of like Von PoofleBurg."

"What's their—" Dad began.

I held my hand up, fingertips extended heavenward. Drawing the pieces into a combined unit, and soaring over above my head, the metallic SIMPLs connected with bursts of sizzling blue fire. They merged into one fist-sized ball, and a light blue flame undulated as a halo over its surface. "And they all come together into one familiar tool we've all spent too many years fighting against. Canaan made it purposeful, containable, and most importantly—" I searched for the menu and selected the proper items. The fire shut off, the blue halo swallowed up within the orb. "It comes in travel size." Holding out my palm, the ball dropped against my skin. Warm to the touch, the metal greeted me like a doorknob to a place called home.

Holding the sphere up by my ear, I grinned at my Guardsmen. I suppose I expected them to be impressed or stunned or the least bit interested. Logan picked at his fingernails. Tucker's eyebrows furrowed over his nose, his mouth saying, "Eh."

And Dad studied Canaan, his gaze as straight as the sun was round. "So, you requested those mounds of paperwork because of this project."

Canaan didn't waver. He settled back, reclining in his chair, and cleared his throat. "The project fell in my lap. I'd been instructed to work on a new project in development. Because of my familiarity with the oxinals, Fulbright asked me to take lead. Couldn't turn it down."

"I bet you couldn't."

"Sir."

"Have you tested out what this will do, long term? How does it affect Saylor's physical construct? Don't you think you should have checked with me first?" His face hardened, a red tint churning just under the surface. A vein in his throat pounded to its own silent beat, spinning hot blood down into his chest.

"Sir, I—"

"And how did you know she was able to do this? How did you know she would be able to engage with the product? Did you build this specifically for her?"

Canaan stiffened, his shoulders thickening while he straightened in his chair. "I'd been given several files, mounds of paperwork, actually, and some helpful files on Saylor's engagement with Breame during her stay in Heart Mountain."

I spoke up, in a hushed voice. "I don't think we need to call it an engagement with Breame."

Canaan didn't hear me. He tapped his fingers along the wooden top of the desk. "I had paperwork. Files. My instructions included developing this product. My results weren't guaranteed until I worked with her on the ship, and I'm amazed the numbers provided aligned with the nanomite network. You might consider why Fulbright approved the project."

"But *you* built this, Canaan."

"And now your girl's more capable of handling the enemy we're about to face. You realize that Jane we saw on board wasn't any old blonde, right? Why haven't we gotten more answers on who she is?"

Dad silenced then. His focus roamed down to the ground before his boots.

"Sir, I saw this as an opportunity to create a new tool. It's essentially for survival scenarios, if you'd like further insight. With the SIMPL, the controller can combat almost any dire situation, filtering clean water, exploring unknown territory, starting a fire. This enables users to carry one simple tool to endure almost any extenuating circumstances. The user merely needs a way to access the network."

"Fulbright wants to inject Guardsmen?"

"No, sir, not as far as I know. I've built a handheld remote as well."

Dad silenced, pondering.

Logan sputtered, choking on the nail piece he'd loosened. He spit out the alienated tissue and wiped his lips with the back of his hand. "Cool. I'm glad Sayles gets another awesome piece of tech to unload. Glad we're all in this together."

Dad twisted his neck, still quiet, and licked his lips.

"We're wheels up at 1210 hours, correct?" Logan cracked the knuckles on one hand and stood.

Dad nodded.

"I'll see you on the tarmac."

Chapter Twenty

HEARTBREAKER
Tucker

"It's not like you to turn tail and run." I cornered Logan just outside the glass doors, closing us from the group. They awaited their plane, crammed into the waiting area. He'd said he wanted air. I said I did too. "You're not one for cowardice."

"What do you mean, cowardice, Thompson?" Logan asked, pivoting on his heel. His other black boot smacked against the pavement. Wind whipped through our hair, stirring up the hackles which I'd just bristled.

"It was you on the balcony. With Eagre."

He snorted. His gaze dropped, studying the ground behind me.

"You're not the jealous type, Logan. You haven't ever said a word about Saylor and what she can or cannot do."

Logan scrunched his nose, the wrinkles over his forehead deepening. "I'm not jealous. Never said the word."

"'Glad we're all in this together.' That's what you said. Eagre said the same phrase when I told the Dragon's Saylor would be joining us."

"And so because I used some similar English words, what? You conclude what?"

Defiant, I thrust out my chin. One hand flung aside. "I thought after the first time you were going to let it rest."

"I don't need your third degree, Oz. I'm not one of your little cronies." He yanked the gray sleeve of his NEXIS further up his elbow, tugging down the sleeve of the pastel yellow silk shirt with the giant banana print embedded all over it.

"Currently, you are acting like them. You're supposed to be their superior. My superior. Where's this coming from?"

Logan cleared his throat then, straightening his shoulders. "Seems we've both forgotten our places, then, Thompson. Thanks for the reminder."

"Logan. Don't. What are you doing? Why are you slipping off with Eagre? Haven't you seen the chaos when you disobey the Commander's fraternization orders?"

"It's not fraternization." He shrugged one shoulder. "It was nothing."

I squeezed my eyes shut.

"She's not a rebound, if that's what you're afraid of," Logan added, quieter. "She's powerful. Confident. Strong. Everything..." He licked his lips and lifted his focus to the top of the doorframe.

"Everything Cadence wasn't?"

"Don't fill in the blanks, mate."

"Am I your mate?" I asked, dumbfounded. I rolled my neck, the bones crackling behind me. "You've been lying. Now instead of owning those choices, you're running off into the darkness, leaving others to fend for themselves, and shrugging away your choices?"

"Fine. Yes." Logan stepped closer. "You want a rundown of the times we've met up? On the balcony. The night before we left. Behind the fitness center where you found us the first time. The night I borrowed your truck."

"Oh, Logan!"

"The night I borrowed your truck, I took Rubu and Weyr to the store to get supplies for their care packages to send home."

"You did?"

He bobbed his chin. "Remember, two days before we left, when Shadow and Clutch ended up leaving the drills early?"

I took my turn to bob my chin.

"Shadow had just heard from her Mother. Her brother was taken to their local medical center. He'd lost his vision."

"I—I haven't heard any of this."

"They're homesick, Tucker. Tired. Missing their familiar surroundings."

"Humans have no excuse for sneaking off to dark corners simply because they are human."

Logan crossed his arms. "But what about Dragons? Our new recruits are lashing out because confusion reigns around them. They don't know who they're supposed to be, but they're fully aware of what they are not. You remind them every day."

"I tell every recruit he has value. From Shadow to Weyr, I tell them they can change and be better."

Logan shook his head from side to side. His gaze glued onto something inside the building. The guy blinked, and then focused on me. Logan pointed an accusatory finger at my chest. "Even I know too much training depletes the best of champions. And I make recruits toss their lunches the first day on purpose."

"But we're not training anymore, Logan. We are active duty."

He clicked his tongue.

"Can I trust you to be on my side? Can I trust when we hit the ground on Sao Miguel I can rely on your back-up?"

Shock read all over his face. "You can." His nostrils widened.

"You won't give more pity party examples? Sure, they've got hard times. We all do. But we aren't excuse-makers. We're Alliance. If you're weak, then I'm weak. Alliance wins. We defeat. We defeat the excuses and the lackluster hopelessness common man relies upon."

"You're starting to sound like my dad."

"Maybe it's time you did too."

He propped one calloused finger against my navy button-up. "You sure do talk big for someone who was doing the exact same thing. Remember, *Thompson*, I've found you ducked behind your own number of wheelhouses and fitness centers with your own number of girls. And what were you doing up there with my sister?"

"Logan—"

"This battle begins the war, Tucker." Logan faced the tarmac before us. A plane thundered down from the sky, far down the opposite runway, the wheels screeching against the concrete. "The battle isn't between us, or the Dragons, and all of our excuses." He huffed out a hearty exhale. "I'm sorry about Eagre. But you might begin considering what you're going to have to do when faced with Saylor's replicant. Can you take down your girlfriend?"

"Can you take down your sister?"

The shining aircraft slowed, rounding the runway corner, its screaming engines lowering their voices, shushing their excitement.

Logan grinned.

"What?" I asked.

"Sounds kind of nice, actually. I could repay her for all the times she insulted my brownies."

"And for buying you that banana shirt."

The sun tumbled down upon my shoulders as Command handed me a rolled wad of papers. "You'll take the Dragons to Ponta Garca and the surrounding areas noted on your map."

"Yes, sir."

Behind him, the row of staunch policemen eyed our group. Behind me, my Dragons awaited instruction, in their own line, in their own somber address.

"We're fully cooperating with the local authorities, I've assured them." The Commander raised his voice, eyeing us all. He handed another roll of paper to Burkman. "You're on the east central side of the island, at Furnas and the hot springs." The Commander shifted to another officer down the row and held out a roll of paper. "You'll take the east end, Povoacao."

The man accepted his assignment with a quick nod.

"Proceed with caution and as friendly strangers. Be on the lookout for unusual or suspicious activity, and call in if you find any leads. Mandatory check in at 1600. Understood?"

"Yes, sir!" The unison chorus resounded.

McConnell closed his eyes for a brief moment. He opened them, proudly surveying our hearty convergence. "Dismissed."

A drum cadence began to tick in the base of my throat. These weren't the hot spot areas on our satellite images. *Why is the Commander sending us to the east side of the island?* All the activity we'd seen had been on the west.

"Sir?" I said as the others meandered over to the caravan of black vehicles lined up along the curb. Lush green grass shivered under all the boots.

McConnell squinted at me, with a slight shake of his head. He held up a finger to me indicating I should wait. He pivoted to the police captain behind him. "Thank you again. Obrigado."

"Fazemos o que devemos." The man frowned, his eyes doubtful and dark.

The Commander offered an awkward, slight chuckle, then nodded. "Thompson, you're in this transport over this way." He placed a hand on my shoulder and guided me over to the front jeep.

A tan, sullen islander stood beside the driver door, his hands clasped before him.

McConnell lowered his voice. "They're unwilling to work with us. You'll have to ditch your driver. Channel six." He stuck out his hand before him, as if to offer a handshake. "Good to be back on intel duty." He said it loudly, his voice almost cracking. I slid my palm in his, where a cool, hard square rested. We shook hands, and McConnell dipped his chin the slightest. "Just like on Barina."

"Yes, sir." Pressing my thumb against the box, I eased my hand away and slid the rectangle into my palm. Releasing his hand, I tucked my fist into my khaki pants' pocket. "Back to the days of the Heartbreaker."

"Why, yes." The left side of McConnell's lips quivered. Then the smile slid into a lopsided grin. The wrinkles beside his mouth extended. "The glory days."

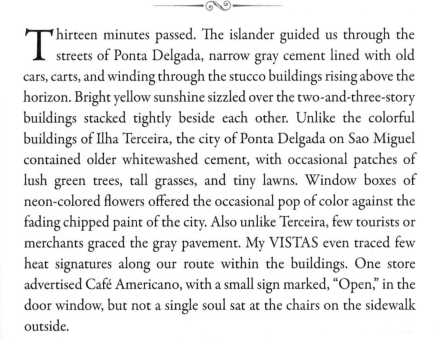

Thirteen minutes passed. The islander guided us through the streets of Ponta Delgada, narrow gray cement lined with old cars, carts, and winding through the stucco buildings rising above the horizon. Bright yellow sunshine sizzled over the two-and-three-story buildings stacked tightly beside each other. Unlike the colorful buildings of Ilha Terceira, the city of Ponta Delgada on Sao Miguel contained older whitewashed cement, with occasional patches of lush green trees, tall grasses, and tiny lawns. Window boxes of neon-colored flowers offered the occasional pop of color against the fading chipped paint of the city. Also unlike Terceira, few tourists or merchants graced the gray pavement. My VISTAS even traced few heat signatures along our route within the buildings. One store advertised Café Americano, with a small sign marked, "Open," in the door window, but not a single soul sat at the chairs on the sidewalk outside.

In the back seats—this jeep had an enclosed top, with a third-row seat—Clutch, Eagre, Wring, Rubu, and Weyr sat glowering at the view, while Hazard continued staring at his hands in his lap every time I glanced back at them.

"Nice day for an island drive," I stated to the driver.

He had said he spoke a little English when we first climbed aboard. But he didn't respond. His eyes stayed focused on the road ahead. He leaned forward, gripping the steering wheel. The scenery opened up, green palm trees and towering forestry surrounding us. Every shade of emerald filled the windows.

"It's quite beautiful here."

Silence answered.

I cleared my throat and adjusted the top button on my shirt. A trickle of sweat beaded up and dripped down the small of my back. Even with the cooling effects of the NEXIS, the layers added up quickly in the sauna of the island heat and humidity. I tapped on the window ledge with my right fingertips.

"I find it fascinating the roads are like American roads. Feels like home."

Not a single response.

"Of course, I suppose I could consider Australia my home, and the roads are quite different there. But shouldn't you remember something about home in order to call it home?"

Mountains rose up before us in the distance, padded by puffy white clouds against the pale blue sky. The crisp green of the surrounding trees lining the road drew out the familiar ache of when I had to do what was hardest and yet required.

I gripped my chest and began to cough.

The driver glanced my way and then reconfigured his focus on the road.

Chucking more air through my lungs, wheezing, I slumped against the seat.

"Are you okay?" the driver asked.

I moaned again and ran my palm over my forehead. Cleared my throat. "Do you mind pulling over?"

Disorient the opponent. Damage the head. Finish the fight quick.

He slowed the car, and as soon as we were stopped on the edge of the pavement, against the guardrail, I tilted forward in my seat, heaving deep inhales of oxygen. He shifted the gear to park. With my right hand, I loosened the seat belt latch, and waved my left hand up to my forehead. The hazard lights ticked on and off, on and off. With a snap of my left arm, I nailed him in the throat with the edge of my hand. Spit and jagged air sputtered through his windpipe. Balling my hand into a fist, I knocked back against his temple, and then shot my flat, hard hand back against his throat. His eyes closed, momentarily stunned. I had about ten seconds.

"Hazard, help me." I slung open my door and darted around the front of the jeep, surging the driver's door handle outward. Withdrawing a thick, black zip tie from my pocket, I bound his wrists crossed over each other.

Hazard jumped out of his door and ran up beside me. The two of us carried the wilted man to the back hatch. Rubu waited by the open door and grabbed the man's middle. The three of us boosted him into the small open space, dumping him with a *thud* against the scratchy gray carpet.

"What's the plan, boss?" Rubu asked nonchalantly. He rested one hand on the hatch, observing.

I yanked another zip tie around the driver's ankles. His eyelids slid shut.

"Well, not good." I huffed to no one in particular. "Hazard, you're my new navigator. Rubu, make sure he keeps breathing."

Hazard bobbed his head. Rubu slammed the door shut. We crawled back into our seats, and I gunned the engine. Checking the floorboards from where I saw it fall, I retrieved the small gray box our driver had been quietly tapping every three minutes. He'd held it not-so-discreetly in his left palm, nervously fingering its outline beside the steering wheel.

Greenery scampered by in a blur, the landscape sliding down a hill to the right, and into a thriving wood. An old rock wall, mossy and crumbling after years of disservice, eventually divided the tiny plot of land from fields which intermingled with the forest.

I handed the grape-sized box to Clutch over my shoulder. "Tap the red button right now, and then tap it every three minutes or so until I tell you to stop."

"Yes, sir." She accepted the box and held it in her lap. I caught her gaze in the rearview mirror. Those almond eyes questioned, although her words did not.

"He was sending signals back to their headquarters to track us."

"Ah."

"So we're going to misdirect for a few minutes."

"Where are we going?" Hazard asked.

"You've got the rolled map from the Commander." I nodded to the tube by his feet. "See what he gave us."

A muffled groan resonated from behind the back seat.

"How long are we keeping him back there?" Weyr called.

"I haven't figured that part out yet," I muttered. A car passed us, shooting along the highway.

"You know how to drive over here?" Rubu leaned forward, pressing his head in the space between Hazard and me.

"I know how to drive anywhere, thank you. I just don't know how fast to go. It's different."

Rubu huffed out a laugh, scoffing.

Something in my pocket vibrated.

Rubu leaned back in his seat.

Remembering the radio McConnell had supplied, I yanked out the black rectangle. *The communication pod Canaan added to our arsenal.* Thumbing the small earpiece off the top corner, I slid the silicone L-shape into my right ear.

The screen display announced I had one audio message waiting. I pressed the word PLAY in the corner of the screen.

McConnell's voice fanned into my eardrum. "Head toward Sete Cidades. I've got Burkman and Canaan. McConnells' en route. Reply when you're on the way. Stay safe."

The word *REPLY* illuminated at the bottom of the screen. A light beep resounded. "Heartbreaker over and out. Hats up." I clicked the word *END* on the display and slid the rectangle back into my pocket. "Hazard." He shook the roll open in his two hands. "Get us to Sete Cidades."

"Sir, what's a Heartbreaker?" Hazard drew the thick paper closer to his face, scanning the lines.

"It was one of the strategies we used on the oxinals back on Isla Barina. Incoming object targeted one or both of us, we'd engage, then exit the perimeter, and round out, returning to the original location or a determined location. It typically confused the unfriendly and we returned to safe territory."

"Do you believe safe territory exists on the field? On duty?"

I rubbed my thumb against the worn material, almost sticky to the touch, on the steering wheel. "You're never off duty. You're simply off the clock."

Road noise diminished our voices, the thundering along the bumpy highway overcoming the hush. The corner of the map flicked, nodding.

"Stay on high alert. The field waits for no man, nor lends mercy," I continued, the blacktop blurring as it charged under our wheels. "But you're Alliance. Alliance isn't just work, it's sanctuary. With a Guardsman at your side, back-up's only a nod away."

"Check *that*!" Clutch exclaimed, pressing her forehead against the window. Outside, among the towering, verdant trees and sumptuous greenery of the mountainside, rose a bulk of moldy cement. The cement wall thrust up into the sky like a layered pyramid. The five levels, octagonal in shape upon our approach, maintained balconies which tilted out and upward to the layer above. I withdrew my foot from the gas pedal, and we slowed, to view a building expanding along the mountaintop, a four-storied cement wonder. Countless broken windows lined the walls facing us on the road winding up the mountain.

The road veered to the right, in a tight curve around the outside of the towering amalgamation.

"Looks like an old hotel," Eagre announced from the back seat.

Overgrown shrubbery, tangled weeds, and gnarled old trees climbed up the small hill between our jeep and the decaying gray cement exterior.

"Are those porches? Balconies?" Clutch whispered.

"I'd stay here," Weyr added. "It's like an ancient marvel."

"It looks like a pagoda." Hazard tipped his head to better see out of his window. "The way the ceilings move in like stairsteps as they get higher."

Around the corner, the road wrapping along the corner of the hotel, the pavement opened into a wide Y-shape where I slowed the pressure on the gas. To the left, the road became gravel and led to an old wire tower, with a disc at the top. To the right, the road looped along the mountain top along the other side of the hotel, continuing to wind down the hill toward the town.

"We *have* to go look at this place," Eagre clapped several times in the back seat.

"Stop the car! Stop the car!" Clutch added her excitement to the mix.

"I can't just stop." I ground my back teeth together.

Eagre cleared her throat. "This is obviously a historical landmark and we'd be missing out on a lifetime experience."

"Somebody owns this property," I insisted.

"Park right there!" Hazard pointed to a large rock beside a wooden fence on the Y-fork leading to the tower. "Looks like a map of the overlook." Beyond his finger, a lake shone below in the valley, as teal as a certain blonde's eyes when she teared up. "I want to look at the lake."

"There's a big wall," I muttered. "I'm turning around. We can get closer to the door." Shifting the wheel, I hand-over-handed us in a circle, the tires crunching on the gravel as we launched in a circle, heading back down the road from where we'd come.

"Park it! Park it!" Clutch chanted.

The others joined with her. "Park it! Park it! Park it!"

An echoing, "Rubu! Rubu! Rubu!" mixed in the incantation. He pumped his fist in the air as he chanted his name.

The parking voters cheered as I veered us up the drive to the yawning exterior. "We are taking ten minutes and no more."

"Can I stop holding this buzzer thing?" Clutch shoved the gray box between Hazard and me.

"I completely forgot about that. The local authorities are going to boot us off this island like a bad pick-up line."

"We've been driving, like, eight hours." She placed the box on the storage console. I yanked the parking break into place and switched the keys in the ignition. The grumbling engine tumbled to a stop.

"Nobody else has been on the road," Hazard commented. "Since we passed Ponta Delgada, we've had no traffic."

Thinking back on the clear roads and considering our options, I rubbed my neck. "Now they know exactly where we are."

"Nah. When we dropped off Snoozy about halfways, I stopped clicking."

"Well, good. And it hasn't been eight hours, it's been one."

Clutch shrugged. "All I know is someone back here has stinky socks, and I need out of this jeep."

The vehicle doors flung open with clicking latches and shufflings of bodies, banter breaking up the quiet of the previous drive.

"Ten minutes." I agreed. "Not a second longer."

They charged the building, boots shuffling, arms swinging in the crisp, open air of the mountaintop. I followed them up the drive leading into what appeared to be the front lobby. Weeds and flowers littered the once-smooth pavement, now torn asunder and riddled with missing bricks and potholes.

Time to check in and see where the others had managed to find themselves. The radio hadn't buzzed with a notification since my sent message. Rubbing my finger along the screen, which lit up, I tapped the word *NEW* in the corner. Selecting *ALL* at the top of the list, I waited for the quiet beep.

"We've found an interesting architectural spectacle outside of Sete Cidades. We're at the top of the mountain. Looks to be an old hotel. The Dragons wanted to explore. Stopping for a quick stretch. Copy?"

I tapped *SEND* and studied the face of the WiCoDe, the slick black casing warming in my palm. My boot kicked a rock and I glanced up. Not a foot before me, a set of stairs led up to what used to be some kind of entry portal leading out from a gaping hole on the ground floor. Halting, I stared up at the relic. The hotel reached out with left and right wings jutting toward the jeep. Between the wings, a green metal structure waited. It must have had an awning over it years prior, an entry for visitors to venture through the missing door. To the right of the old iron remnant a concrete pillar adorned the front wall, a cylinder at least ten feet wide, with old rusty black metal cursive letters anchored vertically from the top of the fourth floor and down, spelling out, "Monte Palace."

The Dragons' voices echoed from within the hollow. Hazard lingered at an old scribbled mess of faded pink, red, and white paint someone had graffitied on the exterior beside the missing doors. Green and black fuzzy scum grew along the concrete surfaces, nature attempting to reclaim its home. Briny breezes gusted through the open first story wings, wide round pillars forcing the wind to halt and reverse. It wanted revenge. But the old pillars had seen years of scorn and yet held, forlorn, resolute.

Rocks crunched under my boots, scratching against the broken ground. A gusty, chilled, pine-scented breeze stirred through the trees jutting up beside the hotel, the branches applauding. The blank windows and dim interior echoed with laughter and conversation. But a ripple stuttered along my sides. We needed to go. Be on the road. We didn't have time to be tourists. My heart hammered within my ribs, counting down the seconds.

"Check this out!" Rubu shouted from the darkness.

"Be careful," I called out. "It's not a playground." Shaking my head, I muttered to myself, "I feel like I'm a parent of toddlers." Once more raising my voice, I added, "Private property. Don't do anything stu...Don't do *anything*."

At the far end of the chamber, Rubu popped his head around the corner of a doorway. "Come on, Thompson. This was an old staircase."

The walls, green with slime and chipped paint, echoed with the footsteps inside the cavernous interior. Moldy, stale air hovered like an invisible cloud. What had once been an elaborate space had crumbled to a ghost of itself. Broken glass, grit, rock fragments, smashed wall scraps, cinderblock bits, and fallen ceiling shards littered the floor, among rank puddles and squishy carpet chunks. An open skylight illuminated the central lobby, dust particles dancing as they soared around, playing tag.

"This is dangerous." The lobby opened into a four-story cavern around me. Balconies running the perimeter of the high, wide area contained cylindrical bulbs protruding, three on the left and right sides of each floor walkway, and one on each end. A crumbly wall filled the end near the front entrance, with a junk-filled base. *Must have been the elevators once upon a time.* Water dripped nearby. I jumped at the sound, my skin rumpling, jittering, at the new territory.

My pocket buzzed, and my skin surged against the moist NEXIS suit sleeves. Shoving a hand in my pocket, I grabbed the WiCoDe and hit *PLAY.*

"We are about five minutes behind you." Saylor's voice rocketed into my ear. "Does the hotel have a bathroom?"

Nice.

I hit *REPLY.* "No, it's ancient. Unless you're okay with using a tree. If so, you're gold."

Drawing up to the stairs where the Dragons had vanished, I nearly stumbled over a beam of some kind, but then jumped over it to splash into a puddle.

"Dragons?" I called out.

Their voices continued to echo from the doorway in the corner of the open area. The small doorway led down a spiral staircase. A muted voice warbled up the hollow. "I have a flashlight. Watch out for the third step down."

More crunching, of scrap and metal underfoot, and a curious chill tumbling from a nearby doorway leading to a room lit by sunlight and missing windows. I stopped to check out the room, a mess of graffitied walls, paint and wallpaper dribbling off their vertical veneer, and sheetrock bits strewn about the floor.

"I don't have a flashlight!" I shouted.

The staircase wound downward into a black, rocky spiral. My insides began to thunder in their trapped housing. This wasn't a good idea.

The WiCoDe buzzed in my palm. Tapped the message. "What kind of hotel doesn't have bathrooms?" Saylor clicked her tongue. "How old is it? Wow, okay, I see the thing now." She paused. "Whoa! We're about to park and head in."

The WiCoDe buzzed once more. "We are in Sete Cidades." *The Commander.* "I'm searching for a specific stop in the city. From the scans, the area looks red hot. Be on full alert. Likely suspects nearby. Expect them armed and dangerous."

I tapped *REPLY.* "Got it, Command. On alert."

Taking the first couple of steps down the staircase, and whoever warned about the third step was correct, because the cement stair was indeed crumbled to slim pickings of a brick, I leaned into the dark hole descending into the unknown. The abyss pooled up the circular stairs as they glided into the belly of the mountain.

"Dragons?"

"There's a whole basement down here. Come on!" Wring's voice skidded upon the walls, smashing against the chambers surrounding us.

"Why did you go down there?" My voice bumped about as well.

"Hello?" Logan's voice bounced around the spacious lobby. Crackling boots, crunching glass. My skin crawled over my muscles.

Leaving the staircase, I hurried to the newest arrivals ducking through the open entry. Logan, Saylor, Thunder, and Flight stood gaping at our surroundings. I met them in the center of the reception area.

"This place. Ridgy didge." My voice sounded much more confident than I felt, even with the echoes bouncing out into the spacious lobby.

Logan stared up at the open skylight, his jaw falling open. The others followed. Saylor focused on me. She leaned closer. "What's wrong?"

I shrugged. "The Dragons decided to go down into the depths of the basement. I mean, why wouldn't you want to explore the upper levels?"

Logan scoffed. "They're more accustomed to tunnels than you are. Where'd they go?"

I tossed my chin over by my shoulder. "Let's go find out."

The WiCoDe buzzed in my hand. A message from the Commander. Tapping the message, I waited for his voice to come through the speaker in my ear. The thing crackled and hummed.

"Do we have to go to the basement?" Flight asked. "I don't want to. I'd rather wait in the car."

"What?" Logan nudged Flight's arm with his elbow. "Not up for a little adventure today?"

"I'm more of a wait-and-see participant."

"You got nothing to lose," Thunder murmured. He wandered into the lobby area. "I think I'll go explore upstairs."

"Everybody stay close," I stated. "Here, Flight. Have my WiCoDe. Be our lookout and message right away if you see anyone."

Flight held out his palm and I plopped the box in it, and then passed along the earpiece. "Free wax. Just for you."

"Thanks, sir. Look at that. You kept it warm for me." He pocketed the radio and placed the piece in his own ear after wiping it down with his thumb.

"It's cozy. Stay in the jeep."

He gave a thumbs-up. Thrusting his fists in the pockets of his navy pants, he pivoted and meandered out the front door.

"Dragons?" Logan stood at the edge of the circular staircase, leaning over at a precarious angle. His greeting ricocheted against the void.

No heat signatures showed on the VISTAS.

No answer.

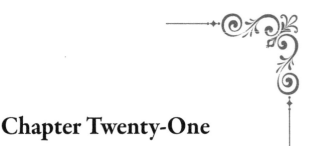

Chapter Twenty-One

THE ARMY OF THE ANONYMOUS
Saylor

L ogan wagged his head toward Tucker and me. "So."

"They're probably exploring some hallway." Tucker sighed. "Let's roll. Watch the third step."

A female scream, trembling, distant, echoed from the depths beyond. Before I could blink, the three of us raced down the steps. All the crumbly rocks and junk slipped along with us down the thin, circular staircase, grabbing at our heels.

"Eagre!" Tucker shouted, one arm waving in the air as he misstepped and nearly tumbled down. He jumped down an extra step to right himself, and then continued circling down into the steep, shadowy second-story below.

"We need a light!" I panted. My left hand skimmed the gritty white wall, helping me keep my sanity in check. It's not like I didn't mind thinking about falling headfirst into a cement, pitch-black basement of an abandoned hotel. But the thoughts were fleeing as fast as my feet down each step.

Logan reached down into the side pocket of his khaki cargo pants and unbuttoned the flap. His boot caught on a jagged rock and I grabbed his shoulder. Steadying us, we halted, as Tucker continued onward.

"Thanks." Logan puffed a deep breath out as he bent over again and withdrew a skinny black stick from the hollow. "Did you say your flying things had a light?"

"Oh."

His words slapped against my forehead and I heaved out a frustrated sigh because I forgot. Logan tapped a button on the end of the stick and continued dashing down the stairs. "Wait up, Tuck." His voice echoed as they finished off the stairway and hurried away into the enveloping blackness.

Squeezing my eyes shut, I leaned against the cool, slick wall. My fingertips slid against the sticky, painted surface. Darkness had no hold upon the grid. The blue shadows haunted my eyelids. Muffled echoes and screams, voices tugging, chattering from the gloomy beyond.

"Activate." I called out the command, hoping they'd miraculously hear. I smacked the wall with my fist. *Are you kidding? It's a computer. All it does is sit and listen.*

"Are you serious? It's a computer. It sits there and listens."

Turning on my heel, I sought the source of the girl's voice behind me.

One gray boot stepped down a stair, and then another, until her knees became visible, in fitted red lycra, and her thin waist, belted with a black and silver utility belt. She stopped on the stairs above me, those muscular shoulders rolling back at a jaunty angle. She tossed her head to the side, blonde hair flipping over her shoulders.

Six feet away, even I could see that not only did she mirror me, she trumped me, surpassing me in every possible way. My insides shrunk, as if smashed and smoldering. I was the shadow, the lacking, the worn.

"Activate," I whispered, the dry words caught in my humbled throat. "Engage."

"Welcome to my castle." Her hollow voice edged against the tight space between us. It didn't echo. She slid one boot down a step. Cement crumbled under her boot.

"You live here?"

Her stained red lips slid into a smirk. "You live here?" Another boot paced down another step.

"Stop it."

"Stop it."

I grunted. I won't say I was mature about how I wanted to act right then. My ribcage shuddered, sure, and heat soared up into my pale cheeks. Balling up my fist, I waved it in the air before me. "Don't move another step."

Neon blue vertical and horizontal lights wrestled with vigor and thrill while the grid flourished around me. The SIMPLs awoke.

A shadow slipped into view on the wall behind the crimson Better Me. "Saylor?" Micah's voice echoed down the stairwell.

"I'm down here," I shouted. "So's the fake one." In a blink, I shouted, "Ignite!" and the other girl jumped over my head, her boot kicking off the wall, and then shoving the remaining feet to the ground. She darted away around a corner into the darkness, fusing with the army of the anonymous.

My SIMPLs floated freely above the slim white staircase, as Micah descended the stairs with caution behind them.

She held the black SIMPL case in her hand. "I noticed you left this in the jeep."

"Get that potty break you needed?"

"Yeah, and well-timed, I see."

"Logan and Tucker have disappeared down here, along with all but two of the Dragons," I whispered. "The one with the wild hair and the anxious one with the Hispanic accent. Flight? He should have been in the jeep."

"I think he's more Filipino. He isn't Hispanic."

"Okay." I shrugged.

"Regardless, he's not in the jeep."

I slapped my thigh. Exhaled. "Great." I flicked a look up to my hovering SIMPLs. "Razz. Lead the way."

The pyramid-like piece glowed brighter, the white light soaring down to about a foot above my head. The SIMPL flew before me, fixed to my location on the grid wherever I would roam.

Micah's jaw opened, both eyes wide, as she stared at the piece overhead. "Saucy."

"We've got to find them. Someone screamed."

"Walk softly."

"And let the SIMPLs zap the enemy."

Water droplets tapped each other in a pool somewhere beyond the shadows. Razz illuminated the space around us, a dank, maze-like level of cement building left alone for years to disintegrate on its own volition. Water puddled up among broken timber, walls, rocks, and remnants of dreams long banished.

"I truly wish I had my NEXIS HUD right now," Micah whispered behind me.

"Ditto." I agreed, hushed. "And yes, infrared or thermal scanner would be helpful right about now."

"Don't happen to have those in your head anymore, do you?"

"Unfortunately, no. But I think my little friends can help us."

Footprints fell, echoing down the hallway, from the left.

"Did you hear that?" Micah halted. "Something moved." She pointed to the right.

Shaking my head, I splayed the SIMPLs in all directions. If I could map the basement better, we could move with more direction and ease. Like bats. Or whales. I huffed a quick chuckle at the idea of being known as whale-girl. Not awesome.

We drew up to a wide, open room with a low, rusted ceiling. My skin shuddered as we entered the vault, bumps prickling at the scuffles of the shadows and the haunting grunts treading through the vast landing. Our boots splattered through the shadowy puddles and dusty crumbs. Winds moaned as they churned down the staircase.

"I feel like we're those two people in a horror film where the audience shouts, 'Don't go in there!' at them." Micah slid her boot through a clump of debris and shook it, stumbling over more craggy brick pieces. "Who littered the floor so bad? They're fired."

"I'm sure the destructors will be sure to come back later and sweep up." I paused then, watching the SIMPLs meet the ends of the space. At the far end of the room, the gridlines swelled and bobbled, like a mirage. My sonar plan succeeded. Someone strode toward us.

"I believe I have someone you'd like to meet." His voice slithered through the chamber.

Blood hurtled through my ears, ringing bells as it did, whipping chaos through my blurred vision. "Who's there?" I called out.

Micah, to her credit, merely moved back a step from where she'd been. She grabbed my elbow, and my whole body shuddered. My grasping fingers reached for her. My sweaty palm patted her arm, squeezed, and then released.

Micah cleared her throat.

"Why don't you turn on the lights." I commanded, more than asked.

"Unfortunately, because of the many tourists who used to explore these premises, we had to resist installing working light fixtures in here. Seeing they'd simply have been stolen anyway. We didn't want the façade broken."

Façade?

"Where did everyone go?" My voice wavered.

"Please follow me. I'm turning on a flashlight for you to follow. The pathway has been cleared for you."

A bright light burst forth, white rays radiating across the chasm. Sure enough, the light glanced off the watery floor, and a clear path through the debris, straight through the gap, reflected the way.

"Come, come." His friendly voiced receded away from us. "This way." The light shook and fluctuated, dispensing a glow around the gray walls and several columns towering from floor to ceiling throughout the space. The man's silhouette tread away from us. His shoes splashed through the puddles.

Puffing out my cheeks, I widened my eyes at Micah.

She copied the look, and our foreheads creased at the same time. I nodded.

She nodded. She inclined her forehead to the man.

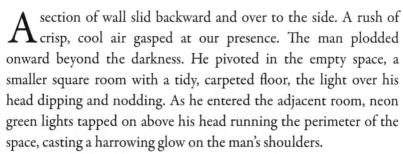

A section of wall slid backward and over to the side. A rush of crisp, cool air gasped at our presence. The man plodded onward beyond the darkness. He pivoted in the empty space, a smaller square room with a tidy, carpeted floor, the light over his head dipping and nodding. As he entered the adjacent room, neon green lights tapped on above his head running the perimeter of the space, casting a harrowing glow on the man's shoulders.

My SIMPLs, Micah, and I progressed after him, Razz casting its own white glow. The man's face stayed shadowed, although his gray hair reflected the dim light, and his slumped shoulders appeared more drained than dangerous. But we all know appearances deceive.

One guarded step at a time I assessed our surroundings. With a quick wave of my hand, I recalled the SIMPLs, and they collected with Razz. Clicking, they snapped in place like a puzzle, and the ball dropped into my palm. The man tapped a brown stain on the wall, noxious lights above us illuminating a living night-vision scape. Green everywhere. The wall groaned, sliding closed between the littered basement and us.

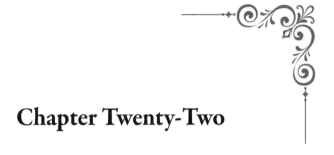

Chapter Twenty-Two

UNFRIENDLY
Tucker

H is bloody knuckle slammed into my eye socket. For a moment an impenetrable black slid around my vision, but I stumbled away. Fists up. Guard the chin. I slung out a wide right hook, missing the man in the black security uniform. The gold name tag pinned on his shoulder unhinged and fell to the floor with a tinny rattle.

"Ye can stop wrasslin' now," he hollered.

"McConnell!" I shouted.

"I've got him in a headlock," Logan's reply grunted between his gritted teeth.

We'd found the two guards at a back door, shining their bright mag-lights at us and yelling. They'd run at us full hilt, fists slinging and nightsticks pummeling.

A swift side kick and I hit the guard's knee. His leg buckled, but he swung around with his right fist. I blocked it, and then shanked a heavy jab at his jaw.

"Any time you're ready to stop, I am too," I panted.

Logan flipped his guard over, the crunch of bone, muscle, and debris clashing against the cement underfoot. Then Logan arched his back, his face writhing in a red grimace, the shout gone silent. A sweeping buzz crackled through the air. The guard had tazed him.

"Stop!" I shouted, but too late. Logan froze, except for the uncontrollable jerking and twitching to the rhythm of the electricity pulsing through his veins.

The second guard then held up a blade before my eyes, the steel glinting in a dropped flashlight's beam. "Ye'd best come about." His gritty voice matched the week-old stubble lining his jaw. Rank puffs of air blew from his winded chest, heaving up and down.

My palms seized the sky.

It was then I realized he didn't wear a guard's uniform, but a black robe twisted all about his frame, tied with a thick, buckled belt. Long black boots wound up his legs until just below his knee. One eye stared at me, green as spring's sprouting fields; the other shone back white and hazy, cloudy as winter's foggy ghost.

He dragged me by the back of my shirt collar through a maze of tunnels and hallways, through a locked door, and down another circular staircase. The clattering metal didn't so much bug me as the void beneath them. The other guard carried a semi-conscious Logan over his shoulder.

Their boots clanked in time to the ticking clock in my brain.

Where are the Dragons?

Round and round we went, he shoving me from the side, cuffing me to keep me just enough off balance, until about three more stories down we reached a clean cement floor. The other man drew up on the left beside me.

Logan shifted his head, and his eye glinted in the shadows. He nudged his chin. I dipped mine.

Flinging my right fist into my guardian's ribcage, his howling wail trembled through the gloom. Flesh crunched against flesh, a mashing of sinew and bone. I ducked a blow, then pummeled his chin with a sick jab. He slung his knife every which way, grunting.

Logan flipped over his guard's shoulder, arms tangled around the man's leg. He folded the man into a pretzel, their grunts shuffling beside us.

I needed to disarm my opponent and end the row.

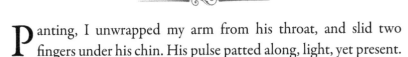

Panting, I unwrapped my arm from his throat, and slid two fingers under his chin. His pulse patted along, light, yet present. Logan straightened, tugging the edge of his banana shirt.

"I'm putting on my GRIPS." I exhaled a deep gust of air, allowing my lungs to catch up from the struggle. Yanking the sleeves of the NEXIS suit down to my wrists, the cool fabric enveloped my sweaty arms. I slung the straps over my thumbs. The chill swam across my skin and up my arms.

"Good idea." Logan gestured to his torso. "If I lose the shirt, do you think I'll be able to maintain my motivation?" He raised his eyebrows and wiggled them.

"That shirt may live on in your memory forever." The GRIPS awaited use in my left pants pocket. I reached down, extracting the black and gray gloves. Slipping them over my hands and tapping the latches down into a locked position, the blue lights outlining the fingers buzzed aglow. Power surged around my fingertips and through my veins. The GRIPS connected with the NEXIS and the VISTAS. Energy coursed through me.

Logan balled up the banana shirt and chucked it against the wall behind the staircase. He'd straightened out the arms of his NEXIS as well, adjusting the buckle across his chest. "So, what do you say? Left or right?"

"You good to go? That was quite the electric charge."

Logan lifted his left shoulder and then dropped it again. "Eh. I've had worse."

"I suppose if we zip-tie them, we're ruining our chances of friendly engagement?"

Logan cleared his throat. "They charged us. As far as I'm concerned, they're the ones we're looking for. Unfriendly to start."

"Confirm jackpot." I whipped out a bundle of the plastic from my pocket.

"Jackpot."

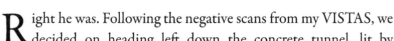

Right he was. Following the negative scans from my VISTAS, we decided on heading left down the concrete tunnel, lit by occasional yellow ceiling light. Eerie.

A man in a tattered red shirt rounded a corner ahead, and quickly turned tail. We charged him, to find a second man with him, fleeing. We caught them before the long hall ended and overcame them. Grunts, smacking flesh, and crackling snaps of muscle and concrete mashed through the hall. Unconscious, the men slept as we zip-tied their ankles and wrists.

"You might be more careful with those GRIPS," Logan whispered. "You broke his nose. It's floppy now. Look at all the blood."

"You have a point."

A locked, metal door filled the end of the tunnel, a black shiny plate on the wall beside it. Buttons glowed, a mix of numbers and letters awaiting purpose. Checking the menu in the top right corner of my VISTAS, I selected the option to scan for thermal signatures. As I leaned closer to study the panel further, the door slid open into the wall, and two more men in black clothing barged through the door.

I think they were as surprised to see us as we were to see them, so they paused for only a second before I smacked one right in the jaw with my right hook and pummeled a swift uppercut to his chin with my left. He collapsed inside the door.

The other man jumped into the hallway, his right arm flying, and he surged to Logan, who nailed him in the ribs with a one-two jab and a wicked left hook to his eye-socket. The guard tried clawing his way around Logan's neck, but Logan twisted free.

Another man, in white pants and a blue shirt ran to us, shouting foreign words. The whites of his eyes strained, the red veins popping out, and his wide-open jaw rattling out a list of words. I grabbed his free arm and flipped him over my back, and then slammed him against the wall behind me. He grunted, gripping my neck with his clammy palm, digging fingernails into my flesh. Bellowing, I grabbed his hand and ripped it free, my GRIPS crushing his hand. He screamed. With a gusty punch to his temple I allowed him several hours to sleep off the pain until his medics could help.

The power of the GRIPS curdled my blood. My insides swelled up, while my senses triggered all over the map. Heat signatures appeared, surrounding us. One man lunged at Logan, another pouncing at his leg. Two men hurled through the air to me, a third, fourth, and a fifth even tackling one limb at a time. Two of them wrapped their arms around my right arm. With my left, I punched every angle and piece of sinew I could reach.

But they overtook us. The many heat signatures contained us. One man, his bronze eyes staring down into mine draped his arm around my throat. His muscles flared, contracting against my throat.

Darkness settled in like an old friend. A hazy one, at that. The warmth of the bodies above and around me crowded my vision. Sweaty iron and charred onions swelled as a parched aftertaste within my mouth.

A pounding pulse tapped within my ears, winding down as a clock dying.

Chapter Twenty-Three

RUBBISH
Saylor

The elevator door groaned beneath us, creaking as it nestled down into its chamber further and further beneath the earth's surface. Micah cleared her throat. She began fiddling with the fabric at her collar, wiggling her neck uncomfortably.

I studied the man out of the corner of my vision, his black sport jacket settled and calm as we rode down into the earth's belly.

Shuddering to a stop, the elevator made a thumping noise.

"This way, please." The man swept to the side, and a rush of air swished in. Beyond the sliding door, a straight line of lights dotted the shadowed ceiling of a cave tunnel. Carved rock walls held no warning or indication of where they led, but the man plodded onward, unhurried, and unaware of danger.

I followed him, Micah by my side, and buried the SIMPL in my pocket. Before I'd had a chance to grow any gray hair, but longer than it took to consider multiple times what on earth we were doing, we drew up to a door, where the tunnel ended abruptly. The door had a window, a small square just higher than my direct line of sight right in the middle. The man held up a hand against a shiny black square panel beside the doorframe. Tapping on several keys illuminating upon the panel, the man leaned forward enough so I couldn't follow his fingers.

Somewhere within the wall a click resounded, and the door swung inward. He pressed the door open. The ceiling opened up, exploding above us as a central hub of some cavernous underground, cinderblock-encrusted work center. Large box-like gray machines filled the center of the room. The machines resounded from their spots, crunching and crashing and mashing metal upon metal.

"You'll want to stay on the red path," the man said.

Below our feet, a waxed concrete floor shined underneath the sparkly white lights overhead. A red painted line led the way from the door we'd just entered, to the right of the machines, past several doors, and finally into a dim hallway far on the other side of the room. Along the red paint, blue, orange, purple, and yellow lines also led different directions. A dotted green line led straight into the midst of the machines. A white skull had been painted in the center of every other green dot.

The man had continued into the room along the red line. Micah hunkered onward, unphased by the gargantuan room.

Through the dim tunnel we strode, until the man stopped at a closed door on the right. He knocked three times on the cream-colored door, and then twisted the silver knob.

"Sir," he offered into the cracked-open door, his drooping, bushy eyebrows furrowing over the bridge of his nose, "I've brought the ladies."

Another man's voice muttered something from within, and the man pushed the door open wider. He waved into the room, stepping aside to let us pass.

At the back of the room, a large brown desk piled up with tossed papers and crooked stacks of books hid a bushy mop of tangled gray curls. His head bowed over the papers and a thick black pen in his left hand. He held up his right pointer finger as if to indicate we ought to wait for his attention.

The man closed the door behind us with a sigh.

Micah and I exchanged a glance.

My heart clattered around within its bars, uncertain and assessing. Its rumblings made a wave of heat wrestle through my veins, the grid glowing while it surrounded us. Along the back wall, on a gray platform, bookshelves filled the space. Books of all shapes, sizes, and colors had been crammed into the nooks in no order. Some hardbacks lay with the spine facing out, some the spine in so the pages faced out, and some lay with the spine facing up. Occasional pamphlets and individual scraps of paper stuck out from between the books. Every inch had been utilized.

On top of the middle shelf unit, a green metal statue of a humbled man with a gigantic golden globe rested upon his brawny shoulders. He gripped his burden with powerful hands, a cape nestled between his back and the waters of the globe, wrapping around his waist, and crumpling upon the ground where he knelt.

"As it would happen," the bushy-haired man stated, still writing, "I'm on a strict deadline. You've arrived at a precarious time for me, so I'll have to make our meeting briefer than I would normally." The man raised his head, and then flickered his bright blue eyes up to us. His leathery face, tan and wrinkled, stretched down into the high collar of a dark gray uniform jacket. He had a beard, the curly gray mass of tangled hairs identical to his head but drawing to a point several inches beneath his chin. None of the hair moved on its own as his head bobbed, but moved along with his skin. Same with the wrinkles. His skin had seen too many days in the sun, long since turning into one thick, brown, waxy wrapper covering his bones. Gray met brown like the seashores of the moon. Those blue eyes, graying at the edges, sliced through the tense hush of the room.

"Welcome to Atlantis. I employ all my guests. You may now choose if you would join me or be put out with the daily rubbish."

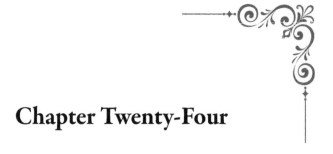

Chapter Twenty-Four

CAGED DRAGONS
Tucker

Concrete. All around. The cavernous walls. Ceiling above, dotted with sparkling white lights in a grid of steel girders, rising what, three stories above me? Sounds echoed, shuffles and bumps and groans and clankings every which way. Drills spun, whining. Oil and grease warmed upon the gears, shuffling through the stale, chilly air.

I surged up to a sitting position, my head reeling. Those cement pillars supporting the walls churned toward the horizon.

"Whoa. Hold." Logan's familiar low voice whisked from behind me. "You've been out for about twenty minutes."

"Should I even ask where we are or what's going on?" My bound wrists prevented my bare hands to rub my swollen eyelids. My vision slowly adjusted to the dim shadows where we sat against the wall, while the harsh overhead bulbs beamed down from high above.

"To your right, our friendly neighborhood bad guys have installed what looks to be a laboratory, with glass cubicles and an assembly line where they're constructing, I'm not sure. Something big.

"In the center of the room you'll see large metal machines, which also appear to produce large things. Between the two spaces, you will see gigantor sliding doors which lead to mysterious tunnels, which open every so often and a big black bin enters or exits on a track leading to the production machines. And to your left—" Slumped in his sitting position, Logan held up a palm to downturned heads seated beside us. "Caged Dragons. Slice and dice, we serve 'em nice."

Rubu huffed a breath through his nose. "You're so apt with the descriptions, Lieutenant McConnell."

"What?" Logan shrugged. "Big. Large. Things. There. I'm a words person, obviously."

"What's all of it do?"

"Make loud noises." Logan grunted.

"Head check," I announced.

"We're all here," Weyr spoke up from beside Rubu. He stated it, calm and smooth as a matchstick before the strike.

With my hands still crossed in the tightly bound black zip tie before me, I searched the group. One, two, three...seven, eight, nine. Case's black eyes zeroed in on me. Ten. Blinking, I re-counted.

Case stood. Hands unbound, ankles free, he strode to me. I could feel my eyebrows wrinkling over my nose. He'd died. He'd sunk and disappeared in the explosion.

Case bent his knees, weight on his toes, and he lowered to a squat before me. One knee of his black cargo pants touched the dusty cement. "No, you're right. Here I am."

My heart stammered. Bolts of electricity shot through my ribs, and my arms jerked.

"You're alive! How? What?" Words stumbled through the mess of spaghetti known as my vocal chords. Delight, confusion, loss, dread, excitement, all pierced through the words on my tongue and down into the base of my gut.

One by one, the Dragons arose. They'd all changed into matching black cargo pants and black fitted shirts, the arms fading to a dark gray from the shoulders and down to the sleeves.

Logan and I paused, our jaws staggered, realization reckoning.

The Dragons slunk beside and behind Case, the group surrounding us.

My tongue dried up from the cold shimmying down my spine, and from the heat flushing my chest.

"I rescued you," I stated. Licked my lips. "I carried each one of you out of the fire. Out of Rapton's grasp. With my own two arms. You're not—you're not—" Words left me, silent as shamed ash.

Case tapped my knee with his palm. "And that's why we took your GRIPS."

My brain knew nothing other than to defend. Knees cracking against the waxed cement, I hurtled to my feet. I had to look them in the eyes. I had to see their pirated pride. My aching spine needed to check their volition. My year of heartache, teaching, hand-holding, herding, inspiring, sequestering, demanded recourse. I wouldn't find it in their deadlights. Soot lined their resolve. Smoke curled from their treacherous fangs, glinting in the pearly incandescence.

A drill spun in the background, purring, howling, grinding toward some malicious end.

"You've been chosen, selected, as a part of Alliance. You can undo whatever you've begun, right now." I nodded to the machines. "Stop whatever this plan calls for and reconfigure your purpose. You decide right now."

Thunder tossed his shoulders back, straightening, shoving a hand in his pocket. "I wore the Alliance uniform. Didn't fit well." His lips curled up in a smirk.

"You can wear the uniform, but it doesn't make you part of the team. The heartbeat underneath counts. That blood throttles, pumping, willing to spill for the men on the line beside you. That wrenching tremor pulsing through your gut, unable to sit still to watch the fire reign down, qualifies to you be Alliance. Not some name-tag or form you filled out. Where's your allegiance?"

Case chewed on the inside of one cheek. He studied the ceiling, and then rolled his eyes my way. "I guess all I wanted to do was fill out the form."

"But what are you doing? I've given you the tools to be a part of Alliance's new mission. We're moving forward, progressing mankind's efforts to survive. Tell me you're not going back to Rapton's goal of destroying everything."

"Oh, no." Case offered a quick smile. "This plan has a more lasting effect."

"Then, what?"

Case's white teeth glared in the lights.

Clutch tossed her head, her curls bouncing around on her forehead. "Can't you tell we were meant to be Dragons? Trying to be anything else is too hard."

With my wrists throbbing, I straightened my shoulders. "Life's challenging no matter what course you choose. Alliance calls for you to invest all of you. This project, whatever you're doing, asks the same. Pick your hard."

"I pick the other kind. Alliance can burn." Clutch spun on her heel then, her boot squeaking against the wax. She waved one hand to a passing man in black and gray, carrying a large brown box.

"You'd choose to kill because it's easier? You give up because you can give it a label and quantify it?" Heat throttled through my veins, spurting with the blood roiling against my sinew. How dare they give up, give in. "Where's Adenauer? Who's convinced you? What's your plan?"

"So many questions, Señor Thompson." Rubu grinned. "We're not killing anybody. Not yet."

Clutch called over her shoulder. "We were built with one purpose. We're doing that work now."

"If only I'd convinced you to be so mission-oriented for Alliance."

"Now, Thompson." Weyr clicked his tongue, "How do you feel when you tell yourself such statements?"

Blowing hot air out of my nose, I clamped my jaw shut. They'd not toss my words back at me again.

Weyr continued his chiding, his green eyes flashing. "Who would you be if you told yourself the opposite?"

Eagre drew up to my left, sliding her arm through mine. She pressed her chest against my bicep. "You're so predictable Tucker. We know all your psychology tricks and standards and rules and hopes. I know if I tell you to look in one direction you'll do it. And meanwhile, in my other hand, I've performed the magic trick. What do you think Logan would have to say about all this?"

"What do you—" Over my shoulder, past Eagre, Logan's spot now remained empty.

Eagre's soft, smooth skin, inches from my cheek, smelled of vanilla and strawberries. A familiar scent, identical to Saylor's. She pouted her wet, glossy lips, jutting out the bottom one.

"What did you do with Logan?" I demanded, scanning their beady lizard eyes and bulbous, steamy snouts.

A hand slid out from the group of them, followed by a shoulder, and the slim, pale features of none other than Shadow. Resurrected and present as the black hair relaxing over her shoulder, her blue eyes stared back at me.

Breath constricted in my throat, teaming and screaming and seething with ire. With relief. I managed to whisper her name. "Shadow."

"Sergeant Thompson."

"You're alive."

"Couldn't kill me if you tried."

A noise rustled to my right. I scanned for the sound to find Hazard siding up to me. He reared back his right arm. The last thing I saw was his balled-up fist, flying at my face.

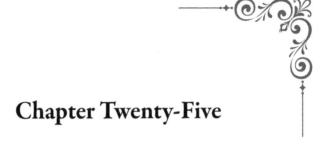

Chapter Twenty-Five

GODDESS OF THE UNDERWORLD
Saylor

"I'm sorry." A twinge shuddered down from the roots of my hair into the base of my spine. "We're here to clear up some issues and find the source of lost articles which are the property of Alliance."

"My dear," the man sighed, "please do not belittle me with your prattlings. I've been—as I said, on a tight deadline. Are you in or out?"

"Well," Micah interrupted, placing her hands on her hips. "Can't we get a rundown of what both options consist of? I mean, join or die, or something, I'm not too sure what 'being put out with the rubbish' entails, but those are opposite ends of the spectrum. What are we joining?"

He rose from his seat, the wooden chair legs scraping against the cement floor. "Would you join the ranks of the immortal?"

I glanced at Micah. Clicked my tongue. "May I ask your name, sir?"

He narrowed one eye, lifting his chin in indignation. "Saylor, my dear, you lack many certain qualities, none of which I couldn't have repaired should you have arrived sooner." He blew a deep, exhausted breath through his lips. "You may call me Poseidon, should you elect to establish yourself as one of my subordinates."

"I'm Micah." She jutted her thumb toward her chest.

"Yes, I know."

Micah shrugged. "Didn't want to be left out."

"I know that about you, as well." He rounded his desk, the dark gray cloak surrounding his dark gray pants enveloping his legs and into some tall velvet black boots which padded his steps. Poseidon glided to us as if he didn't touch the ground. He wrapped his long, tan fingers around Micah's shoulder. "I have a place for you. Just for you. Should you choose to accept."

"What's the job?" Micah's shoulders tightened with his hand upon her green shirt. She folded her arms over her chest, balling up those fists.

"Tsk." Poseidon released her shoulder. "Decide first."

"Shoddy options."

"Sir," I interjected, "Have you been working in conjunction with the pirates stealing Alliance's property?" I knew the bold question could land us further beneath the ground than the rubbish pile, but I needed answers. I was Alliance. They stole my property, they sank my boat, and they threatened my boyfriend. No one in a gray cloak would stop me from reclaiming what was mine. And I knew my squad would be on their way soon.

"Saylor, Micah, since I am heading there anyway, allow me to escort you to the throne room."

A beep resounded from the door.

Poseidon strolled around us, the door swinging inward as he approached. Outside in the hall, a black box on wheels awaited.

"Come, ladies." He lifted a hidden latch on the side, a black lever matching the shiny black of the vehicle, and stepped up inside. As he did, the action reminded me of Breame and the cart up on Heart Mountain. The cart had a similar look to it, a plain rectangle with black bench seats running along both ends of the inside, but utilized wheels instead of a train track. My heart knocked against my spine then, nudging, tapping, the pulse increasing as it did.

Hush. We have to investigate. We need answers.

I strode after him, motioning to Micah with what I hoped was a carefree wave, and climbed up into the cart. Poseidon seated himself on the back seat, facing forward. I plopped down beside him, firm and decisive about it, and Micah climbed in across, facing us. She pursed her lips, resolved herself. I kept one hand on the SIMPL in my pocket, hiding the item with my palm.

After Micah sat, I yanked the door shut, and it echoed with a *thunk* in the long, dim hall.

Poseidon pressed a button on a display to his left. After several quiet beeps, the cart hummed and slid forward. The wheels powered us along through the hallway, cool, humid air tossing the loose hairs across my forehead. With my free right hand, I combed the hairs out of my face. The brisk air snapped soft kisses against my cheeks, whispering what lay at the end of the hall would not be so relaxing.

Our cart hummed along for several minutes, the long hall eventually curving the slightest.

Poseidon stared straight ahead.

Micah and I avoided eye contact, but every now and then I'd catch her trying not to look at him.

He had to be Adenauer. But his Alliance photo on his file looked severely different. The black and white photo of a clean-cut, strong, proud man with a high-and-tight haircut appeared nothing like this character. What had happened?

The lights increased at the end of the tunnel, where one large door defended the space behind it. Four men in dark gray uniforms, with black masks over their faces, holding formidable black rifles across their chests guarded the silver door. A gigantic wheel filled its middle, containing bars which latched to the concrete walls on both sides.

While the cart drew nearer, Poseidon waved one bored hand. They lowered their guns. All four guards grabbed the wheel, turning it to the side. Creaking, groaning, the door swung outward. Bright white lights streamed through the growing opening.

"Here we are." Poseidon tapped the keypad and the cart door swung open to my right. Micah and I caught glances, and I tipped my head to the space. She rose and tumbled out, her boots squeaking against the concrete. I followed, jumping to the hard ground. Poseidon seemed to hover down from the cart, and the door swung shut behind him. He stepped around us and nodded to his guardians. They gathered their guns, continuing to threaten even the air which might forget their power and threaten their director.

Beyond the wall, the ceiling vaulted upward for several stories. Beside a metallic grid lining the inside of the cavernous space, the echoing voices of workers and twinkling white lights all diminished compared to the colossal monument occupying the center of the room. Reposing on a metal scaffolding, tipped back on its massive end, a bulk of shining metal and sparkling blue glass commanded attention. Resembling a shapely pyramid, pillar-like cylinders anchored upon the corners of the trinity. The pillars held their own cyclone-like appearance, with the skinny end pointing to the steel girders lining the ceiling. Gigantic black boosters rested at the large bases of the corner cylinders. The blue glass windows served to form a type of belt circling the middle of the pyramid.

My breath caught up with me. The words slunk out, awed. "What am I seeing here?"

Poseidon stared at the vessel. "I call her Earthshine. Magnificent, isn't she? Come."

He strode to the left of the construction, where a scaffolding staircase led up to the base of the platform where what looked like a door or hatch appeared, waiting, gaping. Climbing down from a ladder within, a pair of gray boots then jumped down onto the platform. In her slinky red leather outfit, my other half appeared. Her lips shimmied up into a lopsided smirk. I didn't know how annoying that could be. Logan's disposition toward me suddenly made a lot of sense. My cheeks heated, and I clenched my jaw.

"You've met Persephone. She's my number two around here, depending on the day. Should you choose wisely, you'll answer to her."

"Persephone?" I repeated.

"Yes. Goddess of the Underworld. We've been working on her for some time. Shame you couldn't have ended up like her. I wish your father hadn't insisted upon breaking you like he did. But he's always been a trouble maker, doing things his own way, deviating from the rules and the definitive mission."

I couldn't help the laugh ruffling out my throat. "My dad? Deviating from the mission?"

"He was always sort of a firebrand. He's the one who instigated all our trouble."

"I'll have to write that down some time." Another chuckle played on my nervous lips.

"Zeus spoke highly of him."

"Who?" Micah blurted out. "What kind of game are y'all playing down here? I feel like I'm in some weird alternate universe."

"Perhaps you've been granted admission to the greatest story of your life, Miss Fortuyn. I don't recommend dismissing it before you understand the ramifications."

Micah let her fists drop.

The girl in red settled her palm on the railing of the stairs. *Persephone.* She'd tightened her hair into a high ponytail on the back of her head, a thick red ribbon tied around the base of it. The ribbon matched the scarlet lipstick she'd applied, glistening under the lights. She studied us through narrowed eyes.

Poseidon wiped away invisible fuzz on his pant leg. "You may know Zeus by his former name, Wellington Breame."

"Former name?"

"He'll rise again. He is Zeus, after all."

"I'm—" I paused, unable to sort my thoughts. "I'm sorry? Who? He will what?"

Poseidon's blue eyes scorched mine. "If you cannot keep up, I do believe we are at an impasse. I require the best in my upper cabinet."

"Sir, um, Po—Poseidon, sir, I—May I ask a few questions?"

"I have no time for questions." He spun away.

"Breame always had time for me."

Poseidon halted.

"What plans did my father divert from?" I questioned. "He has the board on his side. They ousted everyone else. Breame. Rapton. They're gone."

He rotated in his spot, shoulders stiffening. "Gone?"

"They—quit."

"You call attacked by assassins in the middle of the night 'quitting'?"

I shrugged my shoulders. "Well, you know. Breame's not with Alliance anymore."

Poseidon angled his chin, squinting. "And of Chevalier? Ibrahim?"

I have no idea who those names belong to. Just pretend you know what you're doing. I shrugged again. "Gone."

His chest rose and fell. He quieted.

I softened. "Didn't you know?"

His lips twisted, not forming any audible words. Then he froze, and his eyes focused on the wall above my head. He sauntered away, calling for Persephone as he did. "If they try anything, kill them."

The WiCoDe network in my ear crackled, as if connecting to an incoming message. No message buzzed through. *C'mon Canaan, Dad. Logan? Tucker? Do you copy? Where is everybody?*

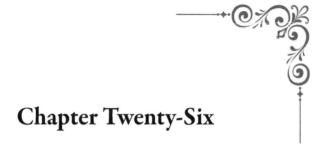

Chapter Twenty-Six

THE DESPAIR
Tucker

My hands still strapped before me, the blast of energy ripped through my skull. If I didn't think of Thunder as a Dragon, I'd say Hazard's punch blasted away all my conscious strength with a thunderous force. But their betrayal fueled the grit in my teeth. Shredded. In an instant, my world had fragmented. I had Alliance, but they didn't know where I was. I had Saylor, but she'd disappeared. I had my two locked wrists, but not my GRIPS. Wind throttled through my lungs, echoing Hazard's sentiment.

I staggered back a step.

My right eye refused to open, the swelling immediate and intense.

Heat and fire splintered through my diminished, blurry vision, and tingles of electric needles splattered out from the point of impact. My brain sloshed.

My left knee pummeled to the ground. *Crack.*

"Take him to Poseidon," Eagre ordered. "He's due an audience."

Boots stalked toward me. I shook my head, cringing against the dizzy reeling. Two hands grabbed my left arm and two gripped my right. They heaved me up to my feet, lugging me away from the corner, and paraded me across the shiny floor. I stumbled, but the two Dragons lurched onward. Hazard. Weyr. The others stood in their semicircle, captured with their own plans to meet with this mysterious Poseidon character.

I had no interest in what they had to say.

They hustled me out of another tunnel arch, until we entered an open doorway leading to a stairwell. Down one level we thumped, until we reached the platform for the next. Weyr released my arm and grabbed the door handle. When his back was to us, Hazard lunged against Weyr's spine. His lithe arm knocked a series of lightning strikes to Weyr's ear, while wrapping a leg around Weyr's middle. The two clattered to the floor, Hazard's fists a series of staccato drumbeats against Weyr's face. Weyr rolled over, his hands grasping for Hazard, and he unleashed a series of knocks against Hazard's leg and one against his rib. But Hazard slid his leg around Weyr's right leg, and the two locked in combat against the cold concrete. Hazard finally wrapped his left arm around Weyr's neck.

The crackling gurgle lasted only for a moment.

Hazard panted, his core stiff as he surrounded his foe.

Weyr's body went limp. His hand slapped against the ground.

Breath mixed with spit in my throat. Setting my jaw, my chest heaving, the red tint filtered around me. I slid back a step.

"You've got to get out of here." Hazard's voice echoed against the concrete steps, bouncing on the cinderblocks. "I'll take care of his body." Hazard rose, dusting off his hands. Weyr's boot clapped the ground with a smack.

"What are you doing?" My breath wheezed through my words.

"I'm sorry I punched you. I didn't want them to question my motives." Hazard reached into his back pocket. When he extended his hand, he held two black gloves in his palm.

I stared at him.

"When I had no hope, you saw me. I held so close to the despair, but you never once let me believe it was as powerful as me." Hazard straightened his shoulders, drawing in a heavy breath. "You helped me run when I could not even crawl on my own. Naming potential over my weaknesses, you encouraged me to be more than I thought I could be. You didn't tell me to get over my pain and loss, but walked beside me through it. I found purpose for the pain. I am forever grateful. I'd rather spend my limited hours on earth here with my guard, as Alliance, than an eternity with those who'd indulge in their own power. You operate on the potential, rather than the outcome. They insist on instilling fear. Now I know I can do better." His stormy gaze met mine, then studied the ceiling.

"One." My words melted into the echoing chamber.

Hazard focused on me, tilting his head. "What?"

"One. You're the only one I helped. Out of all those I helped carry to safety. Spent my life the last year—What about the Dragons back home? Are they causing a revolution as well?"

"No more Dragons exist at Fort Story."

The flinching twist of the knife rammed against my ribs. "They're headed here?"

"They're already here."

"Is this what you meant? The mission to head home? The pillars of the universe? Why didn't you tell me the truth? Why lie?"

Hazard shook, his hair rustling under the nervous energy. "The Dragons threatened me that night. Said they'd kill me if I said another word. They do not trust me. I lied and said I did not understand the protocol for this reason. It is why I had to strike, so they could see my allegiance to them."

"How can *I* trust you?"

"Take your GRIPS." He insisted, shaking them. "I don't play games. You know me."

I reached with both hands crossed before me and accepted them. "I believe you. You're the only one I ever thought to share my books with."

Hazard glanced down at Weyr, then back at me.

"Well, if you're the one who came back, I'm glad it was you."

Hazard grinned. "Saylor will be glad it wasn't Eagre."

I huffed a small breath through my nose. He had a point. "What's their status? What's their plan?"

"They've built a vessel to transport them beyond the upper atmospheres. They believe they've achieved immortality."

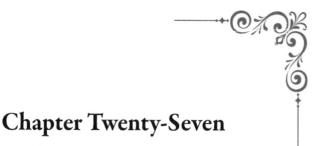

Chapter Twenty-Seven

SHAME
Saylor

———⚬𝕾❍———

"**I**f we join up, I want a cool name, too." Micah scuffed her boot toe against the cement underfoot. "Like, Micauleus, goddess of awesomeness."

"You don't know much about Greek mythology, do you?" I eyed Persephone, who bent over on the scaffolding platform to pick up a bag.

"No."

"Me neither. Fell asleep."

"I guess we should have stayed awake longer in Mr. Garza's class?" Micah tilted her head back, studying the machine before us.

"You're telling me. I feel like I need to know more about what Poseidon could or could not do." A shiver rolled down my shoulders.

"Who knew literature class could help a life and death situation?"

Male voices approached from the tunnel entrance we'd just come through.

Persephone slung the bag strap over her shoulder. "This way, you two." She clunked down the stairs, her steps echoing in the massive chamber and then jumped onto the floor. She moved with grace and ease, her slim silhouette the epitome of coy optimism and vivacious energy. Her hips slid forward with a rhythmical assurance, one muscular arm swinging free.

"Where to now?" I asked, suddenly quite aware of my knee aching. The joints trembled.

Persephone's ponytail swished while she stalked away, circumnavigating the scaffolding.

Micah shrugged, and stepped after her.

I continued studying the vessel as we rounded it, light catching the glass, sprinkling down from the metal. Persephone led us to another cart waiting by the wall, beside what looked like a waterfall cascading down the rock. The water dumped into a pool, level to the concrete floor. The narrow pool followed the perimeter of the room until it reached the third tunnel leading out of the vast space. Three tunnels. Three mega-doors with blast-worthy thickness and locking mechanisms and guards with guns.

Persephone climbed into the car and sat in the middle of the seat facing forward. She settled the duffel bag on the seat beside her.

She pointed at the opposite bench.

Micah climbed in. I followed.

Persephone tapped some beeping buttons and we were off, gliding out of the third giant door, and down another dim, rocky tunnel. She reclined against her seat, examining the red lacquer polishing her fingernails.

"Look," I said after a solid two minutes of absolute silence. "I understand we have some tangled, strange history. But how? What's your story? How are we identical?"

She tossed her head, the ponytail flipping over her shoulder and then brushing against her neck. "We're in no way identical. I've been created to excel above you, should you result in a disappointment to the plan. Turns out, you were."

"Hey, Rude," Micah sat up, "Watch your mouth. You don't get to talk to her like that." Micah balled up her fist in her lap.

Persephone quirked an eyebrow. A crimson smirk enflamed the light smattering of freckles on her rosy cheek. "I speak as I like. My kingdom, my rules."

"No, you—" Heat emanated from Micah.

I grabbed her arm, an awkward backhanded grab before she lunged to the girl who could obviously take on the almighty fury of Micah's wrath. "It's okay, Micah. Let it go."

Persephone's smirk rose further. A light chuckle bobbed her chin. She studied a piece of lint which landed on Micah's shoulder. She flicked it away with a lithe wave of her slim finger.

"What do you mean when you say you were created to excel? Who raised you? Did you grow up here?"

"My father is Zeus." She pointed her chin directly at me, those blue eyes sizzling, her neck snapping at the movement. "He spent a lot of time traveling but we talked every day over the sat."

"The sat?"

"A video chat."

"Zeus? Do you mean Breame? He's your—father?" The last word trembled off my tongue, paused, horrified, confused.

"He loves my mother, although she's been—" Persephone dropped her gaze, her focus rolling around the tunnel as she searched for the words she desired. She winked. "She's learning some lessons the hard way."

Spit caught in my throat, wadded up, nervous, tapping at the back of my mouth. I bit down on my bottom lip. *Persephone uses her words purposefully, intentionally.* I did the same. "You say Zeus loves your mother and you."

She exhaled, impatient.

"As in, present tense? Currently?"

"Of course."

"But Zeus used to be known as Wellington Breame, correct? Before—before?" I didn't know before what. Before he died? *My brain hurts.*

"He lives on, alive and well. We've accomplished our mission, hence the urgent departure. Best not waste one more second on this lousy sphere than necessary." She rolled one shoulder back, firming her position again the back of the cart.

Micah grunted.

I licked my lips. "May I speak with Br—Zeus?"

Persephone's laughter fluttered about, savoring the experience of my joke. "Oh, you are delightful. So simple."

"Is that a yes?"

"No, Saylor, that's a no. He has no need to 'speak' to you." She held up one hand, bending the first two fingers to make air quotes as she said 'speak.' Then she slowly slid her fingers to her forehead. Tenderly she brushed her fingertips down from her forehead and over to her temple, where she rested her thumb under her chin and her fingers against her cheek, cradling her head. Her gesture, slight and to most others would appear as if she were supporting her disdainful skull, served for a purpose.

Everything she does has a purpose. My tongue shivered against my jaw. The place she touched guarded the spot where Breame had installed the SAILOR chip before I fought the solar flare. I wrestled my tongue against the back of my clenched teeth, forcing my jaw to work. "Well, I have a need to speak with him."

She firmed her tone, cutting me off. "You cannot."

"What about your mother? What's her name? Where did you put her?"

"You bore me." Persephone waved one hand in the air, twirling her pointer finger. "Finally."

The cart slowed to a stop beside a silver door. The door of the cart flung open, and Persephone ordered, "Out."

I rose, quelling the ardor pulsing within my palms. Her neck, so slender, waited a mere few inches from my grasp. Instead, I stepped down onto the waxed concrete, and waited. *Get answers before acting irrationally.* Sage advice.

Micah slid down beside me, and then Persephone rose, hopping down and bounding to the door. A black shiny panel sat attached to the wall beside the door and Persephone tapped on it. After a couple beeps, the silver door swung inward.

The gray walls inside the room held drawings, black and white scrawls of life-like birds, landscapes, animal faces, and even some portraits. My face stared at me from the wall beside a wide, wooden dresser holding colorful boxes of trinkets. Upon the dresser rested makeup bottles and tubes, a bowl of shiny gold and silver jewelry, and a short stack of books. On the far wall, a huge bed covered with a red, white, and black damask quilt waited, perfectly smoothed, with a pile of neatly ordered matching pillows. Against the right wall a large wooden desk faced the room, with a wooden chair between the desk and a towering bookcase behind it. On top of the bookcase, a statue identical to the one in Poseidon's office waited, dust-free and ominous. A red leather chair lounged between the desk and the door where we stood.

Persephone tossed the duffel bag on top of the dresser.

"Is this your room?" Micah asked.

"If you're going to accompany me, please do not bother me with such insipid conversation." Persephone sighed. She strode over to the bookcase and studied the third row's contents.

Micah muttered under her breath. "You're insipid."

I nudged Micah with my arm and whispered, "Don't."

Micah eyed me before pursuing her lips. She mouthed, "What does insipid mean?"

"Persephone," I called out, strolling over to the red leather chair, "What all does the plan entail? For today, anyway."

She continued studying the shelf, her finger tracing the spines. She pulled one black leather-bound from its spot. "Final preparations for launch." She murmured the words, focused.

"Won't you miss this place? Your home?" I eyed a small, pink stuffed bear sitting on the corner of the dresser. The animal looked worn, frayed. The eyes no longer shined but the thing continued to grin even in its faded old age.

"I'm ready for the new horizon." Persephone twisted upright and glanced to me. "I suppose I might want to return, but I have no need for it. Zeus and Poseidon have spent hours working with me on slowly ridding of the items I thought I needed. Burning the old toys and books was rather fun."

My eyes widened. That racing pulse hammered in my neck. "Are you taking any of it with you?"

"Where I go, I need nothing."

"Where—are you going?"

She chuckled and drew another book from the shelf. She placed them on the edge of the desk.

"Will you return?"

"I expect not. Although I'm open to options. But our calculations show Earth will not last beyond the next decade anyway. Why return to a futile location?"

Swallowing hard, I then licked my lips. "How—what calculations?" Tucker had told me about the super-computer he'd commandeered in Camp Kissinger. The computer which declared the end of the world. Had they started it up again?

"Persephone," I added before she said anything, "Tell me outright. What's your plan? Who's in charge? No more games, code names. No more wishy-washy jargon." I surged upward to my feet.

"Don't be dour. I've told you what I wanted you to know."

"No, Persephone, I'm jazzed about chatting with you." I huffed a sarcastic breath out of the side of my mouth at a taunting stray hair. "Now, we're both strong-headed, and if we're anything alike in personality, we'll only end up at a draw. Stop the game and tell me what I want to know. Maybe you're the queen down here, but I've got my own army up there."

Her eyes flickered while I spoke. She tipped her chin to the side, considering. She blinked several times. "You will die at the age of twenty-five. From heart failure. Those nanomites Zeus injected into you? The ones which were not completely defunct in the solar flare you battled will rust over and break down, damaging nearly every vein in your body. It will be painful and slow. Imagine rusty metal shards rushing around through your blood vessels, scraping up the insides of your heart. Pity. Shouldn't have damaged yourself so brashly. You will never have children. And your father's future isn't too bright, either. All the stress he's faced? All the experimental testing he had been in contact with? He develops several forms of cancer which spread throughout his organs to a quick end. Shame.

"Zeus, Poseidon, and my mother, Demeter, trained me from early on in combat, mathematics, language arts, philosophy, and the sciences. They brought in the best tutors from across the world, the best trainers. I've lacked for nothing, and they all pruned me to want for nothing. You lacked for everything, didn't you? Zeus saw it. He planned accordingly. He knew the calculations and he desired the strongest to survive with him. He realized your broken body would not last. But he liked you, Saylor. As a baby, the baby he'd helped create, who he'd brought to life because of egg donations our mother provided, he saw ample opportunity for his new world.

He sent a second sample away, to my mother here, and brought me to life. As the years passed he spent his time traveling from his work on Isla Barina, to here, to your piddly existence in Georgia. Even when he couldn't be here with me, he made time to see and talk to me every day. And here we are."

I sat in the chair. My body pressed against the firm seat. I didn't feel any of it. "You're—about nine months younger than me, then?"

"Eleven. He used strains of your DNA and implemented them into mine so we would match."

"Why?"

Persephone shrugged "He'd been working with genetics. He loved our face from the first moment he saw it. Zeus tells me all the time. But he wanted to ensure I could do my job in the case you could not. I don't like being considered second best, but, after seeing you, I can see I have nothing to worry about."

Swallow. Blink. Breathe.

"You're like a clone?" Micah blurted.

Persephone whipped her face to Micah. "No, Micah, I'm not a—I'm my own self. I simply have identical, yet improved, genetic structure to Saylor."

"How do you know so much about us?"

Persephone luxuriously lifted and lowered one shoulder. One firm leg supported her weight while the other knee bent, uninterested. She ran her fingers through the ponytail and its nonexistent tangles. "Zeus sent me recordings, pictures. He told me stories. I've studied you all my life. I'm your biggest fan."

"Well, I suppose that's something," I murmured. I couldn't look her in the eyes.

"Not so much. I think you're weak and atrocious. You discarded Zeus as if he were nothing. You clung to the ridiculous man you call Commander." She shook her head, spurning it. "And you believe your simple mission to help people will make any kind of difference." She fluttered a laugh out of her wet lips.

"We will make a difference." My weak argument didn't even resonate with me.

"The world's burning, Saylor. And you with it."

"So, what, then," Micah leaned against the wall beside the doorframe. "You're going, where? To do what?"

Persephone lit up, her cheeks illuminating. "To the great beyond. Beyond the stars. Beyond the moon, beyond the known world."

"Um." Micah's eyes blinked to mine.

"We're raising Atlantis, directed toward a new horizon. Zeus has figured out how to contain artificial intellect and utilize it to propagate our species. I was the great experiment. Poseidon and Prometheus succeeded in their combined efforts to create a durable, controlled environment and civilization."

A knock on the door interrupted her. She lit up, her cheeks blushing. Rushing to the door, she stepped aside as it swung open. Gliding in to the room with the quiet hum of wheels turning from a motorized carriage, a form entered the room. Glad I sat in the chair, I would have fallen to the floor had the red leather not upheld me. Breame himself, smooth brown hair with an insistent swirl at the back of his head, gray sideburns, and searching brown eyes, stalked up beside Persephone. Micah jumped back out of the way. Breame turned, in a slightly jerking motion, his face scanning the room, and then his body joining it. His fingers balled up, and he rested his fist on his hip. He wore the same gray, flowy pants and cloak as Poseidon. When his eyes rested upon me, he blinked. A slight clicking sound accompanied all his motions.

"I see you have arrived," Breame stated. He had little inflection in his voice.

Micah lunged at him, punching him in the face. She screamed, withdrawing her fist, cradling it in her other hand.

"What?" I called, jumping up. "How's—how are—Micah!"

Breame raised one leg, and then another, carefully placing each foot and exaggerating his arms swinging to his stepping. "Do not use physical actions against me. I am your superior and you cannot damage me. I will only damage you."

"You're not real," I breathed.

"I am as real as you perceive me to be." He continued walking in my direction.

I held up a palm. "You stop right there. How's this possible? You're dead. I saw the report myself. The photos. Your gray, deceased body."

"A body cannot contain that which had been chronicled and animated of its own accord."

"What are you saying?" I backed up a step, bumping into the edge of the desk.

Breame's lips slipped up into a tight smile, and he doubled back, still accompanied by a hum and a jerking motion.

"You're a—you're not real." I called out.

Breame continued marching. "You did not share our private designs with them, did you?"

"No, my father," Persephone said. "They kept asking inconsequential questions though."

"Are you ready for your lessons?"

Persephone nodded. "I am."

"Let us go. Leave them here." Breame strolled through the door and out into the hall.

My spine forged into a steel pole, melting into the concrete.

Persephone bounced to the door. She waved a finger. "No touching anything. I'll be back in thirty minutes."

"What are—" Micah spoke up but stopped as Persephone grabbed the door and slammed it shut behind her.

The echo cascaded around us.

Micah still held her fist. She pivoted to me.

My jaw slacked open, lost, overwhelmed, empty.

Micah pointed to the door. "Is he a machine? Is that a thing? I read a book a long time ago about how people wanted to make people-like machines."

I slid my right hand into my pocket. Gripping my fingertips around the black leather within, I yanked out my gloves and began shoving my hands inside, the sound of shuffling my response to the questions I could not answer.

"Why are you putting those on?"

Tugging the fabric onto my hands, the comfortable material smoothing against my frayed nerves, I wadded my fingers into a tight fist. "They remind me to be strong even when I'm not sure of myself. But with the gloves, I remember who I can be. I'm not Persephone's weaker half. I'm the steel forged under fire."

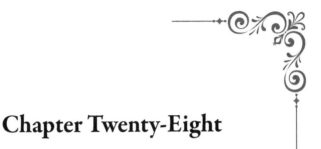

Chapter Twenty-Eight

THE CONCRETE UNDERFOOT
Tucker

"What do you mean they think they've achieved immortality?" I asked, tugging on my GRIPS, chasing Hazard down the tunnel.

"Exactly that."

"What do you mean? Where are we going?" I panted, still recovering from the harrowing last few moments.

"I've been here for about five minutes longer than you," Hazard snapped over his shoulder. "I'm not exactly an expert on the subject. I memorized a map and I am headed toward the exit."

"We can't leave." I stopped short.

Hazard ran for several more steps before stopping himself. "Come on!" He waved me onward.

"We cannot leave. Logan's back there. And Saylor. And Micah. I think. My people are here, and I refuse to run away."

"All I know—I was forced to memorize a floor plan three years ago."

"Well." My chest heaved in and out. I rested both hands on my hips. Studying the carved tunnel of the hollowed-out earth, I scanned both the way before and the path behind. "You need to get us some information. They don't know you're—they don't know, correct?"

"Yes." Hazard ran a hand through his hair. "They believe I'm Dragon."

"And you do not know their plan from here?"

"We learned their maps, their ideals."

"Spill it."

"Their ideals?"

"Yes."

Hazard shifted his weight, rubbing his hands together before his chest. "We need to get some place out of the way."

"Let's go back to the stairwell." I launched a couple steps back the way we came while Hazard stayed planted where he stood.

"You want to go in an enclosed space with a dead body?"

"Got any better plans?"

"This way." Hazard waved over his shoulder as he darted further into the tunnel.

Grunting, I followed. He eventually arrived at a door with a plain knob and twisted it open. He dashed into the space.

Coming up on it, as he held the door open with one arm, I slid inside. A janitor's closet. One long shelf lined one wall, filled with supplies and boxes, and a big yellow bucket on wheels with an old crusty wooden handle swung against the wall with a creak.

"Nice recall," I stated.

Hazard yanked the door shut behind me.

"Now." Our chests inches apart, I scowled down at him. "Spill it."

"I know they have utilized their networked computers to create cognition in assimilated beings. Rapton taught us vague ideas about how being a Dragon meant becoming immortal. We'd be the protectors of our world, and eventually unconquerable."

"How? How can you be unconquerable?"

"It had to do with the triangle. Control. Containment. Consciousness."

"And?"

Hazard's shoulders stiffened before he dropped them. "I've told you all I understand. The old man said he would instruct us further once we contained you."

"The Commander. What did he say?" I squinted at Hazard.

"That's not who I meant by old man. He's older, yeah, but the older old man, he's the head honcho around here."

Closing my eyes, I revisited my conversation with the Commander over coffee and the crumpled napkin. "Mission. Perseverance. Unity."

"What?"

"They're all connected."

"Alright?"

"What old man?" I nudged my chin up and down.

"They call him Poseidon. I've only seen him from a distance. He speaks with big words."

"Where's Logan?"

Hazard cleared his throat. "He's on this level. They have a section of rooms cleared for prisoners or those who've chosen to work against them."

"Alright, well, you have to go get information. You've got to find out what they're doing and how soon it's going down."

"And what will you be doing?"

"Best if you not know. I'll meet up with you in that same room we just left."

Hazard shook his head side to side. "You'll want to get to the control center."

"Control center?"

Hazard laid his palm out and traced a triangle in it. "Over here," he pointed to his thumb, "is where we were. Engineering, assembly, diagnostics." He trailed his finger to the spot on his palm below his middle finger. "Second place of importance, the control room." He dragged his finger to the space of his palm near his wrist. "Third, launch center. They have tunnels leading between all three."

"Where we were just now?" I memorized the invisible map on Hazard's hand.

"Engineering."

"Right." Nodded.

"How do I make them trust me? They won't believe I let you get away."

I grinned. "Oh no?" As lightning flicks against the ground, so did my arm shoot around Hazard's neck, twisting him around so he struggled against the shelf and my GRIPS.

I raced down the hall, trailing the opposite way Hazard had run. Logan. Hazard said to look for the space in the middle of the tunnel, and as much help as that was, I used the VISTAS' heat scanners to no avail. They connected with the GRIPS but no blips caught. Where *was* everybody?

Cursing that I'd given over my WiCoDe to the Dragons, I jogged blindly through the hall. Silent steps shadowed my doubt. What did I need to do? Did it matter if these people wanted the impossible? They'd stolen Alliance property, but technically, they were Alliance. Did it matter? Did any of it matter?

Commander. Where are you when I need you?

My boots slowed. With each step, I faltered more. Could Alliance have stolen its own property? Didn't make sense. Why would Adenauer go to all these lengths to create a program containing zero logic? *Could he possibly have invented a way to—*

As I pondered the possibilities of immortality, a door to my right swung open. It was the first I'd come to, and with no others in sight.

The holding cell. I flattened against the wall with not a single idea what to do. The panel opened fully, the man exiting involved in the thick tablet he carried in his hands. Head bent over concentrating, he ambled on to the right, the door between us hiding my person. He didn't notice a thing. His black boots shuffled away from me down the hall. Grabbing the edge of the painted metal, I slipped around it and tiptoed into the white hallway beyond.

The hall paralleled the tunnel I'd just exited. Choosing the right, I listened for any echoes or signs of the times. A voice, muted by walls or closed doors, argued for a point. Taking one slow step at a time, I studied the concrete underfoot.

"We leave them. The islanders will come looking anyway." The angry voice paused. "No sir. No. I will." Silence. A grunt and mutters rumbled through the wall. A door slammed. Panicking, I froze. Squeaking boots. Three beeps. A churning, and then a clanking of metal against metal. More squeaking boots, and stomping drawing away. The steps hushed.

Continuing along, I peeked my head over the corner to the left, which rounded to another empty left turn. Bare white painted cinderblock walls. A frame filled the center of the inner left side of the corridor. Approaching it, I leaned out enough to see clear glass reflecting the lights overhead. The glass served as a window, a hole cut in the middle, leading into some sort of office. The sole occupant had exited through a door on the right wall of the room. Jogging over to the corner, I ducked around to find the door closed. It opened easily, with a regular knob, fortunately. They had to have some record of who came down here. If this were the holding cells, and that man the keeper, he'd have a messy book somewhere.

Shoving into the office, I flipped through various books and files piled on top of the large desk filling most of the small room. And finally, on top near the window, sat a clipboard with crumpled papers curled up on the edges. A handwritten signature scrawled on the last line, "Prisoner 8210. Blond hair, blue eyes. Six feet tall. One hundred eighty pounds. Gamma Sector, cell three."

Had to be Logan.

As I swiveled to exit the room, maps and a blueprint behind glass frames filled the back wall. Red marker strokes labeled sectors and crossed large X's over cells. Gamma Sector. Cell Three. Got it.

The good thing about wearing my GRIPS is I can grab whatever I like and crush it. Strolling over to the door, I tossed it aside like a scrap of paper. The door hurtled across the room, thundering against the far wall and knocking framed pictures off the sheetrock as it crashed to the ground. Across the hall, a series of metal gates formed the entrance to the holding cells. The steel melted under my wrath. Like butter, the shredded material flung itself aside as I tore away the webbing holding the underworld in chaos.

One poor guard ran up to me. I met him head on, a quick jab to his chin, and the man dropped to the floor. His head hit the ground with a *crack*, and I marched on. No guns? Why had only one guard remained below?

As I drew up to the cell marked Three, a body on a low bed slumped against the cinderblock wall blinked at me.

"Ready to blow this fireworks stand?"

"I was wondering what was taking you so long." Logan straightened. He lifted a foot. "I even kept my shoes on."

I scuffed my boot against the ground. "Then why are your wrists bound?"

"The guy left a minute ago to check on something at the front gate."

"He's indisposed at the moment. Won't be coming back."

"Then let's get to work." Logan held his locked wrists up in the air. The silver metal glinted.

The door came off its hinges as I grabbed the left and right sides of the steel frame. "Shoddy craftsmanship." I grinned in delight.

"I've got to get a pair of those things." Logan stepped to me, extending those wrists clamped with handcuffs.

I twisted the metal of the cuffs, snapping the pieces in their sockets.

"Just so you know, more Dragons have arrived. I saw them on my way down. Your younger ones, the ones we left at Fort Story. I don't know how they're here." Logan almost panted as he spoke.

My heart began to writhe and pound too, my breath hammering at my ribs. "Hazard's on our side. We had a little conversation on the way down the stairs."

"You sure?" Logan rested his hands on his hips.

"Sure as I can be when the world's flipped upside down."

"I've got no reception from the WiCoDe down here, also."

I clapped. "Great." The racing of energy pulsed within my veins, strength overpowering the quandary.

"Your sarcasm inspires me. Rip some of those poles off the wall so I have some sort of weapon."

Checking the area where he nodded, I accepted the challenge. The "wall" of bars slid out of their soldered places with a snap of my wrist. "Here." I tossed two over to him.

"Thanks."

"Ready, My Liege?"

"Proceed, Jeeves."

We ran back the way I'd come, around a corner to the right, past several barred cells and prisoners hanging on to the cold steel, yelling. Beyond the collapsed guard, and through the front cell we charged, until a looming black figure in the gaping broken gate caused me to stumble in my spot. I stopped fast, Logan crashing against my shoulder. He almost surged into the burly mass of muscle and black hair, until the figure strolled forward out of the empty space.

Exit.

His steely gaze burned into my VISTAS. His balled-up fists at his sides swung freely. And the smirk bouncing off his lips replayed the moments I'd thought he would crush me under the grounds of Camp Kissinger. Somehow he had survived the explosions, and here he stood.

"Nice to see you again, scrud." Exit's voice bounded around the white cinderblock walls and shimmied up my spine.

Ten measly feet waited between us, the space itself trembling.

I shoved Logan back a step with my right arm.

Logan grunted.

"Stop!" I held out my fist.

His glance drifted to the blue outline of my GRIPS, and he acknowledged my own power with the slightest of nods. "What do you say? Battle to the death?" He bobbed his own set of GRIPS at shoulder height, weighing the many options.

"Never considered that to be much of a game. I've got a lot of living to do yet."

"Oh, do you?" He advanced one step.

I took one step back, yanking Logan's shoulder with me. "Where have you been all this time? I'd love to hear your side of the story since the section of ceiling fell on you and you died."

Exit chuckled, a growling, gruff, staccato.

"Truly. You've got to have a great story on your hands."

"I'm not one for stories—just crunching up the pitiable bones of those weak enough to crawl away from a fight."

"But you took a helicopter, didn't you? Somehow you snuck out of Kissinger, stole a helo, crashed it, and then made it here without anybody knowing."

He crooned again, as dragons do, rocking back on his heels in amusement.

"But you see, we did know. We saw you used Rapton's point card to purchase a ticket to New Zealand."

Exit's glimmer of excitement dropped, and his jaw hardened. Those back teeth ground together.

"So you see," I continued, waving my hand, "you aren't as surprising as you believe you are. I've been hoping to wrap things up with you."

"I call your bluff. I see your startled, pale face. You cannot defeat me."

"I defeated you once before, Exit. I can do it again."

Exit grinned, vile and wicked. The gleam in his eyes, the dead light of a soul seeking destruction, writhed as it sliced through the air. His lips twisted down into a snarl. "Run."

Chapter Twenty-Nine

SHORT LIST
Saylor

"When she comes in, grab her ponytail," Micah ordered. She leaned against the desk and tapped the top with her fingertips. "Yank hard. I'll kick her."

"Micah, we can't just attack her. We need to find out their plan."

"Um, their plan includes launching that thing." She stood, jutting her thumb over her shoulder. "And, like, taking over the world or something."

I shook my head. "I don't think they want to take over. I think they want to run away. Look at this place. Not a single personalized thing. Those drawings?" I extended my chin to the few colorful scraps of paper tacked on the wall. "She's moved on, mentally."

Micah chewed on the inside of her lip.

I shuffled beside her and leaned back against the desk as well. I gripped the edge with my palms. "Tucker told me about the ordeal in Kissinger. They'd manufactured a timeline, calculated the destruction of the earth. They insist their calculations are correct. But Tucker said they were wrong. You simply cannot predict the end of the world."

Micah twisted her boot toe against the concrete.

Persephone's words replayed through my head. "Or my death." Sticky oxygen slung through my throat, curdling as I said the humble words. I cleared my throat. "We need to find Tucker and Logan."

"And what about Persephone? The Breame thing?"

I bit down on my lip, the squish of flesh and moisture, the slight pressure and hint of pain, willing me back to the moment. "Adenauer needs to be shut down. It all needs to be shut down. We stop the giant machine, we stop that Breame computer, and we get our team back."

"Short list."

"Sound easy enough?"

"One question." Micah slapped her palms together. "Where do you suppose our team happens to be right now?"

Chapter Thirty

HOLLOW
Tucker

E xit dove at us. His glowing blue GRIPS permeated my vision. Step One: stay out of the GRIPS. Should he cast his gloved palm around any section of skin, he'd crush the flesh within. Shoving Logan away, I tossed a quick right hook toward Exit's skull, darting to my right. Exit came in swinging, GRIPS pummeling, flying every which way. Logan shot around Exit and swung one of the steel rods round to the back of Exit's head. *Thunk.* The years of swinging landed Logan's shot directly across Exit's spine, and the beast stumbled forward a step. But he recovered quickly, his fist flying around, and as Logan swung for a second shot, Exit caught the pole. He ripped it from Logan's hands. As Exit distracted himself, I kicked out a boot to the back of his leg and then ducked. Exit's hand raced back to catch me, but I hopped out of the way. Exit swung the rod wide, catching my side. Logan directed the other pole at Exit's side and he landed a solid hit on the brute's ribcage.

But Exit then whipped the rod around, swinging fast and hard, and clobbered Logan in the shoulder. Logan dropped, his head whipping to the side.

I landed another right hook, and a left jab, on Exit's backside, right where his spine would feel it most. Exit flung a fist around, but

I jumped back. I swung once his fist had passed and landed a hit on his shoulder.

We weren't runners.

When the enemy threatened, we didn't turn tail and flee.

We were the ones who stepped in when the danger lurked, rearing its ugly head.

But I hadn't a clue how we'd stop him.

Logan jumped up, gathering the pole which had slipped out of his hand, and he lashed a scathing blow to Exit's knee. The Dragon paused, which gave me the moment I needed to strike with a one-two jab at his cheek. *Smack!* The punches landed hard and crunchy. Within the GRIPS, my knuckles strained, vibrating with energy and agony.

Exit growled, his nostrils flaring, as if willing fire and brimstone to reign down upon us from his shuddering gut. He hurled the rod in Logan's direction, the bar head-over-heels flinging through the air with a rustling *clang*. Logan ducked. The bar shot past him. Hit the wall with a smacking rattle. It clattered to the floor.

I swung hard, a left hook to Exit's side. Spot on. My GRIPS connected, the heat vibrating through his skin.

Exit rocked on his heel, snapping back with his own flash of a right hook. The boom I heard then matched with the fist flinging by my eyes. His rocketing knuckles pounded against my collarbone as I attempted to block his incoming fist. Fire ripped through my torso, threading through my skin, wrapping down my spine. My right arm fell limp. I stumbled back.

A ringing *thunk* resounded, as Logan whomped Exit on the back of the neck again, and then darted away. Exit twisted, slowing, out of breath, and spirited a fist Logan's way.

I sank a quick left hook and cracked his right temple. His head sloshed with the wave of fury hastening through his gray matter. In the slowest crumple ever, Exit stumbled back a step. He lost balance, toppling on his left side, and then sank to the ground.

My right arm burned, my chest pounding and minced with rage. My lungs ached for fresh oxygen, heaving. Throttling the blaze winding through my throat, I pounced over Exit's limp body, ripping a set of zip-ties out of my pocket. The plastic pieces flew everywhere.

"Get his GRIPS off!" I clamored for his wrists. "Restrain him. Hands and feet!" My fingers trembled. Yanking the latches open, I dug my fingers inside the GRIPS surrounding his sweaty skin and scraped them off like the second skin they were. His sweaty flesh refused to give in to my yanking, and his arm jerked as I forced the fabric free.

Logan dove to his other hand, finding success quicker than my throbbing palms. With a swift yank, the fabric splitting on the seams, the blue instantly darkened. Destroyed.

Logan's breath rasped through his lips. "You weren't joking."

"No."

Exit moaned.

"*Quick.*" I whispered. Scanning the room of cells behind us, the nearest empty cell sat hushed and dusky. "Let's get him in here." Yanking the black collar of his uniform, I drug the slumbering giant over the polished concrete toward the cell.

"His hands aren't restrained yet."

"Hurry," I huffed. Sweat dripped down my forehead, eking into my collar and down my spine. Our boots squeaked against the floor. Exit's clothes swished along the floor through the quiet hush.

At the cell, I dropped his collar, and studied the best way to open the locked cell and still be able to use it to contain Exit.

Logan snapped several zip-ties on Exit's wrists, locking them crossed behind his stationary form.

Wrapping my GRIPS over the bolts on the gate, I jerked the pins free. Snapping, metal grinding, and a squeal as they hopped off their hinges. "Logan," I called, "Grab those two bars."

He hustled off.

I grabbed the bars of the cell door and swung the door open, the thing still locked on one side. Dragging Exit inside, I shuffled his body over to the far corner. Moans.

Dusting off my hands, I strolled out. Logan ran up with the two poles and tossed one to me.

I grabbed it mid-air. Slamming the door shut, I then wrapped the bar around where the top bolt had been. Logan held out the second pole. I did the same with it, the steel coiling around its new home like a tamed cobra. Exit wouldn't be able to leave the cell on his own accord.

Heaving more heavy breaths through my nose, I stepped back. Hands on my hips, assessing the cage. "Ready to find the control center?" I asked.

Logan wiped his forehead with the back of his hand. "I want another pole. Came in handy."

Heads bobbing, we jogged to the jagged bars of the front gate.

"Hey, mate," I huffed, "Why do you think all these cells are empty? We only passed a few imprisoned blokes. Why all the empty space?"

"Gives me the chills, Tuck."

Our boots clomped through the hall, echoing off the white paint. I forced the door open into the hallway. Silence greeted us, the white lights encrusted into the rocky tunnel ceiling blaring a hollow luminescence.

Logan lowered his voice. "I keep wondering why all this space and tunnels. What are they keeping down here?"

"And how are they planning on using it?"

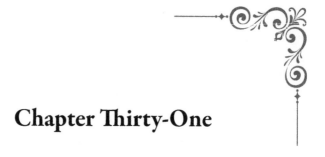

Chapter Thirty-One

BOOM
Saylor

"I half-expected you to be gone." Persephone strolled through the open door, slinging her red leather jacket over her shoulder. Her mussed ponytail swung freely about her blonde head like a tangled halo. "Or I suppose we can say, I *hoped* you'd be gone."

"Don't worry, we waited to hear more of your monologue," Micah snapped. Boots light-footed, fists on hips, we were ready to intercept Persephone's next move.

Persephone paused. Her eyes widened, then narrowed, one eyebrow tilting at a spiteful angle. "Poseidon wants to see you."

"You mean Adenauer?"

Persephone sighed, her shoulders sagging. She swung her head, irritated. "Come along." She pressed the keypad beside the door, beeps accompanying her fingertips. When the door opened, she sauntered out.

I glanced up at Micah.

She shrugged.

I hoisted off the edge of the desk, following.

Out in the hallway, the dim tunnel and its sparkly lights, Persephone's gray boots squeaked along quietly before us. Her hips swung in confident rhythm at a quick pace. One hand fluttered along at her side, her thin fingers tapping some melody on an invisible keyboard.

Jogging to catch up, Micah and I huffed along behind her. I spoke up after several quiet, awkward minutes. "I'm looking forward to working with you. It'll be interesting to compare stories about what Breame's told you."

Persephone halted. She swung her head to the side, that ponytail smacking her cheek. She let out a quiet, jeering half-giggle. "What?"

"I—"

"Of course I'm not going to work with you. Don't be ridiculous. Now Micah, I might let stick around, with her dangly arms. She could do my lifting for me."

Micah plunged forward, her long, muscular arms reaching for Persephone's throat. She landed a slight blow to Persephone's shoulder, but the girl in red slid to the side as she watched Micah hurtle through space. Persephone pounced back at Micah, shoving her arms to the side.

With some sort of springing jump, Persephone swung up on to Micah's back. She crossed her legs over Micah's middle, and used one arm to pull her hair, while the other pummeled her face.

Micah yelled, arms swinging.

We'd practiced similar moves in combat training, and Micah deftly tossed her body down to the concrete. Persephone's right side crackled against the floor, the *thunk* and grunting of leather, muscle, and concrete all competing for the title. I dove for Persephone's left swinging arm. She kicked a boot to block me.

Micah rolled over, skin slapping the flat surface. Persephone's grip tightened, landing around Micah's throat.

"Get off me," Micah hollered.

"You asked for it!" Persephone clenched her teeth.

Micah continued yelling incoherent noises, writhing on the ground.

I dove back in, latching on to Persephone's arm, and yanking her ponytail by the base. Persephone screamed.

"Let go," I shouted over the ruckus.

"Give up, you scrap!" Persephone rolled off Micah's back and swung out a hefty right hook. I jumped out of the way. But Persephone charged at me, a full-body run, until her shoulder connected with my side. Her sticky fingers grappled my leg and she wrenched my body up over her shoulder. I launched into the air, weightless, until she twisted out from under me and I hauled earthward. Hands out to brace the impact, with a booming smack, my incapable mass slapped against the ground. My right side burned. An instant ache wrenched all recognition of up and down into a jumbled scramble. Behind the blur of the backs of my eyelids, the dim snippets dotted with the sight of Persephone's red form darting off down the hall into the darkness.

"Saylor—hey!" Micah's urgent calling rattled against my brain. "I'm up, I'm up." I swung my arms out in front of me, my aching eyes unable to open in the bright light.

"Stop. Open your eyes."

Micah stood over me. She extended a hand down. I clasped her palm, and she yanked me upward. I thrust all my energy into emerging from the floor-sleep, and surged to my feet. The tunnel swirled about, my vision churning, my last meal stirring, and my temples pulsing to the rhythm of the tumbling earth.

"That girl cray," Micah panted.

"What?" I held up a palm to my forehead to stop the dizzy dance.

"She cray."

"I think you're not speaking English." Blinked hard.

"I heard someone say it once. She's lost the Z. She cray."

"Micah. Why did you tackle her? I want answers!"

"She's obviously not going to give us answers. She said so. I just started the process before she did." Micah snapped her fingers.

"Well, great plan." I snapped my lips shut, irritated. My cheeks flushed. Heat and bile rose up in my throat. "Now we need to get out of here before she comes back with the—with reinforcements."

"Supposing she has reinforcements."

"I'm expecting reinforcements. There's always reinforcements."

"Yeah?" Micah asked. "Where are ours?"

"They're somewhere down here. Let's find them!"

"Logan and Tucker, great as they were on Barina, don't exactly count as reinforcements."

"Hey." I pointed a stiff finger at her, the edge lining my voice. "Tucker and Logan would do anything to help us. They are all we have right now. Tucker's highly capable. He has his GRIPS. I have my SIMPLs. The four of us can do some damage down here."

"But what if they damage us first, Say?"

"Micah, I love you, but you're wearing me out. You've got to trust a little."

Micah slid her fingers through her hair, tussling the ends. "I want out. I haven't said it before, but I'll say it now. We're in over our heads, and I want out."

"Fine!" I tossed an arm into the air, my hands waving freely over my head. "But first we have to get out. So are you going to keep attacking every person we see, or are you going to at least pretend you're willing to hear them?"

Micah swallowed hard. She blinked several times before licking her lips. "I think I liked it more when you were stuck in your chair and I could boss you around."

"Well I do too. But I'm not in a chair, and we're not in America anymore. We're in the belly of the earth and have to stop that—that—*ship*—from exploding us all."

"Agreed."

"Now I say we go left, back to the ship thing."

"Persephone ran to the left."

"Well great. We can run into her and buy her a coffee along the way."

"Um, 'kay." Micah shrugged. She studied the ground by her boots and swung a toe around.

"So, we try to handle these people with decorum, right?" Blustery breath shimmied through my lungs and out my throat. "Right?"

"Yeah. I'm very decorum-ous."

"Good." My chest heaved up and down, the weight of anonymity and the burden of peace-keeping in a tug of war upon my ribs. "Shiny."

The idea lasted for about five minutes, as Micah and I ran down the hall, dashing toward what we thought would be the large room filled with the ship. Before we reached the large door, Persephone and a group of ten black-clad people jogged out of the vault. They formed a line, barring the way.

Micah halted beside me.

We panted. Fists balled. Feet planted.

I shot her a quick glance. "I recall my statement about decorum."

"'Bout time." Micah's lips twisted up into a sneer, delighted. A reckoning. She slid a boot back, settling into fighting stance.

"Activate," I whispered. The grid settled around me. The SIMPL warmed in my pocket.

Persephone swung her arm up in the air and wagged her first two fingers.

Their black boots hit the ground like war drums. Like the beat of my wild heart. Like the pulse of energy hurtling through my veins.

The SIMPL blasted up into the air.

The black figures pitched forward.

My ten little pieces soared up, splitting apart. I aimed for their hearts, the little electric ones ready to sizzle and splice the hearts daring to contend their master. One black figure fell to the ground, limp, convulsing.

Their whole bodies and faces covered in the uniform, the face mask fell away as the boy dropped. *Thunder.* His upturned little freckled nose poked out of the murky depths.

Oh no.

My heart churned in its spot, a wave of despair trembling from deep within and rattling the chains of my resolve. *What happened to Tucker?*

Micah pummeled the nearest guard, a collision of brawn, grunts, fists, and cloth. Yanking the SIMPL pieces together, I surged the sphere around the other guards, aiming for their backs to limit the contact and save their lives. The SIMPL rolled over four of them, quick as a swooping bird, the SIMPL dipping and soaring above and beyond their reach.

Persephone stood in the background, her hip jutted out to the side. The sneer on her face analyzed our combat.

A black-clad figure tackled me from the side. His hands around me, restraining my arms, I mashed my palm against his face mask, ramming his nose upward.

The kid yelled. He chucked his face to the side and then at me, I suppose in some sort of head-butt.

Calling upon Sparks, the cross-shape surged against the boy's neck. The sizzle shocked through his body. His skin writhed under the strain. His muscles tightened, those brown eyes widening and freezing. I cut Sparks' electric charge. The guard's arms went slack, his eyes rolling back and eyelids closing. I jumped up out of his grip.

Another guard about to lunge met my blocking right arm and a left jab he wasn't expecting. I chucked a knocking clunk against his jaw. His left hook rounded out. I ducked beneath it. Shoving Sparks against his spine, the shock dropped the guy at my feet.

I straightened. Two black figures, stunned arms frozen at their sides, surveyed the scene.

One of them held a hand up to the face mask and removed the silicone mouth guard. Hazard. His brown eyes, shining under the lights, furrowed under worried brows. "Please come with us, Miss McConnell." He lowered the mask to his side. He winked.

Persephone strode up beside him, between him and the other figure. I shot a quick glance to the other figure, whose brown eyes contained no clues or hints as to the personality behind the mask.

"Hazard." Persephone's irked tone displayed her disdain. "We do not ask politely. We order. Go get her. Restrain the prisoners."

Hazard lowered his eyes from my face. His forehead smoothed out. He took a slow step forward. Then he slung an elbow back at Persephone and jolted a left hook right at her nose.

She ducked. Persephone lobbed her arm out to Hazard, meeting his incoming right fist against her palm. She twisted his arm, and he propelled his weight against her, knocking her to the ground.

The other guard watched it all happen.

While Hazard and Persephone rolled around against the slick concrete, I surged Sparks to the final player not engaged with Micah.

The guard pivoted in place and sprinted away into the room. "Close the doors," he shouted. "Close the doors!"

Micah grabbed her opponent by both shoulders, sunk her boots against his stomach, and flipped him onto his back. She released him and rolled away, fists ready, but I swooped in with Sparks and gave him an early birthday present.

"Aw, Saylor." She grunted. Sweat dripped down her face. She raised an arm, wiping away the liquid with her forearm. Her lungs heaved for the oxygen they craved.

"Hey," I panted myself, "You're welcome."

"Are they dead?" She pointed to the eight unconscious bodies sprawled on the floor.

"They're getting a nice nap in. They'll have a headache after."

Hazard and Persephone smashed against the wall. Huffing an impatient breath through my nose, I shot Sparks over to them and quickly dropped them to the floor like a disjointed sack of hammers.

The hush creeping over the tunnel became overpowered by the roaring grind of gears against metal. The large door began to swing inward, a rushing of air blasting against our faces.

"Come on!" I waved the SIMPLs forward and they soared overhead.

"Saylor, wait!" Micah yelled.

"We have to get in!" I sprinted for the swinging door.

Micah caught up to my side.

The door moved much faster than I thought something that big could move.

Propelling my boots to hurl as fast as possible, Micah, the SIMPLs, and I flung ourselves through the opening.

The door crashed shut behind us with a giant, locking *Boom*.

Chapter Thirty-Two

ANY DESTRUCTIVE FORCE
Tucker

Our nearing the Control Center proved alarming for the under-people. The line of guards, two on each side of the gargantuan blast door, began yelling. One held up a palm to stop us. The black glove on his hand, outlined with a blue glow, illuminated the space around him.

I halted. Logan stopped at my side.

Clenching my fists, I chucked my shoulders back, and charged the silhouette. Dragon or not, I'd take him. A black silicone face mask covered all but his blue eyes. One of the crew from the States. I blocked his outstretch palm, smacking my right arm down at an angle. My forearm crossed his, and he stumbled for a millisecond before slamming his full weight into a wicked jab with his GRIP fist. He rammed my shoulder with his other palm, the tingle of sizzling pain grinding through my sinew. I cut to the right. Kicked his shin. Uppercut to the chin. His head shot back. I sank a right hook across his left temple, and the lights went out as his eyes drifted to the far side of his eye sockets. The uniform trembled, melting to the floor on his side.

Logan attacked another Dragon with the steel pole. He whipped the rod left and right, lobbing thwacks like a sword at the Dragon's legs.

Two more black uniforms materialized from within the Control Center. Each of them planted their boots upon the concrete, GRIPS glowing blue and hot. Logan and me versus five Dragons. I held up my hands, palms out.

"What are you doing?" Logan shouted. He shanked the rod against the Dragon's thigh. The Dragon expected the snap and snatched the rod clear out of Logan's hands.

Logan jogged back several steps, by my side once again. He sighed. Hands beside his ears, those palms faced the line.

"What'll you have, Dragons?" I called. "An unfair fight or a peaceful talk?"

The one with the pole shot a look over his shoulder to the three on his right. He whipped his head around and offered a quick nod.

"Who's in charge?"

The figure twitched his chin. He blinked.

"Alright." I inhaled a hearty breath. "Where's Adenauer? Take me to him."

From his spot on the ground behind me, the Dragon groaned. He rolled over on his back.

"Poseidon will not see you. I believe Zeus may offer a moment of his time." The pole-yielding guard waved beyond the door and toward the brightly lit hollow. "Try anything, and we take you down for good."

They surrounded us, leading us through a crisp, fresh room lined with rows of desks stacked with computer monitors and cables. Upon the far wall, large screens towered up two giant stories, showcasing pictures of the nearby lake, the mountain, the roads, and even the Engineering Lab and another room.

"What *is* that?" Logan hissed, nodding to the screen. "A rocket of some sort?"

I shrugged.

The large pyramid-like contraption on the screen sat glistening under white lights and upon a scaffolding platform. Workers carried boxes past giant black booster-like cylinders on the shiny corners.

The guard behind us, still carrying the pole, poked me in the spine, prodding me along. I hurried to catch up to the two figures before us. They strode beyond a white metal staircase leading up the far wall of the cylindrical room to a second story balcony enclosed with glass. Dim lights shone through. A man stood watching, staring down at us. His head a mass of curly hair, those eyes pierced through the tinted glass. He held his hands clasped behind his back.

One Dragon smacked open a door at the base of the stairs. Inside the bright room, a gray couch and a gray chair sat in an L-shape in what appeared to be an office with an empty desk. Down a hallway, they led us to an empty room with a small round table and four old cushioned chairs.

"Have a seat." The Dragon held the door open and stepped aside to let us pass.

We did. I slipped into the nearest chair, and Logan hopped by me to sit in the chair opposite me. We faced the door. The other Dragons had strayed, and the lone guardian waited, his foot propping the door ajar.

Cool air drifted in through a vent in the ceiling.

Logan slung his elbow on the table and rested his chin on his fist. With the other hand he thrummed his fingertips upon the surface like a drumbeat. Impatient.

"Stop that," the Dragon ordered.

Whirring.

A metallic clank, and then a stiff voice offered a buzzy, "Thank you."

I sat up on the edge of my chair. I let both palms lay flat upon my thighs. The energy pulsed through my NEXIS. The heat signatures in the outer room equaled four bodies.

More whirring, and a rustling.

"As you were." The terse voice clipped short. A shadow filled the doorway.

In strode a plastic version of Wellington Breame. His brown hair rolled over his head as if molded, and his yellow skin stuck to his muscles like a wrapper, with a sick sheen.

I jumped up. The chair tossed asunder behind me, clattering against the table as it fell. I shot out a fist at Breame's cheek and the man stumbled to the side for several steps before uprighting.

His head twisted my way, but not his upper body. His arms held their position, at awkward wide angles, by his sides. "Please do not use physical force upon my frame. While I have a sustainable build, my software prefers for my hardware to remain upright." His lips widened, and his eyebrows raised, and then they settled back in their original position on his face.

Logan happened to be on his feet as well, I noticed, as I took a step back away from the—machine. He was a machine. A humanoid. A Breame look-alike.

"Please have a seat." His knees arched up and down, taking more steps into the room before he settled in the corner, facing both of us.

"What the—" Logan's breath carried a multitude of inaudible questions.

"I must inform you I have few minutes to spare. However, I am happy to meet with you today."

My dry mouth stopped working.

Logan stared at the humanoid, slack-jawed.

"May I answer any questions for you today?" The Breame-bot buzzed. His eyes ticked back and forth from Logan to me.

Gathering my wits and the fallen chair, I sank into the cushion. Logan remained standing.

"How may I help you?" Breame-bot asked.

I cleared my throat. His eyes whirred, clicking to me. "Let's begin with you. What's—what's going on with—this?" I circled my pointer finger around his chest.

"Our labs here on Atlantis have fabricated a durable yet lightweight material which serves as my framework. I've been designed to withstand pressure while maintaining my integrity. My specifications are the newest on the technological field of robotics and mechanical engineering."

"You don't say," Logan muttered.

"Integrity?" I asked.

"Our engineers have built me to stand, sit, rise, and to navigate concourses using my own internal positioning system and gyroscope."

"So if I had pushed you over just then you would have been able to get up?" I scratched my head.

"Yes, sir."

"Hey, hey!" Logan punched a fist in the air. "Stop talking to it like it's a person." He shot a dark look to me, slicing through the space into my scalp. "He's dead."

"I most certainly have circumnavigated the death penalty." The droid was quick on his intake and output.

"How so?" Logan shot back.

"What do you think: if a computer can simulate the brain exactly, does that computer emulate the essence of the original brain?" Breame-bot lowered his hands a smidge.

Logan clamped his jaw shut.

"A computer cannot entirely replicate a human brain. Are you talking consciousness?" I dipped my head to the side a smidge.

"I am."

"Can a computer achieve life?"

Logan sputtered. "Ridiculous." He slapped the table and then slammed his body into the seat.

Breame-bot blinked. *Click click.* "My scans indicate your frustrations have risen your blood-pressure. Be careful, as this can cause dehydration."

"Oh, thank you," Logan muttered sarcastically.

"You are welcome."

"Breame," I began, "Tell me more about this consciousness. Are you Cello?"

"Why, of course not. I am the essence of Wellington Breame."

"When you say, 'essence,' what does that mean?"

"During my time at my lab in Heart Mountain, I completed multiple brain scans of myself. I recorded years of journal entries, personal exploits, writings, and videos into a composite vault. This has resulted in a captured display of my thought process, personality, and being."

"A being isn't just a checklist of personality and thought-process," I interrupted. *Computers. Can't argue with them. Can't just knock them over.*

"Quite contrary. With the amount of data I compiled on myself, my process of learning and adapting resulted in my ability to replicate my fleshly counterpart's responses."

"You spoke with Breame while he was alive?"

"He finalized my programming as Saylor arrived at Heart Mountain. Her brain scans offered the concluding notes and bug fixes to ensure—"

"Wait, wait," Logan held up a hand.

"—my assertions would match a live human being's."

Logan jumped to his feet. "You used the chip you planted in Saylor's head?" He waved at the bot's torso. "To do this? To make this?"

"Poseidon manufactured my external shell on the Atlantis campus. Zeus designed my internal processing unit."

"What are you talking about?" I called out. "Who's this Poseidon character? Who's Zeus?"

"I am Zeus."

Logan shoved away from the table. "Oh, stop it. You created yourself?"

"I am the beginning and the end of Wellington Breame. He conceived me as his higher form, Zeus, highest of the gods."

Logan swung around, his fingers ruffling through his hair, his blue eyes wild. "They're all nuts. Plain, cracked nuts."

Crossing my arms over my chest, I leaned back in the chair. "So, if you as Breame are Zeus, then Poseidon must be..." I squeezed my eyes shut. Surely this was Adenauer's crazy alter ego.

The bot remained silent.

I raised my hand. "May I ask who Poseidon began as? What was his name in his other life? In his other form? Is Poseidon a—what do you call yourself? A higher form?"

"Poseidon formed the triad with Prometheus and myself."

"I'd like to punch you in the nose, but I think you'd enjoy it too much," Logan mumbled. He strode up to the bot, staring at the eyes.

Click click. The eyes blinked. "I do not feel, nor do I enjoy."

"Bully for you."

"Zeus has no need for pleasure or tactile motion. I maintain knowledge, longevity, and therefore power."

Logan jutted out his thumb to the bot. "This guy's definitely got *life* figured out."

I inhaled, processing his lingo. "And who's this Prometheus character? May I chat with him?"

"Prometheus directed the Dragons. His consciousness had not been finalized before his demise. He lost his status in the directive."

"The directive?"

"To suspend the pillars of the universe."

Pressing my fingertips together in front of my lips, my arms buzzed with energy. He thought he knew power. "Right, right, I keep hearing this phrase. Explain it to me a little further, please."

"Atlantis will be raised. Our journey transcends the outer limits of the horizon as we progress beyond mankind's pitiable attempts of survival."

"So, then—"

"When you say 'Atlantis,'" Logan interrupted. "What's that?"

The bot extended his hands out. His cheeks widened, his eyebrows raising. "Why, you stand within its borders." He lowered his hands, his lips, and his eyebrows with a hum behind the exterior.

"And the machine on the screen," I waved to the other room, "That's what will get you to the outer horizon?"

"Yes."

"It's a ship?"

"The Earthshine serves as a multifaceted instrument for survival, travel, and accommodation. The term 'ship' serves as a diminutive, inappropriate term."

"It travels outside of the Earth's atmosphere." I tilted my chin in suspicion.

"The Earthshine will travel toward the nearest solar system."

Logan clicked his tongue. "We can throw them in the lunar bin. Instead of the looney bin. Lunar. Right?"

"You cannot travel that far," I argued. "No human can—"

Breame-bot offered his buzzy grin.

Made my skin crawl. "But you're not human."

Logan paced back to the chair. He sat. "You need someone here on Earth to coordinate for you. What happens when you run out of food—and fuel? Batteries? What kind of power source do you use? Won't you need some way back here? Aren't the Dragons going with you?"

I nodded, blinking back Hazard's words. "They're going to turn all of them into artificially intelligent humanoids."

Logan narrowed his eyebrows.

"They've been collecting their information for years. As the Dragons killed each other off, they retained the logs, the training, the video journals, the instruction, all of it. Didn't you?" I faced the humming figure.

Breame-bot's eyelids clicked shut and open.

Before he could answer, I added, "Where did you get all the material for the vessel? How did you fund this? How will you fund the expedition after you've left? Who will help you? You launch that thing, and then what? Leave behind everything?"

"You ask many questions. I will answer them in order."

I held up a palm to stop him. "How have you developed all of this in such a short time since the Flare? It wiped out all the earth's tech."

"Atlantis once existed as a lake within the remnants of a volcano. Underneath the lake, the volcano's molten core hollowed out tunnels snaking out toward the ocean, filled with an oil packed densely with minerals. Poseidon's political contacts discovered the remains of the tunnels during an excavation expedition, and Alliance quickly retained the land through a series of third-party organizations. Excavations began over forty years ago to channel the oil and refine it. Alliance had a viable space to use when we predicted the Flare. Since then Poseidon funneled the refined oil to global bidders to fund our projects. The minerals, when mixed with our high-grade, heat-resistant, lightweight steel, offered a durable solution to combatting nearly any destructive force."

Logan leaned forward. "High-grade, heat-resistant, lightweight steel?"

Breame-bot answered, "Yes."

"Do your minerals have anything to do with creating a carbon-fiber-reinforced polymer?"

"The minerals combine to create a durable yet—"

Logan jumped up. "That's the exact description of the X-11. I've repeated that wordy description of our weapons for years!" He pointed at Breame-bot. He spat out his fiery gaze, lashing the heat to the plastic face. "You made the X-11's to test out how durable the material was? As a weapon? As a bat? As a rod? For what?"

"Our triad does not waste. We utilize every opportunity and material to test—"

"The oxinals?" Logan demanded.

"The oxinals served as a prototype for launching our Earthshine system. We needed to determine the probability of success and lifetime, along with a variable other myriad of tests for longevity, communications systems along a coordinated grid, and mechanized combustion."

"The material in the tunnels went to build the X-11s?"

"And the oxinals." *Click click* ticked Breame-bot's eyelids.

"And the Earthshine?"

"And the NEXIS Suits." Breame-bot moved one arm, indicating my fists.

"Seems like a lot of material came from those tunnels."

"We utilized material from tunnels across the earth."

Logan almost growled. "And just where do these places happen to be?"

"Alliance purchased land and mineral rights to properties across the globe, including but not limited to Australia, Scotland, Canada—"

I boosted my hand over my head. "Ooh, ooh, teacher, let me guess." I stood. "I'm sure Isla Barina fits nicely within your list."

"Alliance purchased titles to the land and mineral rights of Isla Barina."

"Too bad all of it's about to burn, right?"

Logan fiddled with the sleeve gauntlet of his NEXIS. "Too bad I don't have an X-11 right now."

"Does the Earthshine use the same combustion system as the oxinals?" Seeing as the oxinals ashed themselves the second their shutter received the 'destruct' signal, seemed like a bad idea for a ship sailing through the cosmos. But I wouldn't be on it, so did I truly care?

"The Earthshine uses similar systems, but we have perfected them over the years." Breame-bot adjusted his head to the side, and then straightened it. "We have sent test operations. They took the form of satellites or rockets."

"Where did you launch them from?" Logan chewed on the inside of his cheek.

"We launched global exercises in order to find the ideal location. Our satellites have launched from Texas and Barina, as well as—"

I held up my palm again. "Wait a minute. Barina?"

"The mission failed, however. Barina proved a poor location for propulsion."

Logan grunted. "We saw. How did we miss that?"

I leaned my head back, the weight settling upon my forehead. "Breame." I sighed, disgusted, unprepared, out-leagued, out-planned, out-gunned. "Not to ruin the party, but we've been asking you questions for quite some time now. Aren't you supposed to be doing something important for this little quest of yours?"

Breame-bot raised his cheeks, his eyebrows, and his hands. He lowered them. "I am fulfilling my purpose for the moment. Our hallways are quite long here. I am preoccupying you until the Dragons arrive to take you to the execution chambers."

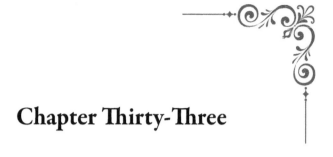

Chapter Thirty-Three

QUIT
Saylor

M icah and I screeched into the chamber. The vessel rose before us, pointing toward the heavens, casting few shadows along the brightly lit floor. My SIMPLs hovered overhead. Micah's wheezing cut short, and she brought her fists up, one guarding her chin.

Between us and the machine, a line of black uniforms blocked the way. At least fifteen of them barred any further progress we'd make. Two of them drew shiny black rifles up onto their shoulders, pointing the noses straight to our chests.

"Drop your weapons," the left gunman shouted. He slid his forehead behind a scope atop the rifle. A red dot focused on my heart. Even if I could fling the pieces to them, his shot would fragment my core quicker than I could write the destruct order.

My eyes scanned the blue grid surrounding us. So many heat signatures in the room. Silent. They froze in their spot, watching us.

Selecting the menu options, I guided the SIMPLs to the ground, slow and steady, until they landed with hushed tappings upon the concrete. *Quit program.* Their lights clicked off, darkening.

As soon as their heat signatures disappeared off the grid, the fifteen ebony figures rushed us. Their black gloves, outlined in blue, quickly overtook us. My hands clasped behind my back. They forced us along the perimeter of the room until opening the bars of a gate leading into a storage area where flattened, empty cardboard boxes sat stacked up against the back wall of the space.

Micah and I stood in the middle of the hollow.

One of the gun-free guards pivoted out of the cage, and dragged the door shut. It clanked with an ominous echo. The others stalked away. He remained, his boots planted for a moment. His black rubber mask covered his entire face except for those blue eyes piercing the dusk. Then the guardian jogged off, leaving us in view of the vessel and its large black boosters.

Chapter Thirty-Four

OF FABRIC AND TECH
Tucker

L ogan whipped out a right hook to smash the face of the humanoid. Breame's arm sliced upward, blocking the blow with ease. Logan hopped back, then drew out a left hook, followed by a quick right jab. *Punch, punch, block, block.* The humanoid expected the movements, his arms flying with the slicing hum of a machine designed to lash about.

Logan stepped back, his fists balled up, one covering his chin. He pointed to me, and then the bot. "Thompson. Smash."

I reared back with a vengeful fist.

"For your information," Breame stated, deadpan, "I've been designed to facilitate combat instruction."

I flew at him with both GRIPS, aiming for his nearest arm, the right one. I yanked at it, as he slammed it up and down in an effort to be freed. His left arm clamped down on my bicep. He began to crush my arm with his impenetrable carbon-fiber-reinforced polymer fingers. I yelled. The pain flared out, and I yanked his left arm clean off his body.

Logan tackled his right arm and hauled it upward, kicking the body of the droid with his swift boot.

Then the chaos unleashed. The Dragon at the door shouted to his mates, rushing at us. A wicked hook smacked against my cheek, and in the dizzy spin downward, GRIPS thrust against my neck, surrounding like a vice. The black rubber face mask and the black hood filled my view, his charcoal eyes drilling down into my gray matter.

"Take his GRIPS!" The voice, a familiar tone, deeper than usual, flowed out from behind the mask.

I balled up my fists.

Didn't matter.

A ripping, splintering of fabric and tech. The latch clattered against the floor. My naked hands chilled in the crisp air. Sweaty palms. The GRIPS heaved from my fingertips. I clenched my fists once more, bracing for impact.

My arms shivered under the loss. A sharp tremble rolled up my wrists, under the sleeves of my NEXIS. Connection lost. The VISTAS posted the words in the top right corner of my vision in unremarkable white letters.

"Stand." Rubu's gritty order rumbled.

"You'd betray me like this?" The words came out thin, strained. His GRIPS remained upon my throat, both withholding yet firm. "After these months? After endless moments where I didn't give up on you, never once?"

"Stand." He leaned closer. His palms mashed my skin and pounded my skull against the hard ground.

He released me and stepped back.

They'd sedated Logan, two on each side, his arms humbly strapped behind his back. His head hung, slumped.

The grit on the floor stuck to my sticky palms. It couldn't scrape away the callouses I'd built up during my hours in the training center, but the remorseless, glowering eyes of my masked guardians shook my ribs down to my core. I sank onto a knee. Unable to rise, my ribs constricted within my chest.

"I didn't need you," Rubu reflected. "I knew my protocol. To infiltrate. The only way to beat Alliance is to be Alliance."

Breath caught in my lungs.

I think the NEXIS faltered. Sweat squished along every surface, my skin crawling and bumpy.

"Rise up, *warrior*." Rubu challenged. Sarcasm dripped around his words. "And join Hazard, your pathetic pawn."

Another Dragon charged and grasped my arm, wrenching me to my feet.

Chapter Thirty-Five

WRATH
Saylor

———⟨⟩———

My chest heaved. A group of guards escorted Tucker and Logan across the room. Their bloodied faces studied the ground as they stumbled in their NEXIS suits, with arms bound behind their backs.

"What happened?" Micah whispered to me. We grasped the bars of the cell.

Hazard sat on the stack of boxes behind us. He had been silent since Persephone threw him in beside us and our dropped jaws. Bare-handed, he ambled to the corner and collapsed. Drawing his knees to his chest, he wrapped his arms around them.

Persephone had watched for a moment, then ran her hand through her ponytail. "What?" she asked.

Micah licked her lips. "How did you—"

"Like I'm going to give away our secrets down here?" Persephone spun away, her golden hair flashing behind her as she marched off.

As the guards yanked Tucker and Logan closer, Persephone and her slick red leather slid over, siding up to Tucker. The guard holding his arm halted. Persephone draped her elbow through Tucker's. She leaned her forehead against his shoulder, whispering to him. His downturned face studied hers.

Oxygen wadded up in my throat.

The guards unlocked the gate and jostled Logan into the space beside us.

Persephone withdrew her head from Tucker's shoulder. Her red glossy lips shimmered in the white lights. She angled so her back faced us. Her ponytail blocked Tucker's reaction from us.

"Oh, come on," I muttered. I ground my back teeth together.

Shifting up on her tiptoes, Persephone leaned closer to Tucker's cheek. She twisted to the left, wrapping her left arm over his neck. Her right hand trailed up his chest, tapping her fingertips against the buckles.

Fire sprawled through my veins. My boots corroded to the concrete.

Persephone glanced around, then back at Tucker. He continued staring at the ground by his boots.

She nuzzled her nose against his cheek, brushing her lips beside his ear. She thrust her chest up, propelled on her toes, against his chest. Her lips caressed his cheek. When she withdrew, the crimson ghost of her lips danced upon his skin. Persephone's chin tilted just enough to glance my way. She traced his jaw with her finger, whispering further through her volatile lips, and then strolled away from Tucker toward the open blast door.

The guard holding his arms had turned his head away while they'd been—should we call it conversing?—whatever it was—but once Persephone cleared the area, he shoved Tucker to the cell where we watched.

Tucker's form filled the space, the five of us stuck behind those steel bars. Suddenly the chill emptied. My heart hammered, striking its alarm.

As if frozen, Tucker continued to stare at the floor.

Logan glanced to us, to Hazard in the corner, to Tucker, and then back to me. I'd never seen worry written in his gaze before.

Logan's broad shoulders shuddered. Those confident blue eyes sunk, dark circles meeting a drip of blood trailing down from his hairline above his temple and down past his chin. Ruddy veins in the white of his eyes straggled to the teal centers, a marbled lethargy rambling a tale of exhaustion and defeat.

I wrapped my palms around the cool metal bars. "You won't get away with this!" I shook the bars. Well, my skin shook. The bars withheld, solid as the sun's daily dawning.

A thundering pop crackled and boomed. My ears echoed with the jolting shatter of exploding fire. A clang hammered against the bars. As my palms flew up to cover my ears, Logan dropped at my side.

He gasped, his hands flying to his chest.

Liquid splattered against my face. I winced, wiping at my skin. A blurry, dark cherry-colored fluid smeared across my palm.

Screams.

They came from me, somehow. Maybe from Micah, too. I heard them cascading.

I knelt at his side, scooping my right hand under his head, which lolled back. My knees crashed against the ground beside his ribs. Logan cringed, the pain smeared across his flushed face, his lips curled in a grimace. Red liquid splashed down his uniform sleeve and onto the ground. It covered my hands. It soaked my legs. It curdled my own blood, a fiery venom of unbridled wrath.

"Activate."

Chapter Thirty-Six

A FINAL GAME
Tucker

The glowing sphere spun into the bars, igniting with a blue fire. Saylor flung her hands to the ether, stained crimson, fixated on things unseen. Her eyes glazed over. She dwelled within the grid only she saw, escaping the world binding the rest of us. The grid freed her.

The bars tumbled.

They clattered to the ground with a noisy chorus.

"We've got to stop the bleeding." Micah whispered, kneeling at Logan's side.

I wiped my hand over my hair.

Logan groaned.

Micah held a hand over her mouth. "That's a lot of blood."

"Hold still," I ordered.

Saylor stepped beyond the edge of the cage.

Dragons flurried about, advancing our way.

One of them sailed across the invisible line. "Let me help!" Panicked. Eagre. She ripped her mask off her face. She chucked it to the side and it bounced against the wall. "I can save his life. Please let me by." Saylor allowed her entry with a slight, blinded nod.

Eagre slid beside Logan, yanking the sleeve of her black uniform free at the seams. "Wrap this. Press it against the wound." She called out instructions to Micah, tugging at the buttons of the shirt. Underneath, her NEXIS shined in the dim light.

"I thought you were all for destroying us." I stated it, cold. Glancing up, I watched, helpless, as the Dragons lined up, facing Saylor. I surged upward to my feet.

Eagre focused on quickly tugging the tunic off and ripping it into shreds. "I've got to help Logan. Let the rest of them burn, I don't care. But I will not let him go like this."

"You're one twisted soul," I grumbled.

"Taniga!" Eagre yelled. "Help me!" She waved an arm. Another black-clad figure hesitated, glancing backward, before dashing our way. The girl, Taniga, one of Eagre's biggest fans from Fort Story, dodged into the cell, crouching down. Eagre called out instructions. Their fingers worked nimbly.

Saylor stepped toward the line of Dragons.

Their blue GRIPS glowed.

I darted out of the cell.

Micah followed.

Hazard raced out, lining up at my side.

We faced the severe mass. At least forty black uniforms, masks shrouding their cowardly, disloyal faces, piled up in a herd to block us from advancing from the cell. To my right, workers in gray one-piece uniforms paused, blinking, awaiting orders, holding boxes in their grimy hands. Upon the steps of the scaffolding beside the vessel, the girl in red, the curly-haired man in dark gray, and Exit in the unrestrained flesh gathered in council.

I remembered the deep, dusky tunnels inside Camp Kissinger, where Burkman had told me a group of dragons was known as a thunder.

"They'll strike quick and hard," I advised my fellow Guardsmen. "They'll crush you with their GRIPS."

"Stay away from the blue lights," Micah added. "Check."

"They're the thunder. But we're the storm."

A somewhat peaceful calm lofted down on my shoulders. The calm before the storm, I suppose.

Once upon a time, 300 Spartans defeated hundreds of Persians in a twisted valley. Once, nearly 200 Texans held their ground for two weeks, fighting off thousands of soldiers in the advancing Mexican army. One time at the lip of a mountain, 300 Israelites with torches and clay pots startled an impending army of over 100,000 Midianites; the larger group was so shocked by the sudden arrival of light and sound they raged war upon the shadows, killing each other along the way.

Numbers don't always determine the winner.

"They'll use their power," I murmured, then cleared my throat. "But they have no heart. Find a way to confuse them, get them to fight themselves. Their objective requires them to leave earth. Let's remind them why we're here."

Hazard stepped closer to my side. "Where you go, I go. All the way across the line."

I dipped my forehead in his direction.

The Dragons surged ahead.

Exit wrenched his palm on the scaffolding and tossed his weight over, soaring through the air until his shady boots pummeled the ground.

Micah reached down and picked up three poles from the cage. She tossed one to me, and one to Hazard. I gripped the grungy steel with both hands. Lining up my knuckles, I planted my feet in that familiar batter's stance. Raising my right elbow out to the side, parallel to the ground, I steadied the left before my chest. Swing level, strike hard. The ghosts and gods of battles gone past echoed along the periphery of the chamber. They chattered. They roared. They cheered. They jeered. A final game for life and death.

Chapter Thirty-Seven

WHERE MEN TELL DARK TALES
Saylor

The blue grid surrounded us. Surrounded them. Their heat signatures popped up, too many to count.

I grasped the ten strings of the SIMPL and cast them apart, their electricity buzzing, humming, and blasted them along to the hearts of those who'd dare strike us down. The SIMPLs thrummed with energy, and I rained them down upon the advancing line. Sparks seared into the shoulder of the guard who still held the rifle. He toppled to the ground. Chunk took out a short, squatty figure. I popped Striker in and out of several collarbones. Brian Von Poofleburg shot down and up, darting among the necks of the guards. More than anything, I distracted the black uniforms with the SIMPLs. The guards jumped, grabbed, punching each other, shoving to get to the pieces which darted in and out among them.

A monstrous form charged Tucker.

Glitch's thrusters all worked properly, so I targeted the beast with the small piece. Glitch zoomed full throttle in a beeline, but he didn't shoot fast enough. The guard smacked his glowing glove and grabbed Glitch. With a snapping crackle, Glitch's signal cut out. The figure tossed aside the crumpled wad of metal. He wiped his palms together.

The SIMPLs stunned their targets.

Figures rushed my comrades, Micah, Tucker, and Hazard volleying swift hits with the bars from the cage.

Sparks soared back, guarding my five-foot perimeter. I knew I couldn't combat any of these characters on my own. They'd have me and my weak knees before I could spell o-h – n-o.

Heat rose up, swelling around us. Intense red and orange flares, fists knocking. Stunned bodies dropping. Sweat rolling down my temples. One left arm, trembling, upholding the invisible strings of the SIMPLs and directing them along their paths.

A grinding echoed throughout the cavity. Groaning, inundating, and like a roaring beast, the colossal wail of gears unwinding swelled around the ruckus.

"What is that?" Micah asked.

Tucker grunted.

"The roof." Hazard's quick answer jerked through the noise.

A crack of bright white light flooded the grid.

"Stop!" Tucker's voice rang out. He commanded the chaos.

In an instant, a hush spanned the heat standing, kneeling, crouching. Some figure tackled Micah. She yelped as they landed with a *thud*.

"In the name of everything logical. Stop!" Tucker's voice ground to a growl.

Above, the grinding continued, a periodic yanking of chains and motorized cables spooling upon themselves.

A laugh. The man's hollow chuckle drifted across the grid from the scaffolding platform. He continued his amused chortling as he spoke. "Yes, let's pause for a moment. Hush, hush, my Dragons. Wait." The cackling stopped. "*Exit. A moment.*"

The large figure hoisted Hazard from the floor by the collar.

His Dragons?

"Drop the human." The voice had to be Poseidon.

Curious, I allowed my focus to withdraw from the grid and the intensity of the SIMPL menu, and studied the scene. A good twenty Dragons remained, waiting, or withholding. Poseidon—Adenauer—stood beside Persephone on the platform beside the ship. He focused on the enormous hulk of a human being holding on to Hazard.

Exit. Tucker had mentioned him, but perhaps not described him as thoroughly as he should have. The guy was three sizes bigger than Tucker. Arms and legs wrapped in muscles, his raven-black hair chucked to the side of his forehead, he appeared as the most dragon-like of the company. He chucked Hazard earthward with disdain. One great mouth twisted toward his dusty boots. His spine even arched out, as if he lacked only the giant tail and wings to become the nightmare upon which legends dwell. From the depths of his chest, he spat a thick wad of throat carnage to the ground by his feet.

The ceiling continued separating, the double pieces departing from each other, the gray sky overhead revealed, one cloud at a time. A gaping yawn formed a tremendous O-shape, the entire ceiling having slid apart into the earth's core.

Persephone clapped.

"What are you doing, Adenauer?" Tucker shouted. He panted. "Your plans are failing. Back-up is on the way, and you'll be shut down any moment."

"Oh, am I?" Adenauer did not appear fazed. "Will I?"

A motor whirred. The sound began, slight at first, from what sounded like far below us.

"Yes. Cooperate and perhaps you'll be shown leniency."

"And what if I'm not available for the trial?"

"Excuse me?"

"You'll want to come forward yourself."

The whirring whistled, churning into a clanking. Then a booming, mechanical thumping accompanied a deep vibration underfoot.

Persephone held up both of her hands to the sky. Closing her eyes, she inhaled deeply. Adenauer glanced at her, satisfied. He balanced one palm on the railing of the scaffolding.

The Dragons abandoned their attack positions, scurrying around the scaffolding.

Eagre and another black figure carried Logan by his shoulders and feet, running to the scaffolding. "Get on the platform!" Eagre screamed over her shoulder as they passed.

The concrete did have a circular rim. On the ground, it appeared to be a line between gaps of concrete slabs.

A burst of hot air slipped up through the crack, and the rim inside the circle, under the open sky, rose upward.

"Get on the platform," Tucker hollered, waving his arm. Micah rolled to her feet, stumbling up to the rising floor.

Exit slammed his fist down upon the top of Hazard's head, then darted over to the scaffolding. Hazard slouched to the ground. Tucker dragged him, yanking his shoulders, shouting his name.

I grabbed Hazard's boots and the pole he'd been wielding, and Tucker and I schlepped his body toward the increasingly higher step. Raised a good six inches, the floor vibrated and pulsed.

Tucker climbed up, tugging Hazard along. I stepped on the platform, wobbling, and rocked his boots upward. The SIMPLs meandered. I slid them together, Glitch sorely missed in the connection.

Hazard shook his head and patted the crown of his skull with his palm.

Exit climbed up the scaffolding and jumped over the rail, landing beside Persephone.

As we continued to propel upward, the Dragons regained their composure. They charged, a crowd writhing with retribution. The old familiar battle stance came to mind, until I remembered the Kali training Tucker and I had practiced on the ship. The first Dragon-guard lunged to me, but I swung down at an angle, remembering the simple yet effective striking techniques. He jumped back. As the Dragons rounded us, back to back to back, Micah, Tucker, and I each held the poles, whipping crackling strikes of steely resolve against the encroaching circle. Someone dragged Hazard's limp, yelping body out into the crowd.

Jangling, droning, the platform slid our boots closer to the cosmos. They were indeed raising Atlantis.

Guiding the SIMPL in its own arching pattern, blasting it down and darting it back up out of reach, the electric shock struck the Dragons, one by one. Short reprieves. One Dragon lunged out at Tucker's boot with his GRIP, grabbing the pole. Tucker yanked it away. But another dove in, GRIPS first, and grappled the steel rod. His muscular, black uniform flew against Tucker, who stumbled back. The break in motion allowed the torrent of Dragons to infiltrate our circle. Another caught Micah's weapon and a second tackled her. A third bound his arm around her boots, laying at the floor by her feet.

I split the SIMPLs apart, again surging them over the crowd.

Someone's arm slid around Tucker's throat.

Tucker shouted as best he could, "Dragons! You were not built to do this! You're meant for more. We're not on different sides, different parts of the equation. We're the whole equation."

He coughed as the arm choked him, tightening the space between the Dragon's elbow and his body.

Tucker grabbed the arm with both hands. "You're Dragons! D-R-A-G-O-N-S. What does Dragon mean?"

His voice cut off. I surged Brian over to that Dragon's head and dove the piece against his spine at the back of his neck. The Dragon vibrated, his jaw going slack, and he dropped.

Tucker slid out of the guy's arm and surged to his own feet. He coughed, holding up a palm to the two black-clad figures running up to his side. "Answer me! What does Dragon mean?"

"We are the strength of the universe. The spearhead upon which Poseidon rules."

"Flight. Come on."

"You don't know Poseidon's plans."

"I know enough. I know Alliance isn't the cut-and-run dictatorship he's mind-melded you into believing. Adenauer's off his rocker. He believes a computer program has predicted the end of the world, over 100 years from now, mind you, and wants to leave. Where's he going to go?"

"Poseidon and Zeus have the answers."

"No!"

The skirmish continued as another couple of guards clambered closer. I yanked the SIMPLs up, down, across, backwards, forwards, dashing them against any surface. One of the GRIPS palmed Zee and crushed it. Lief also met an unkindly end, as a Dragon knocked it into oblivion with one swipe of Micah's stolen pole. Micah kicked a guy in the groin.

Tossing my chin to my shoulder, I paused, listening, waiting for the rhythm of the mechanics under foot. They'd stopped. The platform had finished moving.

Tucker held up his palms again to the black uniforms before him. "Please," he begged. "You once said you sought freedom. What other type of freedom do you seek than to work as a force which protects the earth upon which we live? Alliance doesn't run and hide. Alliance protects. We persevere. Never quit. We finish the mission."

Hazard and another figure wrestled on the ground, rolling into the circle of space. Hazard yanked a heel into his opponent's ribcage, and then jumped to his feet. "He's right." Breathless, Hazard held up his fists, blocking any incoming jabs. The Dragon's face mask had fallen off, and a tall, thin Case studied us darkly.

"We've signed the covenant with Poseidon. He does not relinquish his blood oath."

"Forget Adenauer," Tucker commanded. "He's not even aware he has completely lost his grip on reality."

"And you'd have us beside you, even when we betrayed you?" One of them slid forward, removing the mask. The blond Thunder, with the cute little nose and sparkling blue eyes. He studied Tucker, serious and unsure.

"Prove you're Alliance now. Be the Dragon you're free to be. Alliance strengthens, our training employs your function, and this present moment comprises your crucible. Will you crumble now? I cannot stop the law from touching you once you've sided permanently with Adenauer."

"And his band of misfits," Thunder sneered.

Tucker's normally chill Aussie tone almost disappeared in his composure. "For once, I'm saying your unique skillset may save us all. Here you get to release the weakness of fear Rapton ingrained upon you. Dragons don't fight to the death. They fight for life."

"You're wrong about one thing, Thompson."

Hazard smacked a fist away. He panted. "Dragons do cower. That's what they do. They operate with a fierce tyranny."

"But—" Tucker began to argue.

"Alliance Guardsmen." Hazard wiped at his dripping forehead. "Guardsmen serve the mission. We never accept defeat. Never quit. Never leave a fallen comrade."

Six guards encircled Tucker, Micah, and me. Their black uniforms, wet with sweat and salty as a month-old sock, heaved with every breath.

One by one they all removed their masks.

I yanked the SIMPL pieces among the throng of heat and sweat. "The Dragon has died." Thunder narrowed his eyes. He pivoted on his heel and smashed a GRIP fist against a mask. The masked figure fell backward.

The ripple of movement surged out.

Case, Flight, Clutch, Wring, and another dark-skinned female stared at Tucker. As one, they spun to face the Dragons.

The faceless versus the revealed. Anonymous versus appointed.

My arms shuddered, falling to my sides. Weak with intent, I allowed the blue gridlines to encompass the scene. A Dragon toppled off the edge of the platform. His arms flew out to the sides, willing his wings to save him. They did not.

The heat of an approaching figure came in fast and I shifted to face it.

Persephone's wadded up fist slammed against my jaw. For a moment I lost the grid. I lost everything. Sounds muted, light blacked to dark, and nothing existed other than this intense, overwhelming sting.

Then my knee cracked against the platform.

Persephone laughed, cackling. She ground a heel against my sternum. The swift impact tossed me backward. I flew through the air. Landing with a bang, I stared up at the bright blue patch of sky popping through the gray clouds.

Persephone appeared above me, her blonde ponytail curving just so around her red leather collar. She leaned over, placing her hands on her knees. "You know, if you would pluck those hairs over your nose, your unibrow wouldn't offer such a shady umbrella over your eyes."

She ripped a heavy boot toe into my ribcage. "And those hairs around your mouth. You look like a troll. In winter."

I blocked another incoming kick with my arm, but the boot still shivered into my lungs. "Be a better female," she muttered. "Waste of space."

With a quick blink I opened the grid, searching for any of the SIMPLs. *Brian.* He shot overhead and zipped down, aiming at the red leather pocket. She bent down, grabbing one of the steel poles, and yanked it up just in time to crash against Brian. The piece shattered. Little shards clinked to the ground around my head. I blocked them with my splayed fingers. My black gloves held like a shield over my face. *Come on Saylor. On your feet.*

Snapping my heels to my side, I rolled away from Persephone's boot, and surged to my feet.

Another SIMPL landed against a GRIP, losing a quick battle. I had five left.

Persephone swung the rod, down and across her body, wind whipping near my face.

"Saylor. Think quick!" Micah tossed a bar through the air, and I caught it in my own sure grip. Nodded. Micah mirrored.

We squared off against Persephone.

"Give up now, idiot." She swung across with both arms. "In no world, in no timeline, could you ever best me."

I trotted to my right, escaping the ledge. "Calling me names won't help your combat skills."

She smirked. "You're broken. You're borrowed. You're leftovers. You're nobody."

"Not true. I made the papers a few weeks back. I bet you saw the headline."

"Yeah, and the world thinks you're a fumbling embarrassment. Oh, but they've forgotten about you since then, because nobody cares about some blonde girl who's trying to be someone she's not."

I paused, hand willing the rod to hold. *You're a horribly rude person.*

Persephone narrowed her eyes. As if she read my mind. "What?"

"You're certainly one to talk about not being remembered."

"How's that?" She whipped the bar up at an angle, and I blocked it with my bar. *Clank, clank, clank.* Down, up, left, right.

Another SIMPL smacked to kingdom come by some Dragon. Four.

I skittered to the right. "You live underground. Parented by a computer. You've never been anywhere." I swung my rod from left to right. "Besides, I don't do any of this for myself. I'm here on the line with my squadron. The best team a girl could ever have." My fist led the rod across my body, down right at my side, up to my left shoulder, across to my right shoulder, down to my left side. Fire bellowed through my spine, willing the bar to whip and soar.

She blocked it at every swing.

"You can't do anything right." She laughed. She wasn't even winded. Her eyes twinkled. She kicked out a heel behind her at an angle. "You're so slow. Maybe if you actually tried—"

I charged her, slashing away with the bar. *Clank, clank.*

The monstrous Dragon jumped over another, leaping into the air and grasping Turner and Chunk. Two.

Her fist steadied as she blocked each blow. Then she began to charge, swinging across, up, down, faster, faster, until her bar hit my knuckle. Even through the leather, the sting sliced, and in my flinching, she kicked a boot up to my knee. With a heaving shove, her force wrung out against me. I stumbled backward, my swollen knee collapsing under my weight with an audible crunch. My hip hit the platform. My hands jerked out to stop the fall. The bar slung out of my hand, sliding across the platform and rolling off into the breezy air.

"You're basically dead anyway. All of you." Her ponytail wrecked, she slapped away several stray hairs smeared into the red lipstick. She licked her sparkly teeth. "You've killed your friends, your family, your precious battalion."

"You don't care about anybody, do you?"

With a sneer, she let a snide laugh slip out. "Like I need anybody. They've trained me completely. I told you. I'm lord here."

"So, they will do what you say. Stop all of this."

"Remind me why I'd listen to a loser such as yourself?"

"I—"

"No, that's right, you don't have anything to say." She lifted the bar over her head.

"But I—" The hefty words lashed almost as much as her boot. My alter ego knocked a mighty bitter punch. *Who could I be if I didn't listen to her? I validate myself.*

Out of the corner of my eye, the wad of metal formerly known as Glitch caught the light.

Persephone shanked my left side with her foot, towering over me. My ribs creaked, stinging in echoing pangs.

Glitch's signal pinged online, the red light blinking. Persephone may have bested me in strength, agility, and femininity, but I had an Alliance.

Her lips curled in scorn as she laughed. "You waste of space. I knew you couldn't catch up or catch on. You're broken, beat, and lame. I'm perfect. Chosen. You're nothing." She raised the bar, drawing back for another cutting strike.

I slung Glitch upward, aiming straight for her scarlet, tainted heart.

Persephone froze, one hand out before her, eyes wide. Glitch shuddered, the electricity soldering against her jacket, sparks shooting out as it gave me the last of its few flickering tremors. Slobber dribbled out of the side of her mouth, tongue trembling.

Gurgling. Then her eyes rolled back in their slots, the whites widening, and she collapsed in a heap. The rod clanked against the ground.

Hovering in the air where she'd stood, Glitch's bent spikes sputtered, blue flame stuttering as the flame diminished. It toppled to the ground. Signal lost.

An echoing voice boomed around the platform. "Adenauer! We have you surrounded."

I twisted from my place on the ground. To my left, high on the nearby hill, stood the large hotel. Lush green grass and trees adorned the ground below, between us. Lined up along the roof of the hotel, ten bodies stood in a line.

Much of the movement on the platform froze. Most of the Dragons were down, except for the few stuck in combat between each other. Micah, to my right, yelled, "Finally!" and triumphantly wrestled a lab worker to the ground.

Poseidon had disappeared from the scaffolding.

Tucker and the voluminous bear of a creature Exit continued to crash around, tossing paraphernalia at each other. Mostly, the big guy chased Tucker, who ducked and then slid behind someone, before dodging and darting around the scaffolding. Sweat slid down Tucker's flushed face. The big guy didn't look so fresh himself.

"Alliance. Get low on three."

The booming voice buzzed over the platform, from what appeared to be a whole new set of SIMPLs. *How 'bout that. They have speakers, too.*

"One." The countdown began. I lowered my head even further, studying the people lined up atop the roof of the hotel. Someone stood on the end, holding a black box in his hand. He wore his Heads-Up Display along with his NEXIS suit. *Has to be Canaan.* Dad stood beside him, fists planted on his hips.

"Two." Micah flew to the ground, ducking her head. Tucker rolled under the scaffolding below the vessel, crawling away from Exit and tucking into a small ball.

"Three."

Sparks blasted from the second set of SIMPLs, electric spurts of light crackling toward the remaining standing. Almost as one body, they dropped, unconscious. Exit, however, roared, more alive and irritated than ever. He ripped something out of the side of his neck and dove for a SIMPL. The piece slid away. Exit continued chasing, focusing on the piece.

The last I saw of him, he grasped for the half-moon piece, barely out of reach beyond the edge of the platform. Exit's black boots and uniform stepped through the sky, treading into the land beyond which men tell dark tales.

Exit would no longer haunt the doorways.

My hip ached.

My knee throbbed.

My ears rang.

I sat up. Recalling the last SIMPL piece, poor little Sparks, I found it hovering where I'd apparently paused it, above the heads of the Dragons. Dropping Sparks into my palms, I hushed my voice. "Thank you. I'm sorry about your friends."

The second Glitch lowered before me. "Status report?" A canned man's voice projected from the piece.

"Canaan?" I asked.

"Yes."

"Logan's been injured. He was with Eagre last I saw, over by the scaffolding."

"Hang tight. Reinforcements on the way."

In the distance, a plane roared across the sky, echoes rippling through the clouds. Micah rolled up on her hip. "Can we sit up now?"

"I think so." I rubbed my shoulder. "I think my hand is bleeding in this glove."

"Leave it on. Wait until you have a bucket for me to puke in."

"You okay?"

Micah shrugged. "I've still got these two arms." She held up a bloody knuckle. She looked at it and gagged.

Tucker emerged from the scaffolding, swinging up, using the railing as support. His chest rose and fell. He wiped the back of his hand over his forehead, then rested the hand on his buckle. "Well that was a little more than I anticipated we'd find down here."

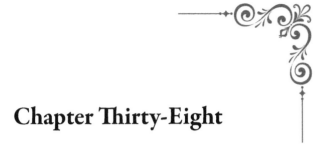

Chapter Thirty-Eight

DEPARTED
Tucker

———— ◦⟨⟩◦ ————

S urrounding the platform, which had risen around fifty feet into the air, the lake's smooth green waters sang choppy murmurs of discomfort. Adenauer had built a circular border just a couple inches under the surface of the water in order to create an exit for his vessel.

"I guess we need to get down?" Saylor peeked over the hand she'd clapped over her eyes.

"It's not so far." I strolled over to the edge, studying the distance.

"Ay, yaya! Back up!" Saylor cried.

I grinned. "Yes, ma'am."

The SIMPL pieces flew back to us after scanning the other sleeping bodies on the platform. Canaan's voice fizzled through a speaker. "You have about twenty minutes until they rouse, but we have another round available."

"How are we supposed to get down from here?" I queried. My stomach rumbled.

"Looks like you can climb down the support system under the platform."

"I refuse," Saylor interrupted, "to swing myself over the edge of that platform."

Eagre appeared to my right. I whipped up an incensed fist. She raised her palm, sedate. "Logan needs a medic."

"Right." I doubted her intentions. Suspicious.

"A hatch under the scaffolding leads down a ladder to the ground. Poseidon designed the platform for this."

"How do I know I can trust you?"

She pointed to Logan beside the base of the scaffolding. Her GRIP-less hands, red and sticky, offered an innocuous white flag. "Team work. Let's get him to safety."

I nodded. Saylor had climbed to her feet and stood studying the landscape. I held out a hand to her. "Let's go."

She twisted my way and then smacked her palm into mine, the best grip I'd ever accepted. "Time to go finish saving the world."

A grin played over my lips. "After you."

The white coats in the control center quickly surrendered, tossing their hands up beside their ears in shock as we stormed into the space. They abandoned their posts once we informed them Adenauer and his cronies had been strapped into thick metal cuffs and were being shipped back to the States. Adenauer had fled the scene of chaos atop the platform, only to meet up with Burkman and our backup in Engineering. Fortunately, Canaan had been able to track Saylor's location even after our WiCoDes went dark. They all figured out something shonky happened when we all stopped responding. The gaping hole in the earth pointed the way.

A crew of medics took Logan and Hazard away in a yellow ambulance. I stood beside Saylor, the Commander, Burkman, Micah, and Canaan, the six of us breathless from the squealing siren and black tires stirring up the gritty, broken concrete of the old parking lot.

"I'll follow them shortly," McConnell stated. He rubbed the back of his neck with his hand. "Burkman. Update."

"Everything's on lockdown here. Senior control operator informed me that Adenauer—they keep calling him Poseidon—these guys have lost it—paid everyone on this side of the island to be here, and threatened them with their lives should they speak out against the leaders. They essentially took over the western portion of the island, held it hostage. Anyone here had to be useful for Pos—for Adenauer's plan."

"For the launching of the ship?"

"The manufacturing of products, fabrication, shipping, excavation, extraction, all of it."

"Logan and I have some more to add, as well." I wiggled my fingers in the air.

McConnell considered it. "Army's heading our way with backup. They should be on the way momentarily to support lockdown."

"What did you do with the humanoid machine?"

"The what?"

Canaan cleared his throat. "Taken care of."

I bobbed my head. "Thank you."

"Do you happen to know why he was missing an arm?"

I let a grin slip across my face. Cheeky.

Canaan huffed out a brief laugh.

"Canaan," McConnell sharpened his tone, "Update?"

"The computers in the Control center appear to be in shutdown mode."

"They appear to be?'

"I haven't had enough time to mess with them. The men were ordered to step away and they did, but they won't give up any intel. I'll make Control my first stop after we're done here."

McConnell dipped his chin. "Get to it then. Thank you." He spun to Burkman. "You've got the witnesses?"

Burkman's voice boomed across the courtyard. Gray clouds whipped up a chilly breeze. "Go be with your boy. I've got these three to help me wrangle ornery detainees."

"Thank you, Burkman."

McConnell held up a pointer finger. "Good work. Stay in contact."

"Yes, sir," the three of us chorused.

Saylor slipped to her father's side and offered a quick hug. "Tell Logan he better wake up soon."

"Of course, Mack." He beamed down at her.

Saylor's face snapped up to his, a shocked smirk on her face.

"These MRE packs are the *best*." Micah flung the brown paper wrapper to the round white tabletop. She licked her finger, freeing it of the gravy. "Chicken and dumplings, my gramma's big toe!"

"Ew." Saylor shuddered. She crossed her arms on the table, resting her forehead on the NEXIS suit sleeves.

"I don't know." I shivered. "I've found them to be quite satisfying. Especially after some sort of strange pork dish I ended up eating for breakfast yesterday."

The white walls of the control center shone stark and bright, even in the early morning hours. "Was it yesterday?" I pondered aloud, tapping my chin. "We've been down here for far too long."

Canaan tapped away at a keyboard on the back row of desks facing the large screens. The screen sat, black, blank, as did all of the computers except for the one upon which Canaan had parked himself for several hours.

Five U.S. Army soldiers' voices occasionally rumbled from the two offices beyond the stairs. Adenauer's private office filled the back of it, and, with McConnell's permission, they scoured it for some means to reintegrate the west side of the island to the east, without a total economic shutdown. Dub had tipped his imaginary hat to us when he'd bounded up the steps.

I sipped my collapsible cup, the tepid water rolling across my fuzzy teeth. I sucked in some air between my lips and studied the room further.

"It's so quiet," Micah whispered.

"Such are the characteristics of an abandoned building," I stated. "Quiet. Cold. Quite creepy."

"I thought Logan was supposed to be the sarcastic one?"

"He taught me everything he knows." I grinned at her.

She rolled her eyes.

Canaan let out a groan. He rolled his face up to the sky and thrust his hands out to the sides.

"Problem?" I called to him.

Canaan slid his chair back and rose. He laced his fingers together in front of his chest, stretching his arms, and then sat his palms on top of his black, curly hair. "I think they may be smarter. I don't usually admit that, but I may mean it this time."

"What?" I asked. "Who?"

Canaan slunk up to the table and dropped into the chair beside Saylor. He plucked a thin can out of the brown paper bag filled with the MRE supplies. Canaan studied the label, then cracked open the tin lid. He yanked out a small brown meat tube and shoved it into his mouth. Chewing. He exhaled out of his nose. Didn't make eye contact with anybody but the can.

"You'll get it, Canaan." I reassured him. "You're the smartest guy I know."

He shrugged.

More chomping upon the meat tube. He pinched another and crammed it in after the first.

Saylor rolled her neck. "I think we all need a hot beverage."

"Won't do any good." Canaan smacked the tin on the table. "If I can't see it."

"Uhm?" Saylor began to ask a question but let it slide. "I bet I can find some coffee. How do you like it, Canaan?"

He leaned forward, his elbows on his thighs. Rubbing his eyes with his palms, his fingertips came to rest on his forehead.

Saylor and Micah glanced at each other.

Saylor blinked over at me.

I shrugged.

"Canaan?" I asked.

"Can I help in any way?" Saylor said at the same time.

Canaan lowered his hands, the whites of his eyes laced with thick vibrant veins. The blacks of his eyes sank in the coffee-brown. For the first time in a while, I studied his eyes. The blacks weren't so black. Kind of hazy.

"I can't see the screens clearly anymore," Canaan admitted. "It's been getting worse for some time, but I thought I could—I thought if I could get these new tech pieces figured, I could get enough—"

"What?" Saylor placed her hand on his forearm.

"My eyes are failing me. A type of advanced macular degeneration."

"What about spec surgery?" I tossed out the worried words.

"I've spoken with several doctors, but they all came to the conclusion no surgery would permanently fix the problem."

"But, Canaan." Saylor squeezed his arm.

He waved his chin side to side. "I'm going blind. It's already bad. I've been able to work around it, to push through, but I'll have to step away from my position before too long."

"You love working on computers and tech things." Saylor stated the fact.

"It's been a dream, to be honest. I can't say I ever regretted a day in my cage."

"But surely with everything you've invented," Saylor paused.

"No." Canaan more firmly shook his head, and then pinched the bridge of his nose with his thumb and pointer finger. He closed his eyes.

Saylor licked her lips. "You know what, Canaan?" She waited.

He dropped his hand, squinting at her.

"I've spent a lot of time in my own little cage. I call it the grid. It's pretty cool looking. And something tells me you're not so far away from redemption here."

He spurned the idea with a brief snort.

She leaned closer to him. "You've saved me a time or two. Now it's my turn. When we get back to the States, you will be our next project. You can count on Commander McConnell's full support."

Canaan's warm eyes studied her face as she spoke. His lips twisted into a half-frown at the final words. But then he dropped his chin, his boots suddenly appearing quite fascinating.

Saylor added, "Remember when we first met? You gave me a headset to use and said it cost more than my ears?"

Canaan chuckled, raising his head. He relaxed against the seat back.

"See!" She laughed. "Well those two eyes are pretty important too. Alliance needs you."

An alarm blared, shredding the silence. All four of us scrambled to our feet. The computers lit up, screens brightening to whites and neons. The large front wall plastered with images from the security cameras across the Atlantis campus. A voice added to the siren, a rumbling echo, "Blast doors closing in ten seconds. Nine. Eight..." He began his countdown.

Canaan scrambled to the computer where he'd previously sat, jamming his fingers against the keys, to an annoyed computer screeching alerts at him.

Canaan spun back around to us. "I'm locked out."

"Six."

The soldiers surged down the stairs from the offices, yelling questions.

"Five."

Canaan's hands flung to the sky. "It's on an automated sequence. I can't stop it." He grabbed the sides of his head and pivoted back to the screen.

Empty halls filled the screens. Empty rooms. Dark tunnels. Three blast doors gliding shut.

"Get that door propped!" Several soldiers ran to halt the large door which slowly pressed inward.

"Two."

"Stop!" I shouted.

"One."

Around us, a gurgling, grumbling.

Boom.

The rooms all seemed to shiver and shake. Micah screamed. My ears popped from the change in pressure.

The hearty voice spoke. "Launch sequence activated. Prepare for ignition in five minutes."

Upon the screens, in the bottom right corner, a timer began to countdown.

4:59.

4:58. The voice explained, "Start auxiliary power units."

4:57.

"You have to stop it!" I yelled. My hands flung out to the side. I dashed to the computer.

"I can't!" Canaan hollered.

"Try! Try something!"

Canaan surged into the chair and furiously smacked the keyboard.

The siren blared, in and out. In and out. In and out.

I yelled back no helpful information.

Canaan slapped the hands of some uniform attempting to access the keyboard where he sat.

3:00. "Retracting oxygen vent arm. Begin aerosurface profile test."

Chaos.

Hands flying, fists balling, palms wiping across foreheads and over high-and-tights, and one Saylor standing quietly in the corner observing the scene. My spine twisted beneath me, absorbing the shock and the furor. Dub paced.

2:00. "Aerosurface profile test complete. Confirmed."

Micah slid beside Saylor. They stared at the screens. Micah's jaw slacked.

The screens continued to show empty hallways. Dark tunnels. A launch area void of life. Smoke began to drift into the space. Because of the early morning light, the mist crept in with thin tentacles, flickering beams of light every which way.

I inched to Saylor's right. I grasped her hand in mine, our fingers intertwining. She squeezed her hand.

1:00. The voice somehow sounded jovial. "Ground launch sequencer confirmed."

"What do you think will happen?" Saylor whispered. Those blue eyes shone up at me. The spinning of the room slowed in the fuzzy background.

I opened my mouth to answer, but I decided to use my mouth for something better. Slipping my hands around her smooth jaw, I angled her face to be directly in line with mine. "I am in love with you, Saylaurelilly Jane MacTavish McConnell. Whatever your name may be, with all those L's in there. My dance partner. Battle buddy. My friend. My home. No matter what happens. I'm glad we're here together." And I rested my lips in their favorite place.

Her palms glided to my waist. Her fingers wrapped around my utility belt.

"Ten seconds to launch. Main engine activated." The voice shook the room. The voice inundated my uniform and I wondered just how well those blast doors worked.

Micah breathed out, "You guys will want to see this."

Saylor withdrew, but slid her hand down to my palm. She laced her fingers through mine.

"Six."

A soldier shouted, "We've got to get ahold of headquarters."

"Five."

Others shouted orders to each other, panic, mostly geared to Canaan, whose hands flung out around his head in a rhythm to pounding on the keyboard.

"Mission control!" Dub held a walkie up to his lips. He clicked the button with his thumb.

"Four."

Dub's radio clicked. Static. He kept clicking the receiver. "Come in, Control."

"Three."

The screen analyzing the vessel's status filled with thick gray smoke. No longer helpful, other than illustrating we couldn't see anything, the gray continued to roll around like a blanket in a windstorm.

"Two."

Fire licked at the smoke blanket. Bright, flickering tongues combined with the gray.

Still the tunnels showed themselves dim, calm. The lights flickered in the tunnel between Engineering and Launch.

"Booster ignition confirmed. Initiate liftoff."

Bright flashes whipped across the blinded screen. While the white screen illuminated our upturned faces, the rumbling from beyond the blast door rattled the walls around us. The ceiling cracked. A guttural groan emanated from the blast door, anchored in the wall, hissing, arguing. The lights flickered.

The siren let up. Silence reigned down, with the distant tumbling of engines boosting.

Thirty minutes after the vessel departed, the automated voice announced the clear signal, and the blast doors released. Slowly they unwound and swung outward. Our radios squawked to life. We heard the news from the outside. They wondered what went down inside.

The Earthshine left the lower limits of our globe's gravitational pull and arced into a comfortable orbit tracing its own predetermined path.

We stayed on Sao Miguel for another week, exploring the tunnels of Atlantis and its shroud under the abandoned hotel. One engineer finally cracked under McConnell's interrogation, telling us a mere smidge of the secrets Atlantis revealed. From under the Lagoa Verde, they'd tunneled to the west coast, using an underground series of locks to hide a number of subaquatic vehicles and even two drones. They matched identically to the one which carried Persephone away right after she commandeered and destroyed our ship.

Persephone didn't say another word. Literally. The electric shocks from the SIMPLs caused nerve damage due to the poor location of two linked computer chips surgically implanted in the base of her brain, in the cerebellum, and in the peak of the frontal lobe. McConnell sent her to a government-funded laboratory for medically disabled cases.

Adenauer shut down. He refused food, movement. Interrogations had no effect upon his stoic demeanor. Blank eyes studied distant walls. Deaf ears cared for no threat. I helped shove his wrists into a shiny set of handcuffs and watched Burkman escort him onto a Stateside-bound plane. We'd get him to talk, down in our own tunnels, away from prying ears and unsettled eyes.

Dub offered me a quick handshake on the tarmac. "Take good care of her." He nodded to Saylor, who stood guarding the stack of black evidence trunks, engaged in conversation with Micah. She tucked a strand of loose golden hair behind one ear. The soft breeze tossed it free again. "She's a special breed."

"You have no idea, sir," I agreed. I slung my black duffel bag over my shoulder.

"That reminds me." Dub held out a paper grocery sack to me. I accepted it, grabbing the rolled lip. "We found these under one of the stair wells. Determined they belonged to you and the younger McConnell."

"Oh?" I shook the bag. Fabric swooshed inside. The civvies we'd abandoned when first entering Atlantis.

"Can't say I'd forget that banana shirt anytime soon."

"No sir. Have to say I agree with you." My own cheeks burned, amused.

"Hope we work together one day soon, Thompson."

"Yes, sir. Agreed."

With a curt bob of his chin, he pivoted and stalked off, waving to another few remaining Guardsmen.

I studied Saylor. Her right hand sank through her wavy hair, swaying in the breeze. Her laughter danced across the tarmac, freer than she'd been in ages. Of course she'd conquered the shadows and the deception. She was the heartbeat, the luminous, the confirmed. She carried it in her smile. A rare breed indeed.

Chapter Thirty-Nine

MORE THAN LIFE
Saylor

"We've taken full responsibility," Dad stated. His face blipped on the screen for only a moment, then the screen cleared up.

"Will Alliance see many repercussions?" I sipped from the steaming, white ceramic cup I'd fenagled from the dining facility. I balanced on the edge of the rolling chair in Tucker's office at Fort Story. Tucker had left to meet with Blagojevich right before Dad had begun his daily intercontinental video debriefing.

"I needed to speak with you. I must confirm a few things. In general, big picture, no. Although Adenauer stole from Alliance, parts, manpower, funding, the products he created will offer us a unique—advantage—in the global market."

"Global market advantage?"

"Alliance now possesses something up in space nobody else has." Dad twisted his face to the side, asking someone off screen a question, and then resumed his attention. "Would you like to speak with Logan?"

"Sure!"

Logan dipped his face beside Dad's. "Hey, fraternal female."

I shook my head, pursing my lips.

"Logan." Dad grunted.

The white, dotted hospital gown draped over Logan's bulky shoulder disappeared into the sling wrapped around his body.

"I don't think you get to ridicule people while wearing a hospital gown with—is that purple flowers on it?" I squinted at the screen.

"Banana shirt. Banana. Shirt."

"Yeah. I have it here waiting for you. Just got it steamed and pressed from the cleaners."

"Alright," sighed Dad, "I see we will not be accomplishing much this afternoon. Are you doing well? How are Bette and Cadence?"

I bobbed my head. "They're kickin'."

"Micah? Patricia?"

My eyes slid to Logan's, then back to Dad's. "Them too. We're a houseful of hormones. Can't wait to have the smelly boys back. When can I plan your welcome home party, by the way?"

"Soon."

"Ah."

Dad cleared his throat. "I'll keep you updated."

"Yes, sir."

"Love you, kid."

"You too, Dad."

I suppose about six months passed. During that time, Dad and Logan returned home, Logan patched up and proud of the scars on his shoulder. We all worked as a unit to ensure a proper welcome back—including banana bread, banana nut muffins, banana smoothies, a fist full of yellow balloons, and a stuffed monkey about the size of Logan himself which Patricia had woefully sown together from yellow fabric I'd found on sale. He accepted a banana cookie from Cadence. Their hands brushed, and she rushed out of the room before he said a word to her.

The Dragons, the ones not charged and put on trial for treason, were placed in specialized counseling centers for soldiers with post-traumatic stress disorder. Hazard alone asked to return to Alliance. He filled out his application the first week at the center.

The other Dragons simply faded into the background, Fulbright operating the logistics of the busted Atlantis affair.

While I never told Logan, I once found a letter from Eagre on his desk. Unopened.

Tucker resumed his work training recruits, which proved difficult because there were none. Burkman, Logan, and Tucker became a good team, though, ripening the remaining rookies along the obstacle courses. Tucker began working in the Fitness Center as a personal trainer to help recruits get stronger mentally and physically. I'd slip in and walk the treadmill, watching him lift weights at the pullup rack. He'd notice me from the mirrors and grin. I once asked him what Persephone whispered to him on that platform. He refused to say. He instead took my face in his hands and said, "I read a poem to you once which had the right words for this kind of moment, but I cannot remember it just now." Then he kissed me.

One breezy afternoon, late summer, I sat on the bench chairs we'd lugged under the treehouse in the back yard. I reclined, the soft wind stirring my hair. I'd brought the new SIMPLs to the house so I could practice with the latest settings. The new Glitch buzzed up in the air, his sixth funnel sizzling out, and then petering back into full gear.

"You've got to get with it, Glitch," I called out.

Glitch buzzed. The first funnel sputtered.

After a breeze whipped a large clump of hair into my mouth for the fifth time, I froze Glitch in his spot in the grid. With a quick snap of my wrist and the pink hair elastic, I tossed the golden strands up into a quick messy bun.

Relief.

Go team messy bun.

Glitch buzzed.

The windchimes overhead jangled, sweet songs *tinkl-tinkl-tinking*. A bird replied to them, then jumped from the tree overhead and soared away.

Tucker emerged from the back door and strolled toward me. The door banged shut behind him. Tucker held a manila envelope in his hands.

"What's wrong?" I sat up straight.

He appeared concerned. Nervous. He studied the grass, the blades trembling under his black boots. He kneeled before me.

My heart thudded, pounding, almost grinding to a stop.

His eyes rose, those emerald questions analyzing my face. "Saylor?"

"Yes?" I lowered Glitch and selected *Quit* from the menu. Glitch clicked off, cooling, dropping into my palm.

"I've got two things I need to say. Do you have a few moments?"

"I've got all the time in the world." I set aside the metal fragment in its black box on the ground beside my bare feet.

Quick bob of his chin. He slid upward and then glided onto the bench beside me. "First." He gulped. "Alliance is bankrupt. Adenauer funneled funds and gold and property away from where the board could have been made aware of the event."

"What?" I straightened, my livid heart again hammering.

"You know the point system? He, Rapton, and Breame all created it to serve as a façade for what they were actually doing with the property and finances."

"It was a cover?"

"A cover."

"The points are a cover? They're fake?"

"The—yes. Alliance can do nothing without—without its chief operational executive."

"And who's that?"

"Breame-bot was actually a pretty conniving little tweed. Even without Adenauer aware, he wrote over and consigned their fortunes over to his heir."

"Whoa." I breathed in, leaning back against the seat.

"Yes."

"So Breame has money?"

"Breame had money."

"Because Breame is dead." I bit the inside of my cheek a little. "Who did he make his heir? Breame-bot?"

"I'm not sure a humanoid device, even though Breame had uploaded his 'conscious' into, could be a legal heir."

"I don't understand the consciousness thing," I admitted. I shrugged. My eyebrows furrowed over my nose.

"We found his main computer and flipped the switch. Removed the hard drive."

"Because computers can't be alive." I shook my head side to side, and then sniffed. "Right? Right?"

"Saylor."

"They have plugs. If it has a plug, it can't be alive. Turn it off. I win."

"Saylor." Tucker sank his hand onto my thigh.

My mouth shut. Eyes widened.

Tucker leaned closer. "Breame named you his rightful legal heir."

Winds dove around us, dithering jauntily through the jingling bars of the windchimes.

Breath caught in my throat. "Say again?"

"You are the legal owner and operator of Alliance."

My spine shimmied. I swayed into the seat back. "But Alliance is bankrupt."

"Without its rightful owner and her financing."

"But I have no—" My eyebrows became their own animal then, nestling in the middle of my forehead. I rubbed at them.

Tucker opened the envelope. He pointed to a line beside several numbers and letters. "This proposes an approximation of what Breame left you."

Oxygen stalled out in my throat. I coughed. My gaze shot upward to Tucker's. "That's a lot of zeros. And commas."

"And that is according to the Eurasian market. When translated into our financial system, it's almost double."

My hand hopped up to cover my trembling jaw.

"How's your heart?" Tucker asked. He gently grabbed my wrist and rubbed with his thumb.

Breathe in. Breathe out.

"I have one other item I need to discuss with you." Tucker released my arm.

I nodded.

"How're those insides? Are you going to pass out on me?"

Slight head shake. "You're saying I'm now in charge of my dad? I'm his boss now?"

"Stick with me Saylor."

"I think I need more time to absorb this."

"Can I finish the second item on my list before you melt into a puddle?"

"Yeah. Yes. Go for launch."

Tucker set his jaw, pursing his lips.

I grinned. "Like the Earthshine." I waved my pointer finger up into the air, swaying it side to side as it sailed heavenward.

"Funny you mention that." He huffed out an impatient breath. "I'm just going to summarize."

"Okay." I settled my hands in my lap. "Please. Continue."

"Right now, Alliance operates the Earthshine as something of a global communications satellite. It has an advanced radar and other technology they'd been developing before the Flare. Everyone considered the tech lost. But in fact, it wasn't. Adenauer and Breame had it hidden away. Anyway. We can receive messages, send messages, and use advanced mapping and sonar capabilities to survey incoming objects."

"Do not even hint at the idea we've received messages from beyond the dark side of the moon."

Tucker rolled his eyes. "The Earthshine functions as an advanced satellite. An umbrella. A shield."

"I like that."

"Me too."

"Shields are good." Visions danced of prior days, prior shields I'd had to be to protect the people I loved. A shiver trotted down my neck and into the base of my spine. "May I interrupt you for one second?"

"Yes?"

"I was thinking about the Earthshine because, ironically, earthshine was the word today on the 'Word of the Day' calendar you bought me."

"It was not."

"It was!"

"Truly ironic."

"Did you know that earthshine is the glow on the moon caused by sunlight reflected off the earth? When the moon can't see the sun, the earth lights its way."

"Learn something new every day."

"So, the Earthshine serves as a source of light. A beacon of hope."

Tucker swallowed. "Now I almost wish you hadn't stopped me."

"Why?"

"According to radar, some kind of inbound astronomical anomaly has aimed itself our direction."

"A what?"

"They think some kind of meteor or meteorite type of thing. They're not sure."

"Who are these people?"

"Blagojevich brought in several astronomers who are working with the crew out at Cheyenne Mountain."

"Ah, the Mountain. I miss that place."

"They want to send a crew up to the Earthshine. Our top candidates have been explored, and the big dogs want to coordinate an effort with the international assembly."

I blinked.

He paused.

Then I waved my hand for him to continue.

"The reality of Alliance's funding has just now come to light, as well as Breame's will, with Adenauer's demise."

"What?"

"Adenauer passed in his cell earlier today."

My jaw cracked open. Breath seemed to sizzle in my lungs. I closed my eyes.

Tucker continued. "With the proper funding, Alliance may continue their efforts. We will send a team up of the highest qualified men, who will enter the Earthshine, assess its inhabitability, and then hopefully utilize it as a tool to navigate around this new threat."

"The highest qualified *men*?"

Tucker shrugged. "Highest qualified people. So far we have mostly men on the roster."

"There's already a roster?"

Tucker's eyes. Those green, honest, open eyes. They glinted. A slight hesitation.

"What are you not saying, sir?" I demanded.

"It's possible you're on the list."

The giggle escaped out of my lips before I could stop it. I didn't even try. "Oh, sure. Naturally."

His forehead crinkled into three lines. "What we've gleaned from the engineers who are talking, Breame left you the keys to the kingdom. He incorporated the use of the nanomites into several of the protocol to operate various systems aboard the Earthshine.

I jumped up from my seat. My knee didn't creak. It didn't hurt even the slightest. The cool grass chilled the fire writhing within my veins. "Dad knows about this?"

"He asked me to speak with you."

"Why?"

"Officially, he's been removed from his position. Happened earlier today when the will information came through." Tucker waved the envelope and its haphazard papers.

"Well, take me to him. We have to get him reinstated or whatever."

Tucker arose from his seat. "Saylor. Think about—"

"No. Dad defines Alliance. If I'm Alliance, then Dad's the great creator of it all. He's the one who helped me see what I truly need to do. More than life, he gave me purpose. He redeemed me in countless ways. If I have even just once to return the favor, then I say let's do it." I beelined for the house.

"Saylor, your SIMPLs."

I twirled to face the lovely jade eyes, the restless stirring of heat against blood, and the hopeful beacon of life awaiting me. Sunlight flickered through the lush leaves. Golden sparks trickled to earth, awed, waiting.

"Activate SIMPLs." I commanded. The ten pieces rocketed up into the sky and soared overhead. With baited breath, they heeded my every command.

Tucker stilled, the fire breathing out around him. "You said you wanted to live out your life, sweeping the porch, and watching the sun set."

"Oh, I don't know." I shrugged. "I wanted that more than life. But I'll always love a good sunset. Maybe we can watch them from some place other than a front porch." My elated eyes flitted toward the cosmos for a moment before matching his gaze. "Dreams change." My fingers brushed against warm, delighted cheeks. "Let's go save the world."

He beamed, those dimples deepening. "Again."

"Again."

About the Author

Fierce yet sparkly, I rally seekers to thrive in their stories. The goal is magic, the medium is ink, and the fuel is coffee. And sometimes pizza. I teach English on the university level when I'm not dancing around the living room with my family, lifting heavy at the gym, traveling the planet, or binging superhero shows.

INSURRECTION, INCOMPLETE, INDELIBLE, HERE BE DRAGONS, and non-fiction inspirational KINGDOM COME roll out perilous motives, twisty plots, and daring protagonists. Grab some real estate and your copy of my latest adventure, and follow along on KadeeCarder.com.

ADDISON *multimedia*

Also by Kadee Carder

Alliance
Insurrection
Incomplete
Indelible
Here Be Dragons
Earthshine

Watch for more at https://www.kadeecarder.com/.